Into the Night

JAKE WOODHOUSE

PENGUIN BOOKS

PENGUIN BOOKS

UK | USA | Canada | Ireland | Australia
India | New Zealand | South Africa

Penguin Books is part of the Penguin Random House group of companies
whose addresses can be found at global.penguinrandomhouse.com.

First published 2015
005

Text copyright © Dark Sky Productions, 2015

The moral right of the author has been asserted

Set in 12.5/14.75 pt Garamond MT Std
Typeset by Jouve (UK), Milton Keynes
Printed in Great Britain by Clays Ltd, St Ives plc

A CIP catalogue record for this book is available from the British Library

B FORMAT ISBN: 978–1–405–91431–4
TPB ISBN: 978–1–405–91432–1

www.greenpenguin.co.uk

in this world
we walk on the roof of Hell
gazing at flowers

Issa

Day One

I

'I can't believe you're doing this. You *promised* you'd look after her.'

Inspector Jaap Rykel stepped towards the edge of the roof, leaving a cluster of forensics fussing over the body behind him.

High in the gas-flame-blue sky a plane glinted its way towards the west coast.

He glanced down and wondered what it would be like to jump.

'I know,' he said, wishing he'd turned his phone off after leaving the message for Saskia, his ex. 'But I've got a dead body here and—'

'There's a *live* body here. Your daughter, remember her?'

Behind him one of the forensics hiccuped, a burst of laughter following from his colleagues.

'Of course I do, you know that. It's just . . .' he tailed off, unable to explain.

Below him, five storeys below, a patrol car pulled out, two officers lifting the red and white tape to let it pass. Sun sparked off the bonnet, a lone cloud cruised across the windscreen. A faint buzzing came on the line, highlighting the silence.

Which was kind of worse than Saskia shouting.

A breeze stroked his face, and he found his free hand in

his pocket, fingers rubbing the smooth brass coins he kept there.

The ones he'd had made specially after his sister, Karin, had died.

Tomorrow would have been her thirty-fourth, he thought.

A distant siren wailed then cut off mid-swoop, and he glanced out north, over Amsterdam, his city.

'Fine,' he eventually heard her sigh, 'but you'll be picking up her therapy bills later on, right?'

Their little joke.

Which often felt too close to the bone.

'I'll do that,' he said, relieved to have got through it. 'Mind you, I might just need some myself.'

'That bad?'

He turned back to the body, watched as the hiccuping forensic lowered something clasped in a pair of tweezers into an evidence bag.

'Kind of. It's . . . Honestly, you don't want to know. I'll call you later. And Saskia?'

'Yeah?'

'I'm going to make sure I can look after Floortje for when you start the trial.'

'I'll hold you to that.'

They signed off and he took one last glance over the edge. He got the feeling that after the first moments of panic the fall might be exhilarating; air rushing, limbs loose, the sensation of speed. He wondered if he'd keep his eyes open or closed.

Coins jangled softly as he drew his hand out of his pocket.

No more decisions to make once you're on your way down, he thought as he turned and walked back to the body. *No responsibilities either.*

He got close and stopped, not wanting to look at it again. It lay there, dressed in expensive white trainers, jeans – ripped by use or design it was hard to tell – and a tight white T-shirt.

Which, considering the body had no head, the neck severed about a third of the way up from the shoulders, was still remarkably white.

He'd just promised Saskia he was going to be finished by Monday. Even as he'd said it he knew it was unlikely to be true.

Looking down at the body now, his own shadow spilling on to the torso, he knew just how big a lie it had been.

'You finished?'

The forensic, on his knees, turned and looked up at him, squinting into the sun.

'You kidding? And I've got a date tonight.'

'Fascinating,' said Jaap, moving to the opposite side of the body. 'And anyway I meant the hiccuping.'

'Bothering you?'

'Kind of.'

The forensic shrugged, his plastic suit crackling like radio static.

'Weird, isn't it?' he said, pointing to the body, another hiccup rupturing the end of his question, throwing the words up high into the air. The breeze whisked them away.

Jaap looked at the figure again and felt his stomach twitch. But he knew there was nothing left to come; he'd thrown it all up when he'd stepped on to the roof for the first time twenty minutes earlier and the forensic had whipped off the plastic sheet with a flourish worthy of a stage magician.

It was at that moment he'd understood the dispatcher's comment about not losing his head on this case.

He's the one who needs therapy, thought Jaap as he looked away again. *He sits there all day sending people out to things like this, and all he can do is crack sick jokes.*

He turned back to look at the body, trying to keep his gaze on the torso. What was in front of him was just so wrong, he found it hard to believe it was real.

'So, what have you got?'

'Not much,' said the forensic. 'Whatever they used for the cut was pretty sharp – the pathologist will be able to tell you more – but I reckon it was serrated, like a saw maybe?'

Jaap wasn't sure he wanted to know more.

'Identity?'

'Nothing on him except for these,' the forensic said, pointing at two clear bags laid out by his kit bag. One had a phone and the other a set of keys.

'Got any spares?' asked Jaap, holding up his hands.

The forensic rustled around before shaking his head.

'Any gloves for the poor inspector?' he called out to his two colleagues, who were on their hands and knees, probing something a few feet away from the door which led back into the building. The nearer of the two tossed over a pair to Jaap; he caught one, the other fluttered down and landed on the body's chest.

It looked like the glove was pointing out the missing head.

He snapped on the first then reached down for the other. He hated their feel, the way they made his hands sweat, the smell which lingered long after they'd been taken off. By now the smell had become synonymous with death.

'I don't like the lack of blood,' he said, the thought of jumping off the building's roof reappearing in his mind.

'Unusual for you lot to want more gore,' said the forensic, pulling off his own gloves and dropping them into a waste sack. 'They must have done it elsewhere, but who the hell would be crazy enough to risk bringing a headless body up here?'

The building was new, brand new. There were still builders on site, fixing up the interior. The security cameras weren't yet operational, and no one had seen anything.

As the foreman had told Jaap earlier, if someone had wanted to take a body to the roof all they'd have had to do was don a hi-vis and get on with it. As long as the body was in a box, or even a sack, no one would look twice.

And the only reason it had been discovered in the first place was an anonymous account had tweeted the official Twitter feed, giving an address where a body would be found. The police assumed it was a hoax and a passing patrol had been asked to check it out. Once the foreman had let them up onto the roof they realized it wasn't a joke and called it in.

'The way I see it,' said Jaap, squatting down and checking the arms for needle marks, 'if you're crazy enough to take someone's head off you're crazy enough to do anything.'

'It gets worse. Turn the right hand over.'

Jaap took hold of the wrist between his thumb and forefinger and twisted it. He hated the feel of dead people, the way the flesh gave without responding. Touching them always seemed like some kind of violation.

Or is it just fear? he thought.

The palm was badly burned, the flesh charred black.

'Blowtorch, I reckon,' said the forensic.

7

Jaap laid the wrist back down carefully, thinking about planned mutilation.

The worst type of killing.

Something moved off to his left, a flicker of light and shadow, and he turned to look above the door. A seagull stood on one leg, head cocked, its one visible eye electric-yellow with a glistening oily black drop at its centre.

It stared at Jaap for a second, then went back to jabbing something near its feet.

'Those things will eat anything.'

'Maybe,' said Jaap standing back up, kneecaps firing. 'But I doubt they'd take off a whole head.'

'Would make it easier for you if it had,' said the forensic as he mimicked a pistol shot at the bird, the recoil exaggerated. He blew across the top of his fingers. 'Then we could all go home.'

Jaap turned to the bags laid out a few feet from the body and picked up the one containing keys. There were three on a plastic key fob, round with a corporate-looking logo embedded in it. When he flipped it over he could see the fob had the name of an estate agent and a number. He punched the number into his phone, saved it, then turned to the second bag.

It held a newish-model phone made by some global company which specialized in underpaying workers in poor countries. Or so he'd heard. He powered it on, expecting it to be locked.

The screen flashed up the fruit logo but didn't ask for a passcode.

Stupid, he thought. *Or arrogant.*

He checked the call lists. Loads of numbers. Didn't look like a drug phone where there'd only be a couple of contacts. A few apps, one for the weather, one for the stock market, and several games, most of them looking like they involved shooting or driving.

He was just about to drop it back into the bag – he'd get the phone company records to see if it was on a contract later – when he found himself hitting the pictures icon.

Behind him the gull squawked, flapped its wings and took off, flying so low Jaap had to duck. He could feel the air beating down on him as the bird passed overhead.

He went back to the phone, a picture on screen.

His lungs froze.

The photo was slightly blurred, as if it had been taken on the move, and showed several people walking through Dam Square. The problem was, he recognized the person at the centre of the image.

He swiped back to see the previous photos, the screen not responding properly to his gloved finger. Then he realized there weren't any more; it was just this one. Sweat oozed between his skin and the gloves, and he still couldn't breathe.

He dropped the phone back into the bag, jammed it in his pocket along with the one containing the keys, and headed for the door.

'Hey, you've got to sign for those if you're taking them now,' called the forensic as the door swung shut behind him and he started down the stairs, his footsteps clattering wildly through the concrete stairwell.

It must be a coincidence, he thought.

But his gut told him otherwise.

The image on the phone had been taken about seven hours earlier.

The face, in two-thirds profile, was his own.

2

The bench creaked as Inspector Tanya van der Mark sat and glanced over towards the pond.

The stone she'd picked up was smooth, its surface pigeon-grey, with one chipped, rough edge. She ran her finger along it, testing the stone, testing her skin, then tossed it into the water, rippling up the calm surface.

Orange fish flickered like underwater flames.

Something, some insect, zoomed past her ear, and a crowd of tulips were just opening on the far side of the water, colour jostling in the breeze.

Her ears picked up surround-sound noise of a warm Saturday afternoon in the park; kids screeching, dogs barking, adults laughing.

It was the laughter that always got her.

But that was going to change. And it was going to change starting now, because she'd tracked him down. She'd been trying for months, unable to find him. Until she discovered the reason it had been so hard.

He'd changed his name to Ruud Staal.

She pulled out a photograph from her pocket and unfolded it, the crease running right through his face.

It's like he knew I'd come after him, she'd thought, noticing the faint tremor in her fingers. *Or does he have another motive for trying to hide? Has he done the same to others? Other girls?*

She felt the soft buzz of her phone in her pocket. The

sun pushed gently against her face, and she put the photo away then leaned back and closed her eyes.

Since transferring down to Amsterdam she'd tried to forget about it all, tried to make a fresh start, tried to live a normal life.

And for a while it worked – new place, new colleagues, new crimes which were at the same time old.

But then the feelings crept back – the bleakness, the edginess, the waking at three in the morning with a wild heartbeat pulsing through her body like a dull electric shock – and she knew she had to do something.

Her phone started up again. She sighed and pulled it out, her eyes momentarily blinded as she opened them.

It was the station.

She really didn't want to answer, she'd been up early on a dawn raid and had left Jaap's houseboat well before sun up. Surveillance had clocked an illegal cannabis farm out in a house in Nieuw-West, the predominately immigrant area to the west of Amsterdam, and the team were short. Her boss, Smit, had volunteered her.

But they'd got there only to find the place had been cleared out in a hurry. According to the unit she'd been with, this was the third time in the last two months. They just kept getting there too late. It was as if the growers were able to move out before they were hit.

'I'm on leave as of midday today, didn't the log show that?'

She figured it was best to be direct, stop anything before it started.

'I saw that, but the thing is something's come up,' said Frits.

Of course it had. It always did. In a city just shy of eight hundred thousand people shoved into two hundred square kilometres there was bound to be a bit of friction. And Amsterdam had the dubious honour of placing first in the list of Western Europe's murder capitals.

'Okay, but seriously I can't do it because—'

'Listen, it's an open-and-shut case. Accident or suicide, and we just need someone to sign it off. Keep things on track and you'll be finished and handing in the paperwork by no later than five tonight. I promise.'

Tanya almost laughed. Promises and the police.

She heard the *thwump* of a football being kicked somewhere close off to her left and instinctively flinched. The ball missed but hit the water just in front of her.

'Uggh,' she said as pond splashed up.

'Hey, it's not that bad. You should see the one Jaap caught a while ago. Guy without a head.'

Tanya didn't want to know. The whole thing with Jaap was complicated. And if Frits, who seemed to have a thing for her, found out about them, well . . .

'Okay,' she said. 'Where is it?'

'Centraal station. Patrol's there at the moment. And the NS are hopping up and down as they want to get the trains moving again – all these people who've come up to town for the day are going to need to get home somehow.'

Great, thought Tanya, *so I'm now responsible for the trains.*

As she stood up she looked down at the wet patches on her clothes, a dribble ran down her right leg from a large dark area on her crotch. She started walking, hoping it would dry out.

'I'm at Vondelpark. Get a car to pick me up at the Van Baerlestraat exit in five minutes,' she said and hung up.

The car was waiting for her when she reached the pick-up point, and got her to Centraal quickly. She could see it was in chaos as they drove up Damrak, siren wailing. Blue and white trams were backed up in every direction, and she had to get out and walk the final stretch.

As she got close she could smell the IJ, the stretch of water just behind the station, which separated old Amsterdam from the modern Amsterdam Noord. She could also hear the frustrated noise of people whose journeys had been interrupted. Pushing through the crowd she came across hippies with large rucksacks and didgeridoos, half the population of Africa and a particularly obstinate old woman who refused to believe she was police, accusing her in a loud petulant bleat of trying to jump the queue.

Inside, past the fluttering red and white striped tape, things calmed down, and she walked through the subway, her footsteps echoing in a space normally crammed with a flurry of people dashing for trains.

On the platform itself she recognized one of the uniforms, Piet. He stepped over to greet her.

'Hey, I thought you were supposed to be on leave?'

'So did I,' said Tanya as they walked to the front of the train and looked over the platform edge at the track.

A woman, who, despite the warm weather, was wearing several coats of varying sizes. Her body was crumpled up on one of the polished rails. Grey and white hair streaked over her face, and one arm was raised above her head along the ground as if she was reaching for something.

'Driver?'

'She's in the main office. It's only her first week.'

'Shaken?'

'Pretty bad, I'd say. And the thing is, if that doesn't get her, all the jokes she's going to hear about woman drivers probably will.'

Tanya shook her head. She'd got used to working in a male-dominated world. It hadn't been easy, but she coped.

Usually.

She looked down at the body again.

I might just get away on time, she thought.

Then she felt guilty. Here was a homeless woman who'd suffered who-knew-what in her life, and all she could think of was herself.

Something struck her.

'Weird she's on the further of the two lines from the platform,' she said, edging closer. 'Did she take a running jump or was she over the other side already?'

Piet looked across at the body and scratched his ear.

'I'd just assumed she was on the other side anyway, looking for something down there. She seems quite the collector judging by her clothes.'

'What did the driver say?'

'She says she only saw her at the last minute. There was some kind of fight on the platform and she was watching that. She slammed the brakes on but . . .'

'Too late.'

'Yeah,' said Piet.

'You've got someone to check the CCTV, right?'

'Bart's supposed to be doing that now.'

14

Tanya looked up at the curved glass and cast-iron roof, the sun rainbowing parts of the glazing.

'I'm going to take a look down there,' she said, looking at the track again. 'Can you go and chase the CCTV up?'

'Sure. You might not want to be down there too long though.' He pinched his nose before turning away.

She moved to the edge and dropped down, her feet crunching on the stones by the track. Stale urine burned her nostrils, and it only got stronger as she stepped closer to the body.

The woman was hard to age. Her face had the skin of someone used to sleeping rough, and her teeth, glimpsed through her open mouth, were standard-issue homeless; black and not many of them left.

Tanya tried to work out what she'd been doing, how she'd got in front of the train.

It can't have been an accident, she thought. *Unless she was drunk or high.*

Tanya had seen colleagues sniff dead bodies for alcohol, but the thought made her feel sick.

I'll leave that one for the pathologist.

Something moved, catching Tanya's attention. A rat was sniffing round the woman's outstretched hand, one paw raised as its nose oscillated, whiskers following suit. Tanya shifted round to see what it was, the rat scuttling off alongside the rail as she moved.

The hand held a phone. A very expensive one.

Tanya was hit by sadness. She could see what had happened; the woman had seen the phone on the tracks, maybe thought she could exchange it for food, drink, or drugs, and had gone down to get it.

'Hey, there's something you should see.'

Tanya was surprised that she had to wipe her eyes before turning to look up at Piet, catching the urgency in his voice.

'What?' she said, already moving back to the platform, springing up to where Piet was standing, agitated, weight shifting from leg to leg as if he really needed to go.

'The CCTV, you've got to see it. C'mon.'

In the control room a fat NS employee sat at a bank of monitors; he gestured to one of them.

Aircon hummed, a radio talk show babbled on at low volume.

'See there,' said Piet, pointing to the lower left corner of the flickery screen, the scene playing out in monochrome.

Alive, the woman was walking on the far side of the track, holding her hand to her head. It took Tanya a moment to realize that she was talking. Talking on the phone she'd seen in the woman's outstretched hand. The train was approaching her slowly, the woman had her back to it, and then, seconds before the train reached her, a figure, which must have been jogging along on the far side of the train, broke ahead and shoved the woman on to the track. The figure then turned and ducked back behind the train.

'Rewind that,' said Tanya. 'Pause it there.'

She looked at the screen.

'Shit . . .'

She couldn't believe it.

'Have you got any cameras which could pick him up elsewhere?' she asked.

'I've got over thirty cameras here,' said the fat guy. 'That would take me hours.'

'Is this backed up on a disk, or a hard drive?'

'Hard drive, the whole thing. We had it installed last—'

'Get it for me. I'm going to get a team on to this right away.'

The fat guy looked unsure, didn't move.

'Yes?' she asked.

'It's just that I'm not sure I'm allowed—'

'You are allowed. I've just given you permission.'

He held her gaze for a second then shrugged.

'Whatever,' he said as he pulled himself up out of his chair and ambled across the floor. Tanya noticed one of his shoelaces was undone. He reached a cupboard, opened it up, fiddled with a computer for a few moments, then pulled the drive out and handed it over.

'This is the only copy, right? There isn't a backup somewhere?'

'It gets backed up automatically online as well, but it stopped syncing yesterday morning and no one's been able to sort it yet.'

'Okay. You're not to talk to anyone about this,' she said to the fat guy. 'It's an ongoing investigation. The press will try to get you to talk but it's really important you don't. Is that clear?'

'Yeah,' he said. Somehow she wasn't convinced he meant it, but she didn't have time to waste, and as she dashed out the room she could feel her pulse pounding.

No one back at the station was picking up; eventually it rang out and she dialled again.

By the time she'd reached the front of Centraal and

pushed her way out through the crowds, she'd managed to get through to her boss's office.

'I need to talk to Smit,' she said to his assistant as she ducked into the patrol car and told the uniform to get moving.

'He's tied up at the moment—'

'This is Inspector van der Mark. Tell him it's an emergency.'

More waiting. The car was heading down Damrak when Smit's voice came on the line.

'Van der Mark,' he said. 'What's the problem.'

'I've got a video showing a woman being pushed in front of a train.'

There was a deep, reverberating silence before he responded.

'So?'

She looked out of the window as they passed through Dam Square. The funfair which had arrived for the King's Day celebration was still there, the Ferris wheel turning slowly. Someone, a kid, was waving from near the top. People queued at a mobile food stall, many of them holding flags on short poles.

High above, an orange balloon powered skyward.

She thought of the man in the image, what was written on the back of his jacket.

The phone felt unreal in her hand.

'The thing is,' said Tanya, 'whoever pushed her was one of us.'

3

'So, I figure this is kind of a celebration,' said Inspector Kees Terpstra as he lowered his head towards the table, guiding the rolled-up note to his nose. 'Here's to nailing the bastard.'

Zamir Isovic sat opposite him on a low 1960s-style chair and nodded. Then he grinned.

'Exactly,' he said as he took the note when Kees had finished.

Kees shook his head quickly as it hit, then relaxed back into the sofa and looked round the flat.

He'd been here pretty much the best part of five days now, someone relieving him for the night shifts only, and the end was in sight. He'd been bored stupid to begin with, and the coke was really a consolation prize for himself. With all the shit he'd been dealing with over the last couple of months he figured he deserved it.

Outside the tiny window he could just make out the tops of the houses on the far side of Herengracht, one of the main canals in Amsterdam with the most expensive real estate in the city.

The flat itself was tiny, nothing more than a studio with a separate bathroom and a damp problem in the low ceiling, and when he'd been told how he was to be spending the week he'd not been happy.

In the movies they always put witnesses up in hotel

suites, complete with a room-service tab, but here he was in an airless bolt-hole with scarcely enough room to move around in.

Not that there was anything he could do about it. Since the shooting – and the cover-up – he'd just not been given any breaks.

It's that fucker Smit, he thought as the coke revved his system up. *I did all that work for him and this is the reward.*

Isovic leaned forward, a necklace with a crescent moon banging the table, and hoovered up his line.

'You know, you're not so bad,' Isovic said, fiddling with his nose. 'For a cop.'

They both laughed.

Isovic had turned out all right. Sure he was a bit cocky, and his accent was so irritating that half the time Kees wished they'd just sit there in silence. But then again, how many foreigners could actually speak Dutch? At least he'd made the effort. And although Kees had managed to find a bit of his background out, he suspected that Isovic had probably only told the half of it.

'This guy, the one you're testifying against, Matkovick—'

'Matkovic.'

'Yeah, Matkovic. So what did he actually do?'

Isovic breathed in deeply and leaned back in his chair, eyes scanning the ceiling.

'He's evil. There's no other way to say it. He was the head of this group of soldiers, part of the Serb army which broke away and set up on their own. After Srebenica he probably realized that it was safer to be a small group. He called it the Black Hands, and one day they arrived at my village.'

Kees waited for more, but the expression on Isovic's face stopped him from probing further.

'So what are you going to do, after the trial?' he finally asked.

Isovic waved his hand in the air, as if trying to catch a fly.

'I don't know really. Maybe some friends have got something lined up for me.'

'Here?'

Isovic looked away.

'I don't think I'll be going back.'

Kees didn't blame him. He couldn't remember which specific part of the old Yugoslavia Isovic had said he came from, but he was pretty sure it was a shit hole. Had to be, the whole area was. Not that he'd ever been.

'Maybe I'll become a cop,' said Isovic. 'You seem to have things sorted out pretty good.'

He motioned to the coke left on the table, enough for a couple of lines each.

Kees looked at it.

It struck him he had no idea what it really was.

Other than goods for services rendered.

And it looked like he was due some more tonight. Which would have to be the last lot. He'd left a message telling them he was out, it was getting too risky. All he'd got in response was a laugh and a reminder about just how much he owed.

And he needed more.

'Man, the last thing you want to be is a cop. Especially on witness protection; you'd have to hang out with people like you.'

Isovic laughed again, then stopped.

'Your nose,' he said, touching his own as if Kees didn't know what a nose was. 'It's blooding.'

'Bleeding. Shit.'

Kees got up and went to the bathroom, ripped a couple of sheets of toilet paper off the roll and looked in the mirror.

It was his left, the trickle like something out of a cheap vampire movie, so he jammed the paper into a tight ball and inserted it into his nostril. He watched as blood blossomed, highlighting fine cellulose fibres.

Ever since the shooting – Kees had pulled his gun on a man who was holding Jaap and Tanya and then pulled the trigger, watching as his head exploded – Jaap had been trying to help him. He'd even got him into an anonymous drug dependency programme. And Jaap could have just shopped him, but he obviously felt indebted to him for saving his life.

They'd even worked a couple of cases together and had got along fine, though Kees got the feeling Jaap never really trusted him.

He would if I stopped, he thought. *But I'm not ready to yet.*

Kees had gone to the meetings Jaap had set up, but he'd not found it was helping. But that was probably as no one there knew what his problem was really stemming from. He'd not shared it with the group, unable to talk about it, and had pretended it was to do with the shooting. They'd bought that, nodding their heads like they knew what it was like, all the while getting some kind of kick out of the story.

He didn't mention the real reason, the reason he'd been forced to up his coke intake.

Just to cope.

The disease, the pain of which seemed to be getting worse every day.

He stepped back into the room and felt anger surge in him. It was all so fucked up. Here he was getting high with a fucking immigrant witness, wasting what little he had left of his career, what little he had left of his life.

And his coke.

Isovic made some joke but Kees hardly heard him. He grabbed the rolled up note and took another line, through his right nostril. He felt the coke hit.

Then something else.

His face crashed into the table, his nose erupting into a flash of pain, the rolled-up note jabbed deep inside his nostril and everything went black.

When he came round his neck ached, and there was a tender spot right on the back of his head. His vision was blurred, and for a full five seconds he didn't even know where he was. His hair was hanging down over his ears, spooling on to whatever surface his face was pressed against.

Then he lifted and turned his head, brushing hair away from his face.

Everything in the flat was the same, the furniture was as it had been. The fridge juddered off, leaving a ringing in Kees' ears. Or maybe the ringing was an after-effect of the impact.

He gradually registered something.

No Isovic.

As he turned his head towards the door, the room swaying, the pulse at his temples like a series of explosions, he saw something he didn't like.

The door to the flat was open.

4

'Get me whatever you've got on Jan Koopman, at this address,' Jaap said as he shot the car out of the tunnel under the IJ, squinting until his eyes adjusted to the light. He yanked the wheel hard on a left-hander, tyres screaming in delight or protest, he couldn't tell.

He was heading to an address in Amsterdam Noord – he'd got bogged down in the approach to Centraal, which had been totally jammed up with traffic and trams – but was now making up for it.

All the time the same thought had been slamming round his head.

Why did he have a picture of me?

The phone, he'd not been surprised to learn, was a pay as you go, no contract and no record of the owner. But the estate agents had been more helpful. He'd spoken to them, and they'd said there would be a code on the back of the key fob. Once he'd read it out they'd given him the name and the address he was headed to now.

'Okay.' Frits' voice came back crackly over the hands-free. 'I'm on it. You need backup?'

'I doubt whoever chopped his head off is hanging out at the victim's flat. But I'll let you know.'

Minutes later he reached one of the estates right on the edge of Ringweg Noord, the ring road which marked the northernmost boundary of the city before flat fields took over. The address he needed was the third road in, and he skidded to a halt just outside the first of the building entrances, scanning for numbers.

Checking up on a victim's identity wouldn't normally require such a rush.

But this wasn't normal.

All he could think about was the image of himself, taken earlier that morning as he walked to work.

He needed to find out why. If he told anyone about it he'd be off the case; Smit would assign someone else. And he figured no one else would have quite the same motivation to find out what was going on as he did.

He stood for a moment before entering the building, aware suddenly of the bleakness of the place, uniform concrete blocks designed by an architect with the express purpose of crushing people's souls.

The flat was on the third floor of four. He rang the bell having taken the stairs two at a time – his muscles stiff from the six-minute Tabata workout he'd done the previous evening – but wasn't surprised when no one came to the door. A baby was crying somewhere, possibly the flat next door, and he could smell spices being cooked up somewhere else in the building. Music pulsed through the ceiling, and he could hear voices, an argument behind closed doors.

He pulled out the bag with the keys in he'd taken from the crime scene, and shifted the keys round so he could unlock the door without touching the key itself. The lock clicked when the key turned.

Inside, boiled meat and cigarette smoke thickened the air. There was a small kitchen, a bedroom, bathroom and a living room which looked out on to the ring road, the dull roar of traffic noticeable despite the closed windows.

Everything was neat.

His phone rang; it was Frits.

'What have you got?' Jaap asked.

'Forty-three years old. Works at the Dronken Brewery by Vondelpark. The only reason he's on our system is a speeding ticket about three months back. Apart from that he's clean as far as we're concerned.'

'There should be a copy of his driving licence on the file; get it scanned over to me.'

Jaap hung up and started going through the living room. A pillow lay crumpled up at one end of the sagging leather-effect sofa, shiny textured black nastiness, and a single bookshelf held a bunch of bootleg DVDs, mostly porn and an original *Dr Zhivago*.

Eclectic tastes, thought Jaap as he turned his attention to the bedroom.

The single bed was half made, the sheets a dirty yellow, and there was a bedside table with an ashtray full of ash and twisted butts. Inside the wardrobe was a bunch of clothes; mainly tatty tracksuits, one pair of jeans, and no white T-shirts.

Under the bed was more interesting. He pulled out a small metal box with a padlock. It was heavy, and something inside slid from one side to the other.

Jaap inspected the padlock. He tried the keys on the fob but none of them worked. He took it to the kitchen, placed it on the table and riffled through the drawers. He found a spatula, the plastic tip melted, but with a thick metal handle.

His phone started up again.

'Yeah?'

'I've got the driving licence photo on the arrest report.'

'And?'

'You can't see anything. It's a really bad photocopy of a photocopy. Looks like the original got lost.'

'Okay, get on to whoever issues them and try and get a better image. I want to see what this guy looked like.'

He hung up and worked the lid. It popped off. Inside, nestling among scrunched-up newspaper, was a stack of photos – and a gun.

Jaap didn't like guns; he carried his own reluctantly and only when he had to. But he really hated to see them out in the wild. He didn't trust half his colleagues with them, let alone random members of the public.

He recognized it, a Walther P5, the model he'd carried since first becoming an inspector, the same model he'd shot and killed with . . .

He stopped his thoughts there. That was past. He had to focus on the present.

The gun was old, but it had that oily smell which spoke of a recent reconditioning. He bent down and sniffed the muzzle, but there was no hint of a recent firing.

Maybe if he'd been carrying this, he thought, *he'd still have his head.*

He'd have to get a trace run on it, check the serial number, and he bagged it up, feeling from the weight of it that the clip was loaded.

He had a photo of me and a loaded gun, he thought. *Why?*

The first thing was the murder itself, the sheer brutality of it shocking. Why had the head been removed and the hand burned? What could it hide, seeing as whoever had done it had left the keys, allowing Jaap to find out the identity of the victim quickly? Or was it a message, a sign to someone else?

The only two groups who tended to use beheadings were jihadists, who periodically posted videos online of Western journalists, and the Mexican cartels.

There are people pushing for sharia law here, thought Jaap. *Is that what this is about?*

He turned to the photos, flicking through them. There were about fifteen, and they seemed to be of men with guns. In some photos they were hanging around some kind of old Land Rover, painted dark green and splattered with mud, and in others a few were shooting at targets. The background was always wooded, the trees a kind of conical pine.

He knew men who did this; went off at weekends to live out some childhood fantasy, or to escape the wife and kids and pretend to be heroes.

Men with guns.

Idiots.

The kitchen sink gurgled once. A shot of sun streamed through the window on to the table in front of him.

He put the photos down and pulled out his three brass coins and copy of the I Ching.

He thought of his tutor in Kyoto, Yuzuki Roshi, who would, in the quiet of the early evening before the last meditation session of the day, devote a few moments to the I Ching. He'd even shown Jaap how the I Ching worked, how to convert coin throws into the lines which made up the hexagrams, despite the fact Yuzuki Roshi's fellow Zen monks thought the I Ching was not an appropriate topic of study, seeing it as little better than ancient Chinese superstition.

At first Jaap had been unimpressed, but just before he'd left Japan Yuzuki had slipped him a small parcel, telling him not to open it until he got home. Months later Jaap had rediscovered it on a shelf in his houseboat – he must have put it there while unpacking and forgotten about it – and he'd unwrapped the delicate plain paper to find a small cloth-bound copy of the I Ching.

He'd started using it, just for fun, and it quickly became a habit.

But ever since Karin had died, Jaap had been using it more and more.

Something told him he shouldn't, and he'd started to feel uneasy every time he did it, but he still couldn't stop himself.

The coins flashed in the light as he threw them up, and he let them clatter on to the table's surface. He noted down the first line of the hexagram, then threw five more times until it was complete.

He looked up the hexagram in the I Ching. The bottom three lines represented Lake, the top three Fire.

He read the overview of Fire over Lake.

OPPOSITION.

Jaap stared at the word for a while.

I need to stop this, he thought as he scooped up the coins and replaced the I Ching in his pocket.

His phone rang again. It was Frits.

'Yeah?'

'You on Twitter?'

'Twitter? Do I look like I have time for that kind of shit?'

I've got time to flip coins though, he thought.

'I dunno, but I think you're going to have to make time.'

'I've got a headless body; why would I want to fuck around—'

'There a TV where you are?'

'Yeah . . .'

'Turn it on. Channel 1.'

Jaap stepped back into the living room towards the TV. He hit the button on the top and the standby light came on but the screen stayed blank. He looked around for a remote but couldn't find one.

'Just tell me what it is.'

'The news, they've got this story going. A tweet got picked up saying there's a man without a head.'

'Yeah, I've seen him already, remember?'

'Not this one. The tweet says the body's out towards Amstelveen, there's a photo too. And the thing is, the journalists are at the scene already.'

5

Tanya was in the basement, a series of interconnected rooms which the Computer Crimes unit operated out of. The rooms themselves were below canal level, and smelt like it.

Everything was buzzing: computers, people, air.

Smit had commandeered the whole unit, telling them to drop everything and get on with scanning the CCTV on the hard drive Tanya had brought in. So far no one had been able to make another sighting of the man who'd shoved the homeless woman in front of a train.

The homeless woman who'd been having a conversation with someone on a brand-new phone.

She'd remembered the phone halfway to the station and called Piet, getting him to check on it. Unregistered, and all the incoming calls were from a blocked number, came the response. And there were no outgoing calls at all.

It was all too weird. Nothing was making any sense.

And the thing was, she needed to get away, hand this over to someone else.

I'll try and get Smit to reassign it, she thought.

'I've got something,' said one of the computer team. Tanya rushed over and looked at the screen.

'Upper right corner. It's kind of blurred, but the time would be about right.'

Tanya watched as a figure wearing a baseball cap, jeans and a dark jacket dropped off the end of one of the platforms and ran across the tracks, and then off screen.

The image was low-res and in black and white. But even so, the word on the back of the man's jacket was clear.

POLITIE. Police.

'Okay, let's get a map of the station up, we can try and trace him back from this,' she said as Smit stepped into the room.

I've got to get him to give this case to someone else, Tanya found herself thinking.

'What have we got?' he asked.

She told him.

'Virtually nothing then,' he said when she'd finished.

He was famous for making his inspectors feel like everything was their fault.

'I've also got people working on the phone, the blocked calls I told you about?'

Smit just grunted, then glanced round the room. 'Let's have a word,' he said jerking his head towards the corridor.

Once outside the room Smit closed the door.

'You contained this at Centraal?'

'The guy who operated the CCTV saw it. I impressed the need for secrecy on him, and I took the hard drive it was saved on to.'

'So it'll probably be on the news already. You know what parasites journalists are,' he said, checking the watch on his pale hairy wrist. Tanya noticed a thin gold chain she'd not seen before. 'Probably the only reason no one's rung me about it yet is they're all over this other case. Some fucking lunatic running around taking people's heads off, then tweeting about it.'

'I heard. Jaap's on that one, isn't he?' said Tanya just as her phone started ringing. It was the phone company. She glanced at Smit, who nodded.

'Where have you got to?' she said into her phone.

'It's going to be tricky, the calls came from the Internet,' said the young-sounding woman.

'So can you trace them online?'

'Not really our kind of thing, we haven't got the expertise here.'

They just don't want to get involved, she thought. *Can't blame them really.*

'Hang on,' she said to the woman and covered her phone. 'Have we got people who can trace calls made over the Internet?' she asked Smit.

'Fuck knows. There must be someone among that lot in there who can.'

The strip light above them flickered once, then died. The corridor went dark.

'We're going to get someone to call you back,' she said and ended the call, wondering how she could hand the case over to someone else.

It's now or never, she thought. *And never's not really an option.*

'There's something else, I—'

'And this other thing, the cannabis farm.'

'Yeah, I think we need to discuss that.' She looked around, checking no one was in earshot. 'Third time? Too much of a coincidence.'

'I agree, and I've got an idea on that.' He checked his

watch, squinting to see it. 'Let's talk about it later; right now I need you to concentrate on this.' He waved a hand towards the room they'd just stepped out of.

'The thing is, I'm supposed to be on leave, and—'

Smit's phone started ringing. He looked at the screen and held it up to Tanya.

The contact's name was the chief crime reporter on *De Telegraaf*.

'Want a bet, headless lunatic or killer policeman?' said Smit before he answered and strode off down the corridor.

Great, she thought. *Handled that well.*

She opened the door and stepped back into the room.

'Anyone here able to track calls made over the Internet?' she called out.

A young guy wearing some kind of heavy metal T-shirt leaned back in his chair, waved his hand. The skull leered at Tanya.

'Depends,' he said.

'On what?'

'Oh, a whole load of stuff. Like, for instance, did they go through a proxy server first? Were they routing round some other—'

'Tell you what,' said Tanya pulling out her phone. 'Call this number and speak to the phone company. And this is top priority now.'

She gave him the number and left the room, noticing the time on the wall clock as she did. Coming up for twenty-five past.

I've got to get away, she thought. *I can't get sucked into this.*

Now that she knew her foster father's new name was

Staal, she didn't want to waste any time before confronting him. She'd held it back for years, and now that she'd made the decision to do it, she couldn't wait any longer.

It felt like a fire in her chest. And there was only one way to douse it.

She made her way up two floors to where Smit's office was, hoping he'd managed to get rid of the journalist.

The police tried to be as open as possible, which meant that although press contacts were usually handled by press officers, for big stuff the station chiefs had to show their faces and assure the journalists that they were doing everything in their power, and all the other clichés which got trotted out at such times.

She knocked on his door but got no answer. Listening for a moment, she was sure he wasn't there and turned to go. Someone called her name from the end of the corridor, and she turned to see the tech with the skull T-shirt.

'Yeah?'

'I've got something, but you're not going to like it.'

If it keeps me here any longer then I'm sure I'm not going to like it, she thought as she followed him back down to the basement.

At his computer he flopped into the chair and pointed at the screen.

'You want the simple version?'

Tanya was torn between telling him that just because she was a woman didn't mean she didn't understand computers, and her hatred of techie-speak.

'Simple's good.'

'Whoever placed the calls over the Internet wasn't very careful about hiding what they were doing. In fact they probably just assumed that what they were doing wasn't traceable.'

'So you've got them?'

'Not quite, but I've got their IP address, and when I run it . . .' He pointed to a number on the screen.

'What?'

He pushed back in his chair and turned to look at her. A stud earring caught the light. A phone was ringing off to her right; no one was picking it up. She suddenly felt sick.

'It traces back to here,' he said lowering his voice, glancing around. 'Someone made all those calls right from this building.'

6

'Are you fucking kidding me?' said Smit once Kees had finished.

It was all going to shit.

He'd had no choice but to call it in, but not before he'd cleaned the place up and got rid of every trace of white powder he could find. Every speck of dust had made him paranoid, and every surface now glinted like new.

He was standing in the flat, phone jammed up against his ear, moving it away when Smit had started shouting.

His hands felt weird, painful, but he was getting used to that. Or if he wasn't yet, then he was going to have to real quick.

'Like I said, I turned my back, and he assaulted me.'

'You let it happen.'

'I thought I was there protecting him from someone else, that's why it's called witness protection, not guarding a suspect—'

'I don't give a fuck *what* it's called. He was the main witness in a major trial, and you've just lost him.'

Kees was looking out the window. A few clouds had formed high up and were moving fast. His head was hammering, the pulse at his temples felt like it might explode on each beat.

Shit shit shit.

'I've put the call out, so with any luck—'

'I know you put the call out, that's how I heard about it.'

It was like the adrenaline had cleared his system out. He wasn't high now.

'So what do you want me to do?'

'I'm dealing with a whole heap of shit today, and now I'm going to have to call ICTY and tell them *you've* lost their main witness.'

Kees didn't have anything to say to that.

'Get back to the station and start doing your fucking job,' said Smit before the line went dead.

Modern management style, thought Kees as he headed down the stairs and out to the canal side. He stood by a bin, overflowing with rubbish, and looked down at the canal. The breeze picked up a blue plastic bag from the top of the pile, and floated it down to the water.

It settled on the surface.

He'd given him some of his coke, and Isovic sat there and took it.

He'd been played.

Anger lashed him. He lunged at the bin, ripped it off the stake it was screwed to, and threw the whole thing back towards the building he'd been cooped up in, narrowly missing a woman cycling past.

She looked at Kees, then turned away and carried on pedalling.

He forced himself to think, trying to remember if there was anything that Isovic had said which might be useful.

The file Kees had been passed before taking on the job had been thin at best, and didn't tell him any more than Isovic had himself. He was testifying against Matkovic, who he claimed had been involved in mass rape and killings, at the International Criminal Tribunal for the Former Yugoslavia, usually shortened to ICTY.

Why did he want to escape anyway? It's not like he was on trial.

Kees forced himself to think. If he was Isovic, where would he go now? Try to leave the country? Or try to hide here? And why disappear anyway? It didn't make sense.

He did mention something about friends in Haarlem, he thought. *Car repairs, or valeting. Some immigrant shit.*

Kees glanced at his phone. It was coming up to quarter to four. There'd be loads of businesses doing that out there, but as he headed back to the station, he realized that he didn't have anything better to be doing.

He signed out a patrol car – all the unmarkeds were out – and called Frits as he left, telling him he needed addresses for all car-related businesses in Haarlem. As he pulled out of Amsterdam – traffic was starting to build up so he slammed on the siren – he wondered what would happen to him if he didn't find Isovic.

His phone buzzed, a text message giving him a location for his collection later.

Kees deleted it one-handed while swerving around a truck which hadn't moved over for him.

The collection was going to be tricky. The message he'd sent, via the woman, had not gone down well.

I could just not go, he thought.

He listened to the sound of the siren for a few moments, watched the road ahead.

Who was he kidding?

If he didn't turn up they'd know where to find him.

And anyway, he seriously needed some more.

7

Total carnage.

And that was before Jaap even got anywhere near the body itself.

He pulled up outside a school playground in the gridded section which joined Amsterdam and its leafy southern neighbour Amstelveen to find it crawling with TV vans. Three uniforms were trying to herd the reporters back but not having much luck.

As he parked and stepped out of the car a journalist he vaguely knew spotted him and dashed forwards, holding a furry mike out in front of her, a cameraman rushing behind her, trying to keep up and not trip over his wires.

Jaap wanted to duck and run.

'Inspector Rykel, is it true that this is the second body found without a head?' she asked as she got into range. The rest of the pack turned to see what was going on, their camera lenses flashing in the sun like wolves baring fangs and moving in for the kill.

'I can't comment on an ongoing investigation, you know that,' he said as he fought his way through the pack to the playground. A uniform had managed to secure the entrance, but the cameras still had a clear sight-line to what was on the concrete.

Jaap stood by the body, trying to block the view of the reporters, and looked down.

Another corpse. Another head removed.

Frits had sent him the tweet, which had simply said there was a headless man at the listed address and gave a link to a photo of the body. The photo itself hadn't shown the missing head, the top of the frame cut off just below the shoulders, but it was enough to get the media's attention. Jaap had no idea how anyone had seen the tweet in the first place – as far as he could tell Twitter was a vast torrent of moronic shit – let alone acted so quickly.

Seems like journalists haven't got anything better to do than surf the Internet, he thought as his phone started ringing.

It was Saskia. His promise to get this case over with quickly was now going to get broken for sure. He let it ring.

'Not another,' said a voice behind him.

Jaap turned to see the same forensic as earlier, then turned back to the body. He checked the hands.

'Burned again?' asked the forensic, putting down his bag.

'Yeah,' said Jaap, turning to the nearest uniform. 'Let's get a screen up around this.'

His phone buzzed a message, Saskia asking him to call her urgently. He touched the coins in his pocket before he called her back.

'I'm kind of in the middle of something—'

'I've just had a call from Ronald,' said Saskia.

Jaap thought Saskia held Ronald, her boss, in way too high regard, and had recently wondered if there was something going on there. She was his ex, so it wouldn't have been any of his business, but for Floortje. He found the thought of her having another father, even if it was only a stepfather, one he didn't want to contemplate.

'And?'

'We've got a really bad situation going on. My main witness has been lost.'

'What do you mean lost?'

'He was under police protection, and someone screwed up.'

'That's the thing, the cops down in Den Haag?' said Jaap, eyeing a reporter who was trying to edge round the newly erected screen shielding the body. 'They're rubbish.'

'This isn't a joke, Jaap. And anyway, it was in Amsterdam. I think it may even have been someone at your station.'

The body was lying at Jaap's feet. His eyes travelled up to the severed neck.

Who is doing this? he thought.

'Look, I'm not sure what I can do, I've got a second body here, and I—'

'I was just hoping you could find something out. Without Isovic the whole trial is going to collapse. That means letting Matkovic get away with it.'

Jaap knew how much this meant to her. She'd been working the case since she'd gone back after Floortje was born. At times he thought she'd been working too hard, but then she was still trying to cope with Andreas' death, and having a child. The same way he was trying to cope with Karin's death and the new reality that the child he thought was Andreas' was actually his own.

They split the childcare as evenly as they could, but given both their jobs it was never easy.

'Surely there's someone working on it?'

'Yeah, they said they had a team. Their best people.

Which basically means they've probably got one washed-up old patrol guy on it.'

Jaap guessed that was the lawyer in her, cynical, unwilling to believe anything she was told. Which was probably why they'd split up in the first place.

But it didn't make her wrong – they were understaffed as it was.

'Okay. I'll make a couple of calls, see what's going on.'

Jaap pocketed his phone – he missed the old clamshell models where you could snap them shut at the end of the call – and looked around. The playground was wedged between two buildings on either side, a wall with primary-coloured murals blocking the far end. One of the images was a large bearded face. It took Jaap a few moments to realize it was probably meant to represent Jesus.

A Christian school.

Jaap wondered about his earlier thought, about homegrown terrorists.

So where are the demands? he thought.

Blue lights flickered as more patrol cars turned up, and the new influx of uniforms busied themselves stringing up police tape between lamp posts, and then pushing the journalists behind it.

Jaap turned back to the body. Like the first, it was dressed in jeans and trainers, but with a football shirt, the red and white of the local team.

Unlike the first victim though, where Jaap had found the lack of blood disturbing, this one was floating on a lake of the stuff, already going sticky from the look of it.

'Has he got a phone?' he asked the forensic, who'd already started work.

He could smell exhaust from one of the TV vans, and he caught snippets of a reporter giving a particularly graphic account to someone over the phone.

Not that it mattered; anyone with an Internet connection could see the photo. It had been retweeted, which Jaap didn't understand, but he'd been told by Roemers that the only way to restrict access to it now would be to shut down the entire web.

Jaap had almost asked him if he could do it.

The forensic rummaged around in the body's pockets and extracted a black phone, same model as the earlier body, a wallet and a bunch of keys.

'Gloves?'

'You should have kept the ones from earlier.'

'I figured I didn't want to cross-contaminate the scene, isn't that what you lot are always on about?'

The forensic sighed.

'Lucky for you I replenished my stock before coming out.'

He pointed to his kit bag a few feet past the perimeter of blood.

Jaap got some and then took the phone.

I hope I'm not on this one as well, he thought as he powered it on.

But this time it asked for a passcode.

He bagged it up, he'd have to get the tech department on to that, and stood back from the body.

Two victims, both killed the same day and their deaths announced on Twitter, which had notified the press. He dialled Frits.

'That tweet,' he said when Frits picked up. 'Any chance of it being traced?'

45

'I already asked someone to look into that, I haven't heard back yet.'

'Let me know the second you do.'

'The thing is, that whole department is kind of tied up, Tanya's got some case on and is storming around like a bitch on heat.'

Jaap had wondered if people at the station had figured out about him and Tanya, but Frits' tone suggested he hadn't. And Frits knew everything that went on there, so if he didn't know, nobody did.

Unless he's baiting me, he thought.

He toyed with the idea of calling Tanya, who must have got roped into something at the last minute. She was supposed to be going away with a couple of friends today – had been talking about it for weeks – and she'd be mad if she missed that.

'Can you check that someone is doing it though? And what's this about a missing witness?'

'Oh man. Smit nearly shat his entire insides out when he heard about that. I tell you what, if Kees doesn't find the guy soon I reckon that'll pretty much be it for him.'

'Don't tell me it was Kees who lost him,' said Jaap, knowing he was going to be disappointed.

'The same.'

Once he'd hung up Jaap shook his head. It was kind of his fault.

Kees saved my life, thought Jaap. *And I thought I was repaying the favour.*

He should have told Smit about Kees' reliance on coke instead of trying to help him on the quiet. But since the death of Inspector Andreas Houten over a year ago and the subsequent cover-up of the murder by Smit, their relations had never recovered.

'Wanna rifle through his wallet?' said the forensic, jolting Jaap back to the present.

'What's there?' he asked, stepping over.

A tornado of flies circled the body, he could hear their buzzing.

'Usual stuff. His driving licence says he's called Martin Teeven. And . . .' said the forensic handing it over '. . . several thousand euros.'

Jaap took the wallet, the brown leather still shiny. It looked brand new. He noticed the lack of any kind of card. He did a quick count of the cash, well over three thousand euros, and a fistful of receipts.

It's usually only dealers who have this kind of cash on them, he thought as he turned to the receipts.

'Hey, look at this,' said the forensic.

Jaap looked down to where he was pointing. The trouser leg on the dead man's left calf was rolled up. An ankle holster made of cheap black leather which looked like it was missing a knife. There was a roundel on the top strap, black plastic with the outline of an eagle in gold.

'Pity he wasn't carrying it today, might have been useful when he was attacked.'

The first victim had owned a gun but had not had it on him, and the second victim owned a knife but again had not been carrying. Unless whoever killed him had taken it.

Jaap turned back to the receipts. The name on one of

them caught his attention. It was a cafe on Bloemgracht, about twenty metres away from where his houseboat was moored.

'How about we split it?' said the forensic. 'I mean, he's not going to need it, is he? I could use a couple hundred for tonight. Flash it around a bit, impress the date.'

Jaap ignored him.

He'd just checked the other receipts.

And his mouth was now Sahara-dry.

He wondered if the forensic would notice his fingers. See the tremor there.

Of the fourteen, twelve were from the same cafe, going back over the last five days.

He turned to the driving licence.

The name was familiar, as was the face.

It took him a few moments to remember exactly.

But then it came.

Jaap had arrested him over eight years ago. He'd testified at the trial, where Teeven had protested his innocence.

Jaap could hear someone calling his name – one of the journalists asking for a comment – but he ignored him, thinking about the trial, remembering the two days with startling clarity.

Remembering the moment the judge announced Teeven was going down for murder and the look Teeven shot him.

Remembering, in a weird kind of slow motion like he was underwater, the threat Teeven had mouthed across the courtroom as he was led away.

8

'You're going to want to see this,' Tanya said as Smit tried to tell her he was busy.

He looked at her for a second, then motioned back into his office, moved round his desk, sat down, and ran his hand over his head.

When she'd first transferred down to Amsterdam Smit had been large, but looking at him now she realized that he'd changed, lost weight. His face was thinner, and his body was almost lean-looking, helped by the well cut suit he was wearing. She knew people called him The Eel behind his back, a reference to both his slippery nature and the fact that his corpulent body had been the very opposite of an eel's. But with the lost weight it was starting to sound less ironic.

There was a smell which Tanya couldn't quite place. Something floral, like lavender. Or roses.

'Make it quick. I've got to brief the mayor on what's going on with these beheadings. And it looks like something else as well?'

'I don't think you're going to want to brief them on this just yet,' said Tanya, sitting in the chair opposite his desk. 'It really is one of us.'

Smit exhaled and flicked something Tanya couldn't see off his desk.

'There was me hoping the guy had just managed to nick a police jacket from somewhere.'

'Me too. But I checked those calls, the ones to the woman's phone?'

He nodded.

'They traced back to here. Someone made them from this building.'

'Seriously?' said Smit, breathing out. 'That's the kind of shit I can do without.' He shook his head. 'Any way of working out who?'

'Not that I can see. We don't have cameras in any of the offices, only the cells and interrogation rooms. I can get the tech team to see if they can pinpoint a specific computer, but I don't think they can.'

I should have said 'someone', not 'I', she thought.

Smit pulled open a drawer in his desk, took out a pot of hand cream and dabbed it on his palms, rubbing it in slowly, before working his way up each finger. Fully moisturized, he replaced the pot and slid the drawer shut.

'You were right. I don't want to brief anyone on this.'

He worked a bit of stray cream around one of his cuticles.

'Normally in this kind of case I'd be obliged to let the Ministry of Justice know – they'd send their own team out to investigate – but . . .' he tailed off.

'I think that's best. The thing is, I'm actually on leave already. I'm going away with some friends.'

The same lie I told Jaap, she thought. *At least I'm keeping it consistent.*

Smit was looking out the window. He didn't give any sign that he'd actually heard her.

'The problem is, getting an internal investigation team in is really unpopular. I've seen it done before, and it just creates chaos. I'd be much happier if you could go forward with this. Treading carefully, of course.'

'I'm not sure that would be a good idea, and like I said, I'm supposed to be on—'

'And I don't want you saying a word to anyone about this. You report only to me. Is that clear?'

Smit stood up, glanced at his watch. He shuffled a few things around on his desk, placing a pen on top of a pile of paper. Adjusted it until it was at the perfect angle.

'And this cannabis farm thing,' he said as if mollifying her. 'Let's just sit on it for now. Concentrate on the killing, then we'll go back to it.'

He stood up, still no eye contact.

'I've got to get going now,' he said as he went to the door, holding it open for Tanya.

'But what about my leave?'

He looked at her as if she'd suddenly popped up out of the floor.

'All leave's cancelled,' he said. 'As of now.'

As she stepped out into the corridor, Smit closing the door on her heels, she could tell she hadn't played it right.

9

After all the shitty luck he'd been having, Kees finally got a break.

Or thought he had. It was only the third place he'd visited, and the people working there had never heard of anyone called Isovic.

So they said.

But Kees could see they were lying.

He was in a shabby office out back. Unusually for a garage, there wasn't a calendar featuring a semi-naked woman hanging from the wall. A window looked over a grimy work area, where three cars were hiked up on large platforms so that men in overalls could do things to their undersides.

The desk in front of him looked post-Hiroshima.

The guy behind it looked even worse.

'But I tell you before, I don't know this man you keep talking about.'

'The thing is,' Kees looked at the guy's name badge but was unable to read it because of the black grease which seemed to permeate the whole place. 'I think you do.'

Kees sought out the man's eyes, but he ducked them away.

Metal hitting concrete clanged out from behind him. One of the mechanics cursed. A tinny radio was playing in the background, periodically obscured as one of the cars was revved up. Kees caught diesel fumes.

'It's simple,' said Kees, figuring that the guy in front of him probably wouldn't understand the finer points of Dutch law. 'You don't tell me where I can find Isovic, then I'll come back later tonight. With some friends.' He smiled.

He'd been finding that smiling was pretty good at unnerving people.

'So what's it gonna be?' he asked, feeling like someone in a movie.

'Okay, okay,' said the guy. 'If I tell you I don't see you again. Okay?'

Kees smiled a bit more. As suspected, the guy came from somewhere where the police had more power, and hadn't worked out that it was different in the Netherlands.

Fifteen minutes later Kees was standing outside a house in Zandvoort, the North Sea at his back. He'd even seen some people on the beach, the sun hanging over the sea reflecting light back off the green-brown water. He'd been here last summer, he remembered as he pressed the doorbell.

He and a few colleagues had made the trip out having seen posters for a world skinny-dipping record attempt. Expectations had been high, and they'd settled in on the beach with large amounts of beer.

But in the end they'd been disappointed. It turned out anyone who actually wanted to take their clothes off in public wasn't worth looking at.

Finishing their drinks, they'd driven back into Amsterdam and gone to a live sex show, which Kees had ducked out from early. For some reason he'd found it depressing.

Nothing much happened in response to the bell ringing, so he walked round the side, noticing how the salt spray was corroding the metal gutters. The garden out back was small, neat, with a few rows of tulips following a white wooden fence. He went through the gate, which he expected to creak but didn't, and walked up to the patio windows, peering inside.

Neat, like the garden. Not the kind of place he'd expect a Bosniak to have friends.

He tried the windows but they were locked. Glancing around he could see the back of the house wasn't overlooked directly, except maybe by the houses on either side. He turned back and stared at his reflection in the glass, the image slightly doubled, out of focus.

Fuck it, he thought as he pulled out his gun, flipped it round and broke the left-hand pane with the butt.

Glass tinkled to the ground. A shard just missed his foot.

Kees brushed off the gun and re-holstered it, his foot crunching glass as he stepped inside.

His search turned up little; there were two bedrooms, one lived in, the other looking like it might have been ages ago but had been left untended for a while, dust on the bedclothes giving it away.

In the kitchen there was a half-eaten burger, congealing in its open wrapper next to a laptop set up on a breakfast bar, and a soft-drink cup. He prodded the bun. It was still warm, the sesame seeds felt like braille against his finger, and a bit of brown glossy sauce oozed out of the edge.

Pushing aside the burger and the large cardboard cup with its swirls of red and white spiralling round the outside, he moved the laptop so he could see the screen. The screensaver showed the pink silhouette of a dancing woman on a black background.

He slapped the space bar and the machine whirred into life, replacing the dancing woman with a plain desktop. A web browser was open, with two tabs. The first tab showed a news website with a story about a headless man being found after a tweet, the second was the Twitter account in question.

Kees had heard all the chatter on the police radio about the beheading as he'd driven over to Haarlem.

He looked at the Twitter page.

The first tweet gave an address in Amstelveen.

The second, posted at 17.46, read, 'More to come?'

Everybody in the Netherlands must be looking at this, he thought.

For a moment he wondered where it had all gone wrong.

This was the kind of case he should be in charge of, not sneaking around looking for missing witnesses.

He heard a noise outside, and looked out of the window, ducking back just in time.

Someone was walking up to the front door.

The footsteps stopped. Kees could hear keys rattling, then one turning in the lock. He stepped quietly behind the door and pulled out his weapon.

The person was in the hallway now and seemed to have stopped dead. Kees was working out if they could see the broken window from there but decided they wouldn't be able to.

Then they started moving – two steps, three – and walked into the kitchen.

Kees slammed the door shut and pointed his gun.

The man jumped, spun round.

'Fucking hell,' he said, backing away from Kees until he bumped into the sink.

'Where's Isovic?' said Kees, wondering if he should try out a smile again.

'I . . . don't know what you mean.'

He was about fiftyish, Kees thought. Short brown hair going grey, pale face and a suit which had probably once looked smart. But it didn't disguise the fact that his body was lean and muscled. The guy worked out, that much was clear.

'I want,' said Kees advancing a step, 'to know where Isovic is.'

'I think there's been a misunderstanding, I don't know anyone called Isovic.'

Kees couldn't quite place his accent, down south maybe.

'You are?'

'I own this place. It's a rental. I'd had a complaint from a neighbour about the tenant. That's why I'm here, to check it out. Can I put my arms down now?'

'Keep them where they are. What's the tenant's name?'

'Who are you?'

Kees fished out his ID and flashed it. The man squinted a bit, then nodded his head.

'The tenant's name is Osman Krilic – he's been here for just over a year now.'

'What does he do?'

'My arms are getting tired.'

'Tell me your name,' said Kees.

56

'Philip Hauer.'

'With your left hand, throw me your driving licence.'

Hauer stared at him for a moment, then shrugged. He lowered his hand, fished around in his right pocket and pulled out a worn leather wallet.

'I can't get it out with only one hand,' he said.

'So do it over your head.'

Hauer did what he was told. Once extracted, he tossed the licence on to the breakfast bar. Kees stepped forward to pick it up. The guy wasn't lying. Or he had a fake ID.

Kees tucked his gun into the back of his trousers, hitching his jacket over the handle once it was in place.

Fucking uncomfortable, he thought. *But it looks good.*

'Catch,' he said as he flipped the licence back to Hauer. 'So, if I wanted to get hold of Krilic, and given that he's not here and it looks like he left in a hurry –' he pointed to the half-eaten burger '– what would you recommend?'

A tapping noise at the window made them both look across.

'Are you okay?'

The face at the glass was hollowed out, the eyes dark rimmed.

Six months, thought Kees. *Tops.*

'I'm fine,' said Hauer. 'I was just checking up. After you complained about the noise.'

'When did you last see him?' asked Kees, addressing the old man direct.

The face at the window looked at Kees, then shook his head.

'He pretends to be deaf,' said Hauer. 'Which is odd as

he complained about shouting here earlier. Which kind of proves he can't be.'

Kees moved towards the window and bent down so his face was right by the old man's.

'When did you see him?' he asked with exaggerated care, loud enough to be heard through the glass.

'About five minutes ago.'

'I was here five minutes ago, and I didn't see him.'

The old man nodded. Kees could see a car with a mattress tied to the roof inching along the road by the sea.

'That's because he ran away just as you arrived at the front door. I saw him jumping over the fence at the back. Him and another man I hadn't seen before.'

10

'Where are we at?'

Jaap hated having to give real-time progress updates. The fact that he had to give this one to Smit made it even worse. That's why he'd chosen to do it over the phone.

'Two bodies without a head. Someone on Twitter who knew about the killings, and there may be another one tomorrow.'

'I saw all that on the news. What I'm asking is how close are you to stopping it?'

You'd think I was responsible for this, thought Jaap.

'I'm pursuing several lines of enquiry,' he said, knowing that was going to piss Smit off, but beyond caring.

It was a couple of hours since he'd stood in the playground, holding the receipts and realizing that he'd put the victim in prison years before.

The receipts could just be a coincidence.

But with the photo on Koopman's phone as well? he thought. *That's one too many.*

'That's the line *I* give to the press. I want something more concrete,' snapped back Smit.

'Well I haven't got anything, yet. And I'm just about to interview someone so I'll get back to you.'

Jaap stabbed the end call button, wishing it was Smit's eye.

'That went well.'

He was down in Computer Crimes, talking to Roemers, the head of the unit.

'The man's an asshole.'

'True. And there's a good chance he may walk through those doors at any moment.'

'I didn't think he liked it down here?'

'He doesn't. But with most of my crew working on Tanya's thing he's been keeping an eye on us all afternoon. Seems particularly keen to get a result.'

Tanya had left the houseboat for work early that morning, saying she'd been roped into a drugs raid. She was hoping it'd be over quickly so she could meet her friends at midday. They'd said goodbye, Jaap still only half awake. Then he'd rolled over to her side of the bed, still warm and smelling of her, and fallen back asleep.

'She still here?'

'She was about twenty minutes ago.'

She really needed that break, thought Jaap. *She's going to be gutted.*

'You're not here just for my company,' prompted Roemers when Jaap hadn't said anything for a few moments.

'Yeah, right. I need you to hack that Twitter account – can you do that?'

'Frits already asked me that.'

'And?'

'I told him that the question really is, am I allowed to do that?'

'Don't tell me you need—'

'—written authorization. Exactly. Like the song says, "fuck the law".'

Jaap didn't know the song, but then Roemers looked like he was into weird music.

Jaap stared at the screen, the tweet taunting him.

More to come?

I don't have time for form-filling, thought Jaap.

'The thing is,' said Roemers, picking up on Jaap's frustration and shifting forward in his seat. 'I know someone who isn't restricted by our very high moral sense. Do you want me to ask him?'

'How long do you think it will take?'

'Hard to say – could be a few hours, could be days – but the sooner he gets going . . .'

'The minute you hear anything—'

'Got it,' replied Roemers, who'd already turned to his screen, fingers scuttling over the keyboard. 'Just setting him off on it now.'

'I'm assuming you can do this though?' Jaap dropped the second victim's phone on his desk. 'It's locked.'

'In my sleep, baby.'

'I'm sure it's off contract, just like the first one, but check it anyway. And once you've got it unlocked cross-ref the call lists in both phones, I want to see what comes up. How long's it going to take to crack?'

'Should be about twenty minutes or so. You want to wait?'

'Just call me,' said Jaap as he stepped out the door. He toyed with going to his desk – he needed to get a start on the initial report, and he wanted to check up on when Teeven had actually been released – but figured the risk of bumping into Smit too great, so he left the station.

Outside the sun was just dipping towards the row of houses to the west. The buildings on the opposite side of the canal were still illuminated, their windows polished gold.

He started walking, trying to think about the victims. Two people, one who had a photo of him and a gun under his bed, the other he'd put away for murder.

The case had been controversial, the dropout daughter of a right-wing politician had been found raped and strangled. The media had been all over it, and Jaap remembered the politician had even used it to his political advantage.

And tricky. Jaap had been under pressure to make an arrest, and while he'd genuinely believed that Teeven, a minor player in a drugs outfit based in Amsterdam Zuid, was involved, he'd had a nagging feeling that there was something wrong, something which didn't quite fit.

But given the outrage whipped up in the press the trial was pressed through fast, and Teeven went down for murder.

And now, before being killed, he'd got out and just happened to spend the last few days sitting in a cafe a clog's throw away from Jaap's houseboat.

I can't have Floortje staying with me now, he thought as he walked.

Saskia was going to be down in Den Haag next week so she didn't have to travel back and forth for the trial. There was a house for prosecutors to use right by the ICTY, and Jaap realized he'd feel a lot happier if Floortje was down there with her.

And Saskia wasn't going to like that at all.

The air was cooling rapidly in the shade on his side of the canal. Skin on his forearms goose-pimpled up. He turned off on to Leidsetraat, heading south. A tram screamed by, metal on metal.

Saskia answered on the third ring.

'Any news?'

'On your witness? No, but I've got something else I need to talk to you about.'

'I can guess already.'

He could sense she was exasperated. She'd been with him long enough, and then with Andreas, to know what was coming.

'Look, I've thought about this. I could see if we could get someone to help out—'

'Hire someone, you mean?'

'Yeah, I'll pay for it, and—'

'I don't want to do that, I'm going to be busy.'

'I know, which is why you need someone. There's room at the house you'll be at, right? So whoever we get could live in.'

'There *are* four bedrooms, but that's not really the point. Why can't Floortje stay with you?'

Jaap took a breath. He could smell something frying in rancid fat from the fast-food joint he'd just passed.

'The thing is, I'm thinking of moving out for a few days, there's that problem with the floor? I had someone take it up yesterday and they think they may have to tank the whole hull. And I'd rather get it done sooner than later.'

Why do I lie so easily? Jaap wondered.

'Well, someone's got to be the responsible parent. I guess it'll have to be me,' she said and hung up before Jaap could reply.

Great, he thought. *Just fucking great.*

Trying to bring up a child which he'd not had time to prepare for was never going to be easy. That he was having to do it with his ex made it even harder.

There were too many people around, too much movement and noise. He needed to think and ducked into the first side street he came to, passing a shop selling bonsai trees. He stopped and looked at one, its delicate branches reminding him of his time in Kyoto.

It'd been tough.

In fact it had nearly driven him crazy, but he'd come out of it with a sense of calm and purpose which he'd not felt before.

And then, with Karin's death, it had gone.

He wondered if it would ever return.

His pocket buzzed and he answered his phone, seeing it was Roemers.

'What have you got?'

'A couple of things. The Twitter maniac has posted again, there's a picture of two heads. I'm sending it over to you now.'

'And what's the other thing?'

'Unlocked the phone, not much on it. But there's something you need to see.'

Jaap got a weird taste in his mouth. His neck felt too long.

'What is it?'

'I don't want to ruin the surprise because it's—'

64

'Just tell me.'

'Okay, fine. It's a photo taken early this morning.'

Jaap knew what was coming.

He didn't want to hear it.

'Looks to me like Tanya, and I'm pretty sure she's leaving a houseboat. In fact, it kinda looks like your houseboat.'

11

Tanya stared at the red letters on the murder board as she slumped into her seat.

Open and shut this wasn't.

Not by a long shot.

This was the kind of case which would be very much open, possibly for a long time, and it had her name next to it on the murder board.

As the most junior member on the homicide team she'd got the shitty desk. The one right by the door, so everyone who came into the room walked right by her back. And when they left the door open, which they invariably did, she got a direct scent line to the toilets just next door.

The men's toilets.

And she didn't know what it was about male homicide inspectors, but for the most part they didn't appear to have the best digestive systems.

Tanya dropped her eyes from the board and stared at her desk. She'd tried to argue with Smit earlier but he'd not been willing to listen, just told her to take leave another time. He'd told her not in so many words but the message had been clear, that he really didn't care.

A uniform walked into the room, looked around for a moment, lost.

'You seen Kees?' he finally asked Tanya when he couldn't find anyone else important-looking enough.

'Not recently. Actually I haven't seen him all week,' said Tanya, realizing how pleasant it had been.

'Urgent package came for him, can you sign for it?'

'What are you, a courier?'

'I know, sucks, doesn't it? Not what I signed up for.'

Tanya signed for the parcel. 'No, me neither,' she said as she handed the pen back and took the parcel.

She took it over to Kees' desk, which was layered with rubbish. It looked to her the kind of place rats would breed. She balanced it on top of the smallest pile and walked back to her own desk, Zen in comparison. Or anal.

It was bad enough that she'd been landed with the case, but the fact that she was now quite possibly going to have to start interviewing her colleagues made it even worse. She was the only woman in the department, and that made most of the men uncomfortable, not quite sure how to behave around her.

This is going to make them even more uncomfortable, she thought.

An idea struck her; she could check the attendance logs for everyone in the building – that way she might be able to narrow down who was present when the calls were made. Meaning she could at least narrow down the number of people she was going to piss off.

She went down to the desk sergeant and requested the logs.

'Not sure I can give them out,' said the young officer, looking uncomfortable.

'It's just that I've been doing so much overtime, and I didn't keep track, you know? I'd really love to be able to put in a claim . . .'

She leaned forward, propped on her elbows, feeling her breasts squeeze together, and watched the guy's eyes slide down her chest. It only took a few moments for her to know he was going to give in.

She felt a wave of contempt.

Only she wasn't sure if it was for him, or herself.

'Yeah, I could do with some of that,' he said, suddenly more animated than he had been. 'We've only got the last two weeks; anything older's been archived already.'

'Two weeks is fine,' said Tanya.

As she got back to her desk with the logs she realized she needed to do this elsewhere; she didn't want anyone seeing what she was up to. She stuffed them into a plastic bag she had in a desk drawer, proof of a hurried lunch from Albert Heijn, and headed for the door, thinking she'd go to the bagel joint she and Jaap sometimes met at for lunch. It was the kind of place cops didn't go, so although it was close to the station they'd figured they'd be safe. And in any case, they were just colleagues, and colleagues sometimes had lunch together.

Jaap had questioned her desire to keep their relationship secret, but she'd been adamant. She didn't want the sleeping-to-the-top jokes, or any of the other shit that would get thrown at her. *Maybe one day*, she'd told him.

She got a table towards the back, ordered a bagel with Oude Kaas and a fresh orange juice, and started to look through the logs for the past two weeks.

It was tedious work, making a list of all the people who were in the station at the times the calls were made, and wasn't helped by the fact that it was all handwritten in various hard-to-read scripts. Legible writing wasn't on the police's list of key skill requirements. But after ten minutes or so a pattern started to emerge, a pattern she didn't much like seeing.

It can't be, she thought.

'Hey.'

The voice startled her – she'd got engrossed – and she looked up to see Frits and his wandering eye.

'Looks interesting,' he said, nodding to the papers.

'Not really,' said Tanya wanting to put them away so he couldn't see but knowing that would look like an invitation to sit. Frits peered over towards the papers. She sighed inside and slid them together into one pile, dumping the whole lot back in the bag.

'Yeah, I mean it's just paperwork, right?' he said, pulling out the chair opposite and sitting down. 'Way too much of that going on.'

Tanya didn't know how old he was, but she figured he must be well into his fifties. His face was open, too open, and that, combined with his eye, made him a non-contender for best-looking cop of the year.

He was the station's main dispatcher, and while in theory he didn't actually assign crimes to specific people – that was Smit's job – more often than not he was the one who decided on who to call. Jaap had warned her about him, saying that she didn't want to get on his wrong side or she'd get all the shit jobs.

Seems like I already have, she thought.

'Mind if I join you?' he asked, despite the fact he was sitting down already. He motioned to the waitress, who came over and took his order.

'Be my guest,' she said once the waitress had left. She got the feeling Frits didn't get sarcasm.

'So, you've been with us, what? Seven, eight months now?' he asked, sitting back in the chair and looking at her.

'Ten.'

'You like it?'

She wanted to get back to the logs. She didn't want to sit here with Frits. 'Yeah, it's all right.'

'So, bad luck about that case you got. The first officer on the scene swore it was a suicide or accident.' He paused while the waitress deposited his coffee and stroopwafel on the table. He picked up the stroopwafel and put it on top of the coffee cup, like a lid. 'If I'd known I'd've called someone else.'

'You said there wasn't anyone else available,' said Tanya.

'Yeah, well. I thought you could probably use a little boost in your clearance rate—'

'You're kidding.'

Frits caught the sharpness in her tone and looked momentarily startled.

'Yeah, I'm kidding,' he said eventually. 'There really wasn't anyone else. And Smit requested you specifically.'

He became interested in his stroopwafel, checking to see if the heat from the coffee had made it more pliable.

Tanya didn't believe him, but knew there was no point in pursuing it.

'Well, it's totally messed up my leave. I was going away with some friends, and now I'm going to miss it.'

He didn't get sarcasm and he probably didn't do guilt either. But she'd try it out anyway.

'That's bad,' he said, taking a bite. A crumb stuck to his top lip, then dropped off when he spoke again. 'I'd hate to miss leave. I've got a holiday booked myself. Next month. I'm going—'

He stopped as Tanya suddenly reached her hand into her pocket.

'I put it on silent, but it always makes me jump,' she said as she pulled out her phone.

She glanced at the screen.

'I've got to take this,' she said and answered, listening for a few moments.

'What, now?' she asked. 'Okay, I'm on my way. Tell me what happened.'

She got up, jamming the phone between her shoulder and ear, grabbed the bag with all the papers in, mouthed sorry to Frits and left.

Outside she pocketed the phone, hoping Frits hadn't noticed it wasn't on, and wondered what to do now.

A horde of tourists cycled past on a guided tour, following the lead bike marked out by a large yellow flag attached to a pole. One of the tourists near the back of the convoy clearly hadn't got used to the fact that Dutch bikes didn't have brakes.

'You've got to backpedal,' she told the woman in English, who looked at her as if she'd just told her to jump in the canal. Tanya shrugged and started walking, her mind back on the attendance logs. What she'd found had shocked her. And she didn't know what to do about it.

Tanya stopped by a tree. The sun was just dropping behind the houses on the far side of the canal, dark shadows devouring their fronts.

She pulled the sheet out again and looked at it. At the names she'd circled.

I need the older logs, she thought. *See if that'll narrow it down.*

I 2

Kees couldn't believe what the voice on the phone had just told him.

'You delivered it where? Are you fucking insane?'

He was crawling back into Amsterdam – an endless stream of people with nothing better to do had decided to get into their cars and block his way.

And there was a speck of dirt on the windscreen right in his field of vision. He'd tried to wipe it off earlier but it wouldn't budge. Then he'd tried lowering the seat back to change his sight-line, but that hadn't worked either.

It was still there, blurring his view.

After the old man had told Kees about the men disappearing out the back he'd searched the area, but it was clear they'd gone. Kees had then put a call in for Osman Krilic, but was still waiting for a hit off the central database. He couldn't quite believe how long it was taking, it wasn't like Krilic was a common name.

As he'd left the house the landlord had asked him about claiming compensation for the glass from the police. Kees had told him it was like that when he arrived, putting the blame on the two men who'd run out the back as he'd walked up the front path.

From the old man's description, one of them was unquestionably Isovic.

'You don't want it?' said the voice that Kees knew as

Paul. He'd figured that wasn't his real name. People practising the art of blackmail generally tended to prefer anonymity.

'Course I fucking want it,' said Kees, lurching the car forward and to the right, spinning the wheel one-handed to make the most of a gap which had opened up. 'But not sent there. I was going to pick it up, like we agreed.'

'Like we agreed,' echoed the voice. 'Is that the same way we agreed that you'd give us the information we need? Because I got a message passed back through our mutual friend that you wanted to stop.'

'Look, it's getting too risky. I think we just need to be a bit careful right now—'

'You seem to forget that you owe us. Quite a lot. What I sent you today was just a little reward – I haven't added it to the bill. But we don't need to have the discussion about what will happen if you don't honour our agreement, do we?'

Kees was about to respond when he heard the click telling him he'd been disconnected.

A V of birds, reflected in the rear window of the car in front, forged from left to right in the sky.

Fuck, he thought. *Fuckfuckfuck.*

They were right, he did owe them.

And now he was screwed.

By the time he made it back to the station garage, dropped the keys off and rushed up to the first floor, he felt like he could really use a line. Just medicinally, just to help put things in focus a bit, give him the clarity his brain needed to sort out what he was going to do next.

At least the sniffer dogs aren't kennelled here, he thought as he stepped into the main office and made his way over to his desk.

There were at least six other inspectors milling around, finishing up paperwork, surfing the Internet, or just staring at the ceiling. Saturday night was usually big, but it was too early for anything really fun to have happened yet. They often took bets on the exact time the first murder got called in.

His phone livened up his pocket with a buzz, and he pulled it out, noticing the number on the screen. It was the guy who ran the weekly meetings he'd told Jaap he was still going to. He let it ring. He'd been leaving messages almost every day, wanting to check when Kees was coming back and hoping that he was sticking to his pledge.

Sanctimonious bastard, thought Kees as the phone buzzed again, signalling another voicemail. He deleted it without listening then turned his attention to what he had to do.

The parcel was sitting there. In plain view of anyone who had two eyes in their head and a brain to process the information. Which made about three by Kees' count.

The whole thing's getting out of control, he thought as he picked up the parcel.

'Hey, Kees,' said one of the men, an inspector whose name Kees had forgotten, just as he was turning round to head out the door. 'What's in there?'

'Oh just some stuff,' he said, suddenly unable to think of anything.

'Yeah? Anything fun?'

'Just stuff.'

'Like porn stuff? A strap-on? That why it's wrapped in plain brown paper?'

'You tell me – seems like you know a lot about that,' said Kees, turning away.

'Or maybe it's one of those rings you put round your—'

'Terpstra.'

Kees turned to see Smit storming into the room, his boss's eyes zeroed in on him like he was prey.

'Got him?' demanded Smit as he came into range, his bulk imposing.

'I've got a strong lead and—'

'Really? What is it? Please tell me,' said Smit as he stopped right in front of him. Kees could smell him, a smell like flowers. Powdery, delicate flowers.

'He went to a friend's place out in Zandvoort, and they left together.'

The other inspectors hadn't stopped what they were doing, but they were all fully tuned in now, Kees could feel it.

He couldn't blame them really. They spent their working lives rocking up to dead bodies, but they very rarely got to see a murder actually take place.

'I see. And now? Where are they?'

'That's what I'm working on. I—'

'It doesn't look like it to me,' said Smit, stepping even closer, right into Kees' face. 'What it looks like to me is you jerking yourself off when you should be out there finding this guy. I've had the big lawyer asshole who's head of ICTY on the phone, and he wants you shipped down there and chucked in a cell with someone responsible for mass genocide, and—'

One of the inspectors laughed. Smit glanced round to see who it was just as a uniform walked in and, unaware of the bollocking in progress, stepped over to Kees.

'Got this for you,' he said, handing over a file.

Kees opened it. There'd been a hit on Osman Krilic.

A brawl in a bar out by Centraal three weeks ago meant he was on the system. Though why it had taken over an hour to find that out was anybody's guess.

Kees slipped a photo and a few sheets out of the file and scanned them, noticing that the home address for Krilic was not in Zandvoort.

It was in Amsterdam.

Surely he'd not be so stupid as to go there now? thought Kees.

But the alternative was to listen to more abuse from Smit.

'Gotta go,' he said. 'This is important.'

He made for the door, holding the parcel in one hand. It was making him nervous and it had made him realize something else; he was going to have to deal with Paul.

'I want to be kept up to date on this, that clear?'

'Sure,' said Kees over his shoulder as stepped into the corridor. 'Absolutely.'

Back in the carpool he was told nothing was available.

'I just brought one back, less than ten minutes ago.'

The guy sitting at the window just shrugged.

'Being cleaned,' he said as he probed between his front two teeth with a key, then, having found whatever it was that was bothering him, started trying to loosen it.

'Cleaned? I didn't shit in it, did I?'

'Look, best I can do,' the guy said, sliding another set of keys over to him and going back to his dental grooming. 'Last on the right.'

Kees scooped the keys up, walked to the end of the space and stopped dead.

He's got to be kidding, he thought.

He pressed the button on the key fob. The lights flashed once, and a soft beep told him the guy really hadn't been kidding.

As Kees motored out he wondered just why the Amsterdam Police Force had a single-seater electric car.

13

Tanya shifted down the seat, a stud on the back of her jeans catching the worn fabric.

The front door of the house she was watching opened, and a man stepped out, pulling the door closed behind him. He turned to fit the key in the lock, his shoulders hunched.

This was the first time in over sixteen years that Tanya had seen Ruud Staal, and he was older, fatter, his posture worse. He turned back to the road and started off down the path. Tanya caught a glimpse of his face.

It was then she felt like throwing up.

This man who had ruined her life was walking down the street, free.

Her hands gripped the steering wheel, which seemed to be vibrating. Then she realized it was her hands shaking, knuckles white from the pressure.

She'd come to confront him, to get him to confess to what he'd done. After that she'd make a formal statement, get him arrested. And while in theory she'd be offered anonymity at a trial, she knew that somehow her name would get out.

She realized that it was that more than anything which had held her back; she didn't want anyone to know what had happened to her, couldn't bear the thought that her life would be laid bare. All because of him. But she knew she had to do this, or the secret was going to kill her, suck all the life out of her, leave her living in black and white, just as she'd been doing all these years.

Do it now.

One of her hands moved from the wheel to the lever which opened the car door. She pulled it and the door opened with a click. He was on the opposite side of the road, his back to her, walking like he was normal, walking like he was innocent, walking like he'd never shoved his cock into a fifteen-year-old's mouth then scared and manipulated them into staying silent.

But Tanya knew different.

And now she was going to do something about it. But just as she opened the door and stepped out a green car, some kind of hatchback with wooden panels on the sides, drew up alongside him, and after a few words with the driver, Staal got in.

Tanya stood in the wedge between her car and the open door, her hand on the metal roof, a thin layer of grime rough under her fingertips, and watched as the car indicated and moved off.

Life went on around her: a motorbike roared by, a group of kids ran down the street shouting, the sun shifted its position closer to the North Sea, shadows crept along the ground, lengthening, reaching out for her.

She felt hot suddenly, a prickling which exploded on her neck and rose up to her face. She turned round, legs unsteady, crouched down and vomited right on to the black asphalt.

Her eyes were closed. She felt splashback on her face.

Back in the car – she was thinking she should clear up

80

her sick but didn't have anything to do it with – she fired up the motor, indicated, checked the mirrors and pulled out slowly, each action deliberate, each movement taking her whole focus.

Minutes later the noise of a car horn being hit repeatedly settled in her mind. She noticed she was stopped at a light, showing green, the man's face in the car behind distorted with anger. She waited until the light changed, then shot the car forward.

If he jumps it I'll book him, she thought, checking the rear-view mirror. He didn't. He just flicked her a middle finger.

She was able to breathe again now even though everything was looking weird; familiar and totally alien at the same time – her hands clasped on the wheel, the blue sticker in the corner of the windscreen – all things she'd seen before, and yet she felt like she was seeing them through someone else's eyes.

Her phone was buzzing on the seat next to her. She glanced across and saw it was the station. She had a murder investigation on, and here she was dealing with her personal life. Or not dealing with it.

Tomorrow, she thought as she reached over for the phone, *tomorrow I'm going to do it.*

14

Jaap handed Tanya the photo Roemers had found on the second victim's phone.

'I don't get it,' she said after a few moments.

She was looking stressed, the muscles in her face tense, and Jaap didn't want to add to it.

But she needed to know.

Jaap glanced around the houseboat, at the *nihonto* hanging on the wall. It had been given to him by Yuzuki Roshi, his old tutor in Kyoto, when he'd left Japan. He looked at the elegant curve of the blade, the wave-like patterns undulating across the steel, and tried not to picture it plunged into Karin's stomach. He'd wanted to get rid of it after her death, but when it came to throwing it out he'd felt torn, unable to make up his mind.

It was the weapon which had killed her. The steel – hand-honed by an artisan using knowledge and skill passed down over hundreds of years – severing flesh so she bled to death.

But although he'd wanted to chuck it into the canal, he felt to throw it out would, in some odd way, be a betrayal of her.

He'd taken it down, ready to do it, but had found himself reaching for the I Ching and throwing the coins instead.

Wind over Water.

DISPERSE HARD ATTITUDES WITH GENTLENESS.

Then he'd put it back on the wall.

'Look, the case I'm on, the two headless bodies? The first one had a picture of me on his phone – he'd taken it this morning as I walked across Dam Square. The second one, Teeven, I put away for murder years ago. And he had these.' He pushed the receipts, jumbled in an evidence bag, across the table to her. He noticed a spot of dried food on the table's old wooden surface and tried to rub it off with his finger.

A boat made up to look like a clog motored past, all yellow plastic and a web address where you could book it. Waves slapped the hull. The houseboat rocked, making the glasses in the cupboard chime like an avant-garde music box.

Tanya was looking at the receipts, which Jaap had catalogued earlier. From the times on each one Teeven had been there for the last five days, and quite possibly for most of each day. She breathed out and handed them back.

'And this was the same guy who had this picture, of me? The one you arrested years ago?'

Jaap didn't want it to be. But it was.

'Yeah.'

They'd been seeing each other for over six months now,

and she'd moved in not long after, though she still hadn't given up paying the rent on her flat up in Amsterdam Noord. He'd said she should, but then dropped it when she'd clammed up on the subject. It was the sensible move from her point of view, he could see that, but it did make him feel that maybe he was into the relationship more than she was.

The problem was probably his daughter, Floortje. He and Saskia had worked out a childcare plan, splitting it as equally as possible, though recently Saskia'd had to do more than her fair share, as had Tanya on occasion. Tanya said she didn't mind looking after Floortje when she could, but Jaap wasn't so sure.

It can't be easy, he thought. *Looking after another woman's child.*

And he'd noticed a change in Tanya over the last few weeks. He was worried it was getting too much for her, that maybe she was deciding being with him was too complicated.

When she'd announced she was going away for a break with some friends, friends he'd never met, he got even more concerned.

Would she make a decision about them while she was away, egged on perhaps by the people she was going to be with?

'And Teeven always claimed he was innocent?' she said, breaking into his thoughts.

'Right the way through. And the actual evidence was pretty shaky, a couple of fairly unreliable witnesses. But I'd interviewed him at least four times, and I was sure he was involved.'

Tanya frowned and looked out the porthole to Jaap's left. He noticed a freckle he'd not seen before, just up by her ear.

'But not necessarily the only one?'

Jaap tried to think back to the case. He'd been younger then, not just in years, but in experience, in outlook. When the chance to join the murder squad had come up he'd made sure he got the place. He remembered feeling on his first day that he had something to prove. And getting such a high-profile case seven months in was just what he'd needed to get him noticed.

Was I wrong? he wondered. *Did I let my ambition get in the way?*

'Hey, you still there?' asked Tanya.

Jaap shook his head.

'Yeah, sorry. I was thinking.'

'I could tell – the grinding sound was awful.'

She flashed him a smile but it faded fast.

'I pulled the file earlier and went through it, just to see if there was anything.'

'Was there?'

'No, pretty much as I remembered it,' he said. 'But the thing is, if he was innocent and wanted to get back at me, then how come he's the one who's dead?'

Tanya got up and walked over to the galley kitchen. She cranked the tap, water hissed into the glass she'd picked up, and she turned back to face him, leaning against the work surface. She hugged herself with one arm and raised the glass to her mouth with the other.

'And the first guy, how's he connected?' she finally asked.

'I don't know. That's the thing – none of this makes any sense.'

'Maybe he was another one, like they met up in prison and found they both harboured a grudge against you?'

'It's really comforting talking to you, you know that?'

Tanya finished the water, rinsed the glass and put it upside down on the drainer. Drips ran down its surface, lines of distortion.

Jaap looked out a porthole across the water to the far side of the canal, where the elm trees had Parkinson's, leaves trembling quietly in the pale dusk. His phone buzzed on the table, moving closer to the edge with each burst of vibration. It was Ballistics.

'The gun you asked for a report on has got a history,' said the woman, once Jaap had answered. 'We've got a match on a case going back quite a few years.'

'What was the case?' asked Jaap.

'It's old so the full report isn't on our system, but I've got the case number here. You can probably access it.'

Jaap took it down and hung up, told Tanya what he'd learned.

'I don't like this,' she said. 'The photos then this gun . . .'

She trailed off, head to one side, pressing an earlobe between her thumb and forefinger.

'I was wondering about telling Smit,' said Jaap. 'What-ever this is . . . well . . . I don't want you to get hurt. And he owes us. We kept quiet for him over the whole Black Tulips thing.'

'It wasn't for him we kept quiet, it was for Floortje. And that was right, you couldn't have done anything else. But if you tell Smit about this he's just going to put some idiot on it.'

She looked straight at him. Jaap was struck by her face, something there he couldn't read.

'Jaap, I'd feel safer if you stayed working on this. And you said the tweet mentioned another killing? So that means there might be someone else linked to the first two victims. And what if he's been watching you – watching us – as well?'

'This is your safety, our safety, we're talking about here. I think we need to take it more seriously.'

'I *am* taking it seriously,' she said, moving away from the kitchen. 'That's why I said what I said. I can't figure out what the hell is going on either, but no one else at the station is going to do any better than us.'

A bike bell tinkled on the canal edge. Jaap turned and saw wheels rush past a landward porthole.

'I thought you had your own case to run?'

'I do, but this seems a bit more important now,' she said, glancing away.

He moved around, trying to catch her eyes.

'Okay. I've got a couple more things to check out, but if I haven't got anywhere by tomorrow then I'm going to have to talk to Smit.'

She nodded, then looked right at him.

'There's something I've got to tell you,' she said.

It's not working for her, the thought detonated in his head. *She wants to leave me.*

He didn't want to hear it.

He wanted to stop her talking, but he couldn't think of anything to say, any way of heading off the moment.

15

'There's something I've got to tell you,' said Tanya.

She'd gone back to the desk sergeant, got the older logs she needed then double-checked them. Then she triple-checked them.

But each time the answer came back the same.

Kees.

Of all people.

How had it turned out that her only suspect was not only a colleague, but one she'd actually slept with?

Their relationship back at the academy hadn't lasted long, but she had the feeling Kees had taken it badly when she ended it.

Not that I can really blame him, she thought. *He got a rough deal, like all the others.*

She suddenly felt angry, all her relationships failing because of her. Or because of what she'd become, what Staal had turned her into.

And now she'd decided to confront him she'd got stuck on a case. Seeing her foster father earlier had opened up something inside her, and she wasn't sure it was ever going to close again.

She needed to focus on the case, put all thoughts of him out of her head. She was going to deal with that tomorrow.

Jaap was looking at her, and she was about to tell him

about Kees but then changed her mind. She knew Jaap had been trying to foster a working relationship with Kees, and he probably wouldn't take the news well.

I need to know for sure before I tell him, she thought.

'You okay?' asked Jaap.

'Sorry, I was just thinking . . . Look, I've got to go, I just realized there's something I forgot to check.'

'Your case?'

He looked relived. Concerned as well.

Why can't I just tell him about my past? she thought as she answered him. *Why is that so difficult?*

'Yeah. You heard the guy who pushed the woman was wearing a police jacket, right? I can't believe it's one of us.'

Despite having made the decision not to, she still wanted to tell him about Kees.

'Could be anyone, you can probably buy a police jacket like that online.'

'Yeah,' said Tanya. 'You're right. But then the question is, who would want to make it look like it was done by a police officer?'

'Someone who hates the police as much as Teeven must have hated me,' said Jaap.

He stood up and walked over to her, putting his hands on her waist. She could feel his touch, the calm firmness with which he always held her.

'Look,' he said. 'Until I've got this thing under control you'll be careful, right?'

'Sure,' she said, kissing him. 'I'll be careful.'

And for a moment it felt good, just being there with him. As if there was nothing else. But the moment passed.

It always did.

He was leaving too, following up on something, but she got out first, heading back to the station. She was going to have to tell Smit about Kees. He'd left a message requesting an update on her case. Once she did that it would be pretty much over for Kees.

She wasn't sure how that made her feel.

Just as she walked off her phone rang. It was Piet, and he'd found two homeless people who knew the victim from Centraal.

'Shall I bring them in?' he asked once he'd explained how he'd discovered them.

'Are you with them now?'

'No, but I know where they're staying tonight. This homeless shelter, out towards Westerpark.'

'I'm going there now,' she said and hung up after she'd taken their names and the address. She then left a message for Smit, saying she was following up a lead.

By the time she pulled into the street twenty minutes later, colour was starting to fade from the sky, blue leaching down to dirty pink.

To her right was the Vredenhof cemetery, graves shielded from view by a line of tall trees. On her left was a row of single-storey industrial units, mostly overflow from the Centraal Markt just to the south. Midway along was the place she was looking for, judging by the clothes of the two people entering via a sliding steel door.

Inside was sparse, a warehouse with a polished concrete floor and blue plastic mats laid out in rows. One of the far corners housed a cluster of white plastic tables and chairs. A collection of people bent over food, intent on eating.

Tanya didn't need to see their clothes, or even the situation they were in to know they were homeless; their postures and movements said it all.

Some of the blue mats were taken already, people settling in for the night. She looked at the nearest, a man, hard to age, lying on his side with a collection of crushed drinks cans next to him on the floor. There must have been at least twenty, all flattened down to the same height. At first she thought he was asleep, but he suddenly spoke to her, his eyes only just open.

'They're mine,' he said in a voice twisted with drink. 'So just fuck off.'

'Can I help?' said a voice behind her.

She turned to see a young woman with blonde dreads, one of them dyed pink, and a sliver nose ring. She wore an oversized ethnic jacket and baggy patchwork trousers, and if it hadn't been for the clarity of her eyes Tanya would have put her down as homeless too.

'Do you run this place?' she asked, getting her ID out and showing it.

'I'm just a volunteer, I generally do a night a week,' said the woman, scrutinizing Tanya's badge. 'Sometimes I'll do more if need be.'

'I'm looking for a couple of people, Katja and Tijmen.'

The woman looked around, then pointed to the back.

'That's them, the table on the far left. They're usually drunk, but they seemed to be relatively sober when I gave them their sandwiches earlier.'

Tanya made her way over; they both looked up as she approached.

Though hard to age – their lifestyle had taken its

toll – she pegged them both around mid-forties. The woman had hair like steel wool, while the man was completely bald. By the way his eyes were bulging it looked like there was too much internal pressure in his head.

Tanya introduced herself. They carried on eating their sandwiches, and Tanya got a waft of too-old tuna, heard the soft, sticky mastication of processed white bread.

'You're the inspector?' asked Katja when she'd finished, dabbing at her plastic plate with a moistened finger to get the last crumbs.

'Yeah. My colleague said you knew the woman who was killed this morning at the station?'

'We knew her all right,' said Tijmen. 'Filthy bitch, she was.'

The phrase jolted Tanya. It was what her foster father used to say to her once he'd finished. He'd tell her she was a filthy bitch with a look of disgust on his face, and then order her to clean herself up.

'You're a filthy bitch, not her,' said Katja to Tijmen. 'And I won't have that kind of language.'

Tanya pulled out a photo of the woman on the tracks whilst trying to suppress all thought, feeling a cascade of sickness run through her body.

'Okay, you filthy bitch,' replied Tijmen, a blob of half-chewed white bread and tuna flying from his lips and arcing down to the table. He grinned before scooping it up with a finger and popping it back in his mouth.

'Don't mind him,' said Katja. 'He's always like this. Doesn't mean anything by it. Just a delinquent by nature.'

'So what,' said Tanya, not wishing to get drawn into a domestic, 'can you tell me about her?'

Katja looked at the photo.

'Why she was killed, you mean? That's easy. I know why she was killed, she'd got a job, spying on someone. And she got paid for it and everything. She even showed me the money she was getting.'

'Who was she working for?' asked Tanya.

'Some guy, she wouldn't say who. He had some stupid nickname, like Wheels or something. To be honest I thought she was making it all up until I saw the money.'

'And who was she spying on?'

'Filthy bitch.'

Both women ignored him.

'She wouldn't tell me that either, but I saw her one day, so I know where she was spying.'

'Where?' said Tanya, keeping her voice level, not wanting to give away her eagerness.

'You know, I like this place,' said Katja, looking around. 'But there would be a great way to make it better.'

'How do you mean?' asked Tanya, not liking where this was going.

'They give us food, which is great. But you know what I'd really like?'

Tanya could guess, but had to play the game.

'What?'

'A drink,' said Katja, scratching an ear and grinning. 'I'd really like a drink. Then maybe we can talk.'

16

The electric car turned out to have its advantages.

Kees managed to squeeze it into a tiny space with only minor damage to the cars parked in front and behind. It hadn't helped that he'd been on the phone to Smit at the same time, his boss finishing off what he'd left unsaid back at the station. Kees figured the odd paintwork scratch wasn't, therefore, his fault.

As he hung up, killed the almost-silent motor, got out and slammed the door – which wasn't satisfying as there was no real weight to it – he could see something was wrong. The address didn't look residential in the least, a huge former industrial block, monolithic concrete painted black, which housed a bar and nightclub. Large smoked-glass doors had 57 sandblasted on to them.

A stray black and white dog ambled across the road, stopping to nose something flattened on the surface.

Kees flicked through the arrest report, double-checking the address. He could see what had happened; whoever filled out the form had put down the address of the incident, and Krilic's, as the same.

Some dumb patrol fuck, thought Kees, checking to see who'd written the report. Turned out to be Piet. Kees was surprised; Piet was all right, he wouldn't normally have screwed up like this. He called the station, trying to get hold of him, but after a few minutes' wait he was told

Piet wasn't answering his phone. Kees told them to keep trying.

Smit had been livid, and Kees could see that if he didn't get Isovic soon then there were going to be some pretty hefty consequences. And now his only lead had pretty much crashed out as Piet hadn't filled in a form properly.

The dog was now sniffing around the pavement by the side of the club. It kept turning in ever tighter circles, nose to the ground like it was hoovering something up, then it stopped, its back legs stiffening as it raised its tail and squeezed out a long one. Kees watched as it turned round again, sniffed at the glistening turd, then gobbled the whole lot down.

You and me both, he thought as he crossed the road, making his way towards the smoked-glass doors.

To Kees, the bouncer looked like the small mean type who'd only gone into bouncing as they'd got some kind of complex. His black leather jacket was a size too large, and his face, or the aggressive expression on it, confirmed the diagnosis. As did the pathetic fake diamond stud in his ear. He looked Kees up and down before jerking his head towards the doors.

As if you were going to stop me, thought Kees as he stepped past.

Inside the space was large, with a huge wall of glass at the far end looking out over the water. Kees could see lights from the far shore of the IJ, streaking down on the black surface of the lake.

The place was stuffed with people. Kees made a quick survey of the women around him and approved. He figured he should check this place out some time. Strictly off duty.

He started with the long bar off to his left, one of the barmen asking what he wanted over the pulse of music, and it took two attempts for the goateed guy to work out what he was saying. And still Kees had to flash his badge before he got any action. Then he was ushered through a door along a poorly lit corridor by another cliché of a bouncer, Big with No Brains.

It's like being in a B movie, he thought as they stopped outside the door at the far end of the corridor. No Brains knocked and waited for the word.

When it came No Brains stepped aside and let Kees through, following him and closing the door, muffling the music's relentless beat.

The room was better than the corridor. Like the main area of the club it looked out over the water, and was spacious with two neon-pink sofas in one corner angled round a massive flatscreen TV showing a rolling news programme complete with a hot young blonde to make it watchable and a middle-aged guy to add gravitas. They were discussing the beheadings.

A large desk was positioned in the other corner. The air was filled with some kind of aromatic, sweet scent. Sprawled on one of the sofas was the source of the smell, half a thin cigar and a man holding it with ring-encrusted fingers.

'What's it this time? A fight? Drugs?' he asked, standing up and walking towards the desk, not even looking at Kees. 'I can't be held responsible for my customers, you know?'

He slid into the swivel chair behind the desk, muted the

TV using a remote and turned to face Kees. He was broad, with a face to match. The scar running across his left cheek hinted at his climb to the top. His hair was lead-grey, cut short apart from a rat's tail, which didn't quite reach down his neck.

'You own this place, right?' asked Kees. The man nodded, taking a draw on his cigar, making a show of tasting the smoke like it was a fine wine. Then he put his head back and blew it out, trying for smoke rings. He failed.

He pointed to a nameplate on the desk, a ridiculously shiny steel strip with THE BOSS engraved on it.

'You have a name?' asked Kees.

'I'd have thought it would be on your records, the amount of times you guys have been round here. But you don't look like the type to read much,' he said with a muscle contraction in his face which would normally be termed a smile. Kees couldn't believe it. But the evidence was there in front of him; the guy actually had a gold tooth. 'I'm Feico.'

'Have you ever seen either of these men?' said Kees dropping two photos on to the desk.

Feico bent forward and peered at them without picking them up. He tried to draw on his cigar again and found it had gone out.

'No. Where would I have seen them?' he asked, rummaging around in his trouser pocket. He finally extracted a silver lighter.

'Here. I think one of them may have been involved in an incident a few weeks ago.'

'We get over eight hundred people in here on a good

night, and I'm increasingly weighed down with paper-work, so I don't get out on to the floor much.'

Kees looked at the desk. Apart from the nameplate and a rectangular block made of perspex with something embedded in the middle, there didn't seem to be an abundance of paper. Feico saw him looking at the block and turned it side on. Kees could see it was a bullet.

'A souvenir from a colleague of yours. She was in here over a year ago, decided to beat up one of my customers and started spraying bullets around. Broke that massive slab of glass you'll have seen out there.' He pointed back to the main room. 'Mind you, she was pretty hot. Fiery, if you know what I mean?'

'Did she have long red hair?'

'That's the one, you know her?'

'Kind of,' said Kees.

He did know Tanya. And since she'd moved down and joined the office he'd been reminded almost daily of their time back at the academy. His face must have betrayed something, as Feico spoke again.

'Didn't put out for you?' Feico laughed. 'Seriously though, she can come and cuff me any time. Just tell her to leave her gun at home.'

'Is there anyone here who might recognize these,' said Kees, ignoring Feico's grin and pointing to the photos.

Feico shrugged.

'Maybe.'

He nodded to No Brains, who left the room and returned a few minutes later with the goateed barman.

'Mark heads up the bar team,' said Feico. He pointed to the photos. 'Have you seen either of these uglies?'

Mark stepped over to the desk. He looked at them for a few moments and started nodding slowly.

'You know, I think I have. This one's been here a few times.'

Kees looked at the photo Mark was pointing out. It was Krilic.

'When was this?'

'I don't know, couple of weeks back?'

'You must see thousands of people, how come you remember him?'

'He got into a fight, with this guy. And the thing is they were shouting in some foreign language.'

'What language?'

'Fuck knows, I'm not a linguist. But something kind of rough, you know? Like Russian or some shit.'

Bosniak? thought Kees. *Is that even a language?*

'And this other guy, the one he fought with. You know who he was?'

'Nah, just some random guy. I think he may have had a beard, can't really remember.'

'And you called us?'

'No. There was a cop here. Off duty, he said, but he broke it up, then arrested them both. Called his colleagues in and everything.'

So that'll be why Piet fucked up the report, he thought. *He was probably drunk.*

'What about him?' said Kees, showing the photo of Isovic he'd taken from the file he'd received a week ago.

'You know,' Mark said, scratching his beard. 'I think I do recognize him too. A couple of days after that fight I'm pretty sure he was in here with the first guy.'

99

So Krilic had tried to beat up someone, and then had come back with Isovic. He already knew that they were linked though, so what did this prove?

'No way,' said Mark, breaking into Kees' thoughts.

They all turned to look at him.

He was pointing to the TV screen, where a blurred image of two heads was being shown. The scrolling tape at the bottom said, 'Two victims identified – Jan Koopman and Martin Teeven'.

'I've seen him as well,' he said. 'The one on the left. He was here just the other night.'

'You sure?'

'I'm sure,' said Mark, stroking his goatee. 'He was here, I remember because he ordered a bunch of drinks then spilt them when he went to pick them up. Fucker tried to blame it on me.'

'Which night?'

'Thursday or Friday, I think. Pretty sure it was Friday.'

'You'll have CCTV of then?'

Mark looked at Feico, who nodded.

'I want to see it. Now.'

Mark led Kees back into the club, then off into a smaller room marked PRIVATE. There were no windows, and a bare bulb hung from the ceiling. A computer squatted on a cheap-looking plastic desk, marked with so many coffee mug rings they looked like scales on a large dirty fish.

It took Mark twenty minutes of skimming through video before he got what he was after.

'There,' he said, touching the screen.

Kees leaned in. The camera was obviously hidden among the spirit bottles behind the bar, and gave an eye-level view of customers' faces, one of which Mark's finger was right by.

'You got Internet on this thing?' asked Kees.

'Sure, what do you want?'

'Compare his picture – check on one of the news sites.'

Once Mark had brought up a news site they could see it was the same man, Koopman.

Kees went back to the video. He saw Koopman buy drinks, four shots in total, and watched as he tried to pick them all up at once, knocking two of them over.

'Clumsy fucker, tried to get replacements for free.'

Kees watched as the scene played out, ending with Koopman buying two replacements and finally turning away, getting lost in the crowd of people pressing towards the bar.

'Any idea where he was headed? I want to see who he was with.'

It took a few more minutes, but finally they had an image of one of the booths at the back. This camera was in the ceiling, so the angle wasn't as good, but it was still possible to make out the three faces of Koopman's companions.

'Bring that web page back up.'

Kees looked at the two victims and then back at the men in the booth.

There was no doubt.

Koopman was there, and the second victim too.

'I need a copy of this,' he said as he pulled out his phone and dialled Jaap.

17

When Jaap returned to his desk with the file corresponding to the case number the ballistics team had given him, he saw he had a missed call, and a message, from Kees. The message didn't say much other than Kees had something which might be linked to Jaap's case. He called him back but his phone was off.

Then he turned to the file and started reading. The case was over nine years old. A man had been shot execution-style and his body dumped in a field of sheep just south of Amsterdam. It turned out, much to the attending inspector's disgust, that sheep weren't always strictly herbivorous.

The victim was ID'd as a small-time crook, and the investigation eventually led to a man called Bart Rutte.

Jaap stared at the name. It seemed familiar, but he couldn't place from where.

Rutte had been interviewed several times in connection with the killing, but in the end not enough evidence had been uncovered. The gun had never been found.

Jaap turned to his laptop and searched for Rutte.

The file was big, Jaap saw as the page count appeared, multiple mentions stretching back to the turn of the millennium.

But Bart Rutte had no convictions; he was always on the periphery of things, a sort of phantom who nobody could quite pin down. He was suspected of at least seven murders, but in each case the investigating officer had been unable to pull together enough evidence to make anything stick.

Behind Jaap one of the inspectors in the office cranked the radio up, a talk show making light of the murders, encouraging listeners to call in with their best headless jokes. It seemed the phone lines were jammed with people heeding the request.

'Hey, can you turn that down?' he shouted across the room after the fifth joke.

The sound eased, allowing Jaap back into his thoughts.

Reading on, Jaap could see why Rutte was still at large; witnesses either vanished or suddenly got a bad case of selective amnesia, and in one case evidence, a gun which supposedly could be linked with Rutte, disappeared somewhere between the police evidence room and the lab it had been sent to for testing.

The most striking failure had been just over three years ago. A woman had been dumped out the back of a van in the middle of a road in the Nieuw-West. Witnesses had seen it skid round a corner, the back doors had flown open, and a woman had tumbled out as if pushed.

She survived, but when the ambulance crew got there, the woman unconscious on the tarmac, they found horrific injuries, knife marks all over her body.

It surprised no one that she'd also been sexually assaulted.

A few days later in hospital she was conscious again, and the story she told was detailed and believable. The description she gave of her main assailant fitted Rutte.

The investigating officer had enough to build a strong case, but when he and his colleague returned the next morning they found she was dead.

She'd been strangled with something thin.

Which turned out to have been the IV tube, ripped out of her arm.

I know his name, thought Jaap. *But where from?*

Jaap leaned back and closed his eyes, running possibilities through his head.

That Koopman had the gun wasn't in itself that surprising; there was a black market, and if you wanted a gun and were willing to pay, there was always someone ready to supply the goods. On the other hand, if a gun was used to commit a murder it was usually ditched; criminals were all too aware of how easy it was to match a gun to a bullet. But then they were criminals, and if they decided to sell the weapon on to someone else, as long as it couldn't be traced back to them, what was there to stop them?

It was a seller's market; if you wanted a gun, you paid your money and hoped that the guy selling it to you wasn't lying when he said it was clean.

Bottom line is, thought Jaap as he opened his eyes and checked the time, *I haven't got a clue what's going on here.*

He had an appointment, and he was now late. He closed down his laptop and left, noticing the headless jokes were still pouring out of the radio.

She was about fifty, Jaap decided when he sat down inside the estate agent's office ten minutes later, and her name was Doutzen de Kok. Her short hair was just starting to show streaks of grey, and she had the eyes of a predator. Jaap thought he recognized her from somewhere.

'Sorry to have kept you so late,' said Jaap.

'Don't worry,' she motioned to a pile of paper on her desk. 'The husband's away on some sad boys-only fishing trip so I figured I'd do some catch up here.'

'You own the business?'

She laughed as she nodded, picked up a cup and took a big sip.

'Oh yes. Don't think I'd be doing this if I was just an employee.'

She put the cup down, and settled back in her chair, as if she was appraising Jaap.

'So, he said. 'This tenant of yours, can you tell me anything about him?'

'I pulled his file when you called, but there's not much in there,' she handed over a few sheets of paper.

Jaap took them and skimmed though. He could see Koopman had started renting the property a year and half ago.

'Problems with payment?'

'No, money came in every month right on time.'

'And you never met him?'

'I don't meet the clients anymore, that's what I have a team for. But there is one strange thing, there's a key missing. We have three for each property, one goes to the tenant, one for use in case we need to get in and one spare.'

Jaap handed the papers back and pulled out the evidence bag with the key and key fob on it, and put it on the table in front of her. She picked up the bag.

'I think this is one of them, let me check.'

She disappeared through a frosted-glass door and Jaap sat back, let his mind start to go over things. The same questions kept coming up, why did Koopman have that photo on his phone? Why had Teeven spent the last five days staking out his houseboat? If he'd been going to get revenge why not do it straight away? And how come they were the ones ending up dead? How had Koopman got hold of the gun? Was he somehow linked with Bart Rutte? And why, just to add to the list, did Rutte's name seem familiar?

De Kok stepped back into the room, saving him from the endless cycle of questions.

'Yeah, that's one of them.'

She handed the bag back. Jaap could tell she was uncomfortable.

'What?' he asked.

'The thing is,' she said, 'I've just been thinking. We had a bit of trouble with one of our staff. She was the one who looked after this property, and I'm just wondering—'

'What kind of trouble?'

'She hasn't been into work for the last two days,' she said as she picked up her cup and stared into its depths as if there was something of enormous interest lurking at the bottom. 'And she hasn't answered our calls.'

18

Jaap stood for a moment next to the quay which led to Saskia's house. Her white Citroën was parked in the designated area, and Jaap noticed it had a fresh scrape on the passenger-side door.

As he walked along the quay he thought about how things might have been different.

It was just over a year ago that Andreas had been killed, and Jaap thought Saskia had been coping well, considering. But maybe that was because she didn't have a choice; she had Floortje, and the demands of looking after her had helped her overcome her feelings.

As for his own feelings, Jaap didn't know what he'd felt about finding out that Floortje was his own child, only days after Andreas' death. He still didn't.

He let himself in, half-hoping Floortje would be asleep and half-hoping she'd be awake to see him. The house was on water, but wasn't a houseboat like his. It was purpose built, two storeys, and floated out in the IJ. It had been Saskia and Andreas' home.

Now it was just Saskia's.

He'd tried to convince her to sell up, move somewhere without the memories, but she'd refused, and he'd stopped mentioning it now. If she was able to cope it wasn't really any of his business.

And he'd not moved out of his houseboat, despite that

being the scene of Karin's death, so who was he to give advice?

Saskia was in the kitchen, and he could hear Floortje starting to cry, Saskia trying to quieten her down with soothing words. Jaap was unsure why everyone's default reaction, including his own, seemed to be to talk mother-ese at babies, because it clearly didn't work. At least not on Floortje.

'Hey,' he said as he stepped into the room, noticing the half-empty glass of red wine on the counter next to a baby cup with two handles in lurid green plastic.

'She's been doing this all day,' said Saskia, handing Floortje from her hip to Jaap. Once unburdened she sat on one of the two bar stools with chrome legs and a flat black seat, and reached for the wine glass.

'We could get her a job as a siren, strap her on to the roof of a patrol car,' said Jaap, gently bumping Floortje up and down which only succeeded in upsetting her stomach, the contents of which shot from her mouth and dribbled down his top.

'Yeah, she's been doing that too,' said Saskia. 'Maybe she's got a bug or something.'

Jaap put Floortje to bed in the wooden cot in Saskia's bedroom, and after cleaning himself up went back through to the kitchen.

'How's it going?' she asked. 'You getting anywhere with it?'

'My investigation?'

'Yeah.'

'It's not great,' he said. 'In fact it's really nasty.'

He thought of the image of himself on the first victim's phone.

He thought of the threat Teeven had mouthed at him across the courtroom.

And he thought, with a twinge in his stomach, about the photo of Tanya leaving his houseboat.

Saskia swirled the wine in her glass. Jaap noticed there was more in it than when he'd first come in. The radio was on low, he could hear some kind of talk show going on, panellists arguing about politics.

'What about you?' He pointed to the glass. 'Do I need to call someone?'

'Shit, Jaap. It's being a pretty tough day for me too, what with her and finding out some dumb ass in your department's lost my main witness, so if I want to have a glass or so of wine then I think I'll do it. Anyway,' she said after a pause, 'it's not like we're married or anything.'

They'd talked about it in the shapeless days after Andreas' death and Floortje's birth, but they both felt it wasn't right. They'd had their time together and it hadn't worked out.

'You're right,' he said, sitting down on the other bar stool. 'I'll just call social services, it's more their kind of thing.'

She punched him lightly on the arm, but he noticed she'd pushed the glass away. He picked up a leaflet from the counter advertising adult swimming lessons.

'I've been thinking about it. I really should learn so I can teach Floortje when she's a bit older.'

'You can't swim?'

'Jaap, we were together for over three years.'

'I know, but I don't remember you saying you couldn't swim ... You live in a floating house and you can't even swim? Isn't that dangerous? What about if Floortje fell in?'

'That's why I'm doing something about it,' she said, snatching it away. 'At least I'm trying here, I don't see you doing much for her.'

They sat in silence for a few moments.

'Sorry,' said Saskia just as Jaap was about to say something. 'It's just this trial, you know? I've been working on it so hard, and I'm sure we can get Matkovic convicted, and then this.'

'Can't you postpone it?'

She looked at him as if to say *Please*. There was a newspaper on the counter and she reached across, pointing out an article. Jaap scanned it.

The article was a profile of a prominent judge who'd come out and said that many of the ICTY convictions for war crimes were based on scant evidence, and there needed to be more robust prosecution cases before people were convicted.

'And?' said Jaap, dropping the paper back down.

'Jesus. Are you sure you're an inspector? This is the judge who's presiding. Meaning my case just got a whole lot harder.'

Jaap wasn't worried. Saskia was as hard as a bullet when she wanted to be, and he knew she was fully gunning on this case.

'Seriously, you're going to be fine. I doubt he's a match for you.'

From the other room they both heard the unmistakable sound of Floortje stirring. Then she started crying again, a high careening noise with a touch of the wild about it.

'Yeah, you're right,' said Saskia as she got up and headed for the door, her hand reaching out for the wine glass as she passed. 'If I can deal with a baby then I'm not scared of a stupid judge.'

Once Saskia had settled Floortje she came back into the room and flopped down next to Jaap.

'Get me another one of these,' she said as she handed him the glass.

He hesitated before taking it, going to the kitchen and pouring some wine into the glass.

'What's this?' she said when he handed it back. 'It's like a quarter full at most.'

'That was all that was left,' he said, sitting down again. He should be going, and he should definitely give Tanya a call, find out where she was, but he felt exhausted suddenly, as if the proximity of Saskia and Floortje helped him relax.

'Liar,' she replied before tipping the glass up, emptying it in one go.

It would be so much easier . . . he thought.

He loved Floortje in a way he never would have thought possible, and it would make sense if they could be a proper family, he and Floortje and Saskia all together.

They sat there in silence, until Jaap realized he was going to fall asleep if he didn't move soon.

Saskia saw him to the door, and just as his hand reached out for the latch he turned back to her.

Their lips met, and Jaap felt like he was falling.

19

'What's this?' asked Tijmen as he scrutinized the label.

Tanya felt irritated. She was pretty sure her duties as a Netherlands police inspector didn't involve supplying homeless alcoholics with vodka. In fact, she was pretty sure it was forbidden.

'So, talk,' she said to Katja, trying to ignore Tijmen as he cranked off the screw cap, sniffed and then took a long swig.

They were hunkered down in Westerpark, on the grass by a large tree, and hidden from view by a row of bushes. Light was fading fast, darkness taking over. Tanya'd followed Katja's directions, skirting the old gasworks and diving into a dense thicket. She'd got scratched by one of the branches as she'd forced her way through, only to find there'd been a clearer route if approached from the opposite side.

The sun had dropped away, the air cooler now.

By the gasworks there'd been some kind of festival going on, ROLLING KITCHENS, the sign had said. About twenty large vehicles were there, each one adapted into a kitchen, each one dishing up different cuisine to hipster Amsterdammers. The smells reminded Tanya she'd not eaten for a while.

Moisture rose from the earth, and a bird burbled liquid song high in the tree above them.

'Not much to tell really,' said Katja as she grabbed the bottle from Tijmen and took an even longer swig.

Tanya thought it might loosen Katja up, make her a better talker. Then again, the speed it was going down it might just make her incoherent.

Or unconscious.

'You said she'd claimed to have a job spying, and you knew who she was spying on?' prompted Tanya when she got sick of the glugging sound.

'Not who,' said Katja, bringing down the bottle. She picked at the corner of the label, trying to prise it off with her nails. 'What.'

'So what was she spying on?' Tanya asked when Katja had leaned back against the tree with her eyes closed.

'This building, somewhere south of that big concert hall.'

'The Concertgebouw?'

'That's the one near that museum, the guy who cut his ear off?'

Tijmen, who'd been sitting watching something on the ground, made a grab for the bottle, but Katja, without even opening her eyes, moved it away and took another long drink. Tanya could see her throat move with each swallow; she gave up counting on five.

'Where?'

Katja lowered the bottle and held it out to Tijmen, then snatched it back just as he reached for it. He howled, a noise like a starving animal, and lunged forward, knocking the bottle over. What was left dribbled into the grass.

'Filthy bitch,' he yelled, trembling with rage. Katja just put her head back against the tree trunk and laughed.

'Please, it's really important that I find the place you talked about,' said Tanya once Tijmen had calmed down and turned away, looking at something in the dirt.

Katja was still leaning back against the trunk, eyes closed.

'I'm not feeling up to it tonight. Maybe tomorrow. And bring something else to drink.'

'I really need to know tonight. How about you show me where this building is, and I'll give you something else to drink?'

Katja's eye's snapped opened and peered at Tanya. They seemed clear.

She must have a huge tolerance for the stuff, thought Tanya.

'Okay,' said Katja as she heaved herself off the ground. 'But this asshole's coming with me.'

It took a full twenty minutes to get them both to her car, and then find the place.

'That's the one,' said Katja, pointing through the open window to a house on the opposite side of the square.

Tanya pulled the car over. A central pedestrian island was ringed with benches.

The building itself was a three-storey red brick, nothing much to distinguish it from any of the others around it.

'You're sure?'

'Of course I'm sure. I caught her sitting on that bench over there. She said she was watching that house but wouldn't say any more. Told me to go away, said I was ruining her cover.' Katja laughed. 'Now, how about that drink?'

'When was this?'

'This morning.'

'What sort of time?'

'Dunno. Just morning.'

Tanya had to drive two blocks before she found some-where open. She ducked in, taking the car keys with her, and emerged with a bottle wrapped in a plastic bag.

Katja and Tijmen were already out of the car waiting for her on the pavement. Tanya handed over the bag and got into the car.

'Hey, what's this?' asked Katja as Tanya slid the key into the slot and turned it, vibration through the seat telling her the motor had kicked into life. She hit a button and the driver's-side window glided down.

'It's a drink,' said Tanya as the motor revved up. 'Enjoy.'

As she moved off she could hear Katja shrieking, Tij-men joining in with his monotonous insult.

She figured they'd need a bit of water after all that vodka.

There were no spaces left in the square when she nosed the car back in, so she had to park on one of the side roads. She killed the engine and the lights. The car's inter-ior still smelt of homeless people and exhaled alcohol.

She got out, pleased to breathe some clean air, and walked around the square, watching the building. There were no lights on, and she decided to try at the back.

A wooden door in a brick wall led off the alleyway; she pushed gently and found it opened. She went through to find a small patio area, concrete slabs and no vegeta-tion at all. Brick walls separated it from the neighbours' gardens, each of which looked neat, like they were actu-ally tended to.

The back door to the property had been hit around the

lock, several blows chipping paint and denting wood. She pulled her gun and torch.

Inside it smelt familiar, the same herbal funk she'd smelt this morning on the raid. Some genetically modified breed of skunk, a *sativa/indica* cross with a THC content off the charts, was her guess. Not that she knew anything about it.

It was crazy that it was legal for registered Coffeeshops to sell the stuff, but not for anyone to produce it. The Coffeeshops weren't, technically, even allowed to buy it in, an anomaly which most people had no idea existed. Tanya knew that a huge amount was smuggled in from abroad, but over the last few years a new breed of gang had decided horticulture was less risky than dealing with Customs.

The house was set over three floors, and seemed perfectly still. Not even the hum of a fridge broke the silence. She checked the downstairs rooms one by one and finding them empty crept up the stairs.

The smell was stronger here, and in the back room she found a bunch of electric cabling which would have been used for the grow lights. The window would have been blocked up so the neighbours wouldn't notice, and a fan had been crudely attached to the ceiling, venting the air up and out through the roof when it was on.

She was just about to leave – she'd need to check if this was one of the places the drug squad had hit only to find it empty – when she spotted something in the corner. Bending down she trained the torch beam on to it.

It was clear the drug squad had not been here.

On the floor was a small knife. A hunting knife with a

curved, jagged blade. The handle was black plastic, with a small round badge on which a gold eagle spread its wings. She looked closer at the blade – there was something dark dried on it.

Tanya didn't need a degree in forensic science to know what it was.

As she left the building she was starting to see why the homeless woman had ended up dead.

20

'. . . and I'm getting all sorts of shit from Smit.'

Jaap had just parked the car when Kees rang. He could still taste Saskia on his lips, or the wine she'd been drinking anyway. It had only lasted a second, then they'd both pulled away. The look in her eyes told him it was a mistake, and he was sure she'd seen the same in his. They'd agreed to forget it, put it down to too much wine on her part and exhaustion on his.

'Nothing compared to what you'll get from Saskia if you don't find him soon,' said Jaap, pulling out the key and swinging the car door open.

'Saskia? Your . . . aahh . . . ex, right? What's she got to do with it?'

Everyone at the station knew about him and Saskia, and their child. For some reason no one was able to really talk about it, they never asked him about Floortje the way they asked after each other's children.

'What's she got to do with it? She's the lead prosecutor on the case.'

'Seriously? Look, I don't know what Smit told you, but I was supposed to be protecting this guy, no one told me he might try and escape. It was his choice to be a witness and—'

'You don't need to tell me. But there's something I want to know.'

'Yeah, I know what you're going to say. And no, I wasn't. And yes, I've been going to the meetings. But, it's like the guy there says, one day at a time, right?'

Jaap watched as a car drove past slowly, like it was trying to find an address.

'Okay, so what was it you wanted to tell me?'

'I was talking to the bar manager out at this place by Centraal, Club 55—'

'You mean 57.'

'Yeah, 57. So I was asking him some questions and he ID'd one of the headless guys they're showing on the TV?'

'Which one?'

'Koopman.'

'When was this?'

'Friday night. I checked the CCTV and worked out he was with three other guys. And the thing is, one of them looked like the other one who got beheaded.'

'Where are you now?'

'Out by the docks.'

'I think we need to talk,' Jaap checked the time on the dashboard. It said 2.57. It was wrong. 'I've just got to speak to someone, should be about half an hour. I'll call you when I'm done.'

If Koopman and Teeven were there with two other guys, he thought as he hung up and got out of the car, *does that mean they're all going after me? And are they also in danger?*

For a split second Jaap wondered if the killer might just be doing him a favour.

Before getting out he placed a call to Roemers, asking if he'd unlocked Teeven's phone. Roemers wasn't answering.

Why's he taking so long? thought Jaap as he sprang up

three grimy steps leading to the front door of a house and jammed his finger on the brass nipple.

A horde of dogs started barking on the inside, and a man's voice yelled at them to be quiet. Behind him, on the opposite side of the road, he could hear the unmistakable sounds of a couple arguing.

Jaap had spent the short drive going over what he'd got.

Which wasn't much.

Two dead bodies, Koopman and Teeven. Koopman had a photo of him and a gun; Teeven, a man Jaap had put behind bars for murder, had been sitting watching his houseboat for the last few days.

It was clear Teeven wanted revenge, and he'd maybe roped some others in to help.

What wasn't clear was why they had died.

And then there was the tweet, hinting that there may be more killings to come.

The others they were at the club with, he thought. *Is one of them the killer? Or were they involved in Koopman's and Teeven's surveillance on me?*

The door opened a crack, the man having failed to quieten the dogs.

He was tall, taller than Jaap, and eyed him with suspicion.

Jaap had managed to track Schneeman, the manager of the brewery Koopman worked at, to his house in Plantage.

'You the guy who called?' Schneeman asked.

'Inspector Rykel.'

'Get down!' he shouted. It took Jaap a second to realize he was yelling at the dogs.

'Come in,' said Schneeman. 'Don't mind them, they just want to play.'

Jaap stepped into the hallway and was inspected by a rolling sea of eyes and teeth.

He followed Schneeman through to a lounge just off the hall to the left, the heavy fug of dog strong in the air. Schneeman managed, through a complicated series of manoeuvres, to keep all the eyes and teeth in the hallway, and closed the door on them. A low growling started up, followed by intense scratching at the door.

'So you said there was a problem with Jan Koopman?'

His voice was hoarse, presumably from all the shouting he had to do around the place.

'You've not seen him on the news?'

'TV bust a month ago, haven't really had time to fix it. So what's he done, must be pretty heavy if it's made the headlines?'

'It's more what someone did to him. He's dead.'

'Oh.'

Jaap waited for Schneeman to say something else, but then gave up.

'He was killed this morning. Someone took his head off and burned his hand. And I found a gun under the bed in his flat.'

'I . . .' Schneeman sat down on a brown sofa by the wall and breathed out. 'This is unbelievable. I mean, I didn't know him that well, but . . .'

'How long did he work for you?'

'Well over ten years. More like fifteen maybe. He was a good worker, experienced, you know? Most of the guys don't tend to stay that long, or they're slackers. But Koopman, he was different.'

He clearly was different, thought Jaap. *Gun under the bed and a photo of me on his phone.*

'He'd never been in any kind of trouble?'

'What, at work? No, no trouble.'

'Acting strange recently?'

'I'm not sure. He got on with people, he was quite good at that really. But I'm not sure about actual friends.'

'Anyone he fell out with?'

'Look, I don't know. I'm not on the floor all that much. But I can't see any of our guys flying out there to kill him.'

'Flying out where?' said Jaap.

Schneeman looked at him with raised eyebrows.

'Somewhere in the Dutch Antilles. He went last week. It's his annual two-week break, takes it every year at the same time.'

Jaap felt like he had a hand round his throat.

He pulled out his phone and showed Schneeman the image of Koopman and Teeven that Frits had sent through to him earlier. Luckily whoever had posted them on Twitter had managed to make them look like mug shots; you couldn't see the severed necks.

'Who,' said Schneeman, 'are they?'

Jaap's phone started ringing, he turned the screen back to him and saw it was Roemers.

'I thought you'd said twenty minutes?'

'Yeah, it took a little longer. But you're gonna love what I've got. I unlocked the second phone and cross-reffed the call lists like you asked.'

'And?'

'And there's a number in common. But the best part is, I've got a live trace running on it now. You mobile?'

'I can be. Where's it located?' said Jaap.

'Van Baerlestraat, heading south-east.'

Jaap did a quick calculation, less than ten minutes away at a gentle drive, he reckoned he could do it in four.

'I'm on my way. I'll call you when I'm in the car.'

He turned to Schneeman.

'I've got to go, but you're telling me that neither of these is Koopman?'

'Never seen either of these guys before.'

'You're sure?'

'Absolutely, Koopman's totally bald, has been ever since I've known him. He always comes back from holiday with a red scalp.'

In the car Jaap fired up the engine and set off, the sound of his mind intermingling with the hum of the motor. If the first headless body wasn't Koopman, then who the hell was he? And why did he have the key to Koopman's flat? He remembered the photocopy of his driving licence, the image too poor to make out the face properly. He'd requested the original, but it'd not come through and he'd forgotten to chase it up. And he'd made the mistake of assuming the photo posted on Twitter was Koopman as he'd already ID'd him from the flat . . .

He dialled Roemers on the hands-free, the ring loud and echoey in the car's interior.

'Where is it now?'

'It's shifted a bit, signal's just approaching Amsterdamse Bos.'

Jaap slammed the siren on and overtook a van painted

with hippy rainbow print on the side. He'd not been back to Amsterdamse Bos, the large wooded area south of the city, since Andreas' body had been found there over a year ago.

'Get Dispatch to check if there's any patrol in the area. I'm still a few minutes out.'

He crossed the bridge at Alexanderplein, cutting in front of a tram, and turned into Mauritskade. Traffic was lighter so he killed the siren and lights.

'No one's closer than you,' came back Roemers' response. 'But they can get someone there as backup, probably arrive same time as you.'

Jaap thought about exits. He'd no idea how many there were, but he knew there were too many to cover.

'Tell them to approach from the eastern end, and quietly.'

As Jaap sped down Hobbemakade his mind was racing. Could the person with the phone he was chasing be the killer? Or were they in danger themself?

About a hundred metres away from the entrance he spotted brake lights, two red flashes in the darkness.

'Shit,' said Roemers. 'Signal's gone. Whoever it is must have turned the phone off.'

'I think I've seen the car, but keep watching in case it comes back on.'

Jaap checked his weapon, hit the siren and hidden lights in the grille of the car, and motored forward. The car in front, a silver BMW, an older model but still probably worth a few euros, was stationary. Jaap thought he saw a door on the passenger side close before the car shot forward, accelerating fast.

He hated car chases. They were nothing like the

movies. And they more often than not ended with the police car standing down as it was just too dangerous to continue. But they were the only two cars on this stretch of road.

'In pursuit, silver BMW,' he said to Roemers. 'Get Dispatch to move the patrol car round to Bosbaanweg and block off the exit.'

If they didn't manage to corner them before they got out of Amsterdamse Bos, it would be so much harder. There were multiple routes, way too many to cover.

'Patrol's in position,' came the response.

Jaap eased off the accelerator. He'd got them. He could even see the flashing blue up ahead now. As could the driver of the car in front, who slowed down then stopped ten metres short of the patrol car, which sprawled across the road, its blue and orange stripes vivid in the BMW's headlights.

Jaap jumped out of the car, signalled to the two uniforms to hold position and edged forward, his gun clasped in both hands. There were two heads in the vehicle in front. Three metres from the car he stopped.

'Driver, get out of the car slowly. And keep your hands visible.'

The door opened with a soft click, and a man got out, struggling to keep his hands up. His movements were not those of a young man. Out of the corner of his eye Jaap could see one of the uniforms trying to stifle a laugh. As Jaap circled round he could see why.

The man's fly was undone, his erection fading fast.

Both uniforms were laughing now, shaking so hard their aim was all over the place.

'Zip up,' said Jaap.

He made the passenger get out, a man dressed as a woman, complete with a ridiculous wig and swooping eye make-up which would make an 80s rocker jealous.

'I need both of your phones,' said Jaap. 'Turn them on and put them on the bonnet.'

As they complied Jaap went back to his car and pulled his own phone out of the hands-free holder.

'Signal still gone?'

'Yeah, hasn't been turned back on yet,' replied Roemers as Jaap walked back to the BMW, stepping in something soft on the way. 'Did you get anyone?'

'Keep watching,' said Jaap, checking out both phones. The old man's was turned off, the prostitute's was on.

'Turn it on,' he told the old man.

'Can you see it?' Jaap asked Roemers once the phone had booted up and found a signal.

'Hang on, let me re-scan,' said Roemers.

Jaap looked around. Sad that people had to resort to this. His neck felt tight and he looked up to the sky.

A cloud sliced the moon in half.

Off in the trees to his right an owl screeched.

Next to him the car bonnet was ticking.

'No,' came Roemers' voice. 'Nothing.'

21

Despite everything, it had worked like a dream.

He watched from the trees as they let the two men go. Jaap Rykel, the one they needed, spoke to one of the uniforms, then got back on his phone, heading back to his car, the streak of white in his hair catching the moonlight.

Something started crawling across his neck, but he didn't move to swipe it off, not wanting to give away his position, and he let it scuttle back and forth, moving up towards his ear. A tremor ran through his body, but he still didn't move.

Only once both cars had gone did he dare shift his hand and flick whatever it was away, just as it was about to crawl into his ear.

He waited for a few more minutes, listening to the sounds, leaves whispering, something scuttling in the undergrowth off to his right. The owl which had made Rykel turn his head and look in his direction for a moment – and his heart had stopped then, but there was no way he'd have been able to see him – screeched again.

The timing had been good. He'd turned the phone on, driven here and waited. The second he'd seen the patrol car move into view he'd switched it off. That still could have been a coincidence, but when the unmarked appeared, chasing down the BMW, he knew it had worked.

He'd had to think fast today, the two deaths complicating

things, and it was still driving him mad trying to work out who it was. He had an idea now, but it wasn't going to deflect him from his purpose, he'd worked too hard for that.

And then it had struck him, his number would have been on Teeven's phone, and he could use that to his advantage.

There'd been no guarantee they'd even make the connection, let alone take the bait.

But they had, which meant that when he needed to, he could get Jaap Rykel exactly where he needed him to be.

Day Two

22

Jaap leaned back and rubbed his eyes.

He'd been staring at the paper on the table in front of him, glowing in a pool of light cast by the lamp he'd flicked on earlier, and the words had started to take on weird shapes, morphing from letters into symbols he didn't know the meaning of.

In essence it was simple; he had two victims, the second of which, Teeven, he'd put away for murder years before. And, given that the first victim had a photo of Jaap on his phone and a gun, and that Teeven had been spending time staking out Jaap's houseboat, it seemed pretty clear what they were planning.

Revenge.

But that was where things started to break down, because Jaap, even if he didn't feel it due to lack of sleep, was alive, and the two men weren't.

There were too many questions, and he'd woken with them swarming around his head like biting insects. He'd got everything he could down on paper, hoping that would help something jump out at him. So far it had raised more questions than answers.

Before going to bed the previous night he'd worked the phone, managing to track down Koopman in Curaçao. It didn't take long for Jaap to feel comfortable that he was who he said he was, confirming that the first victim wasn't Koopman.

Which led him to the gun.

It was the same one used in a killing years ago which had been linked to Bart Rutte, though he'd never been charged. Jaap was sure he'd heard the name before but couldn't place it, just couldn't remember where or when. He needed to find out.

Something else he couldn't place was the phone he'd followed to Amsterdamse Bos; the men in the BMW had simply been in the wrong place at the wrong time. It was almost as if whoever had the phone knew Jaap was coming and had turned it off just at the right moment.

I might even have passed them in the dark, he thought.

Was it possible whoever had the phone had been working with Teeven? The thought that they'd turned the phone on to lure him out into the woods had struck Jaap earlier. If he'd gone on his own, without the uniforms turning up as well . . .

I'm chasing a ghost, he thought as he got up, massaging the muscles in his neck.

The questions kept coming, layering up in his mind.

He walked into the main living area and pulled out his *zafu*, a round kapok-filled cushion he'd brought back from Kyoto, and placed it on the orange mat on the floor.

The only way he could escape was to be in each moment, not get caught up in thought.

Once he'd settled down and set a fifteen-minute timer he closed his eyes and focused on his breathing, feeling the movement of his diaphragm, the rise and fall of his chest, aware of the coolness of the in breath through his nostrils, the warmth of the out breath.

At first his breathing was ragged, but it gradually settled into a rhythm and started to open up his mind. It wasn't clear of thoughts – he'd learned that wasn't possible to achieve – but he was able to observe each thought and let it go immediately, concentrate on the space between them.

Gradually the spaces between each thought seemed to elongate.

His breath became almost imperceptible.

His pulse slowed.

Time expanded.

Space.

The bell on his timer rang clear into the stillness of the morning.

Jaap listened to the liquid purity of it as it faded away, tapered into nothingness.

His eyes opened, he took a few breaths and stood up, stretching his muscles out.

Usually after sitting the first few minutes were filled with gentle surprises, everyday objects looked different, fresh, as if he was seeing them for the first time. He'd get caught up in limescale patterns in the sink, or he'd suddenly notice the lines on the palms of his hands, like channels on the face of the moon.

All things he'd seen a million times before but hadn't really connected with.

He put away the *zafu*, rolled up the mat, trying to do it

slowly, keep his mind on what he was doing, be aware, but already his calm was beginning to be chipped away at.

He stepped over to the kitchen in a corner of the main area and poured a small cup of water into the kettle. The stove fired up, and he watched the fire burst into life, how it spread out as he lowered the black cast-iron kettle towards it, the flames reaching up eagerly, hungrily, a nest of newborn chicks craning to reach their mother's beak.

He'd lost the kettle lid a year ago – he suspected it had gone missing when the forensics were going over the houseboat looking for clues as to who had killed his sister. That was something he tried not to think about much. The man responsible had been killed, by Kees, but it didn't feel like justice.

The flame hissed gently, heat warming his arm as he stood waiting for the water, his mind already detached from the present, the space which had opened up vanishing like the void momentarily created by lightning.

And his thoughts were louder than thunder.

He glanced round the houseboat interior, trying to avoid the spiral of emotion which Karin always kicked into action. A spiral which would leave him angry, frustrated, and exhausted.

He forced his mind elsewhere.

The boat seemed empty. Tanya'd been out late on her case and had ended up close to her flat. At least that's what she'd claimed in her text message. Jaap didn't know what to think of that.

He'd been terrified yesterday when Roemers had told him there was a photo of Tanya leaving his houseboat on Teeven's phone.

And he'd been a different kind of terrified when she'd sat opposite him and said she had something to say; he sensed that she'd backed out at the last minute, claiming it was to do with her case, though Jaap was pretty sure it was about their relationship.

Maybe she's still not decided, he thought.

The first low rumble of bubbles started up, they looked like fleeting fish eyes winking at him from inside the kettle. He reached out and took it off the flame, feeling the steam against his fingers, and tried to think about what he had to do.

Next he pulled a tin of *matcha* out of the cupboard, measured a small heap of the bright-green powder, and whisked it into a froth with the water. He was just putting the can away when he stopped, reopened it and whisked the same amount in again.

It cost a small fortune, but this morning he felt like he needed it.

The chair creaked as he sat down at the round table and sipped the thick, bitter liquid. Before he knew what he was doing he found he'd pulled out his coins and placed them on the worn surface in front of him.

He couldn't remember when he'd slipped from occasional use to doing it every day, but it was some time in the last year. Some time after he'd scattered Karin's ashes at Schellingwouderbreek.

She'd be thirty-four today, he thought as he reached for his copy of the I Ching from the shelf behind him, then picked the coins up, ready to start throwing. He should visit Schellingwouderbreek today.

The noise of brass clattering against wood was loud in

the morning quiet. He built up the hexagram one line at a time, and while he did his mind strayed back to Tanya, to their relationship. He threw the coins for the sixth time, noted down the result and converted it into the final line of the hexagram. Once it was done he looked it up in the I Ching, the pages worn and grubby.

Heaven over Fire.

SEEK UNION WITH OTHERS.

Sometimes this really scares me, he thought.

He cleared up quickly and stepped through the front door on to the houseboat's deck.

The air was damp, and held the tang of tar and wet stone.

He found himself looking around, checking to see if anyone was watching. In the photo of Tanya leaving his houseboat she'd been right where he was now.

A waterbird floated past, clucking softly to itself, head darting back and forth. He watched it as it changed direction, then disappeared around the kink in the canal.

His phone buzzed, a picture message from Saskia. It was of Floortje, asleep on the carpet in Saskia's living room, her head resting on the large fluffy dinosaur one of Saskia's friends had given her. The dinosaur's fur was electric-blue, a ridge of pink spines jutting out from its back. A line of drool spooled down from the corner of Floortje's mouth on to the dinosaur's tail.

Another message from Saskia came in, this one a text:

'cried all night. now she's tired . . . it's like a form of abuse.'

Playful or passive-aggressive, he wasn't sure. He never knew with Saskia. Especially after last night.

He looked at his phone for a few moments before deciding to treat it as playful:

'you should alert the authorities, they take adult
abuse seriously these days.'

As he walked to the shore the metal gangplank swayed with each step. The second he reached dry land bells started up, playing a tune before beginning to strike the hour. They were from Westerkerk, the large church on Prinsengracht whose main claim to fame was its location just south of the tourist hotspot, Anne Frank's house.

Jaap was struck, as he so often was, by just how quiet this part of town was. It was right in the centre, and yet didn't have the noise you'd associate with a busy city.

Elm trees were in bloom along the canal. Their clusters of green flowers frilled like seventeenth-century ruffs, and people on bikes were starting to appear, smooth phantoms gliding through the city.

The sixth bell chimed as he walked up the canal, and he wondered, not for the first time, if the hour was on the first bell or the last.

And then it came to him.

He had seen Rutte's name before.

And he knew where.

23

The train pulled out with its carriage lights off.

Tanya stood on the platform as it moved past, watching her blurred reflection in the windows. The low growl of the engine echoed round the station.

Once it was past she stared down at the track, trying to find the spot where the homeless woman had been hit.

There was no crime-scene halo, no bunches of flowers wrapped in plastic. It was like it never happened.

No one really cared about her death.

It was only because of what the killer had been wearing that she was still on the case; otherwise it would have been open-shut like Frits had originally promised.

Through the curved glass roof she could see the dawn starting, layers of yellow merging up into the fading darkness overhead.

She'd caught the ferry over from Amsterdam Noord and opted to stand on deck despite the slicing wind which had made her eyes water and her nose run. Once docked she'd walked past Centraal and had found herself ducking in.

And here she was. But the platform and tracks weren't giving her anything new. All she had so far was a dead body, a couple of drunk witnesses who claimed the victim had been paid to spy on a house which had turned out to have been a grow site, and a killer in a police jacket. And the possibility that Kees had been calling the homeless woman from the station.

None of it made any sense.

She turned to go, walking towards the stairs which would take her down to the subway, trying to find some kind of logic, some thread which would tie it all together.

Once she exited the front of the station she stopped again and looked around. The usual crowd; a mix of early-morning workers clutching steaming coffee cups, drug addicts walking aimlessly or with extreme purpose depending on what they'd ingested, and the odd homeless person shuffling about.

Her phone buzzed, she saw it was Jaap.

'I went to the estate agent yesterday,' he said when she asked him how he was getting on. 'The one who handles the victim's flat. Turns out it's not Koopman, he's in Curacao. But someone at the estate agent stopped going into work and I wonder if there's a link. I didn't get a chance to check up on her but I've got her address, can you do it?'

'Yeah, sure. I've some stuff to do, but I can fit it in if I get going now.'

'Thanks. Also, I had a message from Kees saying he's got CCTV pictures of some people at 57, he thinks they're Teeven and the first victim.'

Tanya thought about 57. It was the case she'd met Jaap on, and she'd found the man they'd been after there. He'd killed an old couple and stolen their adopted child but had been playing cards like all was right with the world when she'd found him.

He'd tried to escape.

She'd had other ideas.

139

She remembered the way the glass had shattered when she'd fired the shots. And, once she'd finally restrained him, the pain as her foot kicked him hard in the ribs.

He was in prison now, and while Tanya didn't buy into all the macho cop stuff, she hoped that Haak was right now being bent over in the shower by a gang of hairy men, each taking their turn.

Slowly.

That's what people who abused children deserved.

That's what, she thought as the image of Staal exiting his house slammed into her head like a physical jolt, *he deserves*.

'I still don't get why they had the photo of you,' she said, pushing away her thoughts. 'Or the one of me.'

'Apparently they were meeting two other men,' he said.

'You think they might be after you . . . us, as well?'

'I don't know, but I'm beginning to think we should take this to Smit.' He paused for a moment. 'Let's look at them when we meet. Then we can decide.'

Tanya suddenly felt a pang of regret, and the urge to be with him now hit her. They'd not been spending so much time together recently. She'd withdrawn when she'd finally tracked down Staal.

'Did you talk to your friends?' asked Jaap, just as she was about to speak.

She nearly said *What friends?* before her brain kicked into gear.

A motorbike ripped down the tram lane behind her.

'I . . . Yeah. I said we'd arrange another time to meet up. I told them to go on without me.'

She hated herself for doing this, for lying to Jaap. But

what else could she do? She couldn't let him in on what she was planning.

Or is it that I simply don't want to? she thought as they signed off. *Maybe I should trust him more? Maybe it would help?*

'We'll make sure you get another chance,' he said. 'Listen, I should get going. See you at the station.'

Once she'd hung up she walked past the bike stands. They stood in vast rows, so many bikes jammed close to each other it looked like a single mass of twisted metal and tyres.

A man was working his way through them, eyes on the ground like he was searching for something. A few metres away from Tanya he stopped, bent down and picked up an object. When he straightened Tanya could see it was a needle. Used.

The man put it in his pocket and looked around for the first time, suddenly noticing Tanya. His face looked like flesh had been shrink-wrapped on to bone.

'I wouldn't use that if I were you,' she said.

'I'm not you,' he replied.

Tanya saw he had a point. She pulled out a photo of the homeless woman and asked the man if he'd ever seen her.

He looked at it suspiciously, as if something might jump out of the photo and bite him. But after a few moments he nodded.

'I've seen her before,' he said. 'She hangs out here sometimes.'

Tanya pocketed the photo. To her it was pretty obvious the image was of a dead person, but the man hadn't seemed to notice.

Maybe it's all the same to him, she thought.

'I'm trying to find out about her. I think she worked for someone . . .?'

'She did some odd jobs, she certainly had more money than most of us,' he said moving closer, his eyes now trained on Tanya with an intensity which made her uncomfortable. She could smell the deep, unwashed haze which seemed to surround him.

'Maybe,' he said, licking his lips once, the tip of his tongue coated a dirty white. 'Maybe I can tell you something.'

'Like?'

'I might have to charge a fee.'

Tanya sighed. First the drunks wanting vodka, now this. She felt bad enough about that, but she was drawing the line at heroin.

'Tell you what,' she said. 'I'll buy you some food if you tell me what you know about her.'

'I'd prefer money.'

'A meal or nothing.'

He looked at her, squinting slightly. He shook his head.

'Okay,' said Tanya as she turned and walked away.

Five paces was all it took.

'Wait,' he said. 'I am hungry . . .'

In the end she bought him three bagels, two large takeout coffees and a host of chocolate bars. Then she demanded he tell her what he knew.

He rambled, but one detail stuck out. He claimed to have seen her meet a man several times.

'You're sure?'

'Yeah,' he said, taking another bite from the first of the bagels. 'Really. The guy was in a wheelchair. He'd get off the tram from IJburg, they'd talk a bit, then he'd get back on the next tram out.'

A wheelchair, thought Tanya.

This gave her something to work with. Katja had said the man had been called Wheels.

So now she was going to have to talk to whoever ran the trams.

24

Kees was lying on his living-room floor, staring up at the unshielded light bulb.

He'd been stupid, he knew that. It had happened slowly, in increments. Just a little extra one day, just enough to tide him over till the next time. But it was back in September when it had really got out of control. That was three months after the symptoms had started and he finally, unable to ignore the pain, got himself checked out.

And when the test results came back from the hospital and Kees found out what he was facing, he'd needed more and more, and the dealer had been only too happy to oblige – Kees was an upstanding member of society in gainful full-time employment, so if he wanted a little credit occasionally, just to help him at the end of the month, then that was cool with the dealer.

A few months later, just as Kees was starting to come to terms with what was happening to him, he got a call. The man's voice said his name was Paul and that he'd noticed Kees' credit had got a bit out of control. He mentioned a figure which almost made Kees throw up there and then. The worst thing was Kees knew it probably wasn't far off.

But Paul was reasonable. He wasn't the violent type, he said. He valued dialogue, he believed in relationships, in people helping each other out.

Kees had been under no illusion, the threat was there.

Then a call a few days later with a payment plan, a way to consolidate his debt into easy payments.

But, months in, the debt didn't seem to have gone down at all, and Kees was realizing that it never would.

Which was why he'd been lying on the floor. He'd needed to think, to work out what he was going to do. And an idea had come to him; he would get to Paul, and he now knew exactly how. It wasn't going to be pleasant, but he was beyond that now.

He got up, the pain in his limbs bad, but he tried not to think about it, focus on the things he could change.

Breakfast was a line from Paul's package, the thought that it'd been laced with rat poison crossing his mind a nanosecond before the powder hit.

But the high was good, clean, and he didn't keel over, and it even helped his head, which he assumed was pulsing from the knock Isovic had given him yesterday.

He checked his phone, saw Jaap had sent him a message asking to meet at the station. He'd also sent a second message telling him to bring the photos.

He doesn't trust me at all, thought Kees as he felt the coke doing its thing, revving up his whole system. He started to feel a pleasant heat all over his body, seeping through his veins, numbing the pain, making him feel warm, alive.

He scooped up the photos, which after not being able to find he eventually discovered strewn on the hall floor, and stepped out of his flat on Bloedstraat right in the heart of the red light district.

Living here meant he had to put up with noise at night, crowds of tourists who wandered around gawping at the women standing in their glass cubicles in just thongs, waiting for a customer to come along and light up their night.

Or at the very least, their wallet.

It also meant he had to put up with the stench of bleach, the streets being hosed down every morning by a clean-up crew, getting rid of whatever unsavoury stuff got left behind in the early hours.

It wasn't ideal, but it was cheap.

There'd been an article in a newspaper he'd picked up in the hospital waiting room several months ago, in which some rich columnist had argued the way to a happier life was to spend money on experiences rather than possessions.

Well, coke's an experience, he though as he set off across town towards the station.

He found himself laughing, startling a man and a woman crashed out in a doorway. Kees thought they were drunks, but he noticed the label on the bottle clutched in the woman's hand. It said MINERAL WATER.

The coke had lifted his mood. He suddenly thought it was going to be okay, he'd be able to work something out with Paul. Hell, he might even be able to throw a little work into finding Isovic as well.

And as for the disease, well, fuck it.

Everyone's gotta die, he thought. *So why worry?*

But by the time he reached the station he was sinking back into reality. Things weren't so easy to face up to without chemical help.

He made his way to his desk and dropped into the seat, kicking back and putting his feet up. As soon as he'd given

Jaap the photos he'd get out and start putting his plan into action. He could hear a radio on in the office.

'. . . though police sources are staying quiet, unwilling at this stage to give out much information. But it's clear, with the message on Twitter, there could well be another killing today. And . . .'

He tuned out. Not his problem.

His gun and ID badge were sticking into his side. He pulled them out and pushed them on to the edge of the desk. A huge pile of papers, and a half-crushed Coke can, fell to the floor.

They looked better there, he decided after a few moments.

He glanced at the murder board across the room, noticing Tanya was on there at the bottom. He scanned across and looked at her case. Some hobo at Centraal station.

But the thing which stopped his breathing was the victim's photo, which hadn't been there yesterday, pinned up at the far right.

He knew that woman.

He felt a rush not unlike a coke hit, only this was fear.

He dropped his head on to the desk.

25

It was there, in black and white.

Rutte's name had come up in Teeven's case all those years ago.

Jaap was in a glass-walled incident room looking back over the main office. He picked Rutte's file up again and scanned through it. At least six of the killings he was suspected of had been the same – execution-style, bullet to the back of the head. The same way Teeven's victim had died.

He called Ballistics, asked them to check and get back to him if the gun they had matched any of the killings listed on Rutte's file.

Then he peered at the photo of Rutte taken at one of his arrests.

His face was heavyset, thick eyebrows crowded down on his eyes, and his jaw was clenched like he was in pain, or just angry. His hair was low on his forehead, a widow's peak pointing down towards his nose.

Glancing up, Jaap spotted Tanya walking into the office, and waved her over. She nodded and changed direction. He turned back to Teeven and Rutte's files, and wondered just what was wrong with the case, why he couldn't make any sense of it at all.

Tanya stepped through the doorway, her red hair snapped back in a tight ponytail.

'Hey,' he said as he rose. The urge to touch her, hold her, was strong, and he went towards her just as she steered around him, throwing a glance at the glass wall through which he could see Kees was just about to arrive.

It frustrated him that Tanya was so secretive, but he tried not to show it.

She pulled up a chair and placed it opposite him, spreading out some papers on the table between them. Kees pushed the door open and walked over, fanning out a set of photos right on top of the files Jaap had already brought in.

'Okay,' said Jaap, sitting down again. 'Let's get to it.'

He started out by going through the scene reports for each of the two murders, and the autopsy on victim one. All this had come from the new computer system, the images uploaded by the forensic and pathology teams. The switchover from the old Herkenningsdienstsysteem had taken years to implement, but was now fully operational. And much more efficient.

Then he gave it over to Kees, who explained about the photos he'd got from the CCTV at 57.

Jaap leaned across the table and looked at the photo of four men. One of them, just as Kees had said, was the man who he'd previously thought was Koopman, while another was Teeven. Of the remaining two, only one's face was visible; the fourth member of the group was facing away from the camera.

'Did anyone at 57 know these two?' he asked.

Kees shook his head, then grimaced, putting a hand up to his forehead.

The four men had been sitting around a table for a

couple of hours, as evidenced by the digital time stamps in the corner of each photo.

Jaap sat back in his chair. There'd been a few glimpses of something during his morning meditation session, just an illusive flicker of an idea that had stayed tantalizingly out of reach.

He could almost hear Yuzuki Roshi telling him not to search for what he was searching for. Recently Jaap had been wondering if the whole Zen paradox thing was really worth it, if, in the end, it was just all mind games. Fine if you're cloistered up in a monastery in Kyoto, but less useful when you're heading up a multiple murder investigation.

'We've got two dead bodies, and the last tweet yesterday hinted there'll be more,' said Jaap, picking up one of the photos again. 'I still can't see why their heads were removed and their hands burned, or why it's been advertised on Twitter. The killer's not made any demands, so why do it?'

'Not yet, anyway,' said Kees, leaning close to Tanya and jabbing his finger at the photo she was looking at. 'But if there are going to be more killings then it's fair to assume it'll be one of these?'

Jaap watched as Tanya moved subtly away from Kees. She caught his eye for a second before going back to Teeven's file.

Jaap was reminded that Tanya and Kees had gone out when they'd been doing the basic police training course. He tried to stop himself thinking about that, about them sleeping together, even if it was years ago.

'Let's work on that assumption,' he said. 'We need to ID these two as soon as—'

'Hang on,' said Tanya. 'Look at this.'

26

Tanya'd been only half listening to what Jaap and Kees were talking about, she'd been looking through Teeven's file, the man who'd had a picture of her leaving Jaap's houseboat on his phone. But it wasn't till she turned to his autopsy photo that things started to click into place.

The only catch – if Kees was involved, how much could she afford to give away?

'See this here?' she said, pushing a photo of one of Teeven's legs towards Jaap. Both Jaap and Kees leaned in to take a look. The image showed an empty ankle holster strapped to the dead man's calf.

'Kinky leather,' said Kees.

'The thing is,' said Tanya, ignoring him, 'last night I found a knife at a cannabis farm which had been cleared out. And the knife had a round crest on it, with an eagle. That round bit there? It looks the same.'

Jaap picked up the photo. He had the fast movements of a hunter, everything alert.

'I'll get the lab to check it out, but I'm sure we're going to find the roundel on there matches the roundel on the knife I found,' she said.

'I think it will too,' said Jaap. 'I remember looking at it. So you think these four were growing cannabis?' he asked, pointing to one of the photos Kees had brought.

She thought back to the name on the logs. This was

where things got tricky. If Kees was involved, did she really want to play her hand now?

Maybe now's the time to see, thought Tanya.

She paused for a moment before making her decision. She was going to watch Kees carefully, check his reaction.

'That drug raid I was on yesterday? The crew I was with kept hitting these places where surveillance was sure there was an indoor farm, and every time they got there it'd all be gone. I think they're somehow getting tipped off.'

Tanya was looking at Jaap, but she was tuned into Kees, trying to sense if he'd reacted.

Did he react? she thought. *Did he kind of freeze for a second? Or did I imagine it?*

'Okay,' said Jaap. 'Makes sense. Let's see if this knife and holster match up. But that still leaves the question, why are they getting killed? Some vigilante? Or someone trying to muscle in on their business? I . . . Kees, are you all right?'

Tanya glanced at Kees. He was looking pale. Unhealthily so.

'Yeah, I . . . I think I just need a drink,' Kees said, getting up. 'I've been running around and I think maybe I'm a little dehydrated.'

He left the room, leaving the door open behind him.

Tanya got up and closed it, wondering if now was the moment to tell Jaap, but he was already talking.

'Let's divide these up,' he said, picking up the CCTV images again. 'I'll focus on trying to ID these men and see if that pathologist has got any DNA results for the first victim yet. Have you got time to follow up on that knife, see if it is Teeven's?'

'Yeah, I can do that. If it matches?'

'If it does we should check out their customers, most likely the Coffeeshops. See if anyone recognizes them.'

Tanya nodded. It made sense, but it would be a huge job.

'And I should speak to the drug squad,' said Jaap. 'Who were you working with yesterday?'

'Hank de Vries, do you know him?'

'Hank? Yeah, I knew him at academy. Ironic he ended up in the drug squad, he was always partial to a bit of a smoke.'

'Seriously? He seems to really hate the stuff now. He was rabid when we turned up at that place yesterday and found it had been cleaned out.'

'You got his number?'

'I'll call him,' she said, pulling out her phone.

Jaap listened as she got through and told him what they were after.

'Really?' she said suddenly, looking up at Jaap. 'Hang on. They've got another tip-off, they're just about to head there now.'

'I want to be there,' said Jaap. Tanya handed him the phone.

'Hank? It's Jaap. I'm going to need to ride with you on this one. Where are you?'

He listened to the response.

'Okay,' he said, checking his watch. 'I'll call you when I'm close.'

He handed Tanya her phone back. Their hands touched, and he held on to her fingers for a moment.

'Listen, I—'

The glass door swung open behind Jaap before he

could say anything, and they both turned to see Frits carrying a large pile of files. He was looking at them intently.

They'd withdrawn their hands, but Frits looked like he'd noticed.

'Didn't want to disturb anything . . .'

27

Jaap stood, itching to get on.

Smit had caught him just as he was leaving the station and demanded an update. But then he'd asked him to wait outside his office for ten minutes. Jaap had paced around, finally sitting in a chair and trying to read a newspaper he'd found on it. It'd been the business section, a long article about an aggressive takeover bid by some large company. Jaap's eyes had glazed before Tanya had called to say the knife and holster had been checked and the answer had come back. They matched.

When Smit had finally been ready for him, Jaap had stepped into his office and briefed him on the current status.

'So you think the victims might be involved in growing cannabis on an industrial scale?' asked Smit when Jaap had finished.

Jaap nodded, that was exactly what he'd just told him.

'But why are they then being killed?'

'That's what I'm trying to find out, and I've got to get—'

'You've seen the media coverage. We – *you* – need a result on this quickly,' said Smit as if he'd just laid out the answer to a philosophical question which had been bugging mankind since the dawn of time.

'I know,' said Jaap. 'Which is why I really need to go now. And I could use some help.'

'What do you need?' asked Smit, shooting his cuffs.

Jaap paused for a moment. What he was about to request would, if she ever found out, make Saskia angry.

Well, angrier, he thought.

'I'm meeting de Vries from the drug squad. He got a tip-off on another farm, and I want to be there, but I need some help. As it was Kees who came up with the photo of the two victims and the two other men they were hanging around with, I think it should be him. And I know he's working on another case, but . . .'

'Okay, you can have him. I'll give the order he's taken off Isovic and put someone else on it. Not sure he's up to it anyway. But I want a result, preferably before we get another body.'

As Jaap stepped out the front of the police station, he glanced up, looking at the faded blue POLITIE sign jutting out from the building.

For a second he wondered if any of it was worth it.

He heard shouting and watched as two uniforms attempted to bring in a man wearing jeans, T-shirt and an orange clown wig.

The man didn't appear too keen on entering the station.

Once they'd managed to get the clown inside and booked, Jaap co-opted one of the uniforms to give him a lift, and twenty minutes later he was dropped off on a street in Nieuw-West. He spotted an unmarked car midway along.

'Hey, long time,' said Hank, offering up a soul shake as Jaap got into the passenger seat.

He was more compact than Jaap, but lean and muscular. His blond hair was short, the same length and colour as his full beard. He was wearing a stab vest, a short-sleeve T-shirt and gold-lensed wraparounds. Veins coursed along his arms, and Jaap noticed a scar, knotted with stitch marks, cutting across his left forearm. From the pink scar tissue it looked recent.

'So what brings you here?' Hank asked once Jaap was settled in.

'Two dead bodies without heads.'

'Oh man, you got that one? Sometimes I'm glad I got out of homicide.'

'Tell me about it. The thing is Tanya's come up with a possible link between the men that were killed and all these cannabis farms.'

'You have my full attention,' said Hank, turning his head to face Jaap, who could see himself distorted in Hank's sunglasses.

'She found a knife at a grow house which matches a holster one of my victims had, and she reckons the reason you keep getting there too late is they're getting tipped off somehow.'

'They're sure as shit getting tipped off,' said Hank. 'Unless they've smoked so much of their own product they've developed psychic powers.'

A fly started buzzing round the back of the car.

'Fuck, that thing's been driving me crazy,' Hank said as it flew between them and hit the windscreen. He tried to swat it, but missed, his hand leaving a smudge on the glass.

'Tanya's smart,' said Hank, trying to rub the mark off but only making it worse. 'Smart and pretty hot. If I wasn't married I'd slide her on to the bonnet and—'

Jaap didn't want to hear. 'Recognize any of these?' He

handed Hank the photos of the two victims and the CCTV shots from 57.

Hank glanced through them, shook his head.

'So do you have some idea who runs these things?' asked Jaap as he took them back.

'I've got a hunch. There's this—'

Hank's radio crackled into life.

'Two men entering the address now, what's your call?'

Hank turned to Jaap. 'It's a couple of streets away. Wanna join us?'

'What I really need is the name of whoever you think might be behind this.'

'Tell you what. Help me with this, and one of the people there might be able to tell you themselves.'

Jaap weighed it up. He suddenly remembered he needed to let Tanya know that Kees was now working with them. She wasn't going to like it.

'Okay,' he said, pulling out his phone. 'I've got to make a call on the way.'

'I'm moving now,' said Hank into the radio. 'And I've got someone with me. Repeat, I've got someone with me. I don't want one of you morons shooting him. Position yourselves at the back. I'll give you the signal when we're going in.'

He reached over to the back seat and handed Jaap a stab vest like his own.

'Just in case,' he said, as he fired up the car. 'You armed?'

'Yeah,' said Jaap, pulling out his gun.

There'd been a time when he'd thought he'd never carry a weapon again. But last year had changed all that, and he'd got over his reluctance.

'Your arm, that happen on one of these raids?' Jaap asked as Hank fired up the motor and yanked the gearstick.

'This?' said Hank, holding it up laughing. He swung the car out and accelerated faster than Jaap thought was strictly necessary. Sun streamed through the windscreen and they both reached for the sun-guards at the same moment, flipping them down in unison.

'Nah,' he said. 'This was the wife.'

28

Kees was splashing water on his face when his phone started ringing.

'Inspector Terpstra,' said Kees, eyeing himself in the mirror. He'd been trying to get over the shock of seeing that the homeless woman was dead, but the face shower wasn't really doing it.

'Yeah, hi. We spoke yesterday. At 57?'

'You're the barman right?' said Kees, unable to recall his name but recognizing the voice, picturing the goatee.

'Yeah, and I just wanted to say I thought I saw one of those guys last night. From the photo you showed me?'

'What time?'

'I'm not totally sure it was him. It was only this morning I kind of placed him. So I checked the camera we've got on the exit, and I reckon he left just after 10 p.m.'

'You there now?'

'Yeah, just cleaning up, but—'

'I'll be there in five minutes,' said Kees as he headed down to the carpool at a run, water still dripping off his chin.

He managed to secure something a bit more butch than the electric car he'd had yesterday, and was outside the club in less than seven minutes. All the while his mind was racing, faster than the car.

He might be back on track. If this was a sighting of Krilic it could improve his chances of getting to Isovic.

The place where Isovic had hit him yesterday, right on the back of his head, throbbed.

The fact that everyone at the station had heard about it wasn't any less painful.

This time he didn't even bother trying to parallel-park, he simply skidded the car halfway across the road and left it there, siren screaming, lights going berserk and the driver's door hanging open.

People coming off the free ferries which linked the old city to the new northern section were watching him as he ran towards the club door, wondering what was going on. He toyed with drawing his gun, just for show, but decided it might freak the barman out a bit.

But he couldn't resist hammering on the doors and yelling 'Police' as he slapped his ID badge up against the glass.

'Jesus,' said the barman when he let Kees in. 'What's the rush?'

'Let's just see the tape,' said Kees.

29

Hank grinned at Jaap as he nosed the car into the street. He slowed to a stop, leaving the motor running. It sounded like someone had souped up the engine.

The scene out the windscreen was classic Nieuw-West, state housing which ran in terraces. Moroccan and Tunisian flags hung from windows on some of the buildings. A black bin regurgitated junk on to the street for a crowd of unruly gulls, their heads jabbing and pecking in a frenzy of yellow and white.

This was the area that Mohammed Bouyeri, killer of filmmaker Theo van Gogh, was born and raised in, and it was known for immigrant unrest, many of its residents unhappy that the promised land hadn't quite turned out like the dreams which had lured them, or their parents, in the first place.

Jaap had called Tanya as Hank had driven, and told her about Kees, but his reception had gone and he wasn't sure she'd got the message. He tried to send a text but he still had no coverage. Giving up he pocketed the phone.

They're adults, he thought. *They can sort it out themselves.*

'Position?' Hank asked the radio.

'Covering the rear exit,' crackled the response.

'Then we're going in,' said Hank as he lurched the car forward, skidding it to a halt right in front of one of the houses midway along the terrace.

Gulls flapped into the air with angry shrieks.

Jaap sprang out, ran round the front of the car and joined Hank by the door to the property. Hank drew, and Jaap followed suit.

Hank finger-counted down from three then stepped forward and kicked right by the lock. Wood crunched. The door gave.

'Police,' he yelled in a death-metal voice as they ran in.

A short corridor ended in a room to the back, and stairs led to the first floor. The rooms to either side were empty, Jaap clocked as they ran past. Hearing movement above them they took the stairs two at a time, Hank out in front.

On the first floor there was a small landing and two closed doors. It was dark, the one window above the stairs blacked out. Jaap could hear an electrical hum. They picked the room on the right where the hurried footsteps had come from, and positioned themselves either side of the door.

'Police. Come out slowly,' shouted Hank.

Noises from the inside again, whispering.

Jaap caught a herbal hit.

'Come out now,' Hank shouted again.

This time just silence.

He looked across to Jaap, motioned for him to cover and stepped into position ready to kick in the door.

Jaap watched as he raised his foot.

Then he watched as the door seemed to erupt, splinters of wood flying towards Hank, light trailing each individual piece.

It was then he heard the shot. His ears imploded.

Hank fell back, slamming his head on the wall behind

him. Jaap found he'd shifted position, about thirty degrees off the door, his gun held out in front of him. He could hear Hank groaning on the floor.

Through the high-pitched ringing Jaap heard the unmistakable click and pump of a shotgun being reloaded.

He ducked across the doorway, light blaring out of the holes in the door, dust swirling in the solid rays, and pulled the trigger, emptying the clip before he got to the other side.

One of the eight must have hit home; there was a muffled scream and the sound of someone toppling over like a sack of earth dropped to the floor.

He squatted down, out of line of the door and grabbed Hank's left arm, pulling him towards him. Hank groaned again, tried to help by scrabbling with his unhurt leg, but his foot kept slipping in a slick of blood.

Once Jaap had managed to manoeuvre him further away from the door he quickly went over the wound. Multiple shot in the foot and calf. It was messy, and it needed attention.

Quick.

He hoped Hank's men covering the back had heard the shots.

'I'm going to secure the place, then we'll get you an ambulance,' he whispered to Hank, who nodded and handed him his own gun. Jaap took it and moved by the side of the door. With one hand he reached out and gave it a shove, retracting his hand at speed. The door flew inwards, but there were no more shots.

He could hear his own breath, rough as sandpaper, and under that the techno track of his heart, pounding fast and hard. The grip of the gun suddenly appeared to be covered in moisture. He took a deep breath, then burst into the room, gun ahead of him.

It was hot inside, and there was a forest of weed, leaves clustered thick. The hum was louder now, overhead. He looked up to see high-power grow lights hanging from the ceiling. Jaap's eyes were adjusting too slowly. A man lay slumped on the floor about four feet from the door, shotgun just out of his reach. There was a second man, standing several plants deep.

He had his hands up in the air like he was hanging from a cliff.

30

It hadn't taken Tanya long to establish that the girl who'd worked at the estate agent, Esther, had done a runner.

Her housemate, a particularly grim specimen who'd opened the door, bare stomach drooping down over low-slung jeans, had seemed more upset that he was going to be short on the rent for next month. No, he'd not really known her, he'd said with one hand on the door frame, the other fiddling with his outie belly button.

Tanya'd asked to see her room, and had been forced to squeeze past the man to get in. She was sure he'd got some kind of thrill from it. The room itself hadn't yielded much, Esther had either taken everything she owned, or hadn't owned that much in the first place. Just as she was leaving something had caught her eye by the doorway; she'd bent down to look, finding it was a small silver cross on a thin chain. The clasp was broken. She'd bagged it up, then left.

Then she'd talked to someone at the tram company. She explained what she needed and he'd agreed to put the word out; any drivers on the route she specified seeing a man in a wheelchair were to call her.

Now she was in the tech unit reviewing every sighting on Centraal's CCTV of the man who'd killed the homeless woman. The heavy metal T-shirted tech said they'd been through everything.

At no point was his face visible, his cap covering his

features in the few moments when he was actually on camera. There was one short sequence of him, leaving once he'd pushed the woman in front of the train, when the camera caught the back of his head. Tanya could see the man's hair was short. Much shorter than Kees'.

'You okay?' asked the tech.

Tanya realized she must've sighed.

'Yeah, fine,' she said, getting up.

So it wasn't Kees.

Which didn't mean he wasn't involved; he was still the only one who could have made the calls, and she was sure he'd reacted when she'd aired her theory.

She made her way up the stairs from the basement, and just as she turned a corner she heard a man yell out from above. Toilet rolls cascaded down the steps towards her, several unspooling as they came. A man in white overalls stood on the landing, a two-wheeled trolley in his grip, now half empty.

'Sorry,' he called out. 'Not hurt, are you?'

'I've had worse things thrown at me than toilet paper,' she said, picking up a roll. 'At least this looks relatively unused.'

'Normally it's wrapped up, but for some reason when I picked it up at the depot today it was all loose,' he said, starting down towards her, grabbing up rolls as he did, throwing them back up the stairs behind him.

Tanya stood and watched him for a moment. Something had just struck her.

The logs she'd requested had been for police staff only; she'd not thought of civilians. But there were loads of people who came in and out of the station on a daily basis.

Could it be someone from outside? she thought. *Could they have got access to a computer?*

It would be a risk, a huge risk, for someone to take. But then she thought of the night cleaners. There was a crew who passed through, cleaning not only the desks but the computers themselves. She remembered one night she was in late watching a man sitting at one of the inspectors' desks wiping a computer keyboard.

And the calls had all been made at night.

She turned and ran down the stairs, a roll of paper chasing down after her.

31

There was no question in Kees' mind.

He was in the same room as last night, and whoever had been on duty watching the CCTV had a seriously bad body-odour problem. Jaap had called a while back, asking him to help out with his investigation. As if he didn't already have enough on his plate. He'd agreed though, because really, what choice did he have?

But that didn't mean he still wasn't going to try and get Isovic.

He was looking at the freeze-frame on the screen, and despite the poor quality, and the fact that the best shot they could pause on was only a two-thirds profile, he was sure the face was Krilic's.

The fucker, thought Kees as he stared at the image.

Krilic had been there the night before, probably the same time Kees had been, and it looked like he was leaving in a hurry.

'Was he here on his own?'

'I don't know. I'd have to go back through the video, see if I can trace him back.'

'Do it,' said Kees.

'The thing is—'

Kees turned to him. 'Just do it,' he said.

The barman did it.

They managed to work out his route. He'd emerged

169

from the stairs in the main section of the club at 22.11, if the numbers on the bottom left of the screen were correct. He was moving fast.

'What's up those stairs?'

'Another bar. It's smaller, quieter.'

'Cameras up there?'

The barman tapped a few keys, and a new set of images came on screen. A few minutes of searching and Kees spotted Krilic. He was at a small round table at the back. The figure he was sitting with was angled in just such a way he couldn't make out the face.

'Go forward,' said Kees. 'I need to follow his friend there.'

About five minutes after Krilic left, the figure finished off his drink and stood up, turning towards the camera as he headed for the stairs.

Got you, thought Kees.

Ten minutes later he was back at the station, and he bumped into Smit in the corridor. Smit invited him into his office, and from the look on his face his boss wasn't happy.

Smit hadn't even asked him to sit. Which wouldn't have been too bad, but almost as soon as he entered the room his legs started feeling odd, like bone was slowly melting away.

Which was probably something to do with the line he'd had, purely medicinally, before leaving his flat earlier.

'. . . so now you're telling me you still haven't got anywhere?'

'It's not my fault the arrest report, the one good lead I

had, wasn't filled out right,' said Kees. 'If Piet hadn't got the addresses messed up I'd've got them by now. But like I said, I've got a photo of Isovic at 57 last night and—'

'I don't want a photo of Isovic,' Smit exploded, slamming a hand on his desk. 'I can't give a fucking photo to ICTY and hope they won't notice the difference. They can't put a photo on the stand and expect it to answer questions. I want Isovic, the man, the one who can testify in court.'

'Yeah, that's what I'm working on,' said Kees. All of a sudden he felt like laughing. When he used to get bollocked at school he'd often had the urge to laugh. Sometimes he'd not been able to contain it. For some reason that had usually made things worse.

'Actually you're not,' said Smit finally, as if suddenly exhausted. 'I'm taking you off it and reassigning you to Jaap; you'll be working with him on his investigation.'

I see, thought Kees. *That's why Jaap asked for help earlier.*

'Yes sir,' he said and turned to go.

'And Kees?'

'Yeah?' he said, turning back.

'There are serious funding cuts coming our way in the next few months, so I've got to make a case for each and every inspector I've got here. As it stands, I'm going to find it *really* difficult to make a case for you, understood?'

Yeah, yeah, fucking understood, thought Kees as he got back to his desk. *Fucking fucking fucking.*

32

Jaap crouched down by the body, forcing himself to look at the dead man's face.

Adrenaline was still jacking up his system, but the post-action sourness was starting to set in too. He could taste it. Or maybe that was the cannabis stench, heavy and thick in the air.

And he was starting to feel angry. Angry at whoever employed these people to do the job for them, putting them in harm's way. Because it was obvious that neither of the men tending the plants were master criminals. This wasn't their operation. They were just people who needed the work. And one of them had ended up dead.

The bullet had hit his left eye.

Gone straight through.

Jaap had killed two people in his career.

Now the number stood at three.

'Nice shot,' said a voice behind him.

He turned to see Pieter van Dael, one of Hank's crew who'd been out back. They'd heard the shots and barrelled in. One of them was now hauling the uninjured man out. Jaap had tried to question him, but he barely spoke any Dutch, or English. Jaap was starting to think he was a relation of the dead man, as he'd been crying constantly.

He stood up, tried to push all thoughts of what he'd done away. This wasn't the time to deal with it.

Looking around the room, he reckoned there were at least fifty plants, maybe more. The smell was intense, the humidity not helping. High-power grow lights beaming down from the ceiling at regular intervals flooded the room, causing him to squint. He checked a few of the buds, the pistils mostly a dark-brown colour.

Another few days and this lot could be harvested, he thought as he went to the window, pulling down the blackout material which had been taped across the glass. He fiddled with the latch, some cheap UPVC-type material which was bent out of shape, and managed to finally open the glass. Then he went in search of the switch powering the lights.

It was plugged into an automatic timer set for twelve hours at the back of the room; he had to brush past several plants, their sticky resin transferring to his hands. Cannabis was a tropical plant, and it grew best in conditions which mimicked its homelands. He knew that experienced growers would play with the timing of the lights to induce flowering and maximize yields towards the end of the growth cycle.

He flipped the switch and the humming stopped. He noticed the electricity wasn't coming from the mains but a bunch of duct-taped wires sticking out of the wall.

They'd tapped into the neighbour's supply. Their next bill was going to be huge. Of course by then the farm would have moved.

There was also a filter unit venting out the back wall. The new breeds of cannabis weren't called skunk for nothing; the stuff stank and most growers would take precautions to neutralize the smell. It was clear that someone here had messed up; there was a space in the unit which looked like it was missing a charcoal filter.

That's why the neighbours could smell it, he thought.

'Not hydroponics,' said Pieter, stepping beside him, looking at the pots the cannabis was growing in.

'That's fairly unusual, right?'

'We're seeing soil-grown more and more. It's like a premium organic product. Fetches more.'

'Can you tell the difference?' asked Jaap.

'You're asking the wrong guy,' said Pieter, pinching off a bud from the nearest plant. He held it to his nose and inhaled deeply with his eyes closed. 'But I'm told you can.'

A breeze wafted in the window, the plants bowed and bobbed. Leaves rustled.

Jaap walked out to the landing and squatted down by Hank, who was propped up against the wall, his breathing rapid and shallow.

'How's it feeling?'

'Like a fucking nuke just went off in my leg,' he said, forcing a smile. 'Maybe I should smoke a bit, supposed to be good for pain.'

One of Hank's guys laughed behind Jaap. A cannabis leaf spiralled down, landing just out of Hank's reach. It reminded Jaap of autumn in Kyoto, the delicate acer leaves falling gently off the trees.

'Those guys in there weren't even foot soldiers,' said Jaap. 'They're basically hired labour. I'm not sure the one left is going to know anything, even if I can find an interpreter.'

Hank nodded, then grimaced.

Jaap could hear a siren, still a few blocks away.

'So you'll want to know who I think is behind all this?' said Hank.

'Yeah, I'd like to talk to them.'

I'd like to make them pay for what they forced me to do.

'Thing is, I don't want you to scare them off. I fully intend to bring them down –' he pointed to his leg '– especially now.'

'I get that. But if he's the one behind the beheadings we can put him away for much longer.'

Hank grimaced. Jaap watched the blood oozing out of the wounds. It came in pulses.

'Okay,' Hank said finally, his breathing suddenly ramping up. 'But promise me I get to be there when you arrest him.'

'Done.'

Hank's whole body stiffened, his face twisted in on itself with pain. Then his head flopped back against the wall, his mouth working silently.

'So who is it?' asked Jaap after a few moments. Hank's eyes rolled like a frightened horse's. Jaap could see white. Bloodshot white.

Hank's eyelids closed.

Jaap reached out, gave him a slight shake.

'Bart Rutte,' Hank whispered. 'He's the one who—'

Hank's head rolled to one side.

He was still breathing, but he was out cold.

33

'Hey, can you stop that?' called out Frits.

Tanya was sitting at her desk.

'What?' she said.

'That thing you're doing with your leg, it's really annoying.'

Tanya looked down, she was jiggling her right leg, heel tapping the ground in a fast rhythm. She forced herself to stop.

She should be out, confronting Staal, but instead she was waiting.

Always waiting, she thought.

She'd checked in with the tech department, just to see if they'd got anywhere with copies of the CCTV images from 57. So far they'd not ID'd them. She wasn't holding her breath, the task was an enormous one, and probably futile if the men didn't have records.

The requested cleaning logs had still not come through, so she still couldn't rule out Kees as being somehow involved.

She thought of Kees' reaction back in the incident room. She'd been observing him out of the corner of her eye while she'd given her theory some air-time earlier. A split second before divulging it she'd wondered whether it was the right play, showing her hand too soon, but she'd decided that it was probably best to put it out there and see how Kees would react.

And it had rattled him, that much was clear.

Dehydrated, she thought. *Yeah, right.*

Her phone rang, startling her. From the number she could see it was the lab.

'Does it match?' She'd asked them to check the knife she'd found and the holster on Jaap's second victim.

'Yeah, same make, same size,' came the response.

She hung up.

Looks like my theory is right, she thought.

Which meant her next move was going to have to be the Coffeeshops. Which was unfortunate as it meant the only real way of finding anything out was traipsing round them.

Before Jaap had rushed off they'd agreed she should pursue this, but having spent a while listing them, she'd lost track of the number already. She realized it was going to be a needle-and-haystack job.

I'd no idea there were so many, she thought.

Her phone rang. It was Jaap.

'How'd it go?' she asked. 'Too late again?'

'No, this was still running. Hank got hit though, he's in an ambulance now.'

'Shit. Bad?'

'He's out cold. His leg got mashed up with a shotgun, lost a lot of blood.'

'You're okay?'

'Yeah, kind of. But I think we're getting somewhere. Before Hank passed out he gave me a name for who he thinks runs the grow operation.'

'Anyone we know?'

'Bart Rutte,' said Jaap. 'We're going to need to track him down. I'm working on that now, but I just wanted to let you know I spoke to Smit, he's agreed to Kees working on this with—'

'Are you kidding?'

'No ... Look, I know you don't like him, but he did come up with the photos, and I think he could be useful.'

I've got to tell him about Kees, she thought, glancing around.

She looked around. There were too many people here, fellow inspectors whose ears would prick up at what she had to say.

'Listen, there's something I need to tell you,' she said as she headed for the exit, holding her breath as she approached the men's toilets. 'It's about Kees, I don't think . . . Jaap, are you there?'

From behind the toilet door she heard the sound of something being smashed. And whoever was doing the smashing seemed to have a bad case of Tourette's.

It, and this didn't surprise her, sounded like Kees.

The line was dead.

Did he just hang up on me? she thought as she hit the call button. It went straight to voicemail.

She rushed back to her desk, picked up her list and the photos of the people involved with the case. Then she looked up Rutte's file on the system, printed out his mug shot.

Better get out of here now, she thought.

Down in the carpool the desk sergeant had gone AWOL. She waited for a few moments, keen to get on, keen to leave before she saw Kees. After a few more seconds she reached into the booth, grabbed a set of keys, scribbled a note and went in search of a car.

She pressed the unlock button but none of the cars beeped or flashed their lights for her. She dashed back, grabbed a second set, and was this time rewarded by a car right at the end coming to life.

'Hey, wait up,' said the exact voice she didn't want to hear.

She turned to see Kees step into the carpool, the door swinging shut behind him. All she could think about was the name she'd circled on the attendance logs.

Whoever it was had been in touch with the homeless woman. And the homeless woman had been casing one of the places which had been cleaned out.

That can't be a coincidence, she thought, looking straight at Kees.

He didn't look too bad – the colour had come back to his face – but his eyes, always startlingly blue, were bloodshot. His facial muscles were tight, like he was angry.

'Feeling better?' she asked.

'Yeah. Just got a lot on,' he said, rubbing the back of his head. 'So, looks like we're both working on this case now. I guess Jaap told you?'

Tanya tried to think quickly. If he was involved, was it even safe going with him? He was arrogant, she'd seen that during their relationship, and he took risks. But fundamentally she'd always believed he was a good guy. He'd saved her and Jaap's lives last year, shooting to kill without hesitation, or even knowing why he was doing it.

And the man who had shoved the homeless woman

under the train had short hair, nothing like Kees' overly-long style.

It can't be him, she thought. *It can't.*

Tanya turned towards the car.

'He did,' she said, hoping she wasn't just about to make a massive mistake. 'So let's get going.'

34

Jaap was standing just outside the station, leaning back into the car Pieter had just dropped him off in. Petrol fumes wafted up. Pieter was heading over to the hospital, to see how Hank was doing.

'Let me know when you get something,' said Jaap.

They'd worked out the guy they'd arrested only spoke Romanian and were trying to find an interpreter so they could question him.

'Will do,' said Pieter.

'And Rutte, where do I find him?'

'He's got a place in De Wallen, one of those live sex show things. That's his cover, we're pretty sure he launders his drug money through that. We watched him for a bit – he's there every night. We asked if we could bug the place, but they turned us down.'

'Why?'

'Not enough bugs available, apparently.'

As Jaap wrote down the name of Rutte's sex joint he marvelled that he lived in a country where a business specializing in live sex shows could legitimately be a front for an illegal drugs operation.

'Okay, keep me up to date with Hank.'

'Always the fucking hero, getting himself shot like that,' said Pieter with a laugh.

But Jaap could tell he was scared under the bravado.

He closed the door and watched as the car lurched away.

Hank was in a coma. The ambulance crew had been grim-faced, and got him out of there as quickly as they could. He tried to remember if Hank had children. Jaap knew that people who went into comas often didn't come back out.

Or if they did they weren't ever the same.

Before Floortje's birth Jaap had not really thought about the danger his job involved, it was just part of it and he dealt with each situation as it came. But Floortje had changed all that, and he found he was starting to become acutely aware of the possibilities. He could be killed, and then Floortje would be without a father.

She'd have to grow up without me, he thought.

Death.

The inevitable fact of life.

His time in Kyoto had been an attempt to come to terms with it, with the fact that he'd killed two people, and for a while he thought he'd succeeded.

But now he had a daughter everything had changed.

His phone started ringing. He was finding he'd developed a Pavlovian response to it. Each time it went off his stomach clenched, expecting it to be news of another killing.

But when he looked it was Saskia. She'd sent him a text earlier, asking him if he was going to be free to look after Floortje tomorrow and he'd yet to answer.

He could choose between green or red.

He chose red.

The station was quiet, and he went to his desk and sat down.

Things were starting to take shape. Most investigations were simple. The killer was known to the victim, and the average time it took to identify and arrest them was less than twelve hours. Jaap knew from experience that if after the first twelve hours the killer was still not obvious then the case was going to be one of two types. The first could stretch out for days, weeks and months before through either luck or sheer dogged determination the police got a result. The second type were the ones which were never going to be solved.

These were rare, and Jaap had only had one of those in his career.

He wasn't keen for another.

Jaap pulled up Rutte's file again and hit print on the photo. Rutte's face slid out of the printer, twice. He also looked up businesses in the red light district and finally found the one Pieter had mentioned. Jaap grabbed the sheets and made his way towards the incident room, taking them with him. He stood in front of the whiteboard he'd marked up earlier, trying to work out what he was missing.

If Teeven and the other victim were part of Rutte's drug operation, why were they getting killed?

Something pinged in his head. The newspaper article he'd skimmed earlier about a corporate takeover bid.

Is that what's going on here? he thought as a uniform stuck his head round the door. *Is this an underworld takeover? Someone muscling in on the cannabis growing business?*

'Call for you, line three.'

'Who is it?'

'I think she said her name was Sasha?'

'Saskia?'

'Yeah, that's the one.'

'Tell her you couldn't find me,' he said.

He found some tape and stuck one of the photos on to the whiteboard.

As he stared at it he wondered if he was looking at the killer.

Tanya's theory broadly fitted what they knew so far, with one major exception; it did nothing to explain why Teeven and the first victim had been watching him. And Tanya.

His phone rang again.

Okay, okay, he thought as he reached for it, expecting it to be Saskia.

But it turned out to be an unknown number.

'It's Bart van Rijn,' said the voice when he answered. 'I got a message saying you want to know something about one of our ex-inmates?'

'Martin Teeven. I'm guessing you've seen the news?'

'News? I'm coming off shift over two hours late just because one of our *guests* set the fire alarm off. They know that causes huge hassle for us, that's why they do it. We've had people in to try and make them tamper-proof, but there's always some fucker who finds a way to trip it again. Anyway,' he continued, maybe sensing Jaap's lack of enthusiasm for the topic, 'how come you wanted to talk about Teeven?'

'He's dead.'

'Peacefully in his sleep?'

'Beheaded.'

'Oh, I did hear about that. He was one of those? Shit.'

Jaap heard him breathe out slowly. 'He was hard work and all, but beheaded . . . I'm not sure anyone deserves that.'

'Hard work how?'

'He was one of those who always claimed they were innocent. Most of the people in here face up to what they've done, you know? They might not actually feel any regret, but I always think those that deny it are probably the most dangerous. I've seen it a few times, the ones that lie to themselves. It can kind of tear their minds apart after a while. Some of them really come to believe they're innocent, and they get this whole paranoid conspiracy theory thing going on. Which is never good. He used to claim that the cop who put him away had framed him.'

What, thought Jaap, *if he really was innocent? Would that push him over the edge?*

He didn't even want to think about that right now. Because that could be a serious motive for revenge.

'Was he friendly with anyone on the inside?'

'I don't think he was. Kind of a loner. Which again is never a good sign.'

'Did he ever get any visitors?'

'You know, I'm pretty sure he did. There was this guy who kept visiting him, like once a week at least. But the thing is, after a while Teeven stopped wanting to see him.'

'He refused?'

'Yeah, he told us to tell the guy he wasn't home. At least he had a sense of humour.'

'Why did he refuse?' asked Jaap.

'I don't remember. I'm not sure he gave a reason.'

'Who was the visitor?'

'Can't remember that either,' he said. 'Listen, I need to get going, I'm—'

'This is really important. I need you to check the records – whoever it was must have signed in.'

Jaap could hear the man breathe out slowly again.

'Okay, hang on.'

As he waited he thought about revenge. Teeven had been a small, a tiny, part of Jaap's job; he'd done the work, got him convicted, then moved on.

Teeven hadn't.

It looked like all Teeven had done was sit in a jail cell working up his hatred of the man who'd put him away, honing it like a knife.

'Got it,' said Bart. 'The guy who kept visiting him was called Geert Blinker. Mean anything to you?'

Jaap thanked him and hung up.

The name did mean something to him.

Jaap had arrested Blinker several years ago for flashing in Vondelpark.

There'd been reports of a man who'd hide in the bushes by the pond and leap out stark naked whenever a lone woman walked past.

He'd never tried to assault anyone; all of the women had said he seemed more concerned with them looking at his, as one of the victims described it in the official report she filed, piteously small penis.

He'd only been caught when he flashed the wrong woman, a lesbian fitness coach, who'd run at him, chased him through the bushes and pinned him down on the far side until someone answered her calls and dialled the police. Jaap had been closest.

When he'd turned up Blinker was lying there, covered in scratches from the bushes, with only a pair of white trainers on.

He looked up Blinker's file. Given that he'd been convicted of a sex offence, his current address was listed in the register. He scooped up Rutte's mugshot off the table and headed for the door.

35

'Where next?' asked Kees as they got into the car, following another unsuccessful Coffeeshop visit.

Tanya had been letting Keyes do the talking, observing him, trying to work out if he really was involved in her case.

Kees pulled out into the road in a way which didn't surprise Tanya, who was pushed back into her seat by the acceleration. An old couple shuffling along the pavement looked up at the engine's noise.

'Leidseplein,' she said, checking the list she'd made earlier.

'Shit, you should have said.'

'Maybe you should've asked before tearing off,' she shot back.

He glanced in the rear-view before yanking the handbrake up and skidding the car round. Once they were straight again, Tanya bent forward and picked up the paper which had slid from her lap.

'And can we go any faster?' she asked.

Kees didn't respond.

She looked back at the list; she'd crossed off at least fifteen so far. No one had known any of the men in the photos. Or no one had admitted they had, anyway.

'So, how's it going?' she said, dropping the sheets back on to her lap. 'In general?'

'You know,' he said, settling back into his seat and fiddling with the window button on the door as he steered one-handed. 'All right.'

She reached out and flipped the radio on.

'. . . *and it will be tomorrow that Matkovic is finally put on trial. Security has been stepped up here at the ICTY in Den Haag, and prosecutors are expecting—*'

Kees clicked the radio off.

The rest of the short journey was devoid of conversation.

They parked up and walked to the Coffeeshop, a large neon sign of a dog smoking a joint drawing in tourists who'd come to Amsterdam with just one thing on their cultural agenda – horticultural bliss.

Tanya'd never seen the attraction; the few times she'd smoked it'd just made her feel sick. And she suddenly remembered one of those times had been with Kees, back when they were together. Briefly.

They'd been sitting on the roof of her block of flats, watching the night sky, when Kees had produced a joint. At first she'd passed, but then on his third or fourth pull had reached out and taken it from his mouth, the paper damp when she put it to her lips.

And it hadn't just made her sick, it had made her paranoid as well, bringing back her time as a foster child. She seemed to remember that she'd thought Kees had been working with Staal, trying to trap her so he could come back and get her again. She remembered crying, trying to get away from Kees, hitting him when he tried to calm her down.

They'd broken up the next day.

And here she was again, thinking about Staal. She'd been trying not to think about him since her failed attempt to confront him yesterday.

Am I chickening out? she thought as they stepped into the Coffeeshop. *Am I letting myself become distracted on purpose?*

The interior was low lit, and despite the hour, practically full. Groups, mostly men, sat around tables pulling on joints. Some were subdued, staring into space, others more animated, laughing the laugh.

The dull tang of skunk hung heavy in the air, matched by underwater slo-mo bass thudding from the speakers like pumped sludge. Kees went to the guy dishing out joints from behind a long stainless-steel bar and showed him the photos.

'Seen these?' he asked without preamble, raising his voice to compete with the music.

'Who the fuck are you?' asked the guy. He had a tight T-shirt on, military hair with a lightning strike shaved out on one side. Fat rolled on his neck, and his right lobe held a silver earring. Tanya wasn't surprised to see it was the shape of a cannabis leaf.

She flashed her badge at him. He looked at it then begrudgingly turned back to the photos Kees was holding out.

'Can't say I do,' he said after a few moments. 'Should I?'

'They'd be supply side,' replied Kees. 'Not customers.'

'Not my thing,' he said. 'You'd need to speak to Wouter. He deals with that.'

'He here?'

The man shook his head but didn't offer anything else.

'So where can we find him?' asked Tanya.

'Probably at the branch up near Centraal,' he said. 'But I should warn you, he doesn't like cops.'

'You know what?' said Kees, leaning closer to the man. 'I'm looking forward to meeting him already.'

Back in the car Tanya was feeling light-headed. She hoped this was going to be the last stop; she wasn't sure she could take much more smoke. Her clothes smelt of it, and she was starting to think it'd got into her hair as well. She'd insisted on driving this time, but was already regretting it.

'You remember that time we did this?' asked Kees suddenly, not turning to look at her.

She just nodded, not wanting to have the conversation. Something wasn't right with her head, or stomach. The back of her skull, which suddenly felt detached from the rest of her body, found its way to the headrest.

She could smell someone else's perfume on it, something old-fashioned and heavy; musk, rich spice and flowers. It made her feel even worse.

'It was the next day you chucked me,' he said as she pulled to a stop at some lights, tourists swarming across the road in front of them. 'I always wondered what that was about.'

Tanya didn't know what to say.

'Because maybe it would help, you know, clear the air,' he said, turning to look at her.

Tanya concentrated on driving, feeling her hands gripping the wheel too hard.

Not now, she thought. *Please can we not have this conversation now.*

'Turn here,' he said suddenly.

'Left, right?' Relieved to be able to say something mundane, something not connected to their old relationship. But she still didn't manage to keep the irritation out of her voice.

'Left.'

'Too late.'

'Jeez,' he said, throwing up his arms, his voice full of exasperation.

'You didn't give me enough warning!'

'I could say the same thing, remember?'

'So what do you want to hear?' She slammed on the brakes and turned to face him. 'That I was messed up, unhappy, that I didn't know where my life was going and that I thought you were kind of an asshole? That when I tried to talk to you you wouldn't listen? Is that it? Is that going to help clear the air for you?'

Kees stared ahead through the windscreen.

Tanya did the same. She saw a dog sniffing around an overflowing rubbish bin, and watched as a rat darted out from under a crumpled bag on to the tram lines, the dog giving chase.

'Not really,' he said after a few moments. 'No.'

After that they stayed silent until pulling up in front of the Coffeeshop. When Tanya got out of the car her head spun, and she stood for a moment trying to get air into her lungs, hoping it would reach her brain, refresh it, clear it out.

'Better let me do the talking,' said Kees as they made their way inside. 'You seem to have lost your voice.'

Wouter was in, and judging by the look on his face

when they were ushered into his office at the back, his colleague had been right.

He really didn't like cops.

The room smelt of stale air, but was smoke-free at least.

Tanya was thankful for that. She looked around, clocking the general state of the room. Wouter appeared to use the same filing system Kees did on his desk back at the station.

'I'm guessing you know why we're here?' said Kees, picking up a sheet of paper from one of the piles nearest to him and giving it the once-over before looking back at Wouter.

Tanya could see Wouter didn't look well. He was totally bald, she hadn't seen skin tone like that outside of a morgue before, and he didn't appear to have any eyebrows either. His eyes were bloodshot, and a stubble of red, white-tipped pimples dotted either side of his nose.

He's like a rabbit demon, she thought. *An earless, albino rabbit demon.*

She pictured him sitting there, chomping on a massive carrot.

The sick feeling had gone now. In fact, she had to admit to herself, she was feeling pretty good.

She found she was stifling a laugh.

'I got a call saying you were coming, yes,' said Wouter.

'Great,' said Kees. 'So I don't need to explain myself, you can tell me what I need to know, and then we can get out of here.'

He pulled out the photos and flipped them over to

Wouter, who picked them up reluctantly and gathered them into a pile. Tanya watched as he looked at each, hearing the swish as he slid the top one off the stack and replaced it on the bottom.

Third photo in he nodded.

'Yeah, he came here. Trying to sell.'

Tanya took the photo from Wouter, seeing it was Teeven.

For some reason she found this funny and laughed.

'And did you buy?' said Kees, ignoring her.

'Had to. Our regular supplier was having some customer fulfilment issues.'

'Okay,' said Kees, collecting up the remaining photos once Wouter had gone through them and shook his head. 'So who is your regular supplier?'

Wouter scratched one of the pimples. Tanya watched it burst.

Pus oozed, white with a speck of blood.

'I'm not sure I'm really allowed to say, seeing as—'

'You're allowed,' said Kees. 'I promise.'

Wouter sighed, took his finger away from his face, inspected it for a moment before wiping it on his sleeve.

'What the hell, I don't owe them anything. The normal guy we buy from was in here last week, trying to find out where we were getting our current stock from. He was kind of agitated, said some things which made me happy to have switched supply. And anyway, the new stuff's cheaper.'

'Is it the same?' asked Tanya.

'Same cultivars, for the most part. The customers haven't been complaining.'

Tanya and Kees exchanged a look. Tanya realized it was the first time that day.

'Name?' said Kees. 'I want to know his name.'

Wouter sat back in his chair, peered at the ceiling.

Kees thrust a photo of Rutte at him, Wouter glanced down.

Tanya thought she saw him flinch.

'Well?' said Kees.

Wouter shrugged.

'My memory's bad,' he said. 'Must be all the smoke.'

36

The building was a seventeenth-century canal house, still standing strong after all these years, with tall elegant windows, all beautifully proportioned. It was bespoke, built for a wealthy merchant, just as all the buildings along this stretch were, and had been intended as a statement. Jaap wondered what the original owner had traded in; coffee perhaps, or spices or gold.

He also wondered what the original owner would think of the flickery neon sign which had been attached to the wall, a moving outline of a man thrusting back and forth into a woman, who was bent down, clasping her ankles, her head angled towards passers-by.

SHOW STARTS AT 20.00, said the sign on the railings lower down.

Jaap checked the door, but found it closed.

Blinker's address was less than ten minutes' walk away, so he headed there. He wanted to know why he'd been visiting Teeven in jail. And why Teeven had stopped seeing him.

Blinker lived in a houseboat on the quay leading up to the Nemo building, which jutted out into the IJ. The Nemo was a museum, and, judging by the clientele Jaap saw there in the day, it was for kids. But beyond that he had no idea what it was about, what was actually inside.

Guess I'd better find out, he thought. *I could take Floortje there when she's a bit older.*

He loved seeing the look of fascination she got on her face when presented with something new. She was a bold baby, not scared at all, ever curious about the world around her. For a moment he was struck again by the fact that he had a daughter, that part of him had become a separate being. His job involved tracking down killers, people who ended life, and no matter how many of those people he caught it was never going to make up for the deaths they caused.

But now he had actually added something to the world, a life.

Jaap reached the steps leading to Oosterdok and went down, noticing a used needle near the bottom step. Kids came down here on their way to Nemo. He looked round for a bin, then kicked it into the water when he couldn't find one.

On his left large yachts and barges – some converted into houseboats, some still seaworthy – floated. A man was scraping at a rust patch on the hull of one, just above the waterline, a cat sitting watching on the quay beside him. Jaap could hear the quiet friction of the man's work. He suddenly felt a yearning for a simpler life.

Maybe I should give this up, he thought. *Find a job which doesn't mean I'm always chasing people, something which has normal hours. Spend more time with Floortje.*

He found Blinker's midway up, the Somni four-five-one. It was a barge, the hull above the waterline painted in a psychedelic array of colours; swirling rainbows, fantastical creatures and humanoid aliens with placid facial features and dark oval eyes.

Typical, thought Jaap. *He's a sex pest, and he's into hippy shit.*

A hand-painted sign gave times for 'gatherings', which were open to all seekers regardless of age, faith or sexual orientation. Someone had written below this in a much cruder hand, 'Except fucking bankers.'

'Please,' said a voice from the stern. 'Come on board.'

Jaap ascended the wooden ramp, which led at a steep angle up to the deck, and was greeted by Blinker, who looked different, and not only as he was fully clothed.

He'd cut his hair shorter for one, and was wearing clothes which made him look like a waiter in an expensive Indian restaurant, loose flowing trousers and a shirt which went down past his knees.

All white.

'Inspector Rykel! I'm so happy to see you,' said Blinker, his pale silver hair catching the light, sideburns sweeping down each jawline. 'I've thought about you many times over the years, and I've been meaning to thank you for showing me a new way of living.'

'I just arrested you for waving your cock about in front of women, didn't I?' said Jaap, surprised that Blinker remembered him.

Though at least more favourably than Teeven did, he thought.

'It was so much more. I believe that people appear when we need them most, only most are not lucky enough to recognize these meetings for what they are,' said Blinker, showing Jaap an open palm and motioning him to the stern, where a table with five chairs was set out. Buddha heads competed with flower pots on deck, the effect ruined by several bags of fertilizer strewn about.

Jaap sat and looked at the floating palace on the far side

of Oosterdok, a massive Disneyesque interpretation of an oriental pagoda, which on its several floors served up a mismatch of pseudo-eastern dishes mostly drenched in the same gloopy MSG-laden sauce.

Tourists loved it.

'So what, other than the long-overdue opportunity to thank you, can I do for you?' said Blinker, sitting down on an armless chair and pulling his legs into a full lotus. The soles of his feet were dirty.

'Thank me for what?'

'Showing me what I was doing wrong. I didn't see it at the time, but you arresting me, and getting me convicted, was the turning point, the fantastic moment which allowed me to pivot the fulcrum of my life towards more positive energy.'

Jaap knew that hallucinogenic mushrooms, usually imported from South America, had been banned in the Netherlands years previously after a young tourist took some and decided she could fly, testing her skill off the nearest canal bridge. Not only did the mushrooms not give her the power of flight, they apparently robbed her of the ability to swim.

Some must still be getting through, thought Jaap.

'Do you charge for these gatherings?'

Blinker looked momentarily uncomfortable.

'I . . . Just a small donation, to help cover costs.'

'I see,' said Jaap. 'And you're not waving it about during them?'

Blinker put on a hurt look.

'Inspector, I'm a changed man, reborn if you like, a chrysalis which has burst open with the full potential of human life. Surely you of all people believe in the power of redemption?'

Jaap looked out at the water, a large patch of petrol marbling the surface with metallic colours. Having put countless people into the penal system, and seeing how many of them reoffended, he wasn't sure he did.

'Seriously? Come on, drop the act. I can see you've got something profitable going on here, so you just tell me what I need to know and I won't feel compelled to delve into your set-up.'

Blinker sighed, uncrossed his legs, rummaged around in his clothing and pulled out a cigarette and lighter.

'Look, I came out of prison and couldn't get a job. I had to do something,' he said as he flipped the cigarette into his mouth, cupped the lighter and guided the flame until the two met. 'And I'm not hurting anyone, you know? Actually, I think I may have helped a couple of people.'

'Quite coincidentally.'

'Hey, help's help, you know?' said Blinker, blowing out smoke.

Jaap did know. Who was he to criticize? He'd spent all that time studying under Yuzuki Roshi in Kyoto, and there were plenty of people who thought that was downright strange.

'Okay, let's leave it. Tell me about Martin Teeven. I know you visited him in jail.'

'Teeven ... Yeah, I did, until the fucker stopped seeing me.'

A gull swooped down from the sky, hydroplaning webbed orange feet on to the water. Jaap watched the ripples expand out. He thought about small actions with big consequences.

'Why were you seeing him?'

'It's kind of complicated,' Blinker said, fiddling with his cigarette.

'I'm sure I can cope.'

Blinker looked out across the Oosterdok to the footbridge crossing the water like a taut bow.

'We shared a cell for a bit, and despite the fact he was a total asshole we kind of struck up a relationship. And then we found out we'd both been busted by you. I tell you, he really hated your guts. Like serious hate, totally wound up over it.'

'Did he ever talk about getting revenge?'

'Are you kidding? He basically talked of nothing else. He was obsessed, really obsessed. Mania doesn't do it justice.'

I guess I should be relieved he's dead, thought Jaap.

'And the thing is,' said Blinker, 'it was sheer displacement, or whatever the word is.'

'What do you mean?'

'I mean, the person he was really angry with was the one who he'd gone to jail for.'

A picture was starting to form; Jaap was getting the feeling he'd been wrong.

'Bart Rutte?' he asked.

Blinker looked surprised.

'You know him?'

'Not personally. So what did Rutte threaten him with?'

'He never talked about it, there was just one night, he'd got into a fight and had a bunch of stitches. I think they totally overdosed him with painkillers or something 'cause he was all slurred, and he mentioned it, right before going to sleep. Something about he was only there because Rutte had threatened to kill his mother. But he never said anything about that again. And the thing is, I heard his mother died a few weeks before he got out. Some cancer. Probably caused by the worry of her son being in prison, negative energy and stuff.'

Jaap could feel a tingle in his stomach. He'd been wrong, but it was now starting to come together.

'So Teeven had worked for Rutte before?'

'Am I getting paid for this or what?'

'Had he?'

'Yeah, Rutte had a drug thing going, Teeven was kind of like his right-hand man. Funny how these business relationships always go sour in the end.'

The tingle amped up from low to high.

'So when did you last see Teeven?'

'Has he gone missing?'

'You're not a news man?'

'Why?'

'Because Teeven was killed yesterday. Are you telling me you hadn't heard?'

'I . . . Killed? I don't listen to the news. It's all bad, you know?'

Jaap thought Blinker was telling the truth, he seemed genuinely shocked.

'So when did you last see him?'

'Hey, this isn't going to come back on me, is it? I don't want anything to do with . . .'

'If you know anything I'll keep your name out of it.'

Blinker peered out over the water, rubbing an ear lobe between thumb and forefinger.

He turned back to Jaap.

'Couple of months back, I got a call out of the blue and we met up.'

'What did he want?'

'Well . . .'

'He's dead, right? So you need to tell me.'

Blinker went back to his ear lobe.

'Yeah,' he said. 'You're right. Okay, he came to offer me in on a job, but I turned him down.'

'And I'm guessing this job had something to do with drugs.'

'Seemed pretty dangerous to me. He said he knew all these houses where cannabis was being grown, and he needed a few people to help him break in and steal the crop.'

'How did he know where the houses were?'

'I dunno, I didn't ask. But he did tell me they were Rutte's. Not my kind of scene really. Flashing guns around and everything. I heard he hooked up with some people, foreigners, got them interested in it. Looks like it didn't turn out so well.'

37

After the Coffeeshops Tanya suggested they go back to the station, and Kees had driven, in silence, and was now at his desk across the room from her.

She was feeling bad about snapping at him earlier.

But the fact was, he'd provoked her. And she was tired. Tired and frustrated and being pulled in so many directions she didn't know which way to turn.

Which wasn't fair.

But, as Staal had used to say, neither's life.

And maybe it had been something to do with all the cannabis she'd inhaled second hand, opening things up. The effect, she had to admit, hadn't been unpleasant in the end.

The cleaning logs were spread out in front of her. They'd arrived while she was out, and she'd started to look through them, too tired to take them elsewhere.

But she just couldn't seem to concentrate, her head was still too spacey.

She covered them up and went down to the canteen. She grabbed an orange juice and took it back to her desk, the gunk they put in it to convince you it was made from real oranges sticking in her throat.

But it cleared her head, enough to get back to the logs.

A few minutes later she had her answer.

And she wasn't sure she liked it.

Her phone rang, it was Jaap.

He was talking before she'd even got it to her ear.

'Hey, slow down,' she said.

'Teeven and Rutte aren't working together; Teeven was ripping off Rutte's grow houses to get back at him.'

'For what?'

'Teeven went to jail years ago instead of Rutte. For murder. Rutte threatened to kill his mother so Teeven had no choice.'

'We got something too, Teeven wasn't just robbing Rutte,' she said. 'One of the Coffeeshop owners ID'd him. Apparently he was also selling on what he stole.'

'Even more reason for Rutte to want him dead then.'

He gave her an address and told her to get Kees and meet him there.

She scribbled it down.

'Hey, grumpy,' she shouted across the room. 'Let's go.'

38

'So what've you got?' said Jaap.

He'd left Blinker and just as he'd dived into the red light district at Zeedijk his phone registered a call from Pieter.

'More than enough. The Romanian basically gave up Rutte and the whole operation including addresses of all the current grow houses. Seems he and his cousin, that's the one you shot, were in charge of all of them, they spent their time going from one to another making sure everything was growing right.'

'And were any of their houses robbed?' asked Jaap, silently thanking Pieter for the reminder that he'd killed someone.

'Yeah, and that's where you're going to be interested. This guy claims they contacted Rutte – his cousin had been here longer and spoke a bit of Dutch – and told him they wanted protection for when they were doing their rounds. They were scared that someone was going to try and bust one of the houses when they were working there, and he told them not to worry as the problem was being dealt with.'

'When was that?'

'When was what?'

'When did Rutte say that?'

'Friday night.'

'I'll need the transcript,' said Jaap before hanging up

and dialling Smit. Smit had been leaving messages for him, most of which seemed to be demanding a result before anyone else got killed, a point he reiterated when Jaap got through to him. Once Jaap had listened to the character assassination he explained what he had.

'Okay, bring him in. I want this closed down as soon as possible.'

Sure you do, thought Jaap as he hung up and turned on to Oudezijds Voorburgwal. He spotted Tanya and Kees up ahead, standing by the canal, slightly apart. Normally he'd not take two other people to an interview, but he wanted to put the maximum amount of pressure on Rutte. Shock and awe, the military called it.

'Hey, you ready?' he said as he reached them.

Kees took a large drag on a cigarette, flicked it into the canal, and threw his head back, shooting out a jet of smoke into the air.

'Hell yeah,' he said.

Tanya looked at Jaap and rolled her eyes.

They walked across to the building, just as Jaap's phone started ringing.

He checked the screen.

'I've got to take this,' he said. 'Go in and make sure he's there. If he is don't ask him anything until I get there. And don't let him leave, either.'

39

'Police,' said Tanya as she and Kees walked into the room. 'Is Bart Rutte here?'

They were on the third floor; the window facing the canal was blacked out, a large desk stretched along one wall, and a woman sat on a swivel chair surrounded by piles of papers and two computers.

On the wall above the desk were three monitors showing the scene downstairs; two angled at the audience seats, and one directed towards the stage. At the far end of the carpeted room a pair of double doors stood closed, with a sign saying PRIVATE.

The paying public weren't the crowd Tanya would have expected. If someone had asked her who frequented this kind of place she'd have said lone men, not the couples she saw making up a large part of the audience.

The woman swivelled round. She had short hair, and a robust bone structure covered in the leathery skin of a tanning-salon addict.

'You'll have to wait,' she said, indicating the doors at the far end. 'He's got someone in there with him.'

'Let him know we're here,' said Kees. 'I don't want him taking long.'

She stared him down while picking up a phone from the desk. She spoke, listened, then replaced it.

'He'll be five minutes,' she said, indicating a sofa below the blacked-out window.

Tanya sat down and found her eyes back on the monitors. This time she looked at the stage.

A man and a woman were there, the woman completely naked, sitting on a chair with her legs apart. The man walked closer, then dropped his trousers. Kees sat down next to her. He was watching too.

They watched in silence, and it soon appeared that something on stage was going wrong, badly wrong. There was no sound, but it was clear the audience was unhappy.

The woman was trying her best, she really was. But it wasn't the man's night.

'Errr,' said Tanya, attracting the woman's attention. 'I think you may have a problem.'

The woman glanced up at what was happening on stage. Kees had started laughing, and Tanya was joining in. She'd never seen anything so ridiculous.

'Shit,' said the woman. 'He's useless. And he's on the maximum dose already; if he takes any more his heart is going to give out.'

She got up, glanced towards the door marked PRIVATE, then headed out the way Tanya and Kees had come in. 'Stay there,' she said as she disappeared through the doorway.

Kees was laughing so hard he was wiping tears from his eyes.

The crowd were throwing things now, and the man and woman had given up and were heading for the wings just as a fully clothed man burst out in front of them. He was moving fast and ended up colliding with the naked man, knocking him backwards into the woman, who skidded into the chair. The chair swayed on the edge of the stage before toppling over. The clothed man didn't even look at the chaos, he just ran past and jumped down into the audience.

Neither Tanya nor Kees were laughing now.

'That's . . .' said Tanya.

'. . . Rutte,' finished Kees.

He was making for the exit.

Tanya and Kees sprang towards the door.

40

'Look, I know this isn't ideal,' said Jaap, glancing down at the canal water.

It was rippled, each tiny wave picking up neon from the surrounding buildings.

The phone was red hot against his ear. He wasn't sure if it was radiation or Saskia's anger.

'Damn right it's not ideal,' replied Saskia. 'I'm heading down to Den Haag now. And Jaap, if you do manage to tear yourself away from your job early, like tomorrow say, then I'd really appreciate some help with Floortje.'

'The way things are going I may be on track. I'll let you know. I'm sorry this came up, but you know how it is.'

'Yeah, I know,' said Saskia, breathing out. 'Look. I'm sorry we argued over this. I know you don't really have a choice. It's just that this trial is the one chance we've got to put that butcher away, and it's my responsibility.'

Despite their different jobs, they were both on the side of good.

So why do I feel what I'm doing is more important? thought Jaap. *Did I learn nothing in Kyoto?*

'I know, and you're going to do it,' Jaap said as he watched a group of teenagers exit one of the buildings, all buzz cuts and bravado. 'Listen, I've got to go, but I'm really close to tying this up. I'll let you know.'

He hung up and took a breath.

If Rutte is our man, thought Jaap, *I might just make it down to Den Haag after all.*

He turned back to the building, tourists walking past it, laughing, taking photos. Jaap was ten metres away when a figure burst out of the front door, jumped the three steps to the pavement, startling a group of women giggling at the neon sign. The man hesitated for a moment, looking up and down the canal with quick head movements, his whole body primed for flight.

He looked a lot like Rutte: older perhaps, but the heavy eyebrows were still there, and the widow's peak was even more pronounced as the hair either side was receding. He was tall too, taller than Jaap. Which put him well over six foot something.

Rutte swung his head past Jaap, then back towards him. Their eyes met. They stared at each other for a second, each waiting for the other to make a move. A group of tourists walked between them – a bunch of young men on a stag night judging by the fact they were all wearing miniskirts and high heels – and Rutte took advantage of the cover, powering off north up the canal.

More tourists had appeared, and Rutte was having to shove his way through them.

Jaap was after him, trying to stick to the path Rutte was creating through the bodies. He had to jump over one man who Rutte had slammed to the ground, a bag of French fries fanning out in the air, just as Rutte skidded right on to the bridge leading to Oudekennissteeg.

Rutte made it over and dived into the pedestrian passage on the far side, and as Jaap followed he could hear running footsteps behind him, but he didn't have time to turn and check them out. He pumped his limbs harder. Rutte was heading for the next bridge, the one which would take him to the Oude Kerk, where there was more open ground and lots of people.

Jaap was closing in, only five metres or so behind. Rutte clearly hadn't spent the intervening years keeping fit. Jaap could hear his breathing; it didn't sound too good.

Which was better for him.

Two metres now, on the bridge, but Rutte, sensing that Jaap was about to spring, ducked sideways, knocking over several bikes which were leaned against the railing. Jaap tried to go round them but caught a foot against a handle-bar, tripping him up and spinning him sideways. He hit the ground hard, winding himself, and he felt the skin on his hip get shredded on the rough stone.

A figure rushed passed him. It was Tanya.

Rutte was just going down the hump of the bridge when Tanya leaped off the apex, managing to grab a leg just as she hit the ground.

Rutte, off balance, spun round, but his momentum kept him going, and he fell on to his back, his head cracking against a pop-up urinal.

Tanya was on him, trying to flip him on to his front to cuff his hands, but he squirmed free and threw a punch up. Jaap saw her body rear up, and she dropped sideways, clutching her throat, her mouth an O of surprise and pain.

Rutte was up on his feet, moving again. He was bent low, like he'd hurt his back, and he was using one of his hands to help him along, Quasimodo-style.

The crowds, aware that something was going on, were parting for him as he headed towards Oude Kerk.

Jaap sped past Tanya, who was now on her back, still clutching her throat, but she was breathing.

Rutte was upright now, and Jaap put everything he had into his limbs, closing the gap. He barrelled into him, knocking him to the ground. Jaap pinned him in the back with his knee and slipped a plastic tie over his wrists, pulling it tight.

'Guess what,' he said to Rutte as he hauled him to his feet. 'You're under arrest.'

41

'Need a lift?'

Tanya had left Jaap briefing Smit. Rutte had requested a lawyer so they couldn't question him this evening, and despite the fact she was tired and it was late, her throat still aching from Rutte's blow, despite now having to work on two cases, and despite doing this all while she should have been on leave, she had decided to walk through the centre of town to the ferry which would take her over the water to her flat in Amsterdam Noord.

She needed the time to think. About her case, about how Kees was involved, if at all, and about her foster father. She'd heard back from the tram company. Her request had proved fruitful. Several of the drivers on the route the homeless man had singled out did know of a man in a wheelchair, and they all gave the same tram stop that he got out at. Tanya had left a message for Smit and requested surveillance at the stop; she'd not heard back yet.

They always want results, she thought, *but they don't like spending money to get them.*

She was walking up Rokin, travelling north, pressing through crowds of people heading out for the night and wondering what she could do, when she heard a familiar voice and turned to see Kees, his face framed in the lowered window of an unmarked.

'Lift?'

Her stomach flipped like a fish stranded on a drying riverbed.

Now's the time to ask him, she thought.

'Sure,' she said, moving round to the passenger side. As she touched the door handle her fingers sank into something soft.

Someone had stuck gum there.

Once she was in, Kees eased the car forward; she tried to wipe her fingers clean, trying not to think about saliva.

'Where're we headed?'

'Amsterdam Noord. We can take the tunnel.'

'Tough day, huh?' said Kees as he changed lanes quickly, failing to use the indicator.

'Yeah, you could say that,' she responded, knowing she should ask him but reluctant all of a sudden.

'You know, I've got something that might help.'

At a red light he pushed himself up off the seat and reached into his jeans' back pocket. He pulled out two slender objects, moulded to the curve of his backside.

'I got these earlier,' he said, holding out the two joints. 'Purely as research.'

Tanya was about to refuse, but then reached out and took one.

What the hell, she thought.

There was no traffic in the tunnel, and Kees sped through.

Sodium strip lights pulsed down on them at intervals.

As they emerged on the north shore Tanya looked up and saw the moon, surface pitted in the darkness.

They reached her address, but she then redirected Kees

to a small playing field two blocks away. She didn't want smoke in her flat.

Or Kees.

Kees parked and they made their way on to the playing field, a rectangle of grass which was already beginning to wear away in patches from the dry weather. Thin trees, not yet trusted to stand upright without posts, surrounded the area, and a skate park rose up in one of the far corners, its curves and boxes like an alien cityscape.

Beyond that Tanya could make out, over the tops of a row of houses, the upper decks of an enormous ocean liner moored in the IJ.

They made their way to the skate park, clambered up one of the quarter pipes, the metal coping still warm from the day.

The first couple of pulls made her cough, but she gradually relaxed into it and they sat, neither saying anything

A few minutes in, Tanya knew she couldn't put it off any longer.

'Kees,' she said.

'Hey.'

'We need to talk.'

Kees took another hit, holding it in for what seemed like an age before tipping his head back and blowing a pillar of smoke straight up into the darkness.

'Yeah . . . Sure.'

She told him about the calls placed from the station to the homeless woman, but he stayed silent, concentrating on his joint.

'So, you were the only one at the station when all those

calls were made.' She twirled her joint slowly between her thumb and first finger. 'Are you involved?'

Kees took another hit.

'Listen, I'm going to tell you this, but I'd really appreciate it if it, you know, stayed between us?'

'Depends what it is.'

'Yeah, fair enough,' he sighed. 'Okay. I've got into a bit of trouble – debt – and the only way to pay it off was with some information. I did make those calls, but I didn't kill her.'

'It was you tipping the gang off, about where the cannabis farms were.'

She didn't phrase it as a question.

Kees nodded, then rubbed his eyes as if the smoke was bothering them.

'The thing is, victimless crime, right? I mean, some gang rips off another gang, big deal.'

'Except the first gang have now started killing the second gang.'

'I know, but that's nothing to do with me. I just passed on the information.'

'So you know who some of these people are, and you've just stood by and watched it happen?'

I thought this stuff was supposed to calm you down, she thought. It wasn't having that effect on her.

'Hang on,' he said, shifting round to look at her. 'I don't know these people. The person who . . . set this thing up, I don't even know *them*.'

Tanya's head was spinning. She wasn't sure it was from the joint.

'This debt. It's drugs related, I'm guessing?'

'I got behind with some payments, that's all. And I wasn't given much choice in the matter. Basically I had to help out or they'd send some evidence that I'd been using. They'd taken photos of me picking up the stuff.'

'So they let you have drugs without paying, then called it in?'

'Yeah. I . . . I should have seen it coming really. They knew who I was. Or rather what I was. I guess it was planned.'

He finished his joint and pulled out another one.

'I thought you'd only got two?'

'Four. I figured I might need them.'

Tanya's mind seemed to be running down two tracks at the same time, two distinct thought lines.

Kees had got caught up in this, but if what he was telling her was true then he wasn't directly involved with the killing.

But he'd still be, at a pinch, classed as an accessory as he'd been passing information to a criminal.

The other thought line was starting to get out of control, and it had nothing to do with the case.

'The people who set it up are the ones being killed, so whatever you know could help Jaap's case,' she said.

'Thing is, I've never had any contact with the guy behind it all. He called me one day out of the blue and sent me a few photos. He said they'd send me what I needed to my flat, and if I went after his dealer, or him, he'd release what he had on me. So I didn't really have any choice.'

Just like I don't have any choice, thought Tanya.

She finished her joint and then took the second one Kees offered. It was really hitting her now. She was having trouble keeping her mind focused. She didn't know what she was going to do. Unless she suppressed evidence, Kees was going to be in a career-ending smash, with possible jail time thrown in.

She also knew that the world was spinning in a massive void of space, but she'd only just now realized it was possible to feel that lazy spin.

'Look, I know this isn't good, but if Jaap can clear up this case quickly my problem might just go away,' said Kees after a few minutes of silence.

Tanya thought about it, but her mind, just like the last time she'd got stoned, wasn't working rationally.

Years of hatred seemed to have been released inside her, expanding outwards, threatening to explode.

The image of Staal kept flashing in her head.

She kept seeing scenes of what he did to her.

It felt like she was reliving all the times – countless times over the three years she'd been with him before running away – when he'd forced himself on her.

Into her.

Darkness, the feel of the smooth metal beneath her, the smell of grass, the rasp of smoke on her tongue and the distant sound of traffic.

Suddenly she was bent over double, Kees' arm riding the quick rise and fall of her shoulders, tears dripping down the skate ramp.

It was all so fucked up.

She was trapped.

The abuse had stopped years ago, but the echo of it was still there, still strong. Maybe getting stronger.

She'd never be free of her foster father.

There was no way out.

She was trapped.

'Wanna tell me about it?' asked Kees.

Once it was finally spent, Tanya sat up.

Kees took his arm off her shoulder, wondering what he should do. He'd thought she was hard, driven. He'd thought she was a real bitch.

But he'd misjudged her.

Her brittle exterior was just cover.

And now it'd cracked.

A car moved on the road at the far end of the space, headlights flashing on the slender tree trunks.

He looked up, stretching his neck, catching stars and the odd tentacle of cloud, trying to absorb what he'd just heard. When they'd sat down and lit up, the flare of the lighter licking her face as she bent forward towards his hand, the moment bringing back the times they'd spent together before, he'd wondered for a fraction of a second if he could finally tell someone; tell her about what had shoved him towards his high drug intake, tell her about the illness which was taking over, tell her everything, talk to her, finally unburden himself.

But it wasn't going to happen, not tonight at any rate. Tanya clearly had too much on already. He shifted slightly, the metal coping starting to cut off circulation to his legs, and settled again.

He put his arm round her shoulders. Held her tight.

*

Later, when she'd said all she could, when there was nothing left, Tanya let him take her to her flat. As he turned to leave, she reached out and pulled him towards her, part of her unable to believe what she was doing, part of her unable to care.

42

Jaap woke with his head on the desk.

A phone was ringing at the far end of the office.

He had the feeling something was wrong, but couldn't place it.

The phone cut off mid-ring.

He sat up, seeing that Frits had answered and was now listening to the handset, making notes.

Something was wrong.

But he couldn't work out what it was.

They had Rutte, and he had a motive.

And while Jaap had enough experience not to make snap decisions about what people were or weren't capable of, Rutte looked like he was capable of murder. He had that stone-cold quality in his eyes.

But the feeling wouldn't leave him and he sat for a while, trying to work out what it was.

I'm exhausted, he thought, *that's all. I just need to get some rest.*

Jaap checked his phone, one missed call and a message from Pieter. He was at the hospital with Hank, and there was no change in his condition. He also said that there was a problem with the transcript of the interview with the Romanian.

'What problem?' asked Jaap once he'd got him on the phone.

'There isn't one – equipment failure.'

'You're kidding.'

'Wish I was. I've got the interpreter coming back first thing tomorrow so we can get it done again.'

'I'll be interviewing Rutte early, I'll need it.'

Once he'd done with the call he hauled himself out of the chair, tiredness adding weight to his bones, and he suddenly wondered if he was going to make the short walk home without collapsing. Rutte's lawyer had been contacted but was down in Rotterdam. He had said he'd be there first thing in the morning.

There was nothing Jaap could do right now.

Tomorrow he'd have to put his doubts aside, concentrate on getting a conviction.

That would be long, slow work. It always was, but at least the immediate threat of more killings seemed to be over. The tweet yesterday had hinted at another body appearing today, but none had come.

Once he'd interviewed Rutte in the morning and decided on the charge then he might even be able to help Saskia out in Den Haag. He'd like to spend some time with Floortje. Just the two of them.

The outside air slapped him in the face, waking him up as he headed back to his houseboat.

Since the moment he'd found the photo of himself on the first victim's phone yesterday he'd been running on full alert, everything ramped up, every cell firing.

He was paying for it now.

And, he had to admit to himself, he was missing Tanya.

He tried to call her, see if maybe he could catch her up,

perhaps persuade her to spend the night with him, save her having to go all the way out to Amsterdam Noord.

Voicemail scuppered that idea. He spoke to the machine, saying he'd see her in the morning. He paused for a moment, aware that somewhere some computer was waiting patiently for instruction via satellite, waiting for him to hang up or carry on, still recording his breath, the sound of his footsteps, the rustle of his clothes as he moved.

The urge to tell her he was missing her was strong, but the thought of yesterday, when she'd shied away from telling him something, stopped him. He didn't know what that had been about, her hesitancy, the way she was about to say something important but had bailed at the last moment. As he ended the call he turned into Bloemgracht.

Trees sighed in the breeze, a gull cried out above him, and his houseboat floated calmly on the dark water ahead.

Stepping on to the gangplank, the metal creaking as if in greeting, he crossed the deck and wondered how things had got so strained between them. He'd never met anyone like Tanya – her intense energy, her green eyes, which could both inflame and freeze, often at the same time.

He paused a moment, leaning over the rail, looking down at the curve of the hull as it slipped into the water, the faint outline of a stain running from a bilge hole.

He thought about choices and consequences, and felt his fingers itching to grab the coins and flip them, form a hexagram, read what the I Ching had to say.

I need to stop this, he thought.

It had started to take over, he could see that now.

Ironic, really.

Something splashed in the water below him; he tried to make out what it was.

Drunken laughter floated over from the other side of the canal.

He looked up to see a man lifting an arm. A rapid forward movement, silence, then something clanged on the hull. The man laughed a huge fake laugh, bending over as if he was vomiting, then moved on.

Jaap had gone all the way to Japan looking for something, searching, trying to find the path to freedom.

And eventually, through months of frustrating work, he'd glimpsed that freedom inside himself, knew it was there. But at the same time he'd picked up a habit, the I Ching, a reliance on superstition which kept him just as far from freedom as he'd ever been.

Yuzuki Roshi had helped him and hindered him.

And there was a lesson there, only he was too tired now to really think about it.

He stopped his hand, which had started moving, and redirected it to his phone. Voicemail again. After a deep breath he walked to the door, unlocked it and stepped through. Inside he crossed to the bedroom and dropped down on the unmade bed, unable to even undress.

Just as his mind was slipping away he remembered he'd not managed to visit Schellingwouderbreek, where he'd scattered her ashes.

He couldn't help feeling he'd let Karin down.

43

The girl's head bobbed up and down in his lap, her long dark hair tickling his exposed thighs.

She was new; he'd requested her as the one last week hadn't been any good.

Kept catching him with her teeth.

Music, some woman wailing over a jazz funk ensemble, was squeezing out all the space from the room, pushing right up against his eardrums. He took a sip of beer, leaned back in the soft armchair and closed his eyes.

Tomorrow everything would kick off properly, months of planning for just a few days. Once they'd executed their plan they'd have less than forty-eight hours to get it done and get out. But he was confident it would happen. Hell, he was going to *make* it happen. End of.

The girl was powering ahead. She'd started to moan a little, as if that would speed him up. He told her to slow down, take her time, because it was Sunday night, and he needed to kick back and relax a little. Get prepared for the week ahead.

Saliva dribbled down his left groin.

His phone buzzed; he could feel it against his calf where his black jeans had dropped to, and he reached down and pulled it out.

'Did I tell you to stop?'

She got right back to it, though there was something in her eyes he didn't like.

Not enough respect, he decided as he answered, maybe he'd slap her up a bit afterwards.

'Yeah?'

'We've got a problem.'

He listened to what it was then hung up.

He'd gone limp, and the girl, sensing trouble, redoubled her efforts.

He hit her on the side of the head, knocking her off her knees, pulled his jeans up and made for the door.

Day Three

44

'Let me tell you what I know,' said Jaap.

A mass of scratches, lines, and swirls – evidence of a thousand cuffs being dragged across it – covered the surface of the steel table between Jaap and Rutte.

Rutte's lawyer, tanned, fresh-faced despite the hour, with a slick of black hair glinting in the overhead light, picked something off his sleeve with the delicacy of a lutenist plucking a string. Jaap saw him roll it between his fingers before dropping whatever it was on the floor.

'You set up the whole thing. You take leases out on houses using false IDs, rig the place up, illegally tap into the mains electricity and pay some illegal immigrants virtually nothing to do the legwork for you. Once harvested you sell and take home a serious amount of money.'

Jaap paused for a moment, just to see how Rutte was taking it. He'd seen all sorts of reactions over the years: people who broke down almost immediately, people who lashed out, and people who just sat there, impassive, immobile, untouchable.

Those were the problematic ones. Those were the ones who could prove almost impossible to get through to, like they had no emotion at all.

And it was emotion that Jaap needed to elicit now. Cases were built on cold, hard facts. But in the final stages emotion played its part, people made mistakes when they were feeling.

When they had no feelings they tended not to.

And both Rutte and his lawyer were exhibiting signs of being the latter. Jaap might as well have been talking to two stone gargoyles.

And in Rutte's case, a gargoyle might've been easier on the eye.

The lawyer checked his watch.

Behind him, Jaap knew that Smit was standing behind the two-way mirror.

'I know all this,' said Jaap when Rutte still hadn't said anything. 'Because one of your workers has confirmed it. And they will be testifying.'

'Then they're lying. I don't know anything about this,' said Rutte. Despite his size and features, his voice was oddly light, lacking depth.

'Well, that can be settled in court,' said Jaap. 'But that's not all, is it? Someone had worked out what you were doing and decided to profit from your hard work.'

He slid a mug shot of Teeven across the table. Rutte barely glanced at it.

'Recognize him?' asked Jaap. 'Seems like when he got out of prison he wanted to get back at you.'

'Get back at me for what?'

'Threatening to kill his mother unless he went to prison for you? That ring a bell?'

'No bells ringing here,' said Rutte turning to his lawyer. 'You?'

The lawyer shook his head.

'You have proof of this accusation?' the lawyer said to Jaap.

Jaap ignored him.

'So he gets out. Maybe his mother died just before he was released, and he doesn't have anything to lose? So he decides to get back at you. But he's not stupid; he knows he's not going to get a job with his criminal record, so he reckons he can get back at you by disrupting your business. Robbing you then selling it on to your own customers. You with me so far?'

Rutte stared at him but said nothing.

'And that must have been annoying. I mean, here you are, doing all the hard work, and Teeven comes along and starts ripping you off. I'd be annoyed, wouldn't you?' Jaap said turning to the lawyer. The lawyer, too skilled to be drawn, just gave him the fish eye.

'And I can imagine some people would think, *Hey, I had a good run, maybe it's time to call it quits*, and just move on. But I'm not sure you're the type. I'm not sure you'd let someone just get away with that.'

'I'm pretty easy-going,' said Rutte, a smirk creasing up his face.

'Yeah?' said Jaap. He pulled out some photos, fanned them out on the table like a winning hand of cards. He was pleased to see the lawyer's tan fade a notch. 'Or are you the type who doesn't like to be beaten. Entrepreneurial. The type who sees a problem and then deals with it.'

'As I understand it, Inspector,' said the lawyer, keeping his eyes off the photos, 'my client was brought in here for allegedly being involved in the growing of a controlled substance. So I'm not sure what this has to do with anything.'

'I thought I'd just made that clear,' said Jaap. 'Maybe your client would like to enlighten you further?'

'Nothing to do with me,' said Rutte.

'No? You're sure? How about his one?' asked Jaap, fishing a particularly graphic photo of the first victim off the table. 'Or this?' showing Teeven's body lying in the schoolyard. He waved it in front of Rutte's face like a religious nut giving out pamphlets about Jesus on a street corner. Rutte shrugged, glanced away.

Jaap dropped the photos and sat back in silence, counting a slow hundred before continuing. The idea was to increase tension, give the suspect's mind enough space to make them really scared. Jaap had learned how effective silence could be back in Kyoto, the hours of sitting, trying to empty his mind seeming to have the opposite effect, bringing into focus the exact thoughts he'd been trying to escape from.

The lawyer checked his watch again.

'Somewhere you'd rather be?' asked Jaap.

Footsteps marched up the corridor behind the room. They stopped outside the door for a second, then continued.

'Want to know what I think?' said Jaap, pushing the photos around, hoping the wait had unnerved Rutte enough. 'I think that you've been protecting your business and sending a message out to others that you're a hard man, that no one messes with you.'

'Fuck you.'

The lawyer put a calming hand on Rutte's arm, his

expensive watch catching the light from the unshielded bulb overhead.

Getting to him, thought Jaap. *Good.*

'I think my client is a bit upset at this rather extravagant accusation,' said the lawyer.

'Is he?' said Jaap, leaving the photos on the table then turning his attention back to Rutte. 'So you're telling me you had nothing to do with any of these, either directly or indirectly?'

'I already said,' replied Rutte in a monotone.

'Okay. Fine. Then I guess you can tell me where you were at the following times,' said Jaap, listing them off.

He'd been unable to decide if he should go down this route so early on; after all, Rutte could have hired someone to do the killings, leaving him with rock-solid alibis. But the few minutes he'd already spent with the man had confirmed his gut feeling that Rutte was capable of doing it himself. Would have *wanted* to do it himself.

The other option was that Rutte could have bought alibis for the times; if that was the case then Jaap figured he might as well know now, and start the work of breaking them down.

Rutte shrugged. 'I'd have to check my diary, y'know?'

'I think,' said the lawyer leaning forward, pushing the photos away so he could lean his forearms on the desk, 'we're getting ahead of ourselves here a bit. My client doesn't have anything to do with any of this; you've got the wrong man.'

'I don't think so,' said Jaap. 'I know he was in charge of the grow operation.'

'I don't have an "operation",' said Rutte, making air

quotes with his fingers, even though his hands were cuffed on the table.

'My client,' said the lawyer, reaching down to his ankle where a briefcase rested, 'runs an entertainment venue in De Wallen. Here are the documents which show he is a partner in the business.'

Jaap took the sheets from the lawyer.

'And this proves what?' said Jaap, having glanced through the pile.

'That my client is in full-time employment, and so can't have been running a cannabis-growing operation.'

Jaap dropped the papers on to the table, smiled at them both.

'This the best you got?' he asked.

Silence.

Staring.

The smell of the lawyer's expensive aftershave and the hum of an overhead light.

'Good,' said Jaap. 'Because I've got something else to add to the charge sheet as well; the murder of a homeless woman at Centraal station.'

Tanya had told Jaap about her hunch and they'd checked the CCTV image last night. It wouldn't stand up in court – his face wasn't visible – but the hair and build were very similar. And if Tanya's theory was correct – that the woman had somehow been spying on Rutte's operation and selling the information on to Teeven – then it would make sense that Rutte would want her dead as well.

Rutte beckoned to his lawyer, who leaned towards him. The lawyer nodded after Rutte had whispered in his ear.

'I was with someone, a friend of mine. We were away

fishing all weekend down near Gouda,' Rutte said, pointing to Jaap's list and looking straight at him.

'Really?' said Jaap. 'What took you so long?'

Rutte shrugged. 'Guess I didn't seriously think you'd imagine I was involved.'

'So you're denying that you had anything to do with these three deaths?'

'You're wasting time hassling innocent people like me when you could be out there catching real criminals,' said Rutte.

The footsteps were back; they stopped outside the door.

The lawyer checked his watch.

The door opened. Smit was standing outside. He beckoned to Jaap.

Jaap didn't like the look on his face. He got up from the table and stepped out, closing the door behind him.

'What's up?'

'Message from Pieter van Dael. The Romanian man is dead.'

Jaap breathed out and leaned back against the wall.

'How?' he managed after a few seconds.

'He got into a fight with someone in the holding cell and cracked his head against the bars as he went down.'

Jaap walked back into the room.

Rutte was smiling.

45

Tanya stood by the window and thought there was some-thing wrong with her eyes. Their focus wasn't great, and she blinked them a few times.

Is this because of the pot?

She felt a flash of panic, before it slowly dawned on her; her vision was being distorted by rain hitting the window.

Nothing was right this morning. She didn't even know why she was standing at the window, and she didn't really remember getting out of bed and walking across the apartment to where she was now.

She could just make out the gold sickle moon placed on top of the mosque she passed every day on her way to the ferry, its walls covered in turquoise tiles. She turned her head, feeling sick, wondering if it was an after-effect of the two joints she'd smoked or the fact that she'd told Kees about Staal.

All those years the secret had eaten away at her. She was no longer who she could have been. She'd never told any-one before.

Now she had, and to Kees, of all people.

Regret seeped through her body.

Why had she not told Jaap? Was it because she was afraid he'd reject her when he found out what had happened?

She'd heard that unburdening yourself of a deep secret

could help, the act of telling another human being what you'd been through could be cathartic, but she wasn't feeling cathartisized, or whatever the word was. If anything she felt worse.

But that, she had to acknowledge, was probably something to do with what she'd done afterwards.

Why did you sleep with him? her brain demanded as she started moving, finally, and passed the spot where they'd done it. She averted her gaze as she walked past.

In the bathroom she ran the tap, letting the water run over her forefinger, waiting for it to get warm.

The mirror threw back her red eyes.

Jesus, she thought. *I look as bad as I feel.*

She thought back to the moment she'd pulled him to her, how he'd held back at first, but had then taken over. They'd done it up against the wall by the front door, the cream plastic entryphone right by her ear. She'd had a wild image of it going off, and her answering, Jaap's voice coming over the phone.

The weird thing was it had made it even more exciting.

And she didn't want to think about why that was.

The water was still not running warm, let alone hot, so she cupped her hands and splashed her face, the cold sting making her gasp. She dried her skin on a towel which had lost its softness about five years ago but she'd just never got round to replacing, and went back to the bedroom to get dressed.

Telling Kees had done something though: it had made her more determined than ever to confront the man who'd caused her so much pain, and as she pulled on some fresh jeans she stared at her tattoo – the two-headed snake she'd got when she'd finally escaped from Staal, one of the heads destroyed by the bullet wound she'd sustained last January – and started to plan how she was going to do it.

On the kitchen table her phone rang. She checked the screen and saw it was Jaap.

Guilt ruptured her stomach.

She should have told Jaap, not Kees.

She should have been sleeping with Jaap, not Kees.

What am I doing? she thought as she answered.

'Hey, where are you?' he asked.

'Home. Something up?' she said, hearing it in his voice.

'Rutte had the Romanian who was going to testify against him killed. I can't prove it, but I know he did it.'

'Shit . . .' she breathed out.

'And he says he was with someone, a friend of his, all Saturday evening. I'm sure it's some bullshit alibi, but it needs to be checked out.'

Tanya closed her eyes; the last thing she had right now was time.

Knowing what Kees' involvement in her case was had only complicated things.

She was going to have to make a decision. But she didn't like her options, and she had to brief Smit in a few hours' time. Which would be the time to tell him about Kees.

And if it hadn't been complicated enough before, what she'd done last night put it off the charts.

'Yeah, I've got time,' she said, knowing she was just putting off the inevitable. 'What do you need?'

She listened as Jaap gave her the details, and she told him she'd report back as soon as she found out anything.

All the time they were talking she kept thinking of what she and Kees had done, wondering how Jaap would react, hoping she'd never get to find out. By the time she hung up she felt like being sick.

Outside a car was revving, a deep throaty roar repeated again and again. She went back to the window and looked down just as the car, a red middle-age-crisis-mobile, finally moved away. She'd not seen it parked in the street before and wondered what it was doing there.

As it turned the corner and disappeared she realized she'd been making a mental note of the number plate.

Seems like pot still makes me paranoid, she thought as she prepared to leave.

This was official business so she should be taking a car, but to get one she'd have to catch the ferry over to the city centre and sign one out of the station.

She decided on her bike. She'd not ridden it in ages, and as the address she'd got from Jaap wasn't far away, this was her chance.

As she fired up the motor and started out, the mechanical purr comforting somehow, she wondered if she could just keep on going.

Ride away and never come back.

46

Kees' morning was being complicated by several things, and his head wasn't able to cope, pain saturating the area round his left temple.

The first complication was that he was driving fast, way too fast, but he didn't seem able to slow down; he felt gripped, locked in, like the accelerator had been glued to the floor and the brake deactivated.

His hand reached out, fumbling for the window button on the car door. His finger eventually found it, the fresh morning air ramming against his face as the glass dropped down. He hoped that would help clear things out a bit. Spots of rain hammered into his face and he was forced to close it again.

He found he was still going at speed.

When he'd received the call this morning, the man at the garage from Saturday giving him a possible lead on Krilic, and therefore Isovic, he'd jumped in the car and got going.

He knew he'd been taken off the case, Smit had made that quite clear in the debrief/bollocking session he'd had to endure, but this wasn't about the case so much as wanting to get back at Isovic. He'd been fucked over by him, and Kees thought a little payback was in order. And he'd also figured if he could bring him in now then it might at least go some way to mitigating the second complication.

Which was that Tanya had worked out he'd placed the calls to the homeless woman.

The woman who'd managed to end up dead.

The woman who was his only link to finding Paul.

He'd had to tell Tanya what had gone on, hoping she'd be able to keep quiet. But he saw now that was going to be difficult for her to do.

Not for the first time he thought about how stupid he'd been to let himself get into debt in the first place. If he got through this then maybe he'd give those meetings Jaap had sent him to another go.

Chances of getting through this without being fired, thought Kees as he swerved, avoiding a truck which thought it owned the road, *near to zero.*

Wipers sluiced water manically, fighting a losing battle.

Not that it really matters, he thought, *in the long term.*

His thoughts funnelled down a route he didn't want them to go, towards the third thing, towards what was happening to him, the disease which was slowly taking hold, creeping through his body.

Changing him from what he was into something he didn't want to be.

He wound the window right down again and screamed into the wind and rain until his throat was raw.

By the time he hit the outskirts of Haarlem he was feeling more stable; his thoughts were more under control and he'd managed to reduce his speed to a level which would merely be considered dangerous.

He wondered again if bringing in Isovic could be used

to help against the fact he'd been passing information on to criminals.

He thought not. And he knew that Tanya didn't have a choice; she couldn't keep what she knew secret. Which brought him on to yet another thing which was complicating his morning. And this was the one which was really burning a hole in his stomach.

Tanya's foster father.

He'd got the joints as he'd figured he might be able to find out how much Tanya knew, find out if he was in danger or not. There was no way he'd been expecting her to break down and tell him things.

Things which he couldn't get out of his head.

Things which didn't just make him angry; they made him thermonuclear.

He'd listened to Tanya's story, all the while trying to contain himself. And he'd realized something as she told him.

That despite the fact he'd tried to ignore it, he really liked her, and the way she'd dropped him all those years ago at the academy had hurt more than he'd admitted to himself.

Now he knew why she'd done it.

And after what she'd been through he could hardly blame her.

The fucker, thought Kees. *If I ever get to meet him . . .*

By the time he made it to Haarlem itself morning traffic was snarling up the roads and he had to part the wall of cars in front of him with the siren to make it to the garage. As the cars moved out of his way he had a flash of some religious guy parting a sea of metal.

He left the car in the forecourt and made his way to the back office where he'd been two days ago.

The same man was behind the same desk.

'You said you know where Isovic is,' said Kees.

The man nodded, fiddling a grease-covered bolt between his fingers.

'I think maybe.'

'Okay, so where maybe?' said Kees.

The man put down the bolt and handed Kees a folded piece of paper, his fingers smudging its clean whiteness.

Kees opened it, looked at the address. It was on Oude Schans, just round the corner from the canal district's main police station.

'And why now?'

The man shrugged.

'I don't want trouble,' he said, picking up the bolt again. He fished out a nut from a drawer and tried to screw them together. They weren't compatible.

'You should have told me this two days ago—'

'No, I only know this now. I find out. For you.'

Kees looked at him. Had the guy taken his threat seriously? For a moment he almost felt bad.

But there wasn't room left for any more bad feeling. And his head was really starting to kick off.

'How sure are you he's there?'

'He's there, I been told he's there.'

Back on the road Kees felt like he should call Tanya. He pulled out his phone and hit dial. Then he shut down the call.

The thing is, he thought as he dropped the phone into his lap, *what can I say? What can I say that'll make any difference at all?*

245

47

'Yeah, he works here,' said the guy in answer to Tanya's question. 'Or rather he doesn't. He runs the place.'

On the ride over she'd thought more about Kees, his involvement in her case. Kees had been stupid, letting himself get blackmailed, and she'd been wondering what had pushed him to compromise himself so badly. Was it just the drugs – was addiction that strong, overriding any kind of self-preservation? Or was there something else driving it?

'Great. I need to talk to him.'

She'd found the place on an industrial estate on the outskirts of Amsterdam, a large mass of concrete buildings with corrugated-iron roofs showing various degrees of wear.

As she'd turned into the road a fox had darted in front of her bike.

She'd swerved and nearly lost control.

Now she was standing in the building's entrance, walls of breeze block laid on a polished concrete floor. Two doors led out of the room, one going further into the building, from which she could hear the clink of bottles as they sped down a bottling line, and one with a glass window leading back out to the parking lot. The guy she was talking to was wearing a hairnet and a white overall.

A lorry pulled into the lot behind her. It looked like a

petrol tanker but the wording on the side said JUICE CONCENTRATES.

'Ahh . . . that might be difficult,' said the guy, watching the tanker as it turned in a large circle and started reversing back towards the building, beeping as it did so.

Tanya pulled the door shut, but it didn't make much difference; the truck was still visible through the glass pane and the beeping wasn't much quieter.

'Why?'

'I've not seen him today,' said the guy, mid-fifties, stubble going grey, and a paunch that not even the loose white lab coat could hide.

She noticed he wasn't looking at her eyes. Then again he'd not looked at them since she'd first stepped through the door; he'd trained them on her breasts, held tight in her bike leathers, and was keeping them there.

I guess he's not getting any at home, thought Tanya. *He's just another dirty old man. Like Staal.*

'What time does he usually get in?'

'Depends. And it's not really my job to keep track of him,' he said, still not making eye contact. 'Plus, he gets to go in the swanky entrance, not get his feet dirty.'

The tanker had stopped beeping, and she watched as a man in overalls attached a large tube to a fitting on the back end. He then waved to someone she couldn't see inside, jammed a lever sideways and a few seconds later the tube jerked, pulsing as the liquid flowed inside.

The man pointed out the way she needed to go, and she skirted the building, finding the entrance he'd talked about.

It turned out he was in, and a few minutes later Tanya

walked into his office on the second floor, accessed by a metal walkway suspended over the main bottling hall. She'd had to wear a white hairnet; the receptionist had insisted for health and safety.

The man who let her in closed the door behind her, softening the sound of machinery. He was also wearing a hairnet, even though he was totally bald.

'Stupid, I know,' he said as he showed Tanya to a seat. 'But we get unannounced inspections and the rule book says everyone has to wear one . . .'

His laugh sounded forced to Tanya.

Forced and nervous.

'The weekend,' she said. 'You were where?'

'What's this about?'

'Where were you?'

'I was fishing with an old friend of mine. Left Friday night and drove down to Gouda. Took a couple of tents and stayed until Sunday evening.'

'This friend is called what?'

'Rutte,' he said. 'Bart Rutte.'

Tanya looked at him. This was a waste of time.

'Okay. Thanks. I'll leave you now.'

'That's it?' he looked relieved.

'Yeah, we just needed to check up on something.'

She stood up to go; he did as well. She walked over to the door, then turned back.

'You know, there's something else you might be able to help with. There's been a few armed robberies going on at businesses around here. We know who's responsible but we're having trouble tracking him down. I don't suppose you know who he is?'

She pulled out a photo, having to unzip her leathers to reach it, and handed it to him.

'Usual kind of thing,' she said. 'Been in prison for a bit, then they get out and go right back to what they were doing in the first place.'

The man took the photo, looked at it and shook his head.

'I've not seen him, but then we don't exactly carry cash in the business. And it's not like he can steal a large amount of fruit juice. Or not easily, anyway.'

'No, I guess not. Well,' she said. 'Anyway. Better get going. You ready?'

The man looked puzzled.

'Ready for what?'

'Heading down to the police station.'

Alarm flared in his eyes, and voice.

'What for?'

'Oh a few things,' she said, taking the photo of Rutte back. 'Lying to me for starters.'

'What? I—'

'Shut it,' said Tanya, pulling out her cuffs. 'Put these on and follow me.'

48

'So I'm going to announce that we've got the killer in custody, but I'm not going to take any questions,' said Smit.

Jaap had been in his office for the last fifteen, going over everything they'd got.

Which in Jaap's view was enough to put Rutte away for the drugs operation – they'd had confirmation from Pieter that all the addresses they'd got from the now dead Romanian had checked out and were stuffed full of growing plants – but not yet enough for the killings.

'I think we should maybe hold off that for the moment—'

'Have you seen the news?' asked Smit. 'Because unfortunately the mayor has, and he's been on the phone to me twice today.'

Jaap wouldn't really care if Smit was getting his ear chewed off except for the fact that Smit inevitably dosed out double what he got.

'So,' continued Smit. 'I'll announce it, and I—'

Jaap's phone rang, he saw it was Tanya.

'Anything?' he said when he answered.

'He has no alibi,' she said. 'The guy must have been paid to say he was with Rutte, but they didn't prepare him very well. I showed him Rutte's mug shot and he didn't know who he was.'

This could be the leverage we need, he thought.

'Bring him in. We'll see if we can't get him to reveal who set it up,' he said and hung up. Jaap looked at Smit.

'His alibi for the killings is false.'

'Good,' said Smit standing up. 'Let's do it.'

49

Back in Amsterdam Kees slammed the brakes on as he sailed past the house.

The numbering system didn't seem to make any sense, and he'd only caught the number by chance as he'd glanced out the driver's-side window. And maybe he hadn't been paying much attention as his head was worse. Each pulse of blood felt like a depth charge going off in his left temple.

Whoever was in the car behind decided to complain about Kees' driving by putting their finger on the horn and keeping it there. The road was only one lane, with cars parked either side; nothing could get past unless Kees moved. He got out of the car and looked at the house, the address he'd got from the man at the garage. It had stopped raining now, the air several degrees colder than it had been earlier.

'What the fuck do you think you're doing?' yelled a voice behind him.

He turned to see a man, his face wobbling with fat and rage, glaring at him from the car behind. Kees got the feeling he'd seen him somewhere before.

'Fuck you, fat boy,' said Kees. He was sure his head was just about to explode. The man's face registered the words. Kees could see shock, then anger, forcing him to struggle out of the car and walk towards Kees.

Kees estimated his stomach would reach him a good few seconds before the rest of his body.

Then he remembered where he'd seen the man before – it was on the first case he'd worked with Jaap. The man had been outside the house of the first victim, who'd been hanging from a pulley on Herengracht, part of the crowd which always appeared at murder scenes. Kees remembered they'd had words and that he was easily worked up.

Good, thought Kees.

'You can't just stop there; you've got to move it,' said the man as he reached Kees.

'Get back in the car before you get hurt,' said Kees. 'You fat fuck.'

As he turned away and walked to the house he could hear asthmatic breathing following him.

He spun round, noticing the dark patches spreading out on the man's white T-shirt.

He felt like a scrap, but knew he needed to get into the house; if Isovic was there he didn't want to let him go.

So he flashed his ID, snapped 'Police business' at the man and went to the front door.

'I want to see that again,' called the man. 'I want your name so I can report you.'

'Report this,' said Kees giving him the finger over his shoulder.

On the front door, panelled wood with a bubbled-glass panel from about midway up, was the number 19. Kees then spotted a bunch of buttons to the left of the door, nine in total, all featuring the number 19 followed by a letter, starting with A.

Great, he thought. *Either this is the wrong address, or I'm going to have to go through each flat.*

Which considering he didn't have a warrant was going to be tricky.

And he couldn't request one as he wasn't even on the case.

Behind him he heard the fat man start his car. He listened to the whine of the motor as it reversed back along the street. A crunch told him fat boy had hit a wing mirror.

Kees smiled, his head felt slightly better all of a sudden. Just as he moved his hand towards the first button, a shape developed behind the bubbles. He stepped back and waited for the door to open.

A young woman stepped out, shorts, a T-shirt which if it was any tighter would probably be illegal, and large bug-eye sunglasses. A small leopard-print handbag dangled off her right forearm, and a small dog, white fur bunched into a topknot on its head, nestled in the crook of her left. She didn't even look at Kees; just walked right past him and turned left down the road, seemingly unaware of the temperature.

Kees watched her for a bit, breathing in her perfume, before turning back. His head wasn't pounding quite as hard now, but by the time he'd made it to the top of the stairs inside it had ratcheted back up to critical levels.

Pausing for a moment, he wondered what on earth he was doing. It was now near certain he was going to get busted for passing on the locations of the cannabis farms and yet here he was fucking around on a stupid lead on a case he wasn't even assigned to.

He knocked on the first door and waited. No one was in. He went from door to door, going down two floors until 19C yielded a result in the form of an old woman.

Kees showed her his ID and the photo of Isovic.

'Oh, I've seen him,' she said. 'I think he's staying in the flat directly above me.'

'You're sure?' asked Kees.

'Yes. I'd not seen him before, but I passed him on the stairs yesterday. Very polite he was, but I could tell he was a foreigner.'

Kees was sceptical. Isovic hadn't been polite when he'd slammed his head on to the table.

Maybe his headache was related to that, some kind of delayed reaction.

Maybe he was going to collapse with a stroke.

Maybe that'd be best, he found himself thinking. *Get it over with*.

'What time was this?' he asked, rubbing his temple, applying pressure in the hope the pain would ease.

'Just after eight in the evening, I was going to a church meeting, you see. I always go on a Sunday evening, and it takes me twenty minutes to walk there. Do you go to church?'

'Who normally lives in the flat above?'

She peered at him, perhaps taken aback by his abruptness.

'The man who lived there died a while ago. Must be back in December now. It was just after I'd got out of the hospital; they had to do an operation on my colon, you see, and—'

'And since then nobody?'

She seemed upset that Kees wasn't interested in her operation.

'Not until yesterday.'

Twenty steps, each one driving a stake through his head, and he was back in front of the door, but no one was answering the buzzer. He looked at the wood. It seemed pretty solid, and he wasn't feeling up to ramming himself against it.

But he didn't have much choice.

It took four attempts with his foot before it opened, the lock giving way with a crunch.

Once inside Kees knew he was on to something. A short corridor with a polished dark wood floor opened out into a combined kitchen and living area which didn't look like it had been updated since the 50s. There was no furniture, but a sleeping bag was splayed out on the floor, wrinkled like a used condom.

Beside it was a book.

Kees picked it up. He'd never been that hot on reading, but even if he'd wanted to he couldn't have read it.

This must be Bosniak, he thought, *or whatever the fuck their language is called.*

He dropped the book, noticing something in the sink. He stepped over and saw it was a hacksaw.

What the fuck's this for? he thought.

A noise at the window made him turn round. A plastic bag had blown up against the glass. It jostled there for a few moments, before sliding down out of view.

His eyes travelled down with it and he noticed something glinting just inside the sleeping bag. He reached out for it, pulling out a necklace chain with a silver crescent moon, the clasp was broken.

Memories swam around before coming into focus.

He heard voices in the corridor, someone asking if they should call the police.

He'd seen the necklace before.

The pounding in his head was reaching critical levels.

He was sure its contents were just about to splatter all over the ceiling.

Then he remembered where he'd seen it – hanging from Isovic's neck as he had bent forward and, with no hint that he was planning on knocking anyone out, hoovered up a line of Kees' coke.

50

Jaap could feel the expectation coming from the press room like a hot blast.

Standing next to him was Smit, adjusting his suit, getting ready for the cameras.

Once fixed up he nodded to Jaap and stepped towards the door just as his phone started to ring. He answered it, having checked the screen, listened for a few moments, then held it away from his head.

'Something's come up,' he said to Jaap. 'You'll have to take it.'

'I haven't prepared,' said Jaap.

Smit looked at him. 'It's your case, what do you need to prepare?' he said before striding off, phone clasped to his ear.

Jaap pushed the door open, expectation ramping up like water coming to a boil; people shuffled, cameras were readied and throats cleared for questioning. Jaap could already feel his palms moistening, his throat tightening. There was something about press conferences he'd never got the hang of. One on one he was fine, but talking to a room full of people was a skill he'd just never learned. It still made him nervous.

And then he got angry at himself for being nervous, which only made things worse. He had no problem grilling suspects in interview rooms, but this always felt like the tables had been turned.

And he didn't like it.

He walked to the table, each step loud in the now total silence of the room, and sat down, realizing too late that he'd put himself behind Smit's name tag on the desk, rather than his own. He figured most of the reporters present had been to enough of these to be able to distinguish between them. Then he noticed the TV cameras at the back.

He had a fleeting thought, an image of him messing up and it all getting attributed to Smit.

That helped, and he bent forward to the mike, a blow-dried rabbit skewered on a stick, and started talking.

Keeping it brief, he gave the facts and was just wrapping it up when he felt his phone buzz in his pocket.

Then he noticed, through the bright TV lights trained on him, a kind of ripple in his audience. People were also pulling out their phones; there was a general murmur and a sense that something was going on.

He was just reaching his hand down when one of the journalists held up a pen and called out.

'You said you've got the killer, right?'

Jaap glanced towards him, squinting against the TV lights. The man had a trim, almost orange beard, rounded glasses, and was looking down at his phone and then back up to Jaap, his hand still holding his pen aloft like an Olympic torch. 'So how come someone's just posted a third body on Twitter?'

51

Jaap stepped out of the car.

Right on to an empty chocolate wrapper.

His foot slipped away and he had to grab the top of the car door to steady himself.

At least he could see that this time they'd been quick enough; a patrol car had managed to get on to the scene and lock it down before the journalists did.

Only just though, thought Jaap, seeing at least three TV vans forging down the road he'd just driven along.

And given that once again the tweet had contained a link to a photo it was maybe irrelevant. He'd tried to call Tanya as he drove, but her phone kept ringing out to voicemail.

He started away from the car, glancing around.

The docks always looked desolate, but emerging from the centre of Amsterdam with its compactness, its mass of buildings which seemed to jostle up against each other, it seemed even more so.

Across the water a line of low warehouses studded the quay, articulated trucks parked outside, waiting for the latest batch of consumer goods made cheap in the east.

To the north he could see the channel which led out to the North Sea, a container ship just coasting into view, the hull low in the water.

Gulls screeched over to his right. He turned to watch them swarm round the arm of a massive crane moving shipping containers off a ship on to the quayside.

Tugs sliced through steel water.

Trade never stopped.

'Seriously, when are you going to stop this guy? I'm getting sick of these headless bodies.'

Jaap swung his attention back to see the same forensic as before.

'At least it'll give you something to talk about on your next date.'

'Don't . . .'

'Didn't work out?'

'Well, I was late. Didn't get off to a good start,' he said, dropping his bag by his feet. He pulled a packet of chewing gum from his pocket, offered it to Jaap. 'If there's any waiting to be done it's got to be us men, right?'

All I seem to be doing is waiting, thought Jaap, refusing the gum. *Waiting when I should be acting*.

Murder investigations were mainly waiting, long stretches of time when nothing happened, waiting for results to come back, for people to remember things. This one was no different, except the killings kept on happening.

'Actually, I know who did it,' said Jaap.

'Yeah?'

'Yeah. I just enjoy creating work for everyone. You ready?'

Jaap ducked under the red and white of the police tape, feeling it slide over the back of his head. As he straightened up on the other side he was hit with the memory of a dream he'd had.

Or was it déjà vu?

He couldn't work it out.

But whatever it was, in it he'd been standing by the tape, about to go under when something stopped him, and he'd turned and walked away.

'Found something?' asked the forensic as he joined him on the far side of the police line.

'Just thinking . . .' said Jaap.

He had Rutte in custody, and depending on the time of death it might rule him out. Not that that meant he wasn't involved; he could have ordered the hit, though from his violent history it looked like he might want to do this sort of job himself. But it did mean Jaap had less grounds to hold him for murder. Unless he could find something here to link Rutte with the deaths.

'Thinking's seriously bad for you, you know? Causes all sorts of trouble. I think you can get cancer from it. It's like smoking, but worse.'

Jaap watched as the forensic walked over to where the plastic screen shielded the body, right by the edge of the concrete quay.

Following, Jaap stepped around the temporary structure. Portable lights on tripods made it look like a film set, and he could feel the heat coming off them on the side of his face.

It took him only a second to see that this killing was no different to the other two.

Head missing. Hand blackened.

He felt the usual stomach contractions, but they died down quickly.

A ship's horn blared out across the water, booming off

the quayside, reverberating back in waves. He could feel each pulse in his chest.

Jaap looked down at the body, which was clothed in a white tracksuit made of some shiny material with a gold stripe down each leg and arm. The sleeves were bunched up at the elbows, showing skin a few shades darker than the other two victims. Like he'd spent most of his life outdoors.

'Still warm,' said the forensic, touching the man's arm.

Which meant this one wasn't done by Rutte.

Which meant he didn't have the killer in custody.

Which meant the whole thing was fucked.

'Anything on him?' he asked the forensic, who had started to search the pockets.

'Oh man,' replied the forensic. 'This is gross.'

Jaap looked over. The forensic held his gloved palm out to him, on it a collection of tiny white crescents jumbled together. It took him a moment to work out what they were.

'Fingernails?'

The forensic looked sick.

'That's just so disgusting. Not only does he not clip, he rips them off, then stores them all in his pockets.' He looked like he was going to throw up as he emptied them into a bag. 'I tell you, I fucking hate my job sometimes.'

'So the missing head doesn't bother you, but some fingernails do?'

'It's just so gross,' muttered the forensic, almost to himself. He sounded traumatized.

'Wallet, phone?'

'No phone, no wallet. He's got some loose money

though, more than the previous guy,' he said, pulling out a folded wad of notes from one of the pockets. 'Sure you don't want to split it this time? I feel like I deserve it after having to deal with those things.'

If Rutte isn't doing this, thought Jaap, *then who is?*

'Hang on,' said the forensic, pulling out something else. 'Look at this.'

Jaap glanced down into the gloved palm. It was a piece of jewellery, an ornate silver cross.

Jaap moved closer. He'd seen something like it before.

It took him a few moments to remember where. Tanya had brought a silver cross in when she'd searched the place where the girl from the estate agent's had lived. The girl who had disappeared.

It's exactly, he thought, turning it over in his gloved palm, *the same.*

52

'I'm not sure where she was from, somewhere foreign.'

Jaap glanced in the rear-view mirror, saw his own face. It looked calm. Total opposite of how he felt.

The press conference had been a wreck, he had a third body, Rutte was off the hook, – at least for the killings, he'd still go down for the cannabis business – and now Jaap was dealing with someone who didn't do detail.

'Foreign's not helping me, I need something more precise. Have you got her employment record there? Or does one of your colleagues? Surely someone knows where she's from?'

While the guy checked – the woman Jaap had spoken to on Saturday, Doutzen de Kok, was out of the office and not reachable – Jaap's mind was spinning. He now had three victims. Teeven was Dutch; the first he'd been unable to identify but was linked with the girl who worked at the estate agent's; and the third victim had the same kind of silver cross as the girl.

Even an idiot could see that meant victims one and three were possibly from abroad. Which is why he'd not been able to ID them.

'Yeah, hi?' said the guy.

'What have you got?'

'One of my colleagues thinks she was from like the Balkans or something.'

'Okay. Tell you what. Get hold of your boss and get her to call me.'

He hung up.

The Balkans. A small area to search in.

He got the pathologist's office on the phone.

'You ran DNA on the first victim, right?' he asked when he finally got through to someone who seemed capable of helping him.

'Yeah, got the results here. No hits.'

'Was that just national?'

'Uhhh, yeah. We don't run international unless there's a specific request. Takes way too long to do it as standard procedure and—'

'Run it,' said Jaap. 'Run it now.'

53

'Are you saying there is no way someone could have faked this?' Tanya asked the tech.

'I mean, stuff's always possible. I just don't know how someone could do that,' he replied. He was wearing another faded black T-shirt, this one featuring a skull with a snake poking out of one eye, its forked tongue picked out in peeling gold. The words FORSAKEN THORN ran across the chest. It looked like he'd cut the sleeves off himself with a pair of blunt scissors.

'So it could have been set up to look like the IP address was from a computer in this building, but wasn't really.'

The tech tapped a few keys, peered at the screen, then looked up at her.

'It would mean they'd hacked into the police network, which would be pretty serious shit if they had.'

Tanya'd been see-sawing over what to do about Kees all morning, and she had to report to Smit in less than ten minutes.

And Smit expected updates, Smit expected things to have happened, Smit expected investigations to be closed down almost before they'd begun.

As she'd gone to the factory on her bike she'd had to wait for a local patrol to come and pick up the juice company manager who was giving Rutte a fake alibi. She'd used that time to think, and had continued to do so on the ride back into Amsterdam.

It was clear that Kees had been in contact with the homeless woman, although he claimed that he'd been passing info on to her, nothing else.

Her death only made things worse for Kees, so who was benefiting?

Maybe it was the person who had been blackmailing Kees, the person who was employing the woman as a go-between.

She thought about the killer's police jacket. It was too obvious, like it was a message. Could the intention be to frame Kees? And how was the man in the wheelchair connected, if at all?

Kees had said he'd told whoever was supplying him coke in return for information on the grow sites that he wanted out. And apparently they'd not been happy. Could the murder have been a way of telling him to fall into line or he'd be exposed?

She needed to talk to Kees again, and it looked like they both needed to find out who his blackmailer was.

Which was why she'd asked the tech the question – she needed some leeway, something which would give her, and Kees, more time.

'Okay, I just need to know theoretically, that's all.'

'So you don't need me to look into it?'

'Hold off for now,' she said, seeing he looked relieved. 'I'll get back to you later.'

She left the tech department and took the stairs to the main office, noticing the time on the wall clock.

Smit would be waiting. And he didn't like that.

She had to go.

Which meant having to make a decision about Kees. A decision which could basically finish him.

The tech's answer maybe gave her a little wiggle room.

But, she thought as she headed out the door, *is it going to be enough?*

54

Jaap was missing something.

He didn't have time to be standing around on the bridge crossing the Oosterdok, but he was doing just that.

To his left lay the new Conservatorium building, the public library and, further back, Centraal station.

A wet breeze licked the side of his face, and brought the sound of a motorboat from out in the IJ.

Despite the link between Teeven and Rutte, and Rutte's alibi being false, pointing to him being responsible for the killings, Rutte had been in custody when the third murder had taken place.

And the Twitter account had less than ten minutes ago tweeted the number four.

But no location.

No photo.

Yet.

What am I not seeing here? he thought.

Cigarette smoke hit him, and he glanced left. A man was standing at the rail a few metres away, looking out the same way as Jaap. He was a junkie, that was clear from his ragged clothes, wasted muscles and gaunt face. The Dutch policy, pursued since the mid-1970s, of trying to break the link between soft and hard drugs did work to some extent. But there were always people who found their way into that world, a world from which there was, for the most part, only one way out.

The same way out the three victims in his case had faced.

And in the end, whether it came from someone else's hand or from your own, jamming the needle into your arm with an overdose, did it really make a difference?

Rutte could have hired the killer of the third victim to make it look like he was not involved, but if he was being that careful then why had he not worked on a better alibi for the previous two?

It was an amateur mistake. Unless it had been last minute, maybe sorted out by the lawyer once his client was arrested. A botched job. Or maybe it was just a holding tactic until they could work something more solid out.

How long does it have to take? Jaap thought, checking his phone, willing the pathologist's office to get back to him.

Talking of amateur mistakes, he'd made one himself; not checking that they'd be running international on the DNA. He felt like the missing pieces would make sense once he could ID the two anonymous victims.

He watched as a swan slid out from under the bridge. The junkie with the cigarette saw it too, held his arm out and released his two-fingered grip.

Jaap watched as the stub, tip flaring, tumbled through the air, hitting the bird's back.

The swan reared up, wings flashing white against the dark water, its long neck swivelling around in a panic to see what had just bitten it.

'Hey!' Jaap shouted to the man, who looked up at him, already lighting another with scrabbling fingers.

In his job he saw what people were capable of, how they had the capacity to hurt others. To kill others. But something about the man idly dropping a burning cigarette on to a swan . . . He could feel anger fizzing under his skin.

And sure, it was about the case too, and maybe his frustration over how things were working out with Tanya, or his life in general, but before he could stop himself he was moving.

'Why'd you do that?' he said, stepping right into the man's space.

'What's it to you, bitch?'

Jaap reached out to grab him, but the junkie's reflexes kicked in; the man swung his hand round towards Jaap's face, catching his cheek with the end of the cigarette.

Jaap's cheek sizzled as the man darted away. He sprang after him, people crossing the bridge staring at them both.

Jaap was gaining on the junkie, who was running with wild, loose steps, a high, cackling laughter shooting from his throat.

The movement was a release, a relief, despite the pain and despite the anger.

He wanted to run.

He wanted to reach the guy and fight him.

Jaap's phone went off in his pocket; he could feel its buzz against his leg.

He was waiting for the pathologist.

And here he was picking a fight.

Jaap slowed, stopped and answered, watching as the junkie reached the end of the bridge and sprinted past the Nemo centre.

'Yeah?' he said, cursing himself for being so stupid, for losing control.

'Got a hit.'

Jaap reached a hand up to the burn on his check. 'I'm listening.'

55

Smit sat back in his chair and stared at Tanya.

She was sitting opposite him, a cup of coffee, offered as she'd arrived, cooling rapidly on the table between them.

It wasn't the only thing cooling.

'So what you're saying is, you're actually no further on with this investigation.'

'No, not at all. I've established that the killed woman was in all probability working for the people who are ripping off the cannabis growers, so it follows that they, the growers, have a motive for killing her.'

'I get that, but the mode of killing was different to the beheadings, wasn't it? And have you seen the papers this morning?'

Tanya had. All of them.

Each one had the same front-page images: the bodies with the missing heads blurred out and the snapshot of a man pushing the woman under the train. The police jacket was clearly visible.

The leak had to have come from that fat guy at Centraal. Not only had he lied to her about how many copies of the CCTV images were available, he'd also ignored her direct request not to talk to any journalists.

He wouldn't have done that if I'd been a man, she thought.

She'd seen the way he'd looked at her, the thoughts

274

running through his head easy to read in his eyes. As if she'd ever sleep with someone like that.

'Because I'm due to go into a meeting in half an hour,' continued Smit, 'where I have to explain what is going on, and why we haven't managed to find the killer. And then after that I'm heading to a press conference, which is going to be like dousing myself with petrol then jumping in a fire pit. What about the phone logs – you have looked into them, haven't you?'

Tanya was falling through the floor, or at least her stomach was, an echo from the cannabis-induced spin last night.

'Yeah,' she said, her voice catching in her throat. She coughed, reached for the lukewarm coffee and took a sip. 'But I've not been able to narrow anything down. And I've been talking to the tech guy. It's possible someone was able to make the calls look like they came from here but were actually done from elsewhere. Which makes me think someone is actively trying to make it look like us, divert attention away from them.'

Smit shook his head.

'There's also the lead I've got on the man in a wheel-chair. I put a request in for surveillance—'

'I saw it, but I'm not convinced. You're taking the word of a drug addict and expecting me to pay people to hang around at a tram stop. Right now, what with all this other shit going on I just can't spare the manpower.'

He swivelled his chair so he could look out the window.

Tanya felt like saying something, but bit her tongue.

'Anything else?' he asked, still staring out the window.

A bird flickered a shadow across his face.

She could smell his hand cream again, the sweet floral scent making her feel sick.

Tell him about Kees! her mind screamed at her.

'No,' said Tanya. 'That's all for the moment.'

56

'Victim one has a name.'

They were all standing around the whiteboard.

Behind it, through the window, lead clouds smudged the blue sky.

Jaap wrote a name on the board.

'He's from Bosnia, and he has a record.' he said. 'I'm just waiting to get it through. Also the third victim's result should come back any minute now.'

Once Jaap had heard back from the pathologist, he'd called Kees and Tanya in. His cheek was still hurting, a kind of fizzing sting, from the burn. He'd found a plaster and covered it up, the skin already blistered.

'So how does this fit together?' asked Tanya.

'I think Teeven knew what Rutte was up to, and decided to profit from it.'

Jaap's phone rang – the pathologist's office saying they'd got a hit on victim number three. Jaap listened and then hung up.

'Okay, so the third victim was also from Bosnia,' he said as he wrote another name on the board. 'Kees, can you hurry the first one's file up and see what Interpol have got on this one as well?'

Just as Kees was reaching for his phone the door swung open and a uniform rushed in, looked around and settled on Jaap.

'Inspector Rykel?'

'Yeah,' said Jaap. 'What is it?'

'Phone call for you, really urgent. Someone called Saskia? She's in a real panic. I tried to transfer it to that phone,' he said pointing to the unit on the table, 'but it didn't work.'

Jaap started to get up. Saskia should be at the trial, not calling him. His own phone started buzzing as he made for the door. He answered as he stepped out into the main office, following the uniform to a desk right at the back, people watching them as they moved fast.

'Jaap, it's Roemers. That phone, the one you followed on Saturday night, has come back on. I've got a location on it now.'

Victim number four, he thought.

Maybe he was going to be in time to stop at least one killing.

'Where is it?' he said as he reached the desk. The uniform held the landline receiver out for him.

'Amstelveen,' said Roemers.

'Okay, keep watching it. I'm calling you back in two minutes.'

He took the phone from the uniform.

'Saskia what's going—'

He could hear a dial tone.

He tried to call her mobile but it was off.

'What did she say?' he said, turning to the uniform.

'Not much, just it was really urgent. She wouldn't tell me what it was.'

'How did she sound?'

'Uhh . . .' The uniform scratched his head. 'Kind of scared, I'd say.'

Jaap ran to the carpool, trying again to get Saskia on her mobile, but it was still turned off.

What's going on? he thought. *Has Floortje hurt herself or something?*

Driving out, the sky dark and heavy with coming rain, he redialled Roemers, who told him the phone was still on and hadn't moved.

'Listen, I need you to keep track of another number as well – Saskia's. As soon as it comes on tell me,' he said, giving Roemers the number.

As he sped down Stadhouderskade images of what could have happened started spawning in his mind. They'd hired a babysitter to stay at the house and look after Floortje while Saskia was working. She'd been recommended by their usual woman, but they'd not used her before. Maybe they'd made a mistake.

Images of what could have happened continued to multiply in his mind. Floortje could have fallen over, hit her head on something sharp. Or maybe she'd pulled a pan off a stove, the hot liquid pouring on to her head. Or . . .

Stop it, he told himself. *Just stop it.*

He tried to think about the phone he was tracking. He'd no doubt it led to the fourth and last member of the gang.

He hoped he wasn't going to be too late. But he was finding it hard to concentrate. He dialled Roemers.

'Saskia's number come back on yet?'

Roemers took a few moment to reply. 'No.'

Jaap swung a right into a narrow street, clipping a parked car on the way round. But he had to slam on the brakes as he straightened up. Ahead, a white delivery truck was turning, trying to do a three pointer in the road, but had got stuck. He whacked the car into reverse, narrowly missing a woman who'd started crossing the road behind him.

He had to find another route.

Rain started spotting the windscreen.

A vacuum was forming in the car's interior. Opening the window didn't help.

By the time he pulled up outside the address Roemers had given him, a large detached house which was clearly derelict, some of the windows broken and no lights on inside, it was raining hard, bouncing off the road surface.

Further up the road he noticed a car parked up on the kerb, a white Citroën.

Jaap's hand scrabbled around the glove compartment for a torch, dislodging an empty takeaway box and two collapsed water bottles. All cars should be equipped with a torch, only this one wasn't.

He gave up and ran to the front steps, feet slipping on the wet stone. The door was half open. He pushed it with his foot, drawing his gun at the same time.

The inside was a period drama gone to ruin. A large spiral staircase coiled out of the floor, leading up three storeys.

He stopped breathing, listened.

Rain hammered against the domed roof light above the stairs.

There was another noise, intermittent. A kind of groan.

The stairs were solid underfoot, the wood old and thick, not prone to creaking.

Thoughts were jabbing at him, connections forming.

The white Citroën outside like the one Saskia drove.

The victims from Bosnia.

On the first floor he stopped to listen, there were four rooms off the landing, and he thought the noise was coming from the far left at the back of the house. He stepped forward, skirting the doorway.

He pulled his weapon, and poked his head round the corner.

Saskia was slumped on the floor, holding a phone in her hands, her face illuminated by the screen's clinical light.

Jaap could see her features were twisted.

Saskia's trial.

Crossing the room took for ever.

He saw what was happening, what he'd missed.

Then he was beside her, holding her, looking at the image on the small screen.

It was Floortje.

Tied up, with a dirty gag wrapped round her mouth.

Kees could hardly see out of the windscreen, the rain washing down in flowing ridges.

If he'd been moving then he could have had the wipers on, but as he was parked up, outside the house where Isovic had been sleeping, he didn't want to draw attention to himself.

And now the inside of the glass was misting up.

Jaap had left them mid-briefing – it sounded like some

family crisis – and without specific orders Kees had decided he'd best get back on Isovic.

But now he was here he wondered if it was worth it.

Why am I bothering? he thought.

The weakness and pain were getting worse, month by month. There was no denying what was happening to him, the disease which was taking over his body.

So why did he feel the need to get Isovic?

Purely rhetorical, he already knew why; the answer was what they called displacement activity. That's what he was doing, simply not facing up to the inevitable.

A figure was hurrying down the street with a coat pulled up over his hunched head. Kees tried to glimpse the face, but it was too distorted, the water rushing down the glass making it impossible to see properly.

But when the figure ran up the front steps, fumbled with a key and let himself in, Kees got out of the car and followed, making the door just as it was about to click shut.

Wet footsteps rang out on the stairs, Kees tried to remember what floor he'd found Isovic's flat on. Then they stopped for a few seconds before starting up again, faster this time, and coming back down.

It's him, he thought. *He's seen the broken door.*

A few moments later the figure appeared on the stairs, taking the steps three at a time. As his feet hit the floor and he dashed for the door he noticed Kees, who stepped out of the shadows pooled on one side of the hallway from the single central bulb.

It was Isovic.

Eyes locked, Kees could read Isovic's indecision – back up the stairs or straight ahead?

Isovic chose straight ahead. Kees saw the flash of a blade being drawn from a pocket. At the last second Kees dropped down and sidestepped, tripping Isovic, using the Bosnian's momentum to propel him towards the door.

Isovic's face crunched against glass, and Kees heard a scream loud enough to wake the entire street.

He jumped to his feet, hauled Isovic back through the glass pane, kicked the knife away and cuffed him.

He marched him to the car, skull-guided him into the back, secured him, and got into the driver's seat.

'You're going to talk,' said Kees, twisting his head round to look right at him. 'Now.'

Jaap didn't know how the phone got into his hand, but it had. And almost immediately it started ringing. 'Unknown Caller' replaced Floortje's image.

He hit the green button and held it to his ear.

'Inspector Rykel,' said a growling voice in heavily accented English, 'I'm now going to tell you what to do.'

Tanya was looking at the Interpol file which had come in.

Both men were from the former Yugoslavia, Bosnian Serbs to be precise, and both were suspected of being part of a crew, self-styled the Black Hands, which had terrorized Muslims during the conflicts back in the 1990s.

Remembering the burned hands on Jaap's three victims she looked up Black Hand, her pulse increasing, reading that it had been a movement in the early twentieth century fighting for Serbian independence in Serbia.

Nearly a century later, in the conflict which had torn

apart Yugoslavia, these men had taken the name for their own group.

She called Europol, got them to check on the modern Black Hands. They came back with a yes; there was a gang. As she was listening to the names being read out she heard one that was familiar. Her pulse pounded in her veins.

It took her a few moments to place it.

The second she did her hand shot out for the phone, dialling Jaap.

The phone's edges were cutting into Jaap's hand.

'. . . and I'll be watching the news tomorrow evening at 9 p.m. If it's announced that the trial has collapsed and Matkovic has been acquitted then your daughter will be released. If not then you'll never see her again.'

57

He dropped the phone and pulled out the SIM.

Then he reached into his back jeans pocket and pulled out a lighter. The flame scorched the SIM, casting weird dancing shadows on the wooden walls.

Then he broke the phone up, removed the battery and threw it across the room. That started the baby crying again.

He checked his watch.

Things were now coming to a head.

He was the only one left, all his gang had been killed. Which would have been good, saved him the bother of doing it himself later on.

But for the fact that he didn't know who was doing it.

And he didn't have the resources to find out. It'd been driving him crazy for days, ever since the first murder, each further death notching it up even more.

At first he thought they were revenge attacks for knocking off the grow sites, and when the only Dutch member of his crew, Teeven, who was somehow getting the information on the locations, had also wound up dead, he was sure.

Then he'd heard on the news that each victim had had the palm of one of their hands scorched.

That was when he'd really started to get scared. Someone knew about him, knew what he was here to do.

But despite all this, he was still in a position to win.

And no one was going to find him here.

The smell of damp wood was all around him, he could almost feel the mould spores entering his lungs with each breath.

He looked out of the window, on to the pier hovering over the black water.

Rain had been pockmarking the water's surface but it was easing off now.

Turbulence turning to calm.

He checked his watch again.

Just over twenty-four hours.

Not long now.

58

'We need to get a team on this right away—'

'No,' Saskia shook her head, something in her eyes that Jaap didn't recognize. 'You heard what he said. If we tell anyone then they'll . . . they'll kill her.'

'But how's he going to know? I can take this to Smit, make sure it's kept—'

'No!'

'So what's the alternative? You losing the trial? Can you do that?'

They were sitting on the floor, backs to the wall. Outside the rain had eased off but was still falling. Saskia was shivering.

'I . . . Yeah. I mean, Isovic was our main witness. With him gone there's a whole load of testimony we're not going to get. He was really key to our approach. And the judge who got drawn for this trial is the hardest to get a conviction from. When we saw it was him we got worried. So maybe if I mess up there's a chance Matkovic might walk free.'

'But it's not guaranteed, right?'

'Course it's not fucking guaranteed. And where were you?' She turned her head towards him. 'Huh? You're her father. You could have been looking after her, but instead you decided to go off on your case.'

'That's not fair, and you know it,' shot back Jaap.

But is it? he asked himself. *Maybe she's right.*

He couldn't focus properly, too many thoughts running parallel.

The image of him leaving his houseboat on Teeven's phone, was it that Teeven had been part of this plot, scoping him out?

He'd been wrong.

He'd been wrong right from the start and now Floortje was paying for it.

'We've got to think about this,' he said, trying to keep his voice calm, the waver in it telling him he was failing. 'I think I can find out where she is, and—'

'I've already said—'

'This is Floortje's life we're talking about, we've got to look at all the options.'

Jaap could see Saskia was trembling.

'It's just coming up to seven,' he said, trying to sound calm, 'and the trial won't be starting until, what? Ten? Ten thirty?'

'Later, it's scheduled in for twelve.'

'Okay, so that gives us seventeen hours before it even starts. I can find out a lot in that time. We can talk just before you go in. I can let you know where I've got to . . . Saskia?'

He could see she was holding back tears, all the muscles in her face fighting to keep them at bay. Her mouth was open, but there was no sound.

A taught line of saliva joined her lips.

He wrapped his arms around her.

'Listen, it's going to be okay. We are going to get her back. I promise.'

Only I'm not so sure, he thought as he held her. *I'm not sure at all.*

'We have to get her,' she said, her tears spilling on to his neck, echoing the rain outside. 'Jaap, we have to get her back.'

59

'Who's this?'

'This,' said Kees, 'is Zamir Isovic. He absconded from witness protection a few days ago.'

'Don't you need the hospital?' said the desk sergeant. 'I mean, his face and everything? I don't want him bleeding all over one of my cells.'

Kees glanced at Isovic, hundreds of tiny trickles of blood covering his face. It looked full-on horror movie, but he knew it wasn't serious.

Or he didn't care.

He couldn't work out which.

'I want to put him in a cell, I've got a phone call to make.'

'Look, he's cuffed, right? So just chain him to that pipe. I'll keep an eye on him.'

Having secured Isovic to the pipe, which he was pleased to feel was really hot, Kees stepped outside. The rain had stopped and the air was cool, fresh. He breathed in, wet pavements glittering with reflections from the descending sun, and placed a call to Smit, half expecting his phone to be off. But it rang, and Smit picked up.

'Yes?'

'Inspector Terpstra. I've got Isovic in custody.'

Silence howled down the line.

'I thought I'd taken you off that case?'

'I got a tip-off and had to act fast; there wasn't time to let anyone else know.'

A car drove past, a curling wave of water peeling from its front tyre.

'Did you arrest him?'

'Got him cuffed. I haven't done any paperwork, not sure what grounds I'd arrest him on. Other than resisting arrest.'

'Get him down to Den Haag and hand him over. I'll call the head of ICTY and let him know,' said Smit. 'Then he becomes their problem.'

Nice to be thanked, thought Kees as Smit hung up.

He'd hoped to leave Isovic here overnight, get some drone to take him down tomorrow, but that clearly wasn't going to happen.

By the time he'd signed out a car – he'd been picky, rejecting the first two offered – and bundled Isovic into the back it was starting to rain again.

As he headed out of the city, down towards the coast, Kees thought about the next few days.

He had an appointment to go back to the hospital, the latest test results would be in.

The tests which would show how fast the progression was.

The thing is, he thought as he drove, *I'm not sure I'm ready for that.*

It'd been nearly a year ago when he'd first noticed the numbness, but he'd put it down to coke and ignored it. Then the other symptoms started to kick in, but it still took him weeks before he'd decided he had to see someone about it. Even then he'd made the appointment and cancelled it three times before he actually forced himself to go.

The doctor had spent most of the time staring at a computer screen, two-finger-typing Kees' answers on a dirty keyboard. Each answer seemed to prompt another question from the screen.

Once he'd left, with an appointment for a barrage of tests, Kees wasn't sure the doctor had actually looked at him once.

'How you find me?'

Isovic's voice brought him back to the present, and Kees realized that he'd not even been paying attention to the road. He looked in the rear-view, catching Isovic's face behind the cage.

'Someone grassed you up.'

'Who?'

'Does it matter?'

'No, maybe not,' he turned to look out the window, a lazy windmill stood in a field of sheep.

'So why did you run away? I thought you wanted to testify against that guy, what was his name?'

'Matkovic.'

'Yeah, that's the one. So you changed your mind? You don't want him to be brought to justice?'

'Oh, I do,' said Isovic looking back, locking eyes in the mirror, his head nodding as if his seat had transformed into a rocking horse. 'I do.'

60

Tanya was getting worried.

She now knew exactly who the victims were, and had confirmed ID on the remaining man from Kees' photos from 57, presumably the next victim, and she needed to let Jaap know as soon as possible.

Problem was, he wasn't picking up.

After the uniform had interrupted their meeting and told Jaap there'd been a call from Saskia, he had disappeared. At first she'd assumed something had happened to Floortje, an accident maybe. She'd tried to get hold of Saskia but couldn't reach her either. And it had now been hours.

She thought back to when she'd met Jaap, the case which had thrown them together. There'd been something there, between them, right from the start. But then he discovered Floortje was his daughter, and their relationship maybe hadn't worked out quite as well because of that.

He'd changed when he realized he was suddenly responsible for a life.

And he was doing a good job. He clearly loved Floortje, the way his face lit up when he was around her, his attentiveness. Sometimes Tanya felt a pang of jealousy, though she knew that was stupid and tried to dismiss it.

And there were times when Tanya helped out, looked after her for him, and she'd started to wonder if she really wanted to be a kind of mother to a child which wasn't her own.

Not that she'd ever really thought about having children herself; the past, and what had happened there had somehow killed that urge.

She turned back to her computer. She'd managed to match the names to the victims, and the man seen at 57, who they presumed was still alive.

Where is Jaap? she thought, checking her phone again.

They'd been wrong about the case, which was probably her fault; the theory about the cannabis growers had side-tracked them.

She dialled Jaap again, and this time he picked up.

'Are you okay? Where are you?' she asked.

'I had to meet Saskia about something. It's okay now though.'

She could tell something was wrong. His voice sounded different, harder than normal, as if his vocal cords were seizing up. And she could tell he wasn't going to tell her anything, at least not now. She decided not to push it.

'I've found out some more on the two Bosnians and I've ID'd the last man in the photo at 57. The thing is, they were all part of a gang called the Black Hands, who're wanted for war crimes—'

'Where are you now?'

'At the station, I'm just—'

'Can you get to Schellingwouderbreek, quickly as possible?'

He sounded off, stressed, under duress.

'Jaap, what's going on?'

'Just meet me there. I'll explain. And don't tell anyone about this.'

And then he was gone, the intensity of his voice ringing in her ears.

61

Stars pinged off black water.

The sky had cleared, rainclouds heading east towards the continent, and Jaap shivered as he stood waiting for Tanya. He was at Schellingwouderbreek, a small lake in Amsterdam Noord surrounded by woodland.

It was here he'd scattered Karin's ashes, watched as the grey flakes landed on the surface of the water, clung to the reeds at the water's edge.

Something rustled in the undergrowth, before plopping into the water off to his right.

He remembered the famous poem by Basho, the sound of water.

The skin on his arms and neck goose-pimpled up.

But he wasn't sure it was from the cold and damp.

Or something else.

The image of Floortje on the phone screen wouldn't clear from the front of his mind. And then there'd been Tanya's call, confirming just how wrong he'd been.

He'd driven out here after taking Saskia home, and had pulled out the I Ching as soon as he parked by the path which led to the water. He'd made a resolve to stop doing this, but . . .

Coins spun through the air, glinting in the car interior's light. The I Ching had given him Thunder over Lake.

DANCING TO ANOTHER'S TUNE.

He stepped closer to the water's edge, the soil softening underfoot.

How did I let this happen? he thought.

The image of his teacher in Kyoto rose out of the dark, the rounded face, shaved head accentuating the bushy eyebrows, and the placid look in his eyes.

Jaap had woken one morning with the 3 a.m. bell reverberating through his head. It was large, made of copper, and hung in a simple wooden frame in the central courtyard of the monastery. Every day it was someone's job to polish it, to forestall the inevitable greening of the metal, and Jaap had done it many times, his image distorted on the curved, shiny surface as he worked the cloth back and forth.

It was rung every morning, though Jaap had no idea who actually struck it. After listening to it for a few moments he'd got up, dressed and headed for the main hall, where the next three hours would be spent just sitting. Which was purely a warm-up for a much longer session later in the day.

He'd been struggling for weeks. Sitting still and concentrating on his breath only seemed to intensify each and every physical sensation until he felt like he was in so much pain he wouldn't be able to carry on. Yuzuki Roshi had simply smiled when Jaap complained to him of the pain, and said, 'Good, keep going.'

He'd reached moments when he swore he could feel every cell in his body, each one screaming, each one on fire.

But the physical pain was only a mild distraction from something worse.

The mental pain.

That morning Jaap was crossing the courtyard, other monks emerging from all corners like bent beetles, when he noticed Yuzuki Roshi gesturing to him from a side door. Jaap went over to him and, as instructed, followed him through the doorway.

The path on the other side was littered with small round stones which crunched underfoot, and led through a grove of small maples, their branches dripping delicate autumn fire. They followed the path up a small hill, and as they rose Jaap glimpsed through the trees the temple complex spread out below.

He knew it was modelled on ancient Chinese ideas, Zen Buddhism was a Chinese import which had taken root and grown in Japan's feudal society, and the buildings with their sloping roofs which curled up at the corners were testament to that lineage.

Gravel gardens were dotted about, their swirls immaculate and regularly changed, and ornate bridges arched over small streams linking ponds. On the shore of the largest pond a heron balanced on one leg, perfectly still, perfectly calm.

But as they climbed higher, Jaap could also see beyond the temple grounds: the urban sprawl, wires hanging between buildings, a chaos of cars parked on every available flat surface. Neon lights, rubbish, a truck negotiating a corner on a too-tight junction.

He remembered thinking about being cloistered away, wondering if he was achieving anything.

Or simply hiding.

They reached a small building, built in the same style as the rest, and stopped outside. The paper screen which acted as a door was closed, glowing in the early-morning sun. A bird high above them in the clear still air let out a single piercing shriek.

And Yuzuki Roshi spoke to him, which was a rare experience; most of Jaap's questions were answered with the curt command 'Just sit' or a small bow of the head. He told Jaap to enter the building, look at what was inside and stay and meditate on form and emptiness.

Jaap pulled back the paper screen, the action smooth, and entered the room, the tatami mat rough against his bare feet. It was a small space, no more than two metres square, and lying on the floor was a body. The screen slid shut behind Jaap and he sat down, realizing that the figure in front of him was one of the monks he'd seen about the place but never spoken to.

At first Jaap was angry; this kind of thing might work on people who'd never seen a dead body before, but he was a police inspector, his job involved looking at them all the time. And he was about to get up and leave the room, tell Yuzuki Roshi that cheap tricks weren't going to work on him, when he realized the very reason he'd ended up halfway across the globe was because of a body.

A body whose life he'd ended. And that of the child she'd been carrying.

So he sat, slowed his breathing down, and tried to focus on what was in front of him, tried to wrestle with form and emptiness, two polar opposites which were somehow linked.

It took hours, but when, knees aching, his back a twisted rope of pain, Jaap finally emerged into the dusk he felt different.

Felt as if things, life, was suddenly clearer to him.

Felt that, in the end, things were simple.

Form and emptiness.

He'd always assumed the Buddhist concept of emptiness meant nothing, a kind of nihilistic view in a world devoid of meaning.

But as he stood there, watching the orange sun slide down behind the silhouetted mountain range edging Kyoto, the crisp air carrying the savoury smell of miso broth from the kitchens down below, a bird he still didn't know the name of gently squeaking in one of the trees, he knew that was wrong.

Form and emptiness weren't opposites, they were one and the same thing. And that realization was meant to bring the end of suffering.

The black circle on a white background which hung in his room at the monastery, an image he'd stared at for hours, flared in his mind.

But that was then.

Now his daughter was being held hostage, and would be killed if he couldn't find her in the next twenty-three hours.

And it was his fault.

He'd caused suffering, Floortje's suffering.

Saskia's suffering.

His own suffering.

Now form and emptiness seemed like so much mystical bullshit.

No better than the kind of crap Blinker peddled to his willing customers.

Behind him a noise, footsteps, and he turned to see a spot of light dancing through the reeds. It flitted back and forth, hit his legs and travelled up to his face so he had to put his hand up and squint into the beam.

'Jaap, what's wrong?'

Tanya's voice, full of concern, came at him as the light flicked off.

He didn't even know where to start.

He would have laughed.

If he wasn't already crying.

62

Tanya held on to him, held him tight.

As if that would help.

She still couldn't take in what Jaap had just told her.

Jaap shifted his weight and she let him go.

'So tell me about these men,' he said, his voice unable to hide the fear coursing through him.

'They all come from Bosnia, with the exception of Teeven obviously. It seems during the conflict there they were a small terrorist group which specialized in ethnic cleansing. They were part of the Serbian army involved in the Sebrenica massacre but broke away when the UN troops moved in. They probably thought they were safer as a small group.'

'And Matkovic was their leader?'

'Yeah. He got caught, but these guys managed to escape. And they must have come here using false IDs. Easy enough to get.'

Jaap slapped his neck and inspected his hand.

Tanya had been going through their files, and the fact that one of these people was holding Floortje was terrifying; all of their records were littered with deaths, rapes, torture. Europol had a list of crimes they were accused of running into pages. But the one who had Floortje was, apart from Matkovic, the worst.

'And while they were here they needed money so started ripping off the cannabis growers?'

'Looks that way,' said Tanya. 'They needed money to live off, I guess. And it's not like they were going to come here and get normal jobs.'

'So the photos on their phones – that wasn't about us, they were just scoping out Floortje? They needed to know where she would be?'

'Must've been.'

'So who's left?'

Tanya pulled two sheets of A4 from her pocket, unfolded them and handed them to Jaap, training her torch on the paper so he could read. Tanya knew what they said. Goran Nikolic was second-in-command of the Black Hands, answering to Matkovic. And by the look of things he was as vicious as they came.

Jaap scanned down then turned to the second sheet, read that in silence.

When he was done he looked out over the lake.

'This is who has Floortje,' he said.

Tanya noticed the sheets of paper trembled in Jaap's hand, the edges shivering in the torch beam. She wanted to reach out to him again, but he seemed coiled tight, like he might explode if touched.

Not that she could blame him.

From what she'd read in the files, if Nikolic had Floortje the chances were he'd follow through with his threat. Meaning Jaap would never see her again.

Or not alive.

'So what now?' she said. 'How are we going to get him?'

'I don't know,' said Jaap, turning his face towards her. 'But we've only got about twenty-two hours left.'

'I ran his name,' she said. 'Nothing came up. As far as anyone is concerned he's not in the country.'

For a while neither said anything, then Tanya spoke.

'All I can think of is 57. That's the only place we've had a confirmed sighting of him. How about we go there now, flash his photo around?'

Jaap was looking out towards the lake and didn't respond, didn't give any indication he'd even heard.

'I know it's a long shot,' she said, watching his profile, 'but right now I'm not sure what else we've got.'

63

Music pounded, each beat hammering Jaap's head, pressurizing his eardrums, squeezing his brain.

It was nearly midnight, but at 57 things were only just getting going.

He leaned forward to yet another group – stupid, spoilt people out on the town, shrieking, giggling, acting like the celebretards who were everywhere in the media these days – and shouted out the phrase he'd been using for the last twenty minutes. When he'd got their attention he showed the photo.

Faces peered forward, three woman who weren't as young as their dresses would have you believe, and two much younger men, one with a stud in his left ear. Jaap had heard about them – granny snatchers, they were called – who for whatever reason preferred women more mature.

One of the women reached out for the photo, dark roots showing on her blonde middle-parted hair, and Jaap let her take it. She studied it for a few seconds before handing it back.

'I've seen him before,' she said, leaning forward so Jaap could hear her. 'He was trying to rent a building from us.'

Her friends were all looking at her, hopeful that their evening was now going to be considerably more exciting than the fumble round the back of the club they'd been anticipating.

'I think we're going to need to talk in private,' said Jaap. She nodded, got up and followed Jaap and Tanya outside, leaving her friends ablaze with excitement.

'Where do you work?' asked Jaap as they left the building, walking in the opposite direction to the queue which hugged one side of the club. Jaap could see she was older than he'd first thought, maybe late fifties, maybe more. They stopped at the corner of the building.

'De Kok,' she said, pulling her jacket round her and shivering. 'It's on Rozengracht.'

Jaap felt a jolt of energy pulse in his gut.

It was the same place where the girl who'd given the first victim the keys to Koopman's flat worked. The girl who disappeared.

'And what building did he try to rent?'

'It wasn't him, actually; it was a friend of his who I dealt with. But the man in the photo waited in the car the whole time. He was wearing dark glasses, and I kind of got the impression he didn't want to be seen.'

'And the one you dealt with, who was he?'

'Some guy, I don't really remember that much about him. Esther was supposed to be showing them around – she'd made the initial appointment – but my boss wanted me to do it as she didn't think Esther was experienced enough.'

'The man, was he a foreigner?'

'No, I don't think so. He sounded Dutch to me.'

Must have been Teeven, but Jaap didn't have a photo of him to show. Not that it really mattered. They'd got a lead on Nikolic, that was the important point.

'What building were they interested in?'

'Several actually. I took them to probably about five or six, all old farm buildings or industrial units.'

'Did this guy say why they were looking?' asked Tanya.

'He said it was for some project, like a studio or something. To do some kind of metalwork. He wanted somewhere far away from any other building so no one would get disturbed by the noise.'

Jaap's pulse, which had been high since the phone call, notched up again.

That's it, he thought. *That's got to be where they're holding her.*

He tried not to let the excitement show in his voice. He could feel Tanya also trying not to let anything slip.

All he could think about was Floortje.

Being held by Nikolic.

'Which one did they take?'

Shouts broke out from near the entrance. Jaap looked across to see two bouncers piling on top of a man waving a bottle. The bottle left his hand and smashed on the ground, spraying a group of woman at the head of the queue. They squealed, screamed and moved back.

'I don't think they took any in the end,' she said, shivering. 'All too expensive, they said. At least that's what they told me.'

Day Four

Day Four

64

Jaap's eyes followed the blazing swan, each feather a flickering lick of flame in the dark sky.

There were no stars, no planets, nothing against which to gauge depth or distance.

There was just the flying swan.

The swan turned its neck – it was missing an eye – and beat its wings, dislodging a tail feather.

Jaap watched the feather as it dropped, fire flaring towards him, tumbling through space. And he was falling too, he could feel air rushing past him. The feather was close now, and he tried to reach out and touch it, but there was no warmth even as his hand got near. And then he accelerated, or the feather slowed down, and he watched it shrink away from him, watched it until he could no longer see it and there was only darkness.

Something was pounding his skull, arrhythmic, jarring.

He woke with all his muscles firing at once, eyes flipping open, arms and legs jerking, his head lifting off the desk, the world righting from sideways. The pounding he recognized as his heartbeat, the pulse too big, too strong, for his veins to cope with.

He expected to be covered in sweat – that was the cliché – but he found he was stone cold, dry, and his limbs stiff and sore.

Floortje.

He rubbed the side of his face he'd fallen asleep on, the side with the cigarette burn. The plaster was still attached to his skin, but he could feel the edges peeling up, catching and rolling on his fingers as they passed. He found an edge and tore it off, inspecting the pad.

There was blood there, dried and fresh.

He dropped it into the bin by his desk and looked around the office, clocking the lack of people. It was just him.

He checked his watch.

Only thirteen hours left, he thought. *And I'm no closer.*

He dragged himself off the chair, shook his legs out. He needed to be doing something, anything, but he felt weighed down.

And the truth was he didn't know what to do. Nikolic had Floortje and was going to kill her if Saskia didn't get Matkovic acquitted today.

Which, given that Saskia's actual job was to prosecute him, was not going to be easy.

The one shred of hope was the fact that Saskia's main witness had gone missing. That alone gave her a chance of managing to lose the case.

But he couldn't rely on that, couldn't sit around and wait for a verdict which could cause the death of his daughter.

When he and Saskia split up, he'd never imagined that she'd end up getting together with his work partner, Andreas Houten. But they had got together, and they'd made it work, and Jaap had been happy for both of them.

The problem had hit when Andreas, out of town on some training course, had asked Jaap to drop in on Saskia as she was feeling down.

Jaap had reluctantly dropped in. And then spent the night.

When Andreas told him the news a few months later that Saskia was pregnant Jaap didn't think anything of it. Or maybe he had, maybe there'd been a moment of disquiet which he'd quickly quelled?

Then, later on, Andreas had been killed and five days later Saskia gave birth.

Jaap still remembered the beeping of machines in the hospital room as Saskia told him the truth, and the feeling he'd had, like the floor had just dropped away into nothingness.

Now Jaap's insides felt like they were being shredded by something razor sharp.

In the first days of Floortje's life, when he was adjusting to the fact that he was now a father, he'd been forced to confront his thoughts about having a child. Was it the shooting – the one which had propelled him to Kyoto – which caused them?

The woman he'd shot had been pregnant, so maybe it was some kind of internal justice he was trying to impose on himself?

Or was it fear? he wondered. *Fear of something like this happening? Every parent's worst nightmare?*

Meditating was all very well, but when you were responsible for another living human being, detachment from suffering, seeing the true nature of reality, obliteration of the ego – that all seemed impossible. Maybe all he'd been doing in those years was hiding from life under a cloak of spirituality and cheap philosophy?

Maybe, he thought, *I just need to fucking get on with it.*

In the toilets he inspected the burn on his cheek. The blister had burst and was bleeding. He cleaned it up and slapped on another plaster. He noticed he was avoiding his own eyes in the mirror, like the person there was a stranger, looking for a fight.

After leaving 57 he'd told Tanya to go get some sleep and had headed back to the station and tried to force his mind to find a solution. But it was like trying to sift sand with a fork – nothing he came up with led anywhere. He'd eventually fallen asleep some time past five in the morning, despair dragging him down.

Back in the office he started where he'd left off, rereading the files Tanya had found on Nikolic.

It was clear that Nikolic had been Matkovic's right-hand man during the conflict and that they were responsible for a whole host of atrocities.

But what wasn't clear to Jaap was why Nikolic would go to such lengths to free his old boss. It seemed a kind of loyalty way beyond what was normal, and the risk for Nikolic so high. If he was caught then he'd end up on trial at ICTY as well. And from what Jaap had read about him in the file, Nikolic would go down for several lifetimes with no chance of parole.

Was Matkovic really worth it?

Was he worth killing Floortje over? An innocent child?

The razor in his stomach stepped its shredding up a notch.

How has this happened? he thought. *How have I ended up here like this?*

'Rykel.'

314

Jaap turned to see Smit's frame in the doorway, the light from behind him meaning his face was in shadow.

Since the cover-up of Andreas' death Jaap had avoided Smit as much as possible, anger flaring in him every time he saw his boss.

Anger which had been compounded as the only reason he'd had to go along with it was for Floortje's sake.

If Floortje hadn't been my child, thought Jaap, *I'd've gone straight to the press.*

Blowing the whistle would have ended his career in the police, and he'd decided to keep quiet as he knew he had to support Floortje. But maybe that had been the wrong move, maybe he should have gone through with it, exposed the cover-up and then got some boring, normal job where he'd have been a better father, better able to look after her.

'Five minutes, upstairs,' said Smit.

Jaap nodded and turned back to his desk, wondering what he was going to say.

Nikolic had given the standard kidnapper's threat not to tell anyone, and it was highly unlikely he had a network in place which would give him access to internal police communications.

But maybe he does, thought Jaap.

He'd been getting the information about the grow sites, attacking them just before the drug squad did.

Jaap realized he'd missed something.

Who was passing that info on? he thought, *Could they still be in touch?*

Jaap could take this to Smit, ask him to tell no one else,

but then what would he be able to do? Give him more manpower? He already had Tanya, and he could probably enlist Kees as well. He trusted them both. Bringing anyone else in at this stage would just complicate things, make it more dangerous.

And from what the estate agent had told him last night, he had an avenue to explore. He'd have to set Tanya and Kees trawling around other agents, seeing if they could find any trace of Nikolic.

He cleared the file from his desk, burying it in a drawer, and made his way upstairs.

65

Kees willed his eyes to close and his brain to turn off.

But it wasn't working.

He'd got back from Den Haag and had been unable to sleep.

Which was a problem as tiredness seemed to make the symptoms worse, the pain flaring up with exhaustion.

And he felt like he needed a line or two, just to take the edge off.

He'd no idea why coke helped, but it unequivocally did, and had a far bigger effect than the pills he'd been prescribed. The ones he had given up taking as they didn't do a thing but make him sick.

He was sitting on the sofa, looking out at the brickwork of the building opposite. He'd been trying to count the number of bricks, but he kept getting lost somewhere in the middle. The fog wasn't helping.

In all the thoughts he'd had about his future – all the plans, all the fantasies which would blossom in his mind while on long boring stakeouts, the images which he'd play through in those strange moments between sleep and wakefulness – he'd never imagined that he was going to end up with difficulty moving, problems controlling his own body.

But that's what the doctor had said would most probably happen.

317

A decline, the speed of which no one would be able to predict.

Reality washed over him but felt unreal. His mouth tasted weird.

Was this really happening to him? How could it? Why?

He shifted his legs, all senses now attuned to the tiniest sensation, looking for any hint that things might be getting better, that the symptoms had eased overnight, that it was going away.

But things actually felt worse.

His brain, ever looking for a way out, tried to tell him it was simply lack of sleep. Nothing at all to do with the disease. He just needed some rest, that was all.

Fuck it, he thought. *What I really need is some coke.*

After a couple of lines had hit he sat back, already feeling better. He'd laid a third one out, which he might have in a little while. And if he was concerned that it was taking more and more to have the same effect, he wasn't thinking about it, wasn't thinking about it at all.

His phone buzzed on the glass coffee table, vibrating towards the third line. He watched it for a few more buzzes, then snatched it up just before it broke into the slash of white powder.

He could see it was Tanya.

How did things get so complicated? he thought.

'Yeah?' he said as he hit green and held it up to his ear.

'It's Tanya,' she said.

'I know. Caller ID, genius.'

'Listen,' she said, ignoring his jibe. 'Something's come up, we need to talk. Are you free? Now?'

'Where are you?'

'Bloedstraat, that's where your apartment is, isn't it?'

Kees looked down at the line of coke. Less than a second to get rid of that. He reckoned he could manage.

'Yeah, sure,' he said. 'I guess you know the number?'

'Got it from your file.'

If she's got access to my file, he thought as the tiny particles zoomed up into his nose, *then this is serious*.

By the time he'd cleaned up she was at the door. He opened it and let her in, pointing her towards the living room, a moment of awkwardness as to what sort of greeting they should exchange.

Now that they'd fucked again.

They kept it professional, Tanya stepping through the doorway and heading to where Kees had indicated.

'Sorry it's so early,' she said.

Kees felt like he should offer coffee or something, but didn't.

'So what's up?'

She was standing, looking out the window, her figure an improvement on the view. He felt the familiar stirring, but the thought of what was going to happen to him killed it dead.

No one wanted to sleep with someone who couldn't control their own limbs.

He flopped down on the sofa, springs creaking in protest. Sleeping with her had been good though. Great even, the urge coming on so strong that nothing else had existed. For the first time he'd forgotten about his disease, he'd even forgotten about what Tanya had told him, about the abuse she'd suffered. It was only afterwards, as he drove home, that he wondered if he'd taken advantage of her, used her while she was down.

But then she'd seemed to want it, to need it, just as much as he did.

'It's going to come out,' said Tanya, her back still to him.

For a moment Kees wasn't sure what she was talking about.

'Those calls? I asked the tech people if they could have been made to look like they came from the station but were actually from somewhere else. But they said no.'

'And the only person who could have made them was me.'

He didn't even frame it as a question.

'I've been thinking. Maybe the best thing would be to go to Smit now. Tell him about it.'

'Tell him I was passing on information to a drugs gang? I'm sure he'll be thrilled.'

'I never said he's going to like it, but I just think it might be better coming from you,' she said, finally turning round.

He tried to read her face, but it was too much in shadow to see clearly.

'Meaning if I don't tell him then you will?'

'I have to. You know that. The information is there for anyone to see.'

A toilet flushed in the flat upstairs; something rushed through a pipe in the wall behind him. He could tell from her voice she was cut up about it, but she was right; there was nothing she could do.

'Yeah, okay. You're right. And just when I'd managed to kind of get in his good books again.'

'What do you mean?'

'That witness I was looking after, the one that escaped? I found him, took him down to Den Haag last night.'

'Seriously?' She stepped forward, reaching into her pocket. 'You got him?'

'What's going on?' he said, sensing the tension which had suddenly stiffened her whole body.

She pulled out her phone, and already had it to her ear, her free hand held out like a uniform stopping traffic, trying to silence his questioning. She waited, then hung up.

'Shit,' she said. 'Shit, shit, shit.'

66

Jaap stepped out of the station and took a deep breath.

Fog had formed overnight, unusual for May, and the air was like a wet cloth. It didn't seem to contain enough oxygen.

His hands were cold, freezing cold. He tried to work out when he'd last eaten something, but he couldn't concentrate, couldn't remember.

In the end he'd not said anything to Smit; all he'd had to do was listen to a speech about results and then get the hell out of there. Smit had been toying with a nail file as he'd delivered the monologue.

By the end Jaap felt like grabbing it and stabbing him in the eye.

Repeatedly.

He started moving, thinking about what he needed to do.

The woman last night had said Nikolic and Teeven had been searching for an out-of-the-way building, but they'd not taken one of hers. But maybe they were just scoping the places out – who'd actually rent a place they were going to hold a kidnapped baby in for just twenty-four hours?

It would be easier if he could just get a few patrols on to this, let them do the legwork. But then he'd have to explain why, and right now he just didn't see that as an option. Nikolic could have a contact in the police.

And there was also no way Jaap was taking the risk that he could be alerted.

Jaap cursed himself for not previously focusing on how the information on the grow sites was getting out; if he'd done that then he might now be able to hand over some of the search to patrols.

But even so, handing it over meant risking someone making a mistake, missing something crucial. Maybe even barrelling into wherever Floortje was being held and . . .

There was no way he was going to take the risk.

He'd start with the estate agent, the one the woman at 57 worked at, run by Doutzen de Kok. There were too many connections there to ignore; the girl who'd disappeared after giving Koopman's keys to the first victim could have given Nikolic access to other properties.

He checked his phone for the time and saw several missed calls from Tanya. He dialled her back as he headed towards the centre, the rumble of a tram somewhere off to the left. He stepped over embedded tramlines which led into grey fog, the shiny metal beaded like a can straight from the fridge.

Floortje loved trams; she was transfixed by them. Jaap couldn't work out if it was the sound or the motion, or something else entirely that his adult brain couldn't appreciate.

'Jaap, I've got bad news,' Tanya said as soon as she answered.

His stomach plummeted, but his feet kept on taking him up Damrak.

'What?'

'That witness, at Matkovic's trial?'

'Yeah?'

'Kees found him, delivered him to ICTY early last night.'

Ahead of him a traffic light turned red, softened and enlarged by the mist.

He found his feet were no longer moving. But then again his lungs weren't either.

'I . . . Shit!' he said, his voice alien to him. His phone buzzed by his ear. 'I've got another call; I'll call you back.'

He pulled the phone away, saw it was Saskia.

She'd heard. Got a call from her boss Ronald just two minutes before.

'But is he going to testify?' asked Jaap once he'd listened to Saskia's panicked voice. 'He's the one who absconded from witness protection.'

'From what Ronald says Isovic's refusing to talk.'

'Did someone get to him, threaten him?'

'Maybe you'd better ask Kees; he was the one with him before he disappeared.'

'He's refusing to talk, that mean he won't testify as well?'

'I don't know, he's literally not saying a word. But maybe he will when we get him in there and he sees Matkovic. I've spent hours with him; he genuinely hates Matkovic. I don't think I read him wrong.'

Jaap's eyes moved around but didn't take anything in, everything internal now, scenarios running wild.

Maybe Isovic hadn't escaped, maybe someone else had knocked Kees out.

Could it have been Nikolic, trying to get to Isovic to stop him testifying? Maybe Isovic had then got away from Nikolic and gone into hiding? And he'd not turned himself in as the last time he was under police protection hadn't worked out so well for him?

If so, then he needed to talk to Isovic; he might be able to help him find Nikolic.

Jaap made a quick calculation. There'd be little traffic at this time, but the fog was really thick, he didn't want to end up with his car flipped over in a ditch. A good friend of his had wound up in a coma after the car she and her new boyfriend were in did just that. Jaap had visited her in hospital, and two days later she died.

She'd woken up just long enough to discover her boyfriend was already dead.

'I think I'd better speak to Isovic myself. Can you get me in there?'

'Hang on,' she said. Jaap could hear keys being tapped quickly. 'There's a train leaving Centraal in fifteen minutes. I'll meet you there.'

'You don't need to come. Just call them and . . .'

She'd hung up. He knew there was no point in calling her back to dissuade her, so he jammed his phone away and started running.

67

If Kees had raped her pet cat right in front of her he doubted he could've got more of a reaction.

Thinking back, the reaction had come when he'd told her about Isovic; that's when she'd become desperate to get hold of Jaap, constantly trying his phone, not answering the questions that Kees had thrown her way.

The main one being, 'What's wrong?'

She'd left, still trying Jaap's phone, and Kees had slumped back on to the sofa exhausted, the three lines of coke not doing what they should. In fact they seemed to have crashed him out.

His eyelids closed, and he felt himself sinking down, brain slowing and speeding up at the same time, time twisting out of shape.

His phone detonated on the table in front of him.

Fuck, he thought as he jerked upright. *Should have turned the fucking thing off.*

This time it was Jaap, and he wanted to know all about Isovic.

'What's going on?' said Kees. 'When Tanya heard about Isovic she went kind of nuts . . .'

There was noise on the other end, a kind of rushing sound, fast-moving air. Jaap sounded out of breath.

'What did Isovic say when you found him?'

'Not much. He seemed kind of pissed, to be honest.'

'Did he say anything about why he'd run away?'

'I asked him that, he hates that guy he was going to test-ify against so the whole thing doesn't make sense. But when I asked him if he wanted to see the guy brought to justice he said he did. So I asked why the fuck he'd knocked me out and run away.'

'And?'

'And nothing. He just clammed up and wouldn't say anything else. Are you running?'

'Where are you now?'

'Home.'

'I need some help'

'Sure. But seriously, what the fuck is going on?'

'I can't really explain. Just get to Tanya.'

Jaap gave him an address not far away.

Here we go, thought Kees as he hung up.

He reached the address twenty minutes later. The fog was getting worse, denser, and he only saw her when he was less than two metres away.

'His daughter?' he asked when Tanya had finished explaining.

She nodded, her lips tight.

'Fuck,' he said, breathing out.

Traffic was starting to increase, headlights creating a weird effect, catching the suspended water particles and refracting the light till it built up into an Impressionist on acid.

'So what are we doing here?' he asked.

'Waiting for these guys to open up.' She nodded to the shopfront they were standing outside. 'We need to check something with them.'

Kees stared out into the fog. Tram bells clanged twice off to his left, and he could hear the crackle and fizz of electricity on the points. He turned to Tanya.

'Look, about what we were discussing earlier—'

'There's nothing I can do, you know that.'

'I know. All I'm asking for is a bit of time; I think I can straighten things out.'

'Straighten things out? How are you going to do that? The woman's dead—'

'I don't know anything about that. You know that.'

'Thing is, the time she was killed you were doing what?'

'This was what, Saturday morning? I was with that fuck of a witness Isovic.'

'The one who escaped.'

'Yeah, but—'

'So unless he's willing to back you up about the timings then . . . Look, I'm just working the worst-case scenario. Because you know that's exactly what Smit's going to do.'

Kees shook his head. He was beginning to wonder if any of it mattered.

'I've got one lead to follow up on, and after that I'm going to have to report back,' she said, staring out into the nothingness.

'What's the lead?'

She looked at him, held his gaze for a few moments before breathing out and looking around as if checking for something.

He could hear footsteps approaching.

'I'm going to regret this,' she said.

'Regret what?'

She handed him a folded bit of paper.

'You didn't get this from me.'

Kees was about to unfold it when a figure appeared out of the fog and stopped right by them, a look of surprise on her face. Kees thought he recognized her, but couldn't place it.

'Desperate to buy a house?' she asked, looking between them while she got her keys out. 'Let me guess. You've just got married, you're now looking to start a family, and you need a house to get started in?'

'You know,' said Tanya, 'it's uncanny just how wrong you are. But we still need to talk. I'm assuming you're Doutzen de Kok?'

The woman nodded and started unlocking the door.

Inside, once de Kok had flicked the lights on, she invited them to sit at the chairs in front of her desk. The company was one of those who thought having funky designer furniture in bright colours made it look less like an estate agent's.

Kees settled into the lime-green chair shaped like a cupped hand while Tanya took the hot-pink chair which was a pair of gaping, plump lips.

'So you're the cops who found my employee at the nightclub last night?' she asked, sitting opposite them. She was wearing a suit, but the material was a bit shiny for Kees' taste, and had very thin white vertical lines running through the dark-blue fabric.

White lines.

He hated the fact that his mind was so predictable.

Then he placed her. He'd met a prostitute on a case last year who, although younger and more glamorous, bore a strong resemblance to the woman in front of him.

And her surname had been de Kok as well. He wondered if Doutzen knew what her sister did for a living.

'Yes,' said Tanya. 'And I want to know if any of these men have been in here.'

The woman took the photos Tanya offered and studied them. She shook her head and handed them back.

'I haven't seen them, but if you can leave these, I'll show them to everyone else when they get in.'

'I believe they were shown some properties. They were looking for farm buildings, industrial units, basically anything out of the way, non-residential. I'll need a list of what they saw.'

De Kok turned to her computer, tapped away and then reached under her desk, where a printer was whirring.

'Here's what we've got,' she said. 'It's not really our kind of thing, but there are a few. Most of these have been listed for over a year.'

Kees leaned over and looked at the sheets as Tanya held them. There were thirteen, all outside Amsterdam.

'Thanks,' said Tanya, getting up to leave. 'And these are all still available; no one's taken them?'

'All free as of yesterday evening. And frankly, there's not much chance of any of them flying at the moment.'

Kees and Tanya stepped outside, closing the door behind them.

'So what now, we have to check these places out?' said Kees.

'Let me call Jaap first,' she said. She pulled her phone out, but her arm stopped midway between her pocket and her head. Kees looked at her; she was staring at the estate

agent's window. Then she put her phone away, and stepped
back towards the door.

'Hey,' said Kees.

She ignored him.

68

As Tanya stepped inside blood rushed through her head like a broken fire hydrant.

Is it the same house? she thought. *It can't be.*

'The property you've got in your window, the one on Johan Kernstraat. When did that come up for sale?'

'Only a couple of days ago,' said de Kok. 'You interested?'

Tanya didn't know what to say. 'I . . .'

'If you are, now's a great time to look,' she said. 'The owner's emigrating, so it's been priced for a quick sale. I can set up an appointment today if you like?' The estate agent's killer instinct came into play, her hand reaching for the phone. 'Hell, I can take you there now if you want?'

'Emigrating?'

'Yeah, Thailand I think he said. Must have got a job there or something. Though it does all seem a bit last minute; he's actually leaving tomorrow morning – 7 a.m. flight, I think he said. He was asking me for the name of a cab firm to take him to the airport first thing.'

'What's the name of the firm?'

De Kok's face showed a touch of suspicion.

'Uhhm, I'm not sure I—'

Tanya gave her the look.

De Kok told her.

As Tanya turned to leave her legs felt twice as long as

usual and weirdly unstable. Her hands were sweating badly, slipping when she gripped the metal door handle.

Emigrating, she thought. *To Thailand.*

'You okay?'

She glanced up and saw Kees, a cigarette in his mouth, the lighter poised to strike.

'I . . . It's . . .'

He's emigrating, the fucker's emigrating, to Thailand.

Where he'd be able to carry on doing what he did to kids. Where she wouldn't be able to reach him.

She felt Kees' hand on her arm; she shook it off.

'Seriously, what's up?'

'Nothing,' she said, not looking at him, her mind a desperate, scrabbling animal. She took a deep breath, two. 'Really, it's nothing. Just tired. And this whole thing with Floortje being held . . . it's . . . Let's get going.'

They picked up a car from the station. Kees took the keys, but Tanya made him hand them over, she didn't want to be sitting there doing nothing, allowing her brain to go over what she'd just learned. Even though there wasn't much to go over, she either had to act or let it go for ever.

And she wasn't sure she could let it go.

The roads leaving the city centre were clearer than those entering it, but she still had to drive slowly as visibility wasn't great. Once they'd left the city behind them, the fog started to thin out, the odd building morphing out of the greyness – a windmill stuck in a field, a grain silo looming high.

'So what was that back there?' asked Kees as they turned off the small road they'd been following for the last ten minutes on to a tiny track, the surface nothing more than a lunar mass of mud, peaks and troughs.

'What do you mean?'

'You looked kind of spooked. This thing with Jaap's kid getting to you?'

Tanya shifted down and spun the wheel to the left to avoid a deep pothole. The car rocked like a boat side on to a wave. Further on, the track veered off to the left. She killed the lights and pulled to a stop.

'I think we'd better go on foot.'

Kees peered out the window.

'Really? That mud looks knee-deep.'

He wasn't far off, as Tanya discovered when she stepped out of the car. They made their way down the track and after a few minutes caught a glimpse of the first building on the list, emerging from the fog ahead of them.

They both stopped, suddenly aware of how quiet it was.

'I'm guessing it'd be too dangerous to just storm the place,' said Kees after a few moments.

'If you skirt round there –' Tanya pointed to the right of the building, where a broken fence led off into the murk '– I'll take the front.'

She watched as Kees squelched off, impossible to stop the noise of footsteps in the gloopy mud.

Is this where she's been held? she thought as she moved forward, pulling out her gun.

The building was maybe twelve metres long, clapboard wood a dull silver grey, with a corrugated-iron roof splotched with clumps of some plant which was gradually colonizing the surface. She could smell the earth, mud, and also something else.

Cigarette smoke.

She stopped dead. Kees smoked, but even he'd not be stupid enough to light up now. At least she hoped not.

There were no windows, the building had clearly been built to house agricultural vehicles, at least judging by the spare parts dotted around outside; an axle with only a single wheel attached, loose piles of rugged-gripped tractor tyres spilled on to the ground, and cans of motor oil quietly rusting away in the gloom. It all looked like it hadn't been touched for years.

The only entrance was a large double door, big enough to fit a tractor through, right in the middle, and as she got closer she could see one of them had been opened recently, an arc sweeping out in the mud like a fan.

Someone's here, she thought.

She gripped her weapon as the door began to open.

69

The journey had been hell.

Jaap and Saskia had sat, unable to say anything, unable to even look at each other. He knew the fear he'd seen on Saskia's face when they caught the train at Centraal station was mirrored on his own.

Fog had obscured the windows, and there were times when Jaap had wondered if they were even moving.

But now they were getting out of a cab at ICTY and Jaap could feel all the pent-up agitation starting to break loose and fuel his movements.

He'd been thinking about Floortje, about how scared she must be. But then he'd wondered if that would be the case. She was young, just over a year old, and she'd either be crying or asleep. She couldn't possibly know what was going on.

But somehow he was sure she'd have sensed something was wrong.

'So how are we going to play this?' asked Saskia, the first time she'd spoken since they'd boarded the train in Amsterdam.

They were walking around the raised pool towards the main entrance, weird metal sculptures rising out of the water into the fog, both their steps hurried, unable to hold back. It felt to Jaap like they were front runners in a race, each jostling for position.

'You can probably sign me in, put me down as a legal assistant or something.'

'A legal assistant with a gun? I take it you're carrying? They've got airport-style security on because of the trial.'

'Shit,' said Jaap. He'd not thought about that.

I can't let this get to me, he thought. *No more stupid mistakes.*

As they reached the entrance a voice called out Saskia's name from behind them.

'Oh no . . .' Saskia whispered before turning.

The man emerging from the gloom was tall, almost as tall as Jaap. His suit was sharp, enough to cut through any defendant's feeble lies. Jaap had never met him, but he guessed this was Saskia's boss. He'd always thought Saskia had talked a bit too enthusiastically about him, now he maybe started to understand why.

'I need to speak to you,' he said as he reached them, eyeing Jaap. 'My office in five minutes?'

'Yeah, sure,' said Saskia. 'I'll come right up.'

'Ronald Timmermans,' said the man when it was obvious Saskia wasn't going to make introductions. He extended his hand; Jaap reluctantly took it.

'Inspector Jaap Rykel,' he replied as they shook.

This caused a raised eyebrow.

'Oh?' he said looking between Jaap and Saskia. 'So you're Floortje's father? How is she?'

Ronald didn't look like a man who cared about other people's babies, but he gave a good impression. He did however have the air of being highly competent, someone who could get things done. For a split second Jaap felt like telling him everything, unburdening himself, having someone tell him it was going to be all right. But Saskia answered before the impulse carried through to action.

'She's . . . she's fine. A bit cranky this morning. That's why Jaap's here, to help me out while the trial's on.'

'Sounds like a good plan,' said Ronald. 'Because we've got to make sure Matkovic goes down today. And I think we can. Some new stuff's come up and . . .' His hand reached into his jacket pocket, pulling out a mobile. 'Excuse me,' he said, holding the screen away from him as if he were long-sighted. 'Make that eight minutes?'

Saskia nodded and they watched as Ronald strode through the entrance, phone jammed to his ear.

'New stuff . . .?'

Saskia shrugged. 'Guess that's what he's going to tell me about.'

'I need to talk to Isovic while you do that.'

Saskia signed him in, the woman at the security desk mistyping his surname on the badge which she slipped into a credit card-sized plastic folder and handed to him.

Jaap turned his gun over at security and let Saskia find out where Isovic was being held. She talked to the guard and got Jaap into the room before she headed off to find Ronald.

Jaap could tell she wanted to stay, but they both needed to know what new stuff her boss was talking about, and how it might affect their plan.

Not that we really have one, thought Jaap as he pushed the door open and stepped into the room.

It was small, a bed, a desk with no chair, a sink and a wall-mounted TV being the only furniture. Jaap had read criticisms of the ICTY which had surfaced in the media a

338

few years ago; the inmates were kept in too cosy an environment, the sentences, when handed down, were too lenient.

And he'd seen starker cells, that was for sure.

But he knew that it wasn't going to change, Matkovic's trial was to be one of the last before the ICTY was wound up, its mission finished.

Which would mean Saskia would be out of a job.

Not that she'd care much if they lost Floortje.

On the bed a man lay on his back, feet hanging off the end. He raised his head to look at Jaap then lowered it again, apparently uninterested.

A single strip light blared down from the ceiling.

Jaap walked the few steps over to the bed, shoes squeaking on the polished blue floor. The air was still and felt like it had been breathed too many times already.

'I already say. I decide not to testify. That is my right.'

Jaap knew he was right, and that the ICTY was taking a big risk by even holding Isovic here; it had no legal grounds for detaining him. But the prosecutors were gambling on the fact that Isovic had no legal councel.

'Fine,' said Jaap. 'I'm not interested in that.'

Isovic turned his head to look at him.

'I need to talk to you about someone. Someone I think you might know.'

'Who?'

'Goran Nikolic.'

The response was acute, a spasm rippling across Isovic's face.

'So you know him,' prompted Jaap after a few moments of silence.

'I don't know him,' said Isovic, his voice tight. 'I don't know this person.'

'Did you know he was here in the Netherlands?' said Jaap stepping closer, trying to put pressure on him.

'No. Are they putting him on trial too?'

Jaap was watching him closely; he was sure Isovic was lying.

'He's not in custody, no.'

'Then I not able to help you.'

'Nikolic is trying to get Matkovic off, and you're helping him.'

The movement was so swift Jaap was only able to half block the elbow which flew up at him. It still glanced off his cheekbone, just above the burn. Jaap shoved his weight forward, grabbing Isovic's arm and twisting it behind his back as he forced him sideways on to the bed.

'I not help that piece of shit,' hissed Isovic, his jaw clenched with pain.

'No? So why not testify? It looks to me like you're working with Nikolic to get Matkovic off. Which means you know where he is.'

He pulled out a photo with his free hand and shoved it in Isovic's face, forcing his arm further up his back at the same moment. Just to help him concentrate, get him focused.

'See her?' he said, bending closer, whispering in Isovic's ear. He didn't want the guard overhearing anything. He didn't want the guard seeing what he was doing either, but that couldn't be helped. 'That's my daughter, and Nikolic has got her hostage. He's going to kill her if Matkovic isn't released today. So I want you to tell me everything you know about him—'

'Jaap.'

Saskia was in the doorway, the guard looking over her shoulder.

'We need to talk,' she said. 'Now.'

70

Tanya had skirted round the building to where she'd sent Kees.

She found him behind a rusted oil drum lopsidedly sinking into the mud. From what she could see there was no rear entrance.

She crouched down beside him, no longer caring about the dirt, her trousers filthy.

Filthy bitch, she thought.

What Staal always called her after he'd finished doing his thing.

She was still reeling from the news he was leaving the country. She needed to get to him before he did; she needed to tell him what he'd done to her, make him understand the pain he'd caused.

'There's someone in there,' she whispered, trying to cut out the voice in her head.

'You saw them?' he whispered back, his face close but turned towards the building. He had more stubble than the other night. His cheeks had been smooth then; the friction burns were elsewhere on her body.

'Just a glimpse – he came out to go to the toilet. He had his back to me so I couldn't work out if it's him or not.'

'Hair colour the same?'

'He had a hat on, one of those knitted ones.'

Kees looked around, then caught her eye.

'Guess we should ask Jaap, it's his kid.'

Tanya thought for a moment. There was an inherent risk in storming the place, bad things tended to happen when guns were drawn, and she didn't want to be responsible for a disaster.

The kidnapper had given Jaap until 9 p.m. to get Matkovic released. She checked the time. Just over nine hours from now.

'You're right. Get out of earshot and call him. I'll wait back at the front – join me there.'

Kees made his way off into the fog, and Tanya skirted back to the front. There was no movement, and she couldn't hear anything. Floortje had a pair of lungs on her and wasn't usually shy of using them, something Tanya had found out whenever it was Jaap's turn to look after her.

She listened for a moment, but the fog was swallowing all sound.

As she waited for Kees she found herself thinking about Floortje, wondering if it was her who'd come between Jaap and herself.

Certainly they'd not had sex as much recently, their schedules rarely aligning, and often the baby disturbing them when they did. Jaap had seemed less interested, or was it simply that he was exhausted, trying to cope with the situation he found himself in?

And, the question she'd kind of been dodging for a while, did she really want to have the responsibility, even if it was part time, of being a mother to another woman's baby? How could she with all she'd been through still not resolved?

The sex with Kees on Sunday night had been urgent, intense.

She'd only managed to get one trouser leg off before he'd ripped her panties to one side and shoved her against the wall, pushing himself inside her.

It was different to the sex she had with Jaap. He was gentler, less hurried.

But, and she had to admit this, it'd been more exciting with Kees. The intensity of it, the sheer exhilaration of being taken.

The kind of rough treatment she'd grown accustomed to from Staal.

The thought pummelled her stomach.

She bent over and threw up in the mud, a pool of yellow bile in a sea of brown.

Behind her she could hear the squelch of Kees' approaching feet. He squatted down beside her.

'I can't get hold of him. He's not answering his phone and no one at the station knows . . . Jesus, that you?'

'Yeah, I . . . I wasn't feeling too well.'

'What the fuck did you eat?' said Kees. 'That colour? I don't think that's too good . . .'

'Let's just forget it for a moment. What should we do?'

Tanya watched him opening and closing his hand, like he was milking an udder.

'I say we go in,' he finally said.

Tanya looked around; the fog was thick as ever. The place was eerily quiet – no birds, no traffic and no baby crying. If Floortje was inside she might get hurt, or worse.

But if she's not, she thought, *we need to get on to the other addresses and find her.*

'Okay,' she said. 'Let's do it.'

They made their way to the door as quietly as they

could, placing each foot down slowly, mud sucking at their shoes like a hungry predator. They got in position, Tanya by the door and Kees a few feet back, gun outstretched.

On a silent three, counted down on Tanya's fingers, she flung the door open, and Kees jumped forward, shouting, 'Police.'

Tanya rushed in after him, eyes adjusting to the bright light inside. Scanning quickly she saw the top of the hat poking above a hay bale at one end. There didn't look like there was anyone else.

The space wasn't empty though, a series of gigantic canvases lined up against a wall. Lights like those used for TV shows were rigged up to a series of batteries, and shone on to the pictures.

Each one had the same image, but painted in different colours. Tanya couldn't work out what it was meant to be.

Kees had spotted the hat and was advancing. Tanya followed, knowing already that this was a waste of time. They got the man out from behind the bales. He was about mid-forties, with a large tangled beard on a gaunt face.

Kees frisked him and came up with a paintbrush.

'You need to be careful with this,' he said holding it up to the man. 'Looks like you're pretty dangerous with it.'

'I just paint,' he said, accepting it back, his eyes darting between them, shoulders heading for his ears.

'I can see that,' said Kees as Tanya looked at the nearest painting again, realizing what the image was supposed to represent. 'So tell me. When did you get into painting pussy?'

71

'And this judge being suspended affects us how?'

Jaap and Saskia were in a brightly lit corridor deep in the ICTY, the gassy smell of canteen food saturating the air, making Jaap's stomach churn. Saskia had met with Ronald, heard his news.

'Because he has a record of being the hardest to get a conviction from,' said Saskia, her voice tight. 'The one they've replaced him with is much more willing to convict. And I know that he's been gunning for Matkovic.'

'So can't you get him taken off as well? If they're both showing bias then surely—'

'Yeah, but the first judge had a profile done in *De Telegraaf* at the weekend; the one that's been appointed now is smarter than that, I'd have no proof to make any such claim.'

Jaap leaned back against the wall, his heart a series of firecracker explosions in his chest. Saskia had shown him the newspaper report back on Saturday. It seemed like a century ago. If only he'd known then . . .

He forced himself to think. If there was no chance of getting Matkovic off then he was wasting time. He needed to be out looking for Nikolic.

And there was something not right. He couldn't work out what was going on between Isovic and Nikolic, from Isovic's reaction it was clear they weren't friends. And yet everything Isovic was doing was helping Nikolic.

Jaap leaned forward, his heart was still firing, though it didn't feel too regular; he wondered if it was going to hold out. He felt like he was on some kind of high, everything weird, unstable. He thought he was sweating but his forehead was dry when he wiped it with his hand.

'Are you okay?'

Jaap looked up at Saskia. She seemed to be holding up better than he was. But he knew her well enough to see what the calm exterior was hiding.

'I . . . Yeah. Let me try him again.'

Back in the cell, Saskia having negotiated another session with the guard, Jaap stepped right up to Isovic, dragged him up off the bed and slammed him against the wall, pinning him there with his forearm on his neck.

He brought his face right into Isovic's, smelling his rancid breath and fighting the urge to pull away.

'Tell me what's going on, right now.'

'Does Nikolic really have your daughter?'

'Yes.'

'Then I sorry, but I not think you ever see her again.'

'Why do you say that?'

'Because Nikolic is killer – he kill many, many of my people. And he also kill my son.'

Jaap stared into Isovic's eyes. Eventually he nodded and released him, stepping back.

He didn't think it was possible to fake what he'd seen there.

Or maybe I'm just projecting, thought Jaap.

But if Nikolic had been responsible for the death of

Isovic's son . . . Something flashed across Jaap's mind, too fast to catch, but enough to give him the feeling that he might just be able to work out what was going on.

Something which might increase his chances of saving Floortje.

'I'm sorry about your son,' said Jaap. 'But maybe you can help stop him from killing my daughter.'

Isovic rubbed his neck where Jaap's arm had been. Jaap could see there was a horizontal red mark.

'I might be possible to help,' Isovic said. 'But you get me out of here.'

Jaap looked at him, looked at the cell, thought about Floortje.

Breaking out someone from ICTY was not what he'd come here to do.

'I need something better than that,' he said watching Isovic closely.

'Get me out of here,' said Isovic. 'Or I can't help you.'

Twenty minutes later Jaap was in Saskia's office. The door was closed, but they'd still been speaking in whispers. Jaap turned to look out of the window, over the raised pool they'd walked past earlier, and tried to figure out a way. Breaking Isovic out was one thing – he could probably just march down to his cell and do it right now – but his absence would be noted.

Which would put Jaap in a very dangerous position.

It would only take minutes before every police patrol in the country was notified, and that would make any kind of movement so much harder.

'I still don't get it,' whispered Saskia. 'He's been our star witness; I've interviewed him so many times, and he genuinely hates Matkovic, so I can't figure out what he gains from doing this.'

Jaap had been wondering about just that, and was starting to think he did understand. And if he was right, breaking out Isovic might have even larger consequences.

But even so, he thought, *can I take that risk?*

The phone on Saskia's desk rang. They both looked at it, Saskia finally picking it up. Jaap motioned he'd be back; Saskia nodded while listening to the phone.

He asked a guard walking down the corridor where the toilets were.

'Down the corridor to the left,' the guard replied. 'Though you might want to go up one floor. Colleague of mine was out on the town last night and it's not a pretty sight in there.'

Jaap took his advice and went to the floor above. He pulled the door shut behind him and leaned back, staring down at the toilet. Then he reached out, dropped the seat flat and sat on it, pulling out his coins. He took a deep breath, then started throwing. The hexagram built up line by line. Once finished he fished out the I Ching.

Lake over Water

DEADLOCK. CONFINED. EXHAUSTED.

He had a choice; leave Isovic and risk that he changed his mind, decide to testify, or take him away, make sure he couldn't. Trust Isovic to help him find Nikolic.

A toilet flushed in the stall next to him, he hadn't even been aware there was anyone there. He checked his phone for the time.

You've got to make a decision, he told himself. *Right now.*

72

The baby wouldn't stop crying.

It'd been wailing for what seemed like days, weeks, a never-ending death ray of sound which cut through his brain and jangled his nerves so bad he didn't know what to do.

At least he was out of the way. The cabin was right on the water's edge, a small jetty jutting out beyond the window, and the nearest road way down a muddy track. If he'd been anywhere near other people surely someone would have started asking questions.

Like whether he had a licence to run a twenty-four-hour abattoir.

He strode across the small room to where she was, nestled in a cardboard box with bent edges. He looked down, down at her eyes staring back up at him. In contrast to the constant writhing of her body and the noise coming from her mouth, her eyes were still, glacial, timeless.

Like she knew she was pissing him off, was daring him to do something about it.

He pulled out his gun, settled it in his hand, and pointed the barrel towards her.

Nothing changed.

The screams kept coming, the eyes kept staring.

He moved it forward until the metal pressed against her mouth.

The crying ratcheted down until it was nothing more than an occasional whimper.

Her lips explored the object, it looked like she was trying to suck at it.

Then he realized. She was hungry. If he'd given her something to eat hours ago he might've had some peace. He checked his watch.

Only a few more hours to go.

The fact that all the members of his crew had been killed off was starting to look good to him. He still didn't know who had done it, but he was sure he was safe here.

And once Matkovic was out things were going to change. They'd be out of the country within three hours of his release – everything had been lined up.

He was glad he'd sorted that out himself. None of his crew had been involved, so none of them could have given up the escape route, even if they'd been tortured before being killed.

He flicked on the portable radio he'd bought from a shop in the centre of town, and tuned into a news channel. He kept it on in the background.

Then he grabbed one of the chocolate bars he'd brought with him, snapped a bit off, and crouched down, feeding it to the baby.

It worked. He got silence.

When she'd finished it, he gave her another, then another.

73

Jaap watched as the hands hit one.

Only eight hours to go, he thought, staring at the white clock face.

He was standing in the main entrance hall of ICTY, hoping the plan he'd hatched with Saskia was going to work. It was desperate, putting their trust in Isovic's hands, but Jaap didn't see that they had any choice.

And time was running out, Jaap could almost feel it, each second bringing closer something he couldn't even bear to think about. Ronald had pushed the start of the trial back while he tried to convince Isovic to testify, but it was just about to get going now.

It seemed almost certain that Matkovic would be convicted, and then Nikolic would carry out his threat. And if that happened . . . Jaap wouldn't even let his mind go there; he needed to keep focused and fear made that difficult.

He found himself trying to bargain with a higher power he didn't believe in, promising anything as long as he got Floortje back alive.

The doors at the far end of the hall opened and Saskia stepped through, followed by Isovic, hands cuffed in front, being steered by a guard.

Timing was everything.

Their footsteps rang out as Jaap headed over to the

front desk, handing back his mistyped visitor's badge, accepting his gun back at the same time. He shoved it down the back of his jeans in preparation.

Behind him he heard Saskia cry out.

He turned. Saskia was doubled over screaming, the guard looking startled before moving towards her. Jaap started running just as Isovic lunged forward. The guard, sensing movement, turned just as Isovic hit him hard on the side of his head with his cuffed hands.

Even in the confusion Jaap could see Isovic knew what he was doing, the precision of the movement, the practised flow.

The guard slumped down on to the floor next to Saskia as Jaap sprinted back through the metal detector, the alarm bell splitting the air.

As he reached her he squatted quickly down by her body and grabbed the keys from the guard. He flicked them towards Isovic while he pretended to help Saskia, hoping no one had seen what he'd just done.

Seconds later he felt his gun slide out from his waistband and then something hard touch the back of his head.

He was no longer in control.

It was too late to back out now.

He could hear footsteps. Saskia wasn't screaming any more, she turned her head to face him. Jaap could see the desperation in her eyes, as if her screams had liberated the fear he knew she was wrestling with.

'Get up,' shouted Isovic, his voice only just audible over the alarm. 'Hands on back of head.'

Jaap did as he was told. Saskia mouthed *Find her* to him.

'Drop your weapon,' shouted a guard from somewhere off to Jaap's left.

'I will shoot him,' responded Isovic, moving Jaap towards the exit.

There were guards everywhere now; Jaap could even see one in front, who must have stepped outside for a break. He had his weapon aimed right at them.

'I will shoot,' shouted Isovic again, this time his voice taking on an urgency which left no doubt in anyone's mind that he was serious.

Not even Jaap's.

Has he played me? he thought as they moved forward, right up to the scanner.

In his peripheral vision Jaap could see a guard dropping on his knee to help Saskia, and then Isovic shoved him through the metal frame.

The pressure of the gun on the back of his head was intense, Isovic driving him on, fast.

He locked eyes with one of the guards standing by the entrance, a tall man with short black hair and no neck.

A curl of white plastic coiled out of his ear down into his shirt collar.

Jaap tried to show he didn't want any heroics; the last thing he needed was some guard getting trigger-happy.

Once guns started going off it would be over.

Twenty paces away now, and the guard still had his weapon up.

Don't be a hero, thought Jaap. *Not now.*

Isovic yelled again, the gun still pressing against Jaap's skull below his interlocked fingers.

Fifteen paces.

Fourteen.

Jaap tried to shake his head, catch the guard's eye, tell him to stand down.

Twelve, eleven. But the man was stock still, eyes trained on Isovic. Jaap's gaze zeroed in on the man's trigger finger.

Ten paces, nine.

The guard's arm relaxed and he lowered the gun, stepping aside.

Isovic stopped, shouted for him to drop it.

Jaap flicked his eyes to the ground, and the guard did as he was told, placing the gun on the floor.

'Back, move back,' said Isovic, and waited for compliance before they moved forward again, rushing past the guard and the gun on the floor, its barrel pointing back into the building.

Outside the fog hit their faces like a cold wet blanket.

A flag, Jaap couldn't work out the country, writhed on a high pole.

All they had to do now was find the car Saskia had parked.

If Isovic was still following the plan and hadn't decided to screw Jaap.

Isovic took the gun away from his head.

They turned left, skirting a grey metal fence, and came out on to Johan de Witlaan, where the traffic was building up, lunch rush hour getting going. Dodging cars they reached the central grass reservation, Jaap looking for Saskia's white Citroën.

She said she'd left it just down the road to the left, but

he couldn't see it. Using a break in the traffic, he ran, followed by Isovic, across the next lane. And then he spotted it, about a hundred metres away. He started sprinting, Isovic by his side.

They reached it – Jaap had fired the remote unlock a few feet away – and flung the doors open, the wail of sirens hitting Jaap's ears as he jammed the key into the slot and slammed his foot down.

'You outrun the police in this?' asked Isovic, breathless.

Jaap skidded the car out into traffic and accelerated, his hands tight on the wheel. He glanced at the rear-view mirror, adjusting it so he could watch the flashing lights appearing in the distance behind them.

'I don't know,' he said, spinning the wheel left to avoid a motorbike up ahead, 'but you'd better hope so.'

74

'Let's hope this place hasn't got a crazed painter in it,' said Kees as he slowed the car down.

It was another agricultural building, not dissimilar to the first, but it looked in worse condition, the wood weathered and pitted. This time a whole combine harvester was parked outside, rust rupturing the paintwork, and a row of water butts stood sentinel along one side of the structure. Tanya was brushing mud off her jeans in the seat next to him, the sound just audible over the engine. She'd been silent all the way, ever since she'd acted all weird at the estate agent's. But then he had seen she'd been throwing up in the mud, so he figured she wasn't feeling too good.

I hope it's not catching, he thought as he parked the car up on a verge and they both got out. *Now that we've shared fluids.*

He could hear ticking from the bonnet. Trailing his hand on the metal as he walked round the front of the vehicle he could feel its warmth – for a second he found it comforting.

Things had got complicated, but despite the fact that they'd slept together he knew she wasn't going to be able to drop her investigation, even if she wanted to.

And then, outside the estate agent's, she'd handed him a bit of paper with a name written neatly across the centre, and an address.

The name was not one he recognized, but after it she'd written, 'Paul?' When he'd tried to ask her about it she'd refused to talk.

Was she doing this because they'd slept together? Because she liked him? Or was it a way to end anything before it'd even started? Pay him off.

And one thing he'd not really even considered in all of this was Jaap.

If she tells Jaap what we did . . . The thought trailed off. It wasn't even worth thinking about.

The only chance he had was making sure that he was never linked with Paul.

So he had to get to the address and find out if Tanya's lead was right.

The question is, what if it is Paul? he thought. *What do I do then?*

They were walking down a track, a small ditch with flowing water hugging the left-hand side, the soft trickle as it filtered through the grass overhang from the verges like something from a New Age relaxation track.

'Same again?' Tanya said in a hushed voice when they were about fifty metres away.

'Why's it always me that has to go round the back? And anyway, it looks like the other place; I don't reckon there'll be another way in or out.'

She looked at him – he figured she wasn't able to tell if he was joking or not. He wasn't sure himself.

'Okay, *I'll* go round the back,' she said, and she split off to the left before Kees could say anything.

He watched as she jumped the ditch and skirted the field. There were sheep dotted around, heads down. One raised its head to look at Tanya as she passed about five metres from it. Kees could see its lower jaw moving, a swaying, circular motion.

He was struck by the thought that the woman walking away from him into the fog meant a lot to him.

Meant more than he'd realized.

And yet she was seeing another man, and Kees had an illness which in all likelihood was going to kill him, or at the very least leave him unable to do the most basic things for himself.

There'd probably be a stage when he couldn't even wipe his own ass.

He wasn't sure he should get Tanya involved in that. He wasn't sure she'd be up for it either.

Not unless she had a hidden kinky side, which given what he knew she'd been through with her foster father, he thought unlikely.

How did everything get so fucked? he wondered as Tanya disappeared around the back of the building.

The day he'd had the first test results back he'd been off shift, and he'd sat around for ages, staring at the bit of paper.

Then he'd screwed it up into a ball and chucked it in the bin.

Then he'd taken it out of the bin and uncrumpled it, ripped it into tiny pieces, emptied them into an ashtray and torched the lot with a lighter.

He'd left the flat, walking fast, not really seeing what was around him, too caught up in images of his future.

Or what was left of it.

He'd been going to the meetings Jaap had told him to

and had been working at it. He'd done the whole confessional thing – Hi-I'm-Kees-and-I'm-a-drug-addict – sat and listened to the other people in the circle, put on a contrite face when required, murmured supportive noises at the right moments and generally behaved like a model citizen trying to get his life back on track.

Fifty-seven days he'd reached, not a bad number for a first attempt. But day fifty-eight had been when the letter arrived, and after hours of walking he'd found himself back at his flat with enough coke to pay the Swiss finishing school fees of a South American drug baron's daughter.

And it didn't take long after that for things to really get out of control.

He knew he should never have accepted the offer of credit, knew that there would be some kind of payback required, but had gone ahead and said yes anyway. The way he felt in those days and weeks after the diagnosis – he even hated the very word – wasn't conducive to long-term thinking.

So he needed to put aside thoughts of Tanya. She was with Jaap for a start, and Kees didn't have a future he could offer her.

Fuck! I could use a line right now, he thought.

His phone buzzed a message, Tanya saying there was no exit at the back and that she was coming back.

He looked over at the building. Nothing was moving anywhere. He couldn't hear a sound. Wherever Jaap's kid was, it wasn't here. He felt thirsty and headed back to the car, hoping there'd be an unopened bottle of something. Anything.

He cranked open the door and was rummaging around under the front seat when he heard Tanya's footsteps behind him. Just as she reached him the radio shot out some static. Kees automatically put his hand out and turned the volume up.

'. . . officer kidnapped at the ICTY. Last seen proceeding with the suspect north out of Den Haag in a white Citroën, licence 9JCW76. All units in the area report in.'

Kees turned to look at Tanya; her face said what he was thinking.

'You think it's . . .?' she said.

He pulled out his phone, dialled Jaap. It kept ringing out to voicemail.

He called the station over the radio.

'Who's the kidnapped officer?'

While waiting for an answer he looked over to the field of sheep again, this time noticing that one of them was lying on its back, four feet in the air like an upturned footstool.

'Inspector Jaap Rykel,' came the response.

Kees sat back and turned his head to Tanya.

They just looked at each other.

75

Jaap couldn't believe they'd made it out of Den Haag without being caught.

But the small size of the car had proved useful, able to nip through gaps the larger police cruisers hadn't. And the fog had helped.

Now they'd switched. He and Isovic had dumped the car and boosted another, and although it probably only gave them a half-hour advantage – it wouldn't take the police long to work out what they'd done – thirty minutes was better than nothing.

Now he didn't need to concentrate so much on driving and had blocked out all thoughts of what he'd just done, he was able to try and get more from Isovic.

'So now I've got you out I think you need to start talking. This person you're taking me to, how come he knows where Nikolic is?'

'He just does.'

'Why did you change your mind about testifying against Matkovic? You said he killed your son; don't you want to see him punished?'

Isovic didn't answer at first, staring out of the side window at the fog.

'Is sitting in warm cell for the rest of life punishment? Food three times a day? Medical care? Is that punishment?'

Jaap was still trying to work out what was going on.

Seeing the look in Isovic's eyes back in the cell when he'd told him about the death of his son had sparked something off.

A truck's headlights zoomed out of the fog ahead of them, the light blinding. The car rocked sideways as the truck sped past. Something was pooling in Jaap's stomach.

He figured, based on some thoughts which were going on, that it was dread.

'We heard rumours that they were coming to our village. But we had nowhere to go. And then one day we saw them coming. They had army jeeps, and they were driving up the main road towards us. It was in the evening – they'd arrive in about two hours, maybe less – so we had big decision. We didn't have many weapons, so we decide to move out, further up the mountain. Maybe they turn up, see no one and leave.'

'And this was Matkovic who was coming?' said Jaap, his fears being confirmed. The flashes he'd had earlier, the ones which had stayed out of reach, suddenly came together.

He knew what was going on, which made his breaking Isovic out even worse than it already was.

'Yes, him and his men. We only find out later who he was when he . . . when he kill my son. We got women and children together and we leave, into the night, higher up the mountain. But they follow us.'

Isovic stopped talking, his story broken off. But it didn't take a genius to work out what happened next.

And Jaap now knew what that had led to, what had pushed Isovic to the Netherlands, at first to testify against

Matkovic and then to change his mind and try and secure his release.

He glanced across at Isovic, catching his profile.

Would he be capable of that? he thought as he flicked his eyes back to the road.

There was a question he needed to ask Isovic, but if he did he risked showing his hand; if Isovic knew what Jaap thought he'd worked out – that Isovic and maybe his friend had been responsible for the headless bodies – then he'd most likely duck out at the first opportunity.

Being held for contempt of court was one thing, multiple murder was quite another.

Red brake lights flared in the fog ahead. Jaap slowed down, the high whine of the motor dropping as he did so. He checked the route on Saskia's phone – they'd switched back at ICTY – but he knew he couldn't risk keeping it live for much longer. If someone reviewed the CCTV images, which they were undoubtedly doing by now, there was a chance they would have worked out he wasn't exactly the classic kidnap victim.

From there it was still a couple of steps to realizing that Saskia had been involved and thinking of tracking her phone, but he needed to stay ahead, not get caught out on something stupid.

He also needed to be reachable, if Tanya and Kees found something he had to know.

Saskia should have called them by now, he thought. Meaning that they had nothing to report; they hadn't found Floortje, otherwise they'd have called him. He wondered how many addresses they were having to search.

A few minutes later Jaap pulled up at the end of a road

in Amstelveen, Amsterdam's prosperous southern neighbour. The fog was thinning slightly, allowing the trees on either side of the residential street to narrow into the distance. He killed the engine, letting his ears adjust to the silence.

He was relying on the word of a grief-stricken man. A man who'd let that same grief turn him into a killer, someone capable of cutting other human beings' heads off.

And he was about to meet his partner.

76

The fog was so thick it was like dusk.

Tanya flicked down the rear-view mirror; a car behind was giving her the full-beam treatment.

It'd only taken them three minutes to establish the building was clear, all the while her brain absorbing the news of Jaap's kidnap.

She'd been trying to work out what had gone wrong, and her working theory was that Nikolic had somehow got into the ICTY and taken Jaap, maybe to further pressure Saskia into losing the trial. But she didn't know how that could have happened.

How could Nikolic have known where to find him? And why would he, already having got Floortje, risk a move like that just to get Jaap?

Too many questions for which she couldn't get answers, and time was running out.

So she'd made the decision to head back into town; they needed to increase the speed they were covering the remaining buildings and the only way to do that was to split up. For that Kees would need a car.

'Fuck,' said Kees leaning forward to look in the wing mirror. 'What's wrong with this guy?'

'Guess he doesn't know we're cops,' said Tanya, torn between slowing down just to really piss the driver behind off and the need to get on with the search.

'Tell you what,' said Kees reaching into the glove compartment.

Tanya thought he'd go for the detachable roof light, but he left that and fished out a torch. He flipped it over, whacked the beam on and shone it over his shoulder.

'Careful you don't make him crash,' said Tanya, glancing in the rear-view again.

'How'd you like that, you fucker?' whispered Kees as he jiggled the torch around.

The car eventually flicked its beams off full.

Kees put the torch away.

'I must be getting wise in my old age,' he said. 'There was a time I'd've just waved my gun around.'

Tanya knew he was trying to draw her out, but she just couldn't raise the energy to respond. He'd changed since they'd slept together, and she wasn't sure she liked that.

Which only meant her earlier thoughts about rough treatment probably held true, and that was definitely not something she wanted to think about right now.

'I'm sure he's okay,' said Kees after a while. 'Jaap can take care of himself, you know? Shit, what with all that Eastern stuff he can probably meditate his way out of whatever he's got himself into.'

'I . . . There's something you should know,' said Tanya, her throat and mouth drying out, the pit of her stomach dropping away from her. 'About Jaap. I—'

'You're fucking him, right?'

Tanya kept her eyes on the road, the central line bobbing up and down.

'No big surprise. Everyone knows,' continued Kees when she didn't say anything.

'Really?'

'Yeah, there've been rumours going round the station for months. Did you think people didn't know?'

She had. And she'd been stupid to. She saw that now.

'So when we . . .' She couldn't bring herself to say it. 'You knew?'

'Uhh . . . look, about that,' he said, suddenly interested in something outside his side window.

'It's all right, let's not say anything,' she said, clicking the car radio on, twisting the dial to find something. Anything.

'. . . .and the so-called Twitter killer looks to still be at large. Sources close to the police aren't giving much away, though the unofficial word here is that they may soon be making an arrest. But I've just received unverified reports, and I must stress they are unverified at this stage, that the inspector in charge of the investigation has been involved in some kind of incident at the ICTY in Den Haag. This is Inspector Jaap Rykel, who held the disastrous press conference earlier today claiming he'd found the killer just as another body was discovered. I've not been able find out any precise details as of yet – the police are staying tight-lipped at present – but one unofficial report suggests the stress of the failure of his investigation may have some bearing on this troubling incident.'

'Thank you, Annette. Our reporter there, Annette Groot, in Amsterdam. And now we're going to our weekly agricultural show, where a special investigation into the genetic lineage of the Friesland cow is unravelled, with surprising results.'

'I've been worried about that,' said Kees, reaching out and snapping the radio off.

'What?'

'The Friesland cow.'

'Yeah. Keeps me up at night.'

By the time they made it to the station, traffic had intensified. Tanya dropped Kees off at the front after they'd split up the remaining properties. The plan was to scope them out, see if there were any signs that Floortje was being held.

'If you think you've found her give me a call; don't go in alone unless you have to.'

'Same goes for you,' he said as he turned, heading down to the carpool.

Now she was here she suddenly got the urge to go in and tell Smit what was going on. She checked the dashboard, just over five hours to the deadline. That gave them just enough time to get to all the properties.

She sat there for a few moments, fingers drumming on the tacky steering wheel, before jamming the indicator on and pulling out.

The best thing she could do for Jaap was to find his daughter.

Find her before Nikolic followed through with his threat.

Which, having read his file, she had no doubt he'd do.

77

Jaap watched as Isovic walked up the front steps to the building and pressed the buzzer.

The fog had seemed to intensify, absorbing the trees and buildings into its depthless grey mass, digesting them so only parts remained.

He was taking an enormous risk: all Isovic would have to do once inside was duck out the back, and Jaap would have lost him, and his friend. Or he could go inside with him, and be in a room with two killers. Either way, the risk was he'd end up losing Floortje.

It had been a rough year. Normally people had the months of pregnancy to get used to the idea of being a parent, but Jaap had gone from not knowing to knowing with a few short words from Saskia. He'd also had his life saved by Kees, working one of the hardest cases of his life, which had ended with his sister's death.

For a moment, when Saskia had told him, he'd wondered if it was really true. Then when he looked down at the baby he knew it was. Despite the freshly boiled skin, the wrinkles, the closed eyes and open toothless mouth, he recognized something familiar, something he looked at every morning.

Up ahead Isovic turned round and gave the thumbs up to Jaap.

Minutes later Jaap was sitting in a tiny one-room flat

with Isovic, a man he'd introduced as Krilic sitting on a dark sofa, and a small electric heater, which was doing its thing. An unmade bed took up a third of the room. An old-fashioned TV with a curved screen perched on a side table, and two wooden-framed chairs and a white plastic kettle plugged into the wall completed the ensemble.

Krilic was older than Jaap had expected, with grey hair and bony cheeks, below which shadows hung. He was holding a pea-green mug in both his hands, the surface crackle-glazed, and had a look in his eyes which Jaap had seen many times before.

Jaap had no doubt in his mind now that these two were responsible for the beheadings. Which meant he was in a room with two cold-blooded killers, and no one knew where he was.

'Your daughter,' said Krilic, after Jaap had explained what had happened. 'I might be able to help.'

His Dutch was better than Isovic's, fluent but with an accent.

The words were what Jaap had wanted to hear.

'But we need something in return.'

Those less so. Jaap shifted his weight.

'I got Isovic out, that was the deal I made with him,' said Jaap, keeping his eyes locked on Krilic. 'He said you'd be able to help me find my daughter.'

'Deal's changed,' said Krilic, shrugging. 'I know where Nikolic is, but first you have to do something for me.'

It struck Jaap that whereas Isovic had helped kill for a purpose – revenge – Krilic looked like he'd tipped over into a far scarier reason; he'd grown to love killing.

The window behind Krilic was covered in condensation, drips running in vertical channels.

'What?'

'I have to visit Matkovic, in his cell. Alone.'

'I've just busted this guy out of there,' said Jaap, pointing to Isovic. 'What makes you think I can get *you* in? Pretty soon they'll realize I wasn't being held hostage. I've probably got all of my colleagues out looking for me already. So there's no way I can get you in there.'

Krilic held his gaze for a few moments, then brought the mug to his mouth, still not breaking eye contact.

'Then there's no way I can tell you where Nikolic is.' He took a breathed-in slurp, like the liquid was too hot.

Jaap wondered if he could beat it out of him, but even if he managed to put Isovic out of action before going to work on Krilic, something in the man's eyes told him he wouldn't be easy to break.

His muscles must have tightened, or Krilic had read some other sign. He shook his head.

'That won't work,' he said.

Jaap hated violence. He'd realized several years ago that it was this, in part, which had drawn him to being a cop. He needed to make sure it didn't go unpunished. But now with less than five hours to go until Nikolic killed his daughter he was starting to lose a sense of self.

He nodded his head, forced himself to relax. Krilic smiled.

The movement was quick, so quick that Krilic was taken off guard, the mug smashing against the wall as Jaap slammed his body forward, twisting Krilic's torso so he could get him in a full headlock, his face squashed up against the window.

'Don't,' Jaap shouted as Isovic moved behind him. He pulled Krilic, spinning him round and forcing him to his knees.

Isovic was five feet away, but he had stopped, his eyes flicking back and forth between them, trying to read the situation.

Jaap could smell Krilic, damp clothes and fermented sweat, and felt the grease of his skin against his own. He'd made the wrong move, he knew that even as he was going for Krilic. He felt like he was losing control.

'Where is Nikolic?'

Krilic had his mouth clamped shut, the muscles in his jaws like snakes under his skin.

Jaap raised the arm hooked around his neck, forcing Krilic's head up and back.

'Where is he?' he asked. He found his teeth were locked together, lips pulled taut, making his voice hiss.

Nothing. No movement. No answer.

Stupid, he thought. *Really, really stupid.*

He'd read Krilic right the first time – he was not someone you could break easily – and yet he'd still gone down the road which lead to nowhere. The hexagram had warned of deadlock. He'd not heeded it.

Isovic was still watching them. He'd not moved, and for a moment Jaap saw all three of them staying in position for ever, locked in some stupid battle while the world went on around them.

While Nikolic killed his daughter.

'Okay,' he said, forcing himself to talk calmly. 'I'm going to release you. Then we can talk about this.'

Krilic nodded with what little room he had, and Jaap loosened his grip. Half a second later Krilic sank his teeth into Jaap's forearm, going for the kill. Jaap kicked out, hitting Krilic's shin, his mouth opened in a cry, allowing Jaap to break free.

He'd taken his eyes off Isovic. Which, he realized when he glanced back up, was a mistake.

Isovic had moved over to the right, and now had something in his hand.

To Jaap it looked very much like a gun.

Krilic got up, grinned at Jaap, a flash of white teeth coated with blood, then stepped forward. Jaap tried to block the blow, but Krilic saw his move and switched up.

Pain exploded on Jaap's cheekbone and nose.

Then, as the room whirlpooled, everything went dark and the pain stopped.

Saskia felt like a passenger in her own body.

She shifted in her seat. Or her body did and she observed it; observed the way the muscles, tendons and bone all worked together, thousands of minute, delicate interactions which she normally wasn't aware of.

Ronald had been on fire today, presenting all the evidence they had in such a way that left little doubt as to Matkovic's guilt. Isovic's absence had brought something out in him, a kind of deep primeval power with which he was holding the court spellbound.

And there'd been a time recently when she'd started to think about him; he wasn't with anyone and neither was she.

But all that was gone now, those thoughts seeming so facile, pointless.

Her daughter was gone.

Nothing else mattered.

So she sat there, watched as all the work she'd put in over the last few months, the careful accumulation of evidence, the complicated web of information she'd spun to make sure the man sitting less than ten metres away from her would get what he deserved, gradually inched her closer to her worst fear.

It was hours since Jaap had left, and she'd not heard anything. She'd felt her phone buzz in her pocket a million times, but each time she'd checked had found she must have imagined it, like the pain amputees often felt in missing limbs.

And now it was all over, the judge about to deliver the verdict.

Suddenly there was no air in the room. She felt panicked and looked around, but nobody else seemed to have noticed, all seemingly breathing as normal.

'The court,' said the judge, having gone through the legal preamble, 'finds Bojan Matkovic to be guilty of the charges laid against him. Sentencing will occur at a later date.'

79

Kees didn't know if it had been intentional on Tanya's part or not, but when they'd divided the addresses they were going to check he'd got one very close to the address she'd given him earlier on the scrap of paper.

It would only take a matter of minutes to get there.

He was at a junction; he could go left or right.

He knew he should be moving on to the next property, looking for Floortje, but he found his hands spinning the wheel. Right.

Two minutes later he stopped the car, parked and walked to the address on J. F. van Hengelstraat. The north side of the street consisted of a row of brick houses with large windows on the second and third floors.

The one he needed had been converted into flats. He checked the number and pressed the buzzer, not expecting anything to happen.

But even over the crackly intercom he recognized the voice he'd heard many times on the phone.

It was, without question, Paul.

80

Tanya was just pulling away from building number four on her list, a property just outside Leiden, when her phone went off.

The road was quiet so she flipped on the hazard lights, stopped the car and reached into her pocket, hoping it was Kees saying he'd found Floortje. But the screen said Jaap.

'Jaap, where are—'

'Tanya?' The voice at the other end was strained, and the reception was bad. It took a few moments for Tanya to place it.

'Saskia?'

'Have you heard from Jaap?'

'No . . . Where are you?'

'Listen, he's got my phone, but I've been trying to call it and he's not answering.'

'Saskia, I've got bad news. Jaap's been kidnapped and—'

'No, that was planned. He had a lead. Isovic said he knew someone who could help him find Nikolic.'

Tanya took a moment to absorb what Saskia was telling her.

'Okay, so where is he now?'

'That's the thing. He took my phone so we could keep in contact – he didn't want anyone tracking his phone. But I keep calling him on it and he's not answering.'

'Text me the number,' said Tanya.

'The thing is, Matkovic has been convicted, and I don't know what to do, and—'

Tanya checked the time on the dashboard, almost expecting to see the numbers flying by.

'When will it be announced?'

'What?'

'The conviction?'

'They're going to kill Floortje . . .'

'We're going to find her. Hang up and text me that number.'

The text came in a few seconds later.

She tried the number but got nothing.

Where is he? she thought as she put her phone away and started the car, the fog making the windows look like frosted glass.

Without speaking to him the only thing she could do was continue. She checked the address of the next property on her list.

It was a boathouse on the Braassemermeer, a lake halfway between Amsterdam and Leiden, and, according to her satnav, was pretty close by.

If that didn't yield anything then she had one more place to try.

And if she struck out there, and Kees did the same, then she didn't know what else they could do.

I don't think Jaap will cope if Floortje dies, she thought as she neared the address, fields stretching off to her right and a narrow strip of water on her left. She pulled out the torch Kees had used earlier and trained it on the far bank as she drove.

A heron perched on the grass, stark grey and white against the dark green trees, feathers hanging off its chin like a beard, its reflection choppy on the water's dark surface.

According to the sat nav the trees obscured the Braassemermeer itself. She slowed down, trying to work out where the boathouse would be. A car was cruising towards her. She flipped off the torch before it passed so as not to dazzle the driver.

Five minutes later she realized she must have gone past it – she'd now reached a town called Rijnsaterwoude – so she swung the car round and prepared to look again. Darkness surrounded her. The sun wasn't due to set for another hour or so, but the fog was so dense it might already have for all she could tell. She could only see what was directly in her headlights, and she felt totally alone.

Something had been opening up inside her since she'd found out Staal's house was for sale – an enormous space, an emptiness which had gradually filled with anger.

She had to help find Floortje, of course she did. But she also knew that time was running out for her to deal with her past, that if she was ever to be free she had to act before her foster father left tomorrow.

She'd called the cab company and discovered he was being picked up from his address really early the next morning. She didn't have long before he was gone for ever.

The thought churned her anger more. She could feel it – a kind of cold heat, an acid burning.

I could go there now, she thought. *Who'd know?*

She was passing the heron again when she saw something she'd not noticed the first time round. It was a small track which led over a flat wooden bridge to the far bank and then off into the fir trees. She drove past, stopped the car, and was just getting out when static burst from the police radio. She reached back into the car and turned up the volume, listened as a call was put out to detain Inspector Jaap Rykel on suspicion of kidnapping.

Top priority, the voice was saying as she clicked the radio off.

She hesitated for a moment, then headed towards the bridge.

The wood sounded hollow as she walked over it, and then she was in the trees, a slight wind rustling the needles together. The path, more mud, curved round and made it out the other side of the trees, giving a view of the large expanse of the Braassemermeer, where the fog was thinner.

The track carried on along the shoreline, and less than twenty metres away was a wooden boathouse with a low jetty projecting out over the water, a cluster of small boats moored along one side.

Stark light shone from two windows.

Then she heard it. The unmistakable cry of a baby.

Ducking back into the trees she pulled out her phone and her gun, and stared at them both for a second.

She hit dial, but nothing happened.

No signal.

81

Kees had pretended to be a falafel delivery guy trying to reach another of the flats, which, he said, had a broken buzzer.

Paul's flat was at the back of the building, off a corridor with five other doors. The place wasn't exactly opulent; only one overhead light was actually working, and Kees could hear the sounds of a TV spilling into the space from more than one flat.

It's like a retirement home, he thought.

Paul's door was at the far end, and had a peephole. Kees pressed the buzzer and turned towards the corridor as if looking at something, trying to hide his face. Not that Paul had anywhere to run, but he didn't feel up to breaking down the door.

As it opened Kees could see that even if there was an escape route it wouldn't have mattered.

The man in front of him was in a wheelchair.

He nodded at Kees, wheeled himself back and pirouetted round with surprising grace. Kees followed him into the flat, his heart thudding. Over the last few months he'd thought about this meeting many times, thought about what he'd do to Paul.

'How did you find me?'

The room was neat, a low computer desk on one wall, and filing cabinets along another. It looked more like an office than a home. The air was stuffy, too warm, too lived in.

'Does it matter?'

'Not really,' said Paul. He sat there looking at Kees, something going on with his face. It took Kees a moment or two to work out it was a kind of smile.

A chair scraped across the floor in the flat above, finally stopping just above Kees.

'Are you doing this to other people?'

'A few.' He shrugged, pointing to the cabinets, the smile more pronounced now. 'I deal in information. And before you get any ideas you've got to know that everything is duplicated. If I die then the whole lot gets released. It's funny, there seem to be a lot of people concerned for my well-being these days. And before you ask, yes, the woman had to go.'

'Why?'

'She'd started to get ideas of her own.'

'And why the police jacket?'

Paul laughed.

'Oh that?' he said once he'd stopped. 'That was just a bit of fun.'

Kees looked at him. He was trying to hold back a thought, but it broke through.

This is what I'll end up like.

It set something off in his brain, and his stomach came to life, like the two were linked, like the two were actually one.

He felt like he'd been turned inside out.

'Why me?' he managed to say after a few moments, wondering if he was going to be sick. Paul was observing him, his eyes watery and full of something Kees couldn't place. Hate? Disgust? Or just a coldness which reached right down into the man's lack of soul.

'Why not? Your dealer owed me a favour, told me he had a cop on his list of clients.'

'So you're blackmailing him as well?'

'Not at all. I've been paying him for everything you've taken.'

'You've been paying *him*?'

He reached over to one of the cabinets, pulled open a drawer, his fingers skipping over a row of files. He reached the one he wanted and pulled it out, offered it to Kees.

'Here's every gram that's gone up your nose – you can see the transaction amounts, dates. I simply pass these on and get reimbursed. Some of the photos you've seen before of course.'

Kees didn't move to take it, he didn't doubt what was there. Beyond the offered file he could see the poke of the man's legs; just bones in a tracksuit, wasted muscle.

'So what, you then sell on the information you get from me?' he asked, trying to fight down the feeling he had rushing up at him from his stomach.

I'm going to be like him, he thought. *I'm going to be a cripple.*

'Exactly,' said Paul. 'But the best part is there's a plan for you. Someone's been very interested in what you've been up to, in your activities. A benefactor, let's say. He's actually been the one giving me the money to pay your bills. You belong to him now. He'll be contacting you, I'm sure.'

The room swayed drastically to the left, but it only

seemed to affect Kees; Paul was still in his wheelchair. Kees reached out and put his hand against the wall. When the room had righted he turned and headed for the door.

He no longer cared what Paul did.

Losing his career seemed so insignificant now.

Now that he'd finally allowed himself to acknowledge what his future was going to be like.

As he stepped into the corridor he was sure he could hear Paul laughing.

82

Sound came back first.

Jaap could hear them talking but he couldn't make out the words.

It took him a few moments to work out why. It wasn't anything to do with his hearing, or his brain; they were talking in a language he didn't understand.

Feeling came back second in the form of pain, his nose and cheekbone throbbing. From his position he figured he was slumped on the floor, head on the carpet. He opened his left eye, slowly, trying not to give away that he was conscious. All he could see was some dark fabric, probably the back of the sofa Krilic had been sitting on when he'd entered the room.

How long ago was that? he wondered, trying to work out if his hands had been tied.

They had.

Behind his back.

He listened to the voices, mainly Krilic's, Isovic contributing only when it seemed required. There was little doubt as to who was in charge.

Then there was movement, the sound of keys being scraped off a solid surface, and something heavier – Jaap pictured the gun Isovic had been brandishing earlier – and finally the slamming of a door, the voices instantly muffled before receding.

His brain was still slow, and there was something about the gun which he just wasn't getting. He shifted position then realized what it was; his own wasn't in its holster. He was lying on his left side and he'd be able to feel it if it was.

Then he remembered he'd not taken it back from Isovic after they'd left ICTY. He'd been too busy driving, trying to avoid the police.

He should be able to feel Saskia's phone as well, but couldn't.

Realization hit him. He'd put it in the car-door pocket when he'd been driving and left it there when he'd followed Isovic inside.

He struggled into an upright position, hampered by his bound hands, then stood up, scanning the room. Whatever was binding his wrists was thin, he decided after a few moments of exploration, so at least it wasn't cuffs. He might be able to cut through, but there wasn't anything he could see that would be immediately useful.

I've got to get after them, he thought. *Now.*

Looking round again his eyes fell on the TV.

Two strides and he was in front of it.

One hard kick and it was on the floor, but the screen remained intact. He tried kicking the glass. All he got was more pain.

He moved the small side table the TV had been on in front of the screen, pushing it with his foot. Once he'd lined up the corner of the table with the screen he gave another kick.

The reward was a few shards of glass.

He kicked the table away and sat down on the floor, back to the TV, his hands searching for the shard he'd singled out, his fingers probing the carpet like a hungry spider.

Once in his hand, he could feel sharp edges running along his palm and the insides of his fingers, he tried to manipulate it round to connect with the binding.

His breathing was heavy now. He was battling panic, knowing that every second spent here and not going after Krilic was a second of Floortje's life running out.

Getting the shard into position was proving difficult, and he had to twist it several times, nicking skin, before he thought it was in position, between his two palms, pointing up at his wrists. He tried a sawing motion, but that didn't seem to achieve anything other than a cut in his hand.

Next he tried shifting the angle, trying to get the point of the shard on the inside of whatever the binding was, then putting pressure against it, hoping it would slice through.

The glass broke, he felt a bit of it slide into a wrist, he wasn't sure which one.

Blood oozed, slick and sticky at the same time. Pain was shooting up his arm, he wasn't sure he could feel his hand.

He grasped the shard with his left and tried again, willing the glass to stay intact.

This time it worked.

Neither of his hands looked like his own, both glistening with blood. Glass poked out of his right wrist. He watched as his drenched fingers gripped the end of it and gently pulled it out, the volume of blood rushing from the wound increasing the further out it came.

He dropped the glass on the floor, clamped his left hand over his wrist and made for the door, trying to work out how long it'd been since Krilic and Isovic had left.

He listened for footsteps in the stairwell, but couldn't hear any, so he ran down, his head starting to whirlpool again. He didn't know if it was an after-effect of the punch, or the loss of blood, or both.

A trail of dark fluid spooled out behind him.

Outside it was getting dark.

Which meant he was really running out of time.

Every second he wasted put Floortje in more danger.

He checked for the car they'd switched to once they'd ditched Saskia's Citroën but it was gone. They must have taken the keys off him while he was knocked out.

He put his left hand on to a car bonnet to steady himself, but the blood starting to pulse out of his wrist again. He slumped down, back against the car's front wheel, and re-clamped his hand over the wound.

A couple were walking towards him. They looked Algerian, the man thin, the woman less so. They saw the blood on his hands – Jaap saw alarm flare in their eyes – and started giving him a wide berth.

'Police. I need your phone,' said Jaap, fumbling for his ID, his right hand definitely not working the way it should. The couple hurried on, eyes averted.

He tried to get up, struggling to his knees, then standing, one leg at a time.

How hard did he hit me? he wondered as everything swayed, *or is it that I'm losing too much blood?*

'Hey, you all right?' came a man's voice from behind him.

Jaap tried to turn, tried to say that he needed help, that time was running out.

His legs dissolved.

All he could think about was Floortje.

The ground zoomed up at him, fast.

83

Tanya got a signal way back up the road.

But she couldn't get hold of Jaap, the phone just kept ringing out to voicemail. On the fourth go she left a message explaining where she was.

She hung up and wondered what she should do.

There was less than an hour until the conviction was announced. She needed to make a decision. She could go in on her own, but the chances were Floortje might get hurt – or worse – if things went bad. And despite all this, her mind kept swerving back to Staal, a sickness pooling in her stomach.

Maybe Saskia has been in contact with Jaap, she thought.

She called and Saskia picked up, her voice frantic.

'Jaap?'

'Saksia, it's Tanya. I really need to speak to Jaap – do you know where he is?'

'What is it, have you found her?'

Tanya thought for a moment, scenarios running through her mind. The rule book was clear; civilians should not be involved in cases. But she didn't know what the rule book said about kidnapped babies.

'I think I might, so I really need to tell Jaap.'

'Where are you? Have you seen her? Is she—'

'Look, I know this is tough, but the best thing we can do right now is to get Jaap here.'

'He's due to call me any minute now. Tell me and I'll let him know.'

Tanya thought for a moment. She didn't want to tell Saskia the details, but she also wanted to get back to watch the boathouse, and there was no reception there.

'Okay,' she said, and gave Saskia the address. 'You wait where you are, we'll let you know as soon as we've got her.'

One she'd hung up and headed back over the wooden bridge, the uneven planks slippery underfoot, she couldn't help feeling she'd made a mistake.

84

The siren was really starting to bug Jaap.

He wished it would stop, but it kept repeating its cycle – up and down, up and down. Then he felt a hand on his shoulder, shaking him gently. Reluctantly he opened his eyes. It seemed to require a huge amount of strength, and it took him a few seconds before his brain kicked in; Floortje, the cut on his wrist, losing Krilic and Isovic.

A second later he worked out where he was.

'Take it easy,' said the paramedic sitting by his shoulder, his right arm braced up against the side of the ambulance. 'We'll be there in a few minutes.'

'How long has it been?' said Jaap, trying to sit up, his head spinning so much he had to drop back against the stretcher. A clear IV bag hovered above his head, the tube snaking down into his arm like an alien parasite.

For a moment Jaap pictured a goldfish in the bag.

'We got a call eleven minutes ago, and we picked you up –' he glanced at his watch '– about three minutes back. Not bad really.'

Not much time lost then, thought Jaap.

He'd been worried he'd been out for longer, that he might already be too late. Moving his arm up he could see the bandages, the rough white fabric blooming with blood.

'I've got to go. Can you stop the ambulance?'

'You've just lost a bucket load of blood, and it looks like you might still have some glass in your wrist,' said the paramedic. 'The only place you're going is the hospital.'

'I've got a situation on my—'

'Yeah? I kind of wondered if you'd done it yourself. Then I noticed the tie marks on your wrist, figured you weren't trying to kill yourself after all.'

'I need to get moving.'

'Hey, I know. Don't worry. I found your ID and I've let your colleagues know, so I guess they can take care of whatever you're working on. Your case.'

'You gave them my name?'

'Name and rank. They seemed pleased to hear you were okay, especially some guy called Smit? Said he'd been looking for you, was worried about where you were. He said someone'll be waiting for you at the hospital.'

They know, thought Jaap. *They've worked out I helped Isovic escape.*

Another thought came to him just as the ambulance slowed down and hung a right.

Maybe I should tell Smit, get more people working on finding Floortje.

'Have you got a phone?'

'Someone you want me to call?'

'There's someone I need to speak to. It's urgent.'

The paramedic looked at Jaap for a moment, before fishing in his pocket. Jaap sat up, his head spinning, but less than previously.

Jaap got put through to Roemers.

'Roemers, I need you to track a number for me.'

'Jesus, Jaap,' whispered Roemers. 'Things are going apeshit

here, they're saying you abducted someone. Last I heard they've put a warrant out for you so I really should be hanging up at—'

'Listen, I'll explain later, but I really need your help now.'

'I'm not sure.'

'I'm about to give you a number. I need a location on it – can you just do that?'

Roemers paused; Jaap could hear him tapping keys.

Is he sending someone a message? he thought.

'Okay, go ahead,' said Roemers.

Jaap gave him the number of Saskia's phone and waited. The ambulance was speeding up again.

'How long before we get there?' he asked the paramedic.

'Less than two minutes now.'

'How's it coming?' Jaap asked Roemers.

'Got it,' came the reply. 'You want the location?'

'Course I fucking want it,' said Jaap. The paramedic glanced at him.

'Okay, okay. No need to snap. It's out towards Leiden somewhere, just getting the exact position now. It's moving.'

Jaap swung his legs off the stretcher, jammed the phone between shoulder and ear and yanked the IV tube out of his arm.

'Stop the ambulance,' he said.

'I really think you need to get to hospital. If you go out there you're going to risk all sorts—'

'If I don't there's an even bigger risk,' said Jaap as he lurched towards the back doors, trying to work the latch.

The paramedic banged on the partition separating them from the driver.

'Roemers, I need Tanya and Kees' numbers. Can you send them to the phone I'm calling you on?'

'Thirty seconds, they'll be with you.'

The ambulance stopped. Jaap hung up, got the door open just as the paramedic reached out his hand for the phone. Jaap leaped out on to the road, scanning the street. Houses lined both sides of the road. More importantly there were cars, plenty of them. He turned back.

'I need to take your phone, but I'll get it back to you.'

'You're kidding, right?'

Jaap shook his head. It felt light, floating up from his neck. He put a hand out to steady himself on the door. He thought of Hank, dropping into a coma.

'Actually it's a shit phone,' said the paramedic, shrugging. 'I reckon given the circumstances you can get the police to buy me a new one, like a serious upgrade? But my number,' Jaap heard him say as he turned away, scanning the cars, choosing one which looked fast enough. 'I'll want to keep my number.'

85

Neon streaked in the fog.

Which meant Kees was driving too fast.

But he couldn't think of anything else to do.

Seeing Paul in the wheelchair had flipped something inside him, unleashed the fear he'd been trying to strangle for months.

Now it was running riot, every cell in his body on fire, something trickling down his cheeks, his hands shaking on the wheel, legs vibrating, dancing to some unknown, erratic rhythm. He was having to tense his muscles hard just to keep his foot down on the accelerator.

The road was only half clear, and he kept having to swerve to avoid other cars, people going about their everyday lives, people who weren't afraid of the future. He glimpsed their faces as he flew past each car, and he hated each and every one of them.

He didn't know how long his phone had been ringing, but he gradually became aware of it. He let it go. It rang again. Then he slowed down, pulled off the motorway he had no memory of getting on, and looked at the phone, still ringing on its fourth attempt. A mobile number he didn't recognize.

He hit answer and heard Jaap's voice.

86

'. . . and I just spoke to Saskia. Apparently Tanya thinks she's found where Floortje is.'

Jaap was driving hard, one hand on the wheel, the other clasping his phone.

'Okay,' said Kees. 'I'm on my way. I reckon fifteen minutes.'

As Jaap hung up on Kees – who had sounded weird, but Jaap was so jacked up by adrenaline that the thought hadn't really registered – he dropped the phone on to the seat next to him and started slowing. His eyes kept glancing at the dashboard clock. Each time it moved he felt a jolt to the stomach.

He'd driven south out of Amstelveen and was now among fields. Not that he could see much, the fog was still thick. Or thicker.

If Tanya'd found Nikolic, Jaap didn't care about Krilic or Isovic. Roemers was still tracking them via Saskia's phone. He was sure they'd taken her car, and he could get someone to pick them up later.

He was only a few minutes away now, and despite the faintness which kept hitting him – the last wave had threatened to pass him out at the wheel – he was feeling a kernel of hope.

If Tanya'd found Floortje then he might just be in time.

The announcement would be making the news soon however, so he tuned the radio to a breaking-news channel.

Now he was on the south side of Braassemermeer, heading east towards where Saskia had said Tanya was. The landscape was flat, a ditch to his right. On the far side of the ditch trees hid the body of water which he knew must lie beyond. He was looking for a wooden bridge. Two white pinpricks appeared in the rear-view.

His phone went off, Roemers calling. He had the location of Saskia's phone.

'Give it to me,' said Jaap, watching as the pinpricks grew in size. 'It's on Zwetweg,' came Roemers' voice. 'The road that runs south of the Braassemermeer.'

Isovic and Krilic, he thought as he checked the mirror again. *They're going after Nikolic now.*

Up ahead he spotted a bridge with a car parked by it, an unmarked, he saw as he got closer.

Tanya.

He checked the rear-view again. If that was them he didn't want to lead them to Nikolic.

Have they followed me? he thought, trying to work out if that was possible, *or did they already know where Nikolic is.*

He should try and stop them.

But Nikolic had Floortje, and he didn't have time to lose.

He swung the wheel towards the bridge, accelerating hard.

87

Tanya'd heard the car coming and ducked back into the woods, still keeping an eye on the boathouse.

She was sure she'd heard a child crying, and was wrestling with herself, unable to decide if she should wait any longer or just storm the place now.

Her gun was gripped tight in her hand.

The car stopped before it got round the corner; she could just make out headlights through the trees.

Jaap must have got my message, she thought.

A few seconds after the engine died the lights flicked off.

She found herself dodging through the trees, body low to avoid the branches, a sense of relief that she wasn't going to have to go in by herself flowing through her.

But as she got closer she could see the figure getting out of the car was a woman.

Tanya ducked behind a tree, then peered round.

Despite the darkness, she could tell it was Saskia.

I told her to wait.

Tanya crept forward, whispering Saskia's name as loudly as she dared. Something snapped underfoot; Saskia's head jerked round. Tanya leaped forward and made a grab for her, clamping her hand over her mouth. She managed to cut off the scream, but not before it had torn open the night.

It was less than half a second, but Tanya reckoned it was long enough, and loud enough, to have alerted whoever was in the boathouse.

She pulled Saskia backwards into the trees, whispering in her ear, and got her to nod that she'd understood who she was before uncovering her mouth.

'Is she here?' said Saskia the second Tanya took her hand away.

'I think so, I'm just—'

'In that place?'

Tanya nodded. It was hard to make out the boathouse through the trees, vertical lines obscuring the view, but she thought she caught a glimpse of movement.

Saskia started forward. Tanya put a hand out, clasping her arm. Saksia shrugged it off and carried on, weaving through the trees. She didn't seem to care how much noise she was making. Tanya sprang after her, again grabbing her arm just as Saskia lowered a hand to scoop up a fallen branch, the wood twisted, knotted.

'We need to wait,' she said as Saskia spun round to face her. Despite the dark Tanya could see something in Saskia's eyes, something she didn't like at all.

'They've just announced it,' she said. 'We've run out of time.'

'Okay,' said Tanya, thinking fast. She didn't want to be the one responsible for starting a firefight which ended with Floortje getting injured or worse. But if the announcement had been made then she had to act now. 'I can't let you go in there, but I'll—'

The movement was quick, too quick. She felt the air

rushing at her, then her ear exploded. As she fell to the ground she could see Saskia was already running, the branch still clutched in one hand.

88

Jaap had skidded the car to a stop.

He was out and over the bridge, running into the trees.

Up ahead he saw two figures, wrestling.

One knocked the other down.

He sprinted forward, feet crunching twigs, branches clawing at him, scratching his face. One jabbed an eye. He ran with one eye open, the closed eye watering, the stream cold on his cheek.

He reached the spot where the first figure had fallen, slumped against a tree. It was Tanya, the side of her face cut from the rough bark as she'd slid down, her ear bloody and swollen already from where she'd been hit.

She had a pulse. He wanted to tend to her but didn't have time. The figure who'd knocked her out was just breaking out from the tree line, heading for a wooden boathouse, its windows lit.

He grabbed Tanya's gun from her holster, his eyes still on the figure heading for the boathouse.

As she reached the light he could see it was Saskia, and she was only feet away from the door.

It swung open and a figure stepped out.

It was Nikolic.

He was pointing a gun.

And he was holding Floortje.

89

Yuzuki Roshi had talked of a state where thought no longer existed, where life simply opened up, millisecond by millisecond.

Jaap was there now. He saw everything clearly as he rushed out of the woods just as the door closed, Saskia dragged in at gunpoint.

He could smell pine on the cold air, hear his breath ratcheting in and out of his lungs, blood rushing in his ears, small insects marching through the trees behind him, fish swimming in the water ahead, something rustling off to his left, moist earthworms burrowing deep in the soil. He could feel the curve of the earth, the pull of the moon way out in space, every proton and electron in every atom in his body spinning in the timeless frenzied movement which was the basis of life.

And none of it mattered.

He was at the door, listening, Tanya's gun in his hand. Saskia was screaming, Floortje following her lead.

Inside he could see why.

Saskia was on her knees.

Nikolic had his back to Jaap, but he could see he'd put Floortje down – she was on the floor by his feet – and had grabbed a clump of Saskia's hair instead, shaking her head like a rag doll, hair flying loose. But he was aiming the gun down at Floortje. Jaap moved forward slowly, not wanting to startle him.

All it would take would be a tiny electrical impulse firing deep in Nikolic's brain, sending the command to pull back the trigger.

Nikolic was shouting at Saskia, but Jaap couldn't make out the words. He took another step forward. Saskia noticed him, her head moved and Nikolic spun round, the gun moving up to Jaap. Their eyes locked. Jaap held his gun steady. He could get a head shot, he was close enough. His finger started applying pressure to the trigger.

But Nikolic had already swung his arm down, the weapon aimed back at Floortje. She writhed on her back, screaming. It looked like she was reaching out to clasp the barrel of the gun only inches away from her.

Nikolic motioned to Jaap with his head.

Jaap put the gun down.

Nikolic stared at him.

Jaap shoved it away with his foot, out of reach.

'Just let them go,' said Jaap, his voice unrecognizable in his own ears.

'You both fucked up,' said Nikolic. 'I told you to get Matkovic released and I've just heard on the news that he's been convicted.'

Saskia started to say something, Nikolic jerked the hand holding her hair, snapping her neck back. She cried out in pain, in despair. Jaap saw the arch of her neck, skin held taut.

'Loyalty's fine,' said Jaap, 'but you don't have to kill anyone else. It's over.'

'You think I'd do this out of loyalty?' Nikolic laughed. 'This isn't about loyalty, it's about something I like far more.'

90

Tanya's eyes flicked open.

It took her a few seconds to work out what was going on. She was slumped down, her face pushed against something rough, the other side of her head on fire. As she struggled to her feet everything came back in a rush. She felt for her gun. It was gone.

Saskia took it, she thought as she darted forward through the trees, hoping she wasn't too late.

If she was it would be her fault. She'd been the one to tell Saskia.

The boathouse was up ahead, the door open, a wedge of light forging out into the darkness. As she pushed her legs to go faster she heard a noise, somewhere behind her. A car.

Maybe it's Jaap, she thought as she swung her head round.

Headlights shone into her eyes.

She couldn't wait. She turned back and ran for the boathouse.

The car slipped to a stop metres behind her.

Just as she reached the doorway shots exploded.

From behind her.

She dived through the door as wood splintered into the air.

91

Jaap heard the footsteps, the car.

Then he heard the shots.

He hurled himself towards his gun as Tanya flew in through the doorway. As he hit the floor he twisted and rolled, swinging the gun round, shooting blindly back out the door. Tanya, lying a few feet away from him, glanced across the room. Jaap followed her gaze, saw Nikolic making a move.

Golden sparks rained down from overhead as the light went out.

The gunfire outside ceased. Jaap's ears were ringing. He scrabbled to his feet just in time to see the door at the far end of the boathouse swinging closed.

He dashed towards it, shouting to Tanya to stay down though he wasn't sure she could hear any better than he could, and slammed through the door.

On the jetty, planks loose underfoot, he could see Nikolic had already got Saskia and Floortje into the furthest boat. As Jaap sprinted towards them Nikolic was yanking a starter cord with one hand, foot braced on the side of the boat, the gun still aimed in their direction.

Jaap heard a dim roar and saw Nikolic shift position. The boat moved out on to the water.

Seconds later Jaap jumped off the jetty into another boat, fumbling for the outboard's starter cord while trying to untie the mooring rope. The fog was clearing now, and he could see Nikolic's boat out on the black water trailing a white wake.

He felt the motor come to life more than heard it, deep vibrations rattling his chest, and turned his full attention to the mooring, thick marine rope spotted with tar. He could feel the distance between them widening, but his fingers were struggling to release the rope. Petrol fumes teased him.

He knew the shots had been fired by Isovic and Krilic; he just hoped Tanya could cope.

He'd put her in danger too.

The mooring finally slipped away, and he grabbed the rudder, twisting the throttle round to full.

The increased air pressure on his face told him he was moving.

His boat was going to be lighter, but he didn't know if that was enough to close the gap.

Water sluiced off the bow.

The boat started to bounce as it hit the wake from Nikolic's craft.

He tightened his grip on the throttle.

92

After Jaap ran out Tanya crawled to the left of the door, glad of the darkness inside the boathouse.

She let her eyes adjust before very slowly poking her head out, trying to establish who had been shooting at them. At first all she could see was a car, one door opened, puncture wounds in the metal. Then she saw something else; a foot poking out from behind the vehicle.

The toe of the shoe pointed skyward.

There has to be at least one more, she thought, her eyes scanning back and forth.

Then she saw it – movement a few feet away from the car.

Movement on the ground. A body was moving, slowly.

With her fingers she explored around her, eventually finding something. It felt like a short plank. She grasped it, checked the weight, then threw it out the door.

Nothing happened.

No shots.

She slowly got to her feet and stepped through the doorway.

She wasn't sure if she saw the muzzle flash first, or heard the crack, or if both of those only came after she felt the numbness in her right hand.

93

The growl of the motor and the ringing in his ears didn't stop the sound of a single shot reaching Jaap's brain from somewhere behind him.

The fog was still clearing, and now the cloud parted above, moonlight hitting the surface of the water like a switch had been flicked on.

Jaap was focused on the boat ahead forging across Braassemermeer, heading north-west. He was close enough now to feel the spray on his face, catch the fumes from the outboard whining ahead of him.

Now the shore was coming into view. Nikolic would be there in a few more minutes.

Further round, to the left, the lights of a small town glowed in the darkness. To the right Jaap could see a road, headlights moving towards the water.

The boat ahead swerved left, the arc of its turn throwing a curl of water into the air, backlit by the headlights.

94

Kees punched the satnav with his hand, knocking it out
of the holder growing from the dashboard.

It had brought him to the wrong end of Braassemermeer, he could see that now. Which meant he was going
to have to go right round, adding another ten minutes at
least. As he shot the car forward he glanced out of the
side window and saw a boat skimming across the surface
of the water, heading towards the narrow waterway which
led from Braassemermeer to who knew where.

He started a three-pointer, the boat passing in front of
him, streaming through his headlights for half a second.
Then he saw a second boat chasing the first.

It took a couple more seconds for his brain to work
it out.

Both boats were now in the waterway, only forty or so
metres across, and the second was gaining. He didn't need
to see the figure up close to realize it was Jaap. Kees completed the turn and shot the car forward. There was more
light from the buildings lining the water, and he could see
now that the man in the front boat had a gun.

The second was only metres behind now, and the man
in the lead boat swung his hand round and fired.

Kees saw the spark, saw Jaap's boat swerve hard to the
left then back again.

Kees had one hand on the steering wheel; his gun was in his other.

He couldn't get the window button to work.

He lashed out at the glass with the gun.

A storm of glass bit into his arm.

His head was flicking back and forth from the road to the lead boat, trying to get a sight on the man, who he saw was firing again.

Then he saw movement, a figure sprang up from the front of the boat and lunged at the man, her long hair flowing wildly in the air.

95

Jaap saw Nikolic turn at the last second, swinging his arm round to deflect Saskia, smashing his elbow into her face while keeping the other on the outboard throttle.

She staggered back. The boat swerved, and for a second Jaap thought she was going to lose her balance, go overboard. Nikolic was off balance too, and Saskia recovered quickest, lunging at him again, her scream of rage shooting out above the snarl of the motors. Nikolic tried to swing the gun round at her, but she caught his arm in time, forcing it away with both hands.

Nikolic had to take his other hand off the throttle. The motor revved down and the boat started to slow, rocking from side to side as he struggled with Saskia.

Then Nikolic dropped down, Saskia jolting forward.

Jaap could see what he was doing.

Nikolic used Saskia's momentum and his low centre of gravity, forcing her over his back.

Jaap watched as she toppled overboard, her arms splayed out like she was doing a cartwheel.

As she hit the water Nikolic grabbed the throttle again, shooting the boat forward, white water rearing up in its wake.

Jaap's mind shut down for a few seconds before reigniting.

Saskia couldn't swim.

But Floortje was still on the boat with Nikolic.

He was going to have to make a decision, quickly. He was fast approaching the spot where Saskia had fallen in. He could see her, arms hitting the surface of the water; he could hear her scream.

Jaap glanced at Nikolic's boat, then at Saskia.

The time required to stop and get her aboard would give Nikolic the chance to get away.

He had to choose.

His hand was tight on the throttle.

It stayed there.

The boat rocked as it sped over the expanding ripples from Saskia's plunge into the water. As he passed her he thought he heard her voice, only he couldn't work out what she was saying.

96

Tyres shrieked into the darkness.

Kees was out of the car before it had fully stopped, rushing down towards the water. He'd not been able to see the hair colour, but it was Tanya, he was sure of it. He threw himself in, the cold hitting him, paralyzing his lungs.

He had tried to fix where the body had entered the water, but the waves from the two boats meant he wasn't sure. He struck out, pumping his arms, kicking his legs, clothes dragging him down. He called out but got no response. He trod water, circling. Nothing. He dived again and again, feeling with his hands, empty water rushing through his fingers.

Just as he thought he couldn't go under again his hand felt something – flesh. He dived, reached out, grasped an arm. He kicked to the surface, trying to get her head above water.

97

Jaap heard a noise he didn't like.

The motor had been sounding different for the last thirty seconds, but he'd not really paid any attention, all his focus on the boat ahead.

The motor misfired, losing power.

He released the throttle then jammed it on again. The motor caught and he felt the pull of acceleration. Up ahead Nikolic's boat was powering away.

Seconds later his own spluttered again as if low on fuel. He willed it to keep going.

Not now, he thought. *Please not now.*

He did the same again, quickly releasing the throttle and re-engaging it.

But this time it didn't work; it just cut out.

His boat was losing speed fast.

The distance between his boat and Nikolic's was growing. In less than a minute Nikolic would be out of range.

Jaap spun the wheel towards the shore, hoping the residual speed would get him to dry land, and putting him side on to the back of Nikolic's boat. He raised his gun, the moonlight bright, but Nikolic a fast-receding shape in the night.

He couldn't see Floortje at all.

He sighted on Nikolic just as the boat in front veered away to the left before swinging back to the right.

A few more seconds was all he had left.

You're going to have to do better than that, thought Jaap as he sighted Nikolic again.

His finger touched the trigger, but didn't pull it in.

If he fired he risked hitting Floortje.

But if he didn't fire Nikolic would get away.

He could feel his finger against the metal, feel the trigger's resistance.

Now he was down to the last second – any longer and Nikolic would be out of range.

His finger pulled back. The shot rang out and Jaap felt the recoil.

For a few moments everything became still, frozen into place.

He was sure he'd missed.

Then the motor on Nikolic's boat flashed like a firework. Jaap could see fragments exploding out from it, flying towards Nikolic.

Nikolic went down, one arm thrown up in the air, a scream of pain breaking through the sound of the motor. His gun flew into the air before disappearing into the water. As he fell he knocked the rudder and the boat veered towards the right-hand bank.

As Jaap dived into the water, gun still in his hand, he could see flames starting to lick the outboard on Nikolic's boat.

98

Kees heard the shot and the scream behind him, but he ignored them. He had her head cradled under his arm like he'd got her in a headlock, and was using his other arm to scoop at the water, trying to pull them to shore.

She was heavy, unconscious, and he knew he had to get her breathing again quickly.

He reached the water's edge and dragged her out, his clothes sucking at his flesh. On the grass he rolled her on to her side, her hair stuck to her face.

He'd done basic CPR – it was part of every cop's training – but he couldn't remember what to do. As he tilted her forward water spewed from her mouth, and he was hoping for a cough, hoping that clearing the water out would somehow start something going deep inside.

He'd seen that happen in films.

But it wasn't working here.

He rolled her on to her back, her body movements floppy, loose, and he noticed something. He reached out, his hand shaking badly, and brushed the hair away from her face.

It wasn't Tanya.

His mind spun.

But he didn't have time to think, to try and work out what was going on. Whoever she was she probably only had seconds to live, and he had to do something. Right now.

He took a deep breath, pinched her nose and bent forward.

The impulse to recoil hit him hard as his lips touched hers; they were so cold, and didn't feel alive. But he pressed harder to form a seal and blew hard into her mouth.

Then he put his hands one on top of the other on her chest, palms down, and started to push in rhythmic pulses.

He pushed again and again until he heard a crack.

It was then he knew she wasn't coming back.

99

Nikolic was hurt, shrapnel from the motor buried deep in his leg. He was limping across an impossibly flat lawn right by the water's edge, heading for a large house, windows blaring light out on to the meticulously trimmed grass.

Floortje was slung under one of his arms like a sack.

Something seemed wrong about that, but Jaap didn't know what.

He swam past Nikolic's boat, his arms aching, slicing into the water, the choppy surface coloured orange from the blaze consuming the outboard motor.

He could feel the heat on his face as he passed it, contrasting with the cold water.

Seconds later he was scrambling out of the water and taking off after the Serb.

He could get him now, he knew it.

Five paces out Nikolic sensed he was close. He stopped and turned. Jaap saw a small knife, flames flashing on the blade's surface.

Jaap kept the gun by his side.

'Put her down,' he said, his voice barely a whisper.

Nikolic stared at him, then moved the knife up towards Floortje, holding his gaze.

Jaap raised the gun, sighted Nikolic's head.

'Don't do it,' he said.

Nikolic stood there, breathing heavily, then began to lower the knife.

Jaap watched as Nikolic's hand opened, the knife falling to the grass, the blade slicing into the earth.

Nikolic took Floortje in both his hands.

It was only then Jaap realized what was wrong – she wasn't making a sound.

'Give her to me,' he said, taking a step closer.

Nikolic threw her at him, two-handed like she was a basketball.

Jaap caught her, grabbed her into his chest, wrapped his arms around her.

His eyes were off Nikolic for less than a second, but it was enough for the Serb to make his move. He swung his wounded leg round, knocking Jaap's from under him, screaming with the pain of the impact. As Jaap went down he knew he had to drop the gun or risk hitting Floortje with the barrel. His hand released the weapon.

Then he was on the ground; he'd narrowly missed falling on the knife. Floortje was in his arms, Nikolic standing over him, pointing the gun he'd scooped up right at him.

Jaap stared at it, the dark centre from where the bullet would fly out, the side of the barrel milky white from the moonlight.

In his arms Floortje wasn't moving.

Behind him the outboard motor exploded, the light flaring on Nikolic's face, allowing Jaap to finally get a good look at him, see the rage and frustration and the fear.

Nikolic didn't even flinch, kept the gun trained right at him.

Jaap watched as the Serb's trigger finger curled back,

squeezed his eyes tight, waiting for the blast, waiting for it all to be over.

He heard a click.

He knew that sound. It was the sound of an empty chamber.

Jaap swung an arm out, grabbed the knife by its handle and threw it straight at Nikolic.

100

When Tanya came round she was on her back. She rolled her head sideways, felt her ear ease into cold mud, plugging it shut. She opened her eyes, looked at the moon leering out of the sky at her.

She'd been shot. In her right hand.

She felt for the entry point in the back of her hand. As she sat up she turned her hand over. The exit wound was right in the centre, ruptured flesh like a flower blooming in her palm.

When she tried to move her fingers she gasped. They hardly moved, and the pain was electric.

She looked around, suddenly aware that whoever had shot her might still be there.

He was, slumped against the car, but his arms were flopped down by his side. She got up slowly and made her way over to him.

The man was breathing heavily. She recognized him from the file photo. Krilic. He looked up as she approached, Tanya could see he'd been hit in the stomach, blood pooling in the wrinkles of his jacket. His face was gaunt, the bone structure visible. For a second she saw him as the skeleton he was soon to become if he didn't get medical attention quickly.

She picked the gun he'd used to shoot her out of the

424

mud with her left hand. It felt alien, wrong, but her right was useless, throbbing with pain. Then she cuffed him to the car door handle with a plastic tie – tricky with one hand, but he barely looked at her. She walked back to her own car, sliding into the driver's seat. Her breathing was heavy now, the pain in her hand increasing.

She reached out for the radio.

The ambulance would be seven minutes, the dispatcher told her.

Her head fell back against the headrest. She inspected her hand again. It was still bleeding. Badly.

She fumbled in the glove compartment, pulling out the first-aid kit. She had to unzip it with one hand, the case wedged between her legs. She wrapped a bandage around her hand, pulling it tight. By the time she'd finished the fabric was already soaked with blood.

There was a box of painkillers. She fumbled with it.

Then dropped it back.

Right now she needed the pain.

She reached out with her left and twisted the key, the angle awkward, and once the engine had fired up started to drive.

She'd waited years to do this, constantly putting it off, constantly afraid.

Now was the moment.

Now was when she made things right.

Now.

She pulled up outside the house just over half an hour later, her right hand in her lap, useless.

But she wasn't thinking about that.

Her thoughts were full of her past. It was like she was seeing her life played out on the inside of the windscreen.

She was a teenager again, standing by the window in her bedroom, watching her foster mother leave the house to go to her weekly knitting circle. The feeling of dread was heavy in her stomach, because she knew what was going to happen next. She'd hear Staal downstairs; he'd go to the wooden cabinet they kept in the living room. Then she'd hear the scrape of the key being taken off the top and being inserted into the lock.

The click.

The creak of the door opening.

The sound of a bottle being pulled off a shelf, liquid glugging into a glass.

At that stage she knew she had less than ten minutes left; he only ever had one drink before coming upstairs. But the time didn't matter, she'd nowhere to run. She bunched herself under the duvet, closed her eyes tight, as if that might work, as if, for once, it might stop him, or make him decide that tonight he'd just drink, stay downstairs, away from her.

But it was always the same. The sequence of noises would reverse, the bottle being put back, the door locked and the key replaced on top. He'd take the glass to the kitchen, a hiss of water from the tap as he washed it out. Then the footsteps on the stairs would start. There were eleven in total, and Tanya knew the sound of each one. She would tighten her eyes even harder with each step, curl tighter into a ball, not breathing, willing herself away.

Then the door would open slowly, and he stepped into

the room. She could smell him, smell the alcohol on his breath, smell his sweat.

And hear the rasp of his breathing.

Which was getting faster and tighter as he got closer.

Tanya shook herself, refusing to relive it again.

She got out of the car, legs unsteady, her hands freezing but her brow covered with sweat, and walked across the road.

The doorbell sounded, and she stood there.

Further down the street a dog was barking, each bark a shot in the darkness. A breeze cooled one side of her face.

A light flicked on inside, footsteps approached the door.

It opened just a crack, an eye appearing, scoping her out. She could tell by the quick dilation it recognized her.

She had her toe in the gap before he could close it. She shoved it open as he stepped back into the hall.

Tanya walked in, closed the door behind her, and looked into her foster father's face.

101

Jaap laid Floortje on the stretcher, and the paramedic got to work, telling him to step back.

He tried to explain what had happened but the paramedic wasn't listening; he was bent over, focusing on Floorjte, checking for a pulse, shining a torch into her eyes, his gloved hands a flurry of movement.

Another paramedic stepped over, guided Jaap back a few steps and asked what had happened. Jaap started to tell him but saw the first paramedic straighten up.

He had only to see the small shake of his head, the deflation of his shoulders, to know what was coming.

He stepped away, as if by avoiding hearing it he could make it not happen.

And then he saw Nikolic, who'd collapsed on the grass, the knife blade buried in his throat. He was still alive – just – restrained on a stretcher while a third paramedic tended to him.

Every atom in Jaap's body exploded.

He lunged, knocked the paramedic away and grabbed the knife handle, jerking it sideways. Blood spurted as two uniforms pulled him off, a strange rasping sound coming from Nikolic's throat.

They pinned him to the ground, Jaap thrashing like a wild animal, twisting and writhing, pure reflex.

No thought.

No existence.

Just rage.

Later, he didn't know how much later, but certainly after they'd taken Floortje's body away, Jaap found himself sitting in the back of a patrol car, blue lights strobing the darkness.

He had a paper cup of coffee in his hand. It was full, and cold. He'd no idea how it had got there. His hands were cuffed.

He looked out the open door and saw someone walking towards him. It was Kees. The thought of Saskia burst into his head. But the look on Kees' face told him everything.

A uniform intercepted him, and they spoke briefly.

Once he'd finished Kees walked over, helped Jaap out of the car and undid his cuffs.

Jaap found himself walking, each footstep an age, down to the water where the boat was still on fire.

As he stood a few metres away, just enough so it was warm, he fished the I Ching from his back pocket.

The pages were soaking wet, the paper swelling and fanning out. He thought about Kyoto, thought about Yuzuki Roshi, thought about how he'd tried to escape but hadn't.

Because the thing he was trying to escape from was himself.

And that just wasn't possible.

A siren started up. People were moving behind him, around him.

He held the book in his hand for a moment, feeling the wet paper, its weight, what it represented.

Then he tossed it into the flames.

102

Kees watched as Jaap stood by the water, his frame a silhouette in front of the blaze.

He'd just listened to what the two uniforms had told him, and he turned back to them.

'So, when you come to write your reports what are you going to put?'

One of them, the shorter of the two finally spoke.

'We'll have to report that Inspector Rykel assaulted the victim when he was restrained and that—'

'You've got to be fucking kidding me,' said Kees stepping right up to him. 'That man was responsible for the death of his child, and her mother. He was also a mass murderer. Your report is going to state that Nikolic's death was a result of self-defence on Inspector Rykel's part. You got that?'

Both uniforms looked at the ground.

'You got that?' said Kees again.

Slowly both uniforms nodded their heads.

'Yeah,' said the shorter one. 'Got it.'

Kees stared at them for a few moments more, then turned away.

He had another problem, Tanya was missing.

Kees left Jaap with the paramedics; they'd given him a sedative but it didn't seem to have done much. He'd never seen such anger and rage and despair on another human's face. He didn't ever want to see it again.

Through talking to the ambulance crew Kees learned of the boathouse and rushed there, driving fast, all the while thinking of Tanya. He found Krilic, still cuffed to a car door handle, being tended by more paramedics, the blue lights flickering intermittently through the trees on his approach, but neither of the paramedics had seen Tanya.

He tried calling her phone but it was off.

Kees walked into the trees, away from the shoreline – he'd seen enough water recently – and tried to think where she had gone. Sitting against a tree trunk he closed his eyes and tried to think it through, about what she'd told him.

Then it hit him.

He got back into his car and drove off, hoping he was wrong.

Outside the estate agent's something had spooked her. She'd seen something in the window and gone back in.

When he got there he left the car on the kerb and went to the window. There were seven properties displayed. He noted down the street names of each and got back in his car.

He'd driven past the first three, but there was nothing obvious and he was starting to wonder if he'd got this wrong when he turned into the street with the fourth address on his list.

He wasn't sure if he was pleased to see her car or not, parked up opposite the property.

As he drove past slowly he noticed a light on in a downstairs room, the view obscured by curtains.

He parked two streets away and walked back. There was no traffic, and his footsteps seemed impossibly loud in the night.

The car was definitely hers, and he stood there a few moments, his hand on the still-warm bonnet.

The path leading to the front door seemed to stretch away from him as he walked it, the door receding further with each step.

Finally he was standing in front of it.

He wanted to go inside.

He wanted to turn back.

His hand reached out, fingers making contact with the painted wood. He gave a little push. The door cracked open.

The hallway wasn't lit, but light spilled into it from a doorway further down on the right. He couldn't hear anything, any sign that anyone was here. He walked down the hallway, his footsteps silenced by the carpet, and made it to the doorway.

He looked through and saw her perched on the edge of a large suitcase, her head resting on her hands, her eyes staring ahead.

She didn't even look up when he stepped into the room.

He followed her gaze, her line of sight, and saw the man, lying on the floor.

She didn't know how it had happened, but here she was, in the passenger seat of her car, with Kees driving. She looked out of the window, gazed at the fields of tulips stretching out on either side of the road, their petals just catching the first rays of morning light.

She reached for the door. Kees put a hand out to touch her, slowed the car down.

He watched as she walked out among the tulips. The flowers in the field he'd stopped by were all black, a massive sea of identical blossoms, soon to be harvested.

The horizon was a smear of candyfloss pink.

He watched as she stopped about twenty metres away and stood still, the light just catching her hair.

He thought about what he'd seen at the house, what it would mean.

He watched as she started walking again, one hand trailing down, her right hand, touching the flower heads with her fingers.

Epilogue

Matkovic looked up from the desk he was sitting at, crossword book open in front of him, as Jaap stepped into the cell. Two guards followed him in.

After several phone calls Ronald had agreed to allow a meet with Matkovic.

In the days following Matkovic's sentencing the story had come out about the kidnap and the events at Braassemermeer. Smit had already told Jaap he was suspended and that a full investigation would have to take place, even though he understood there had been mitigating circumstances.

Jaap had told him he didn't give a fuck.

The visitor's badge he'd got at reception had 'Inspector Jaap Rykel' typed on it, 'Inspector' crossed out by hand.

'Tell me about Nikolic,' said Jaap in English – he knew Matkovic spoke a little.

'What's to tell? I hear on news he's dead.'

'I want to know why he did it all, why he'd do all that just to help you.'

Matkovic laughed.

Jaap felt something.

Not anger.

More like emptiness.

Floortje was gone. Her neck had snapped some time during the chase, probably when Nikolic had grabbed her from the boat. Jaap would never see her again, never touch her hand, cradle her to sleep.

Floortje no longer existed.

Except as a massive void at the very centre of his being.

'He's a loyal dog, no?' Matkovic's voice broke into Jaap's thoughts.

Jaap didn't respond.

'Okay, I tell you. You're right. It wasn't loyalty. It was greed. I needed his help, and I promised money, lots of money, if he got me released.'

'And where's this money?'

'Ahhh,' said Matkovic, laughing the soft laugh of a grandfather recounting youthful follies.

Emptiness turned to anger.

Jaap wanted to jump across the room and throttle him. One of the guards moved forward, sensing Jaap's rage.

'There is no money now. But the important thing is he thought there was money.'

He shrugged, and went back to his crossword.

Jaap had listened to Krilic's statement, made after he'd been released from hospital and taken into custody earlier that morning.

Isovic and Krilic had also planned to get Matkovic released, hoping that once they'd got the prosecution to rely on Isovic's testimony the trial would collapse with his disappearance.

Once released their plan had been to kill him.

But then Krilic had seen Nikolic and his gang at 57, and they'd decided to get revenge on the whole crew, while increasing the pressure on Matkovic by tweeting the murders.

Krilic's plan was that Matkovic would hear the news and work out what was going on, maybe even get scared.

But here he was sitting in his cell, and despite having been slapped with several life sentences, seemingly unconcerned about his fate.

Krilic had spat about justice at the end of his statement.

As Jaap left the cell he was starting to wonder himself.

Tanya gazed out over the pond. The water was marbled with colour, flower reflections bobbing about in the cool breeze. Small clouds churned in the sky, changing shape continuously, and a siren burst into life in the distance.

Two weeks ago she'd sat in the very same spot.

It seemed like two millennia.

Jaap was next to her on the bench, and she tucked up against him, their shoulders touching.

In the days after Floortje's death she'd moved in with him, trying to help, trying to get him out of the darkness he was sinking into. She'd stayed with him, made sure he was eating, sleeping, held him when he needed it, even though for the first few days he'd been so unresponsive she'd got scared. But gradually, to her relief, he'd started to come out of it. Bit by bit the life was coming back.

The real turning point however had been his meeting with Matkovic three days ago. She'd been unsure if it was a wise idea, but Jaap had insisted. And he'd come back calmer, like he was accepting how things were. She knew it wasn't going to be quick, and it probably wasn't going to be a linear improvement, but she was now sure he was going to make it. She'd seen flashes of his old self returning, and right now she could hardly ask for more.

But as her relief about Jaap grew she found herself

thinking about something which she'd been avoiding, something that caring for him had allowed her to push to the back of her mind.

The trail would be easy to follow. When she'd gone to Staal's house she'd wanted to confront him, put to rest the years of pain she'd suffered. Over those same years she'd imagined that meeting, but never really thought it would happen.

Or what she'd do if it did.

Then she'd been on Staal's doorstep, looking into his eyes, seeing the recognition there, the sudden fear which dilated his pupils till they were nothing more than black, shiny orbs. She'd not planned it, but it was like someone else had taken over her body – a raging fire unleashed inside her which had made her feral, wild.

The trail would be easy to follow. And it led to her.

She shivered.

'You okay?' asked Jaap.

'Yeah,' she said. 'Just a bit cold.'

She looked down at her hand, the bandages wrapped tight. The surgeon said she'd been lucky. But he also told her she'd probably lose control over her thumb, index and middle fingers, the tendons obliterated by the bullet as it tore through her flesh.

She didn't see how that was lucky.

But she didn't seem to care either.

Jaap put his arm around her shoulders, and she let herself be pulled closer.

When she'd stood in the field of tulips, dawn opening up the sky, she'd resolved to turn herself in. It was the only thing she could do.

But then she'd heard what had happened to Jaap, to Floortje, and she knew she needed to be there for him, knew that she was the only person who could see him through.

So she'd spent her days caring for him, afraid of the knock at the door, the summons which would take her away from Jaap.

Now time was ticking on, and still no one had come. Surely they would soon. And when they did it was going to devastate Jaap.

She'd made a mistake. She'd wanted to help him, but in the end she was just going to hurt him more.

A swan flapped down from the sky and landed in the water just in front of her, tucking in its wings when it had come to a stop. It swivelled its neck around, and Tanya saw a dark mark on its back.

'C'mon,' Jaap said, standing up. 'Let's go.'

As they walked away Tanya wondered just how much time she had left.

'Come in,' came Smit's voice through the door almost as soon as he knocked. Weirdly, Kees noticed, there was a uniform standing next to the door, who hadn't even acknowledged him.

He stepped into his boss's office.

'You might want to close that,' said Smit.

Kees did, and then sat in the chair indicated by Smit in front of his desk. There were two files laid out in front of him.

'A total mess,' said Smit.

The news outlets had been covering the story for the

last few days, too many violent killings for the media to let it go. Kees had given up watching or listening.

'If you'd not lost Isovic in the first place . . .'

Kees didn't see how that would have changed much, but he kept quiet.

'Anyway,' said Smit, 'that's not why I wanted to speak to you. Open it.'

Kees picked up the file indicated by Smit, and started to read. After a few moments he put it back down.

'I'm not sure I understand.'

'I need someone in that organization, someone willing to go deep undercover—'

'That's not undercover, that's a suicide mission.'

Smit stared at him across the desk. Then he pointed to the second file.

Kees picked it up, opened it to a photo of a scene he'd already seen.

'She's a good inspector,' said Smit, 'but it's clear that she killed a man. And that we can't have.'

Kees had been thinking of virtually nothing else, wondering what would happen to Tanya if anyone traced it back to her.

'Now, you'll see from that there's no conclusive evidence she had anything to do with it. But the man killed used to be her foster father, and a CCTV camera caught her number plate in the area at the right time.'

Kees felt like swallowing, but his Adam's apple seemed too big.

'The thing is,' continued Smit, 'another of our cars was also picked up, and according to the logs it had been signed out by you. It's all in there.'

Kees didn't even bother to look. He wasn't sure anything mattered any more.

'There are many ways to serve,' said Smit, 'and I think you're ready for a change. Of course, to be undercover you're going to need a story.'

'And that's where all this comes in,' replied Kees, putting the file back on the desk.

'You'd have to do some time, but we'd move you around the system. You'll probably be in for four months at the most.'

Kees sat back in his chair.

He'd finally acknowledged to himself just how ill he was.

Or would become.

Seeing Paul in his wheelchair had brought it home. Did he want to spend time in prison just so he could work undercover? But if he didn't then Tanya was going down, that much was clear.

She had a future; he didn't.

'No more than two months,' said Kees.

Smit looked at him, sizing him up.

'Okay,' he finally said, calling in the uniform who'd been standing outside.

Smit stood, and motioned to Kees to do the same.

'Inspector Kees Terpstra, I'm arresting you on suspicion of murder.'

Kees tuned him out, waited until he felt the cold metal of the cuffs slap over his wrists, heard the clicks of the ratchets. They were closed too tight but Kees figured complaining wasn't going to get him anywhere.

He let himself be led down to a cell, shoved inside.

Smit walked down with him.

As the metal bars clanged behind him the uniform left.

When they were alone Smit spoke again.

'And you'll be able to indulge yourself a little in prison. I hear coke's quite readily available. Despite our best efforts.'

Once Smit had left Kees sat on the metal bench attached to the wall and put his head back on the cool concrete.

His mind was whirring.

Then he saw it.

Smit had known all along.

Paul had said someone was interested in what Kees was doing – a benefactor, someone who Kees would soon belong to.

It was Smit.

Smit had sat on the information Paul had passed to him. He'd been planning to use it, to get Kees exactly where he was now, force him into an undercover mission which no one would volunteer for.

But Smit had got lucky: murder was a better cover than a drugs bust.

Murder would give him more respect undercover.

The cell smelt. Fear, stale urine, who knew what else.

He'd been singled out for this. Smit had seen what he was. Smit had manipulated him. Smit had made him his bitch.

Kees' laugh echoed round the cell.

He closed his eyes.

Once his heart had settled he found he was thinking of Tanya.

Author's Note

The ICTY continues to prosecute individuals involved in the Balkan conflict which raged throughout the 1990's leaving more than 100,000 people dead, and millions more displaced. It hopes to have completed its work by the end of 2015.

Acknowledgments

At WME my thanks go to Simon Trewin and Annemarie Blumenhagen, and at Penguin Rowland White, Emad Akhtar, and Sophie Elletson.